A Book of

PHYSICAL

PHARMACEUTICS - II

For

S.Y.B. Pharm. (Semester - IV)

As Per Revised Syllabus

Mr. Prashant H. Khade

M. Pharm. (Pharmaceutics)
Assistant Professor
PDEA's Shankarrao Ursal College of
Pharmaceutical Sciences and Research Centre
Kharadi, Pune 14

Mr. Sujit S. Kakade

M. Pharm. (Pharmaceutics)
Assistant Professor
PDEA's Shankarrao Ursal College of
Pharmaceutical Sciences and Research Centre
Kharadl, Pune 14

Ms. Trusha Y. Puttewar

M. Pharm. (Pharmaceutics)
Assistant Professor
PDEA's Shankarrao Ursal College of
Pharmaceutical Sciences and Research Centre
Kharadi, Pune 14

NIRALI PRAKASHAN
ADVANCEMENT OF KNOWLEDGE

N1701

PHYSICAL PHARMACEUTICS - II   ISBN 978-93-5164-991-5

First Edition : **January 2016**

© : **Authors**

Published By :   Polypate

NIRALI PRAKASHAN

Abhyudaya Pragati, 1312, Shivaji Nagar
Off J.M. Road, PUNE – 411005
Tel - (020) 25512336/37/39, Fax - (020) 25511379
Email : niralipune@pragationline.com

✦ DISTRIBUTION CENTRES

PUNE

Nirali Prakashan : 119, Budhwar Peth, Jogeshwari Mandir Lane, Pune 411002, Maharashtra
Tel : (020) 2445 2044, 66022708, Fax : (020) 2445 1538
Email : bookorder@pragationline.com, niralilocal@pragationline.com

Nirali Prakashan : S. No. 28/27, Dhyari, Near Pari Company, Pune 411041
Tel : (020) 24690204 Fax : (020) 24690316
Email : dhyari@pragationline.com, bookorder@pragationline.com

MUMBAI

Nirali Prakashan : 385, S.V.P. Road, Rasdhara Co-op. Hsg. Society Ltd.,
Girgaum, Mumbai 400004, Maharashtra
Tel : (022) 2385 6339 / 2386 9976, Fax : (022) 2386 9976
Email : niralimumbai@pragationline.com

✦ DISTRIBUTION BRANCHES

JALGAON

Nirali Prakashan : 34, V. V. Golani Market, Navi Peth, Jalgaon 425001,
Maharashtra, Tel : (0257) 222 0395, Mob : 94234 91860

KOLHAPUR

Nirali Prakashan : New Mahadvar Road, Kedar Plaza, 1st Floor Opp. IDBI Bank
Kolhapur 416 012, Maharashtra. Mob : 9850046155

NAGPUR

Pratibha Book Distributors : Above Maratha Mandir, Shop No. 3, First Floor,
Rani Jhanshi Square, Sitabuldi, Nagpur 440012, Maharashtra
Tel : (0712) 254 7129

DELHI

Nirali Prakashan : 4593/21, Basement, Aggarwal Lane 15, Ansari Road, Daryaganj
Near Times of India Building, New Delhi 110002
Mob : 08505972553

BENGALURU

Pragati Book House : House No. 1, Sanjeevappa Lane, Avenue Road Cross,
Opp. Rice Church, Bengaluru – 560002.
Tel : (080) 64513344, 64513355, Mob : 9880582331, 9845021552
Email:bharatsavla@yahoo.com

CHENNAI

Pragati Books : 9/1, Montieth Road, Behind Taas Mahal, Egmore,
Chennai 600008 Tamil Nadu, Tel : (044) 6518 3535,
Mob : 94440 01782 / 98450 21552 / 98805 82331,
Email : bharatsavla@yahoo.com

niralipune@pragationline.com | www.pragationline.com

Also find us on f www.facebook.com/niralibooks

Acknowledgements

We take this opportunity to express sincere gratitude to our parents and family members for providing their moral support and enabling us to utilize the crucial spare time for successive completion of this book.

We would like to thanks Hon. Shri. Ajitdada Pawar, President, Pune District Education Association, Shri. Sandip Kadam, Secretary, Pune District Education Association, Shri. Rajendra Ghadge, President Representative, Pune District Education Association and Shri. A. M. Jadhav, Joint Secretary (Administration), Pune District Education Association.

We are thankful to our Principal, Teaching Staff, Non-teaching staff and students of PDEA's Shankarrao Ursal College of Pharmacy, Kharadi, Pune, for encouraging us to venture into writing this book.

We are sincerely thankful to the Publisher Mr. Jignesh Furia and all the Staff of Nirali Prakashan, especially Dr. S. B. Gokhale and Mr. Nitin Thorat.

Authors

■■■

Preface

We take pride in presenting this book of Physical Pharmaceutics-II for the Second Year Pharmacy degree course as per revised syllabus. We have written this book in such a fashion whereby students can acquire the knowledge required for Second Year B. Pharm.

The subject of Physical Pharmaceutics has been associated with basic of Pharmaceutics and give ideas about theoretical principle which can be applied in the formulation development of any dosage form.

This book contains five chapters and an attempt is made to provide point by point account of syllabus which has been meticulously arranged to make the overall studies easier and more enjoyable. The suitable figures have been included to give good illustration of text. A special efforts based upon previous university examination have been taken during the frameworks of each topic.

Every chapter includes a question bank containing questions from earlier university question papers to help students to prepare better in the examination.

We have made every attempt, strived hard to present a good book. We would appreciate any suggestions and criticism from the teachers and students for future improvement of this book.

Authors

■■■

Syllabus

■■■

Contents

■■■

Chapter 1 ...

Surface and Interfacial Phenomenon

Syllabus ...

(A) Introduction to Surface and Interfacial Tension, Surface Free Energy, Measurement of Surface and Interfacial Tension, Spreading Coefficient.

(B) Adsorption at Liquid-interfaces, Surfactant Classification and HLB Scale, Micellar Solubilization, Krafft and Cloud Point, Soluble Monolayer and Gibbs Equation, Insoluble Monolayer and Film Balance, Adsorption at Solid Interfaces, Adsorption Isotherms, (Langmuir and Freundlich).

1.1 INTRODUCTION

All the liquids have a tendency to assume a shape having the minimal surface area exposed. For a drop of a liquid, that shape is the sphere. The boundary that forms between two phases [e.g. solid and liquid] is called **Interface**. The term **surface** is normally used to denote interface, when one of the phase is gas [e.g. gas and liquid]. Surface tension is the property of liquids arising from the intermolecular forces of attraction. Interfacial phenomena is important property in the formulation of various dispersions like:

- Suspensions [solid in liquid]
- Emulsions [liquid in liquid]
- Foams [vapour in liquid].

Interfacial phenomena is significant in pharmacy and medicine that affects absorption of drugs from solid dosage forms, penetration of molecules through biologic membranes and stability of emulsion and suspensions.

The interfaces can be classified into six classes as given in Table 1.1.

Table 1.1: Classifications of interfaces

Phase	Example
Gas – Gas	No interface possible
Gas – Solid	Solid exposed to atmosphere
Gas – Liquid	Water exposed to atmosphere

contd. ...

Liquid – Liquid	Emulsion
Liquid – Solid	Suspension
Solid – Solid	Powder particles in contact

The combinations given in Table 1.1 can be divided into two groups, namely liquid interfaces and solid interfaces and can be illustrated as shown in Fig. 1.1.

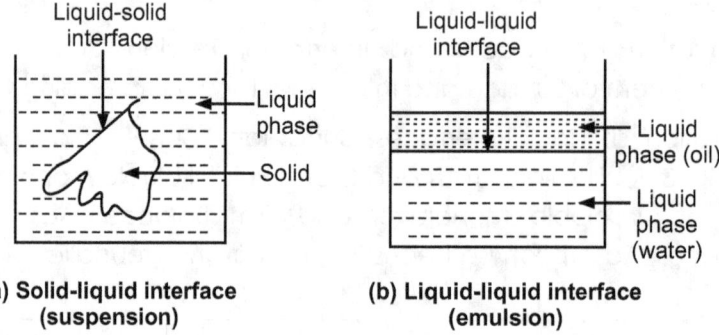

(a) Solid-liquid interface (suspension)

(b) Liquid-liquid interface (emulsion)

Fig. 1.1: Representation of (a) solid-liquid interfaces, (b) liquid-liquid interfaces

The term surface is generally used to denote interface, in which one of the phases is gas. i.e. either a gas-solid or a gas-liquid interface. E.g. Table top forms a gas-solid interface and the rain drop constitutes a gas-liquid interface. This phenomenon can be illustrated as shown in Fig. 1.2.

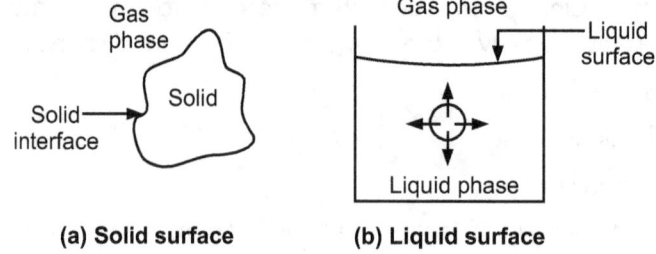

(a) Solid surface

(b) Liquid surface

Fig. 1.2: Representation of (a) solid-gas interface, (b) liquid-gas interface

1.1.1 Surface Tension

Surface tension is defined as 'the force, in dynes, acting on the surface of the liquid at right angles to any line of length of surface, 1 centimeter'.

Surface tension of liquids can be explained by considering the inter-molecular forces between the molecules in the neighbourhood.

In a liquid, molecules experience greater attraction from the neighbouring molecules. Such intermolecular attractions between like molecules are called **cohesive forces** while attractions between unlike molecules are called **adhesive forces**.

Surface tension denotes the cohesive forces of interaction in a liquid because its interaction with air is less. The concept of surface tension can be illustrated by accounting for these interactive forces at molecular level.

Consider an example of water in a beaker (Fig. 1.3).

Bulk molecules (B): A molecule present in the bulk phase of water (say B) is attracted equally from all sides by neighbouring molecules. Therefore, a molecule in the bulk of the solution is disturbed more or less symmetrically. Hence, the net pull (force) acting on the molecule 'B' is zero (Fig. 1.3).

Surface molecules (S): Now, consider a molecule say 'S' that lies on the surface. It is partially surrounded by other molecules. There are no molecules above it. This molecule is attracted by the molecules below it and experiences downward pull. The adhesive forces between the molecule 'S' and the air above it are weaker than the cohesive forces and cannot balance the inward pull on molecule 'S'. These unbalanced molecules acting downward tend to draw the surface molecules into the bulk of the liquid. This type of behaviour tends to reduce the surface area to a minimum.

The force acting on the surface of the liquid is called **Surface Tension.**

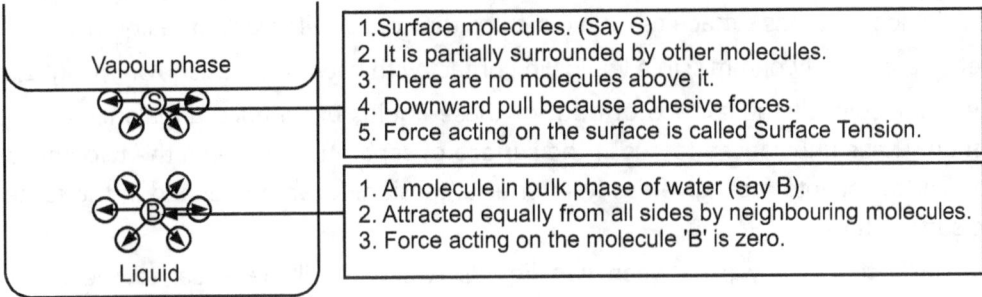

Liquid (water) phase
contained in a vessel

Fig. 1.3: Representation of unbalanced forces of interaction of molecule (S) at the surface of a liquid as compared to that of the interactive forces on the molecule (B) in the bulk of the liquid phase

In principle, the above arguments also apply to solids. It is easier to visualize surface in terms of the unbalanced forces projecting from the surface, rather than net inward attractions exerted on the molecules residing at the interfaced.

The phenomenon of surface tension is responsible for following process.

(a) Formation of spherical globules in emulsions.
(b) Formation of nearly spherical shape of falling water droplets.
(c) Formation of spherical shape of mercury particles on a flat surface.
(d) Rise of liquid in a capillary tube.
(e) Formation of hemispherical surface, i.e., lower meniscus, when water is filled in a glass tube.

Units of Surface Tension: The units of surface tension are dyne/cm in CGS system and Newtons/metre in MKS system.

1.1.2 Interfacial Tension

Interfacial Tension is defined as 'the force per unit length existing at the interface between two immiscible liquids'.

- **Miscibility:** When two liquids are completely miscible, the interface cannot be observed and hence, do not possess interfacial tension. Examples are water and ethyl alcohol.

- **Immiscibility:** When benzene and water are mixed together, these remain immiscible and form a boundary. Hence, benzene and water system has interface and shows interfacial tension.

Interfacial tensions are less than the surface tensions.

Because,

1. The adhesive forces between two liquid phases at the interface are greater than when liquid and gas phases exist together.

2. Interfacial tension indicates the strength of the adhesive forces between immiscible liquids, whereas surface tension indicates the cohesive forces in the liquids.

Let us consider two immiscible liquids in contact with each other as shown in Fig. 1.1 (b).

The molecules at the surface of both of these liquids experience unbalanced forces of attraction. These unbalanced forces at the surface of separation between the two immiscible liquids (i.e., at the interface) give rise to interfacial tension. It can be defined in the same way as the surface tension.

Interfacial tension (γ_{AB}) between two liquids A and B will be equal to the difference between the respective surface tensions (i.e. γ_A and γ_B).

$$\gamma_{AB} = \gamma_A - \gamma_B$$

Therefore, the interfacial tension should be between the surface tensions of the two liquids. This is indeed found to be true for many liquids (e.g., water and carbon tetrachloride). However, for many liquids, this prediction does not hold (e.g., water and cyclohexanol).

Unit:

The units of interfacial tensions are same as that of surface tension, dyne/cm (CGS system) or Newtons/metre (MKS system).

1.2 SURFACE FREE ENERGY

Surface tension maintains the surface area of a liquid to a minimum value. The surface area can be increased provided some work is being done against the force at the surface.

Surface free energy is defined as 'the work required to increase the area of a liquid by 1 sq. cm.'

As per the definition, surface free energy is equal to the surface tension.

The derivation to estimate the surface free energy is as follows:

1. ABCD is a rectangular wire as shown in Fig. 1.4.
2. The side of AD = L and is movable.
3. A drop of soap solution is placed on the frame, so that it forms a film within the frame.
4. The side AD remains stable on account of surface tension exerted by the soap film.
5. When force (such as hanging mass) is applied downward, the film gets stretched as the movable bar AD goes down until the film breaks.
6. When the applied force is less than that is required for breaking, the film would retract on account of surface tension.

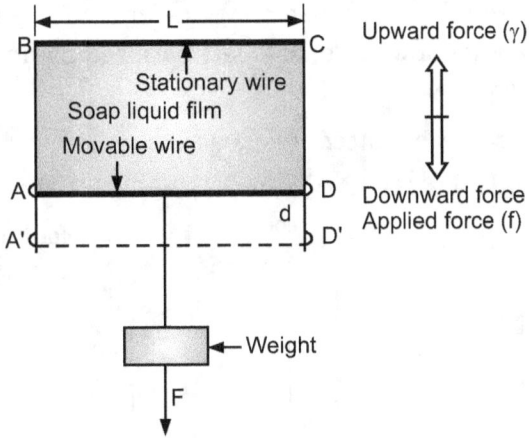

Fig. 1.4: Wire frame apparatus

If force 'f' is applied on AD (downward component), it shifts the movable wire from AD to A'D' (i.e. it is shifted by distance d). Then, the work done W is given by

$$\text{Work done (W)} = \text{Force} \times \text{Distance moved}$$

$$W = f \times d \qquad \qquad \text{... (1.1)}$$

The above force acts against the surface tension (upward component) 'γ' of the liquid, since surface tension tries to contract the liquid. There are two surfaces of each length 'L' on either side of the wire. The force acting on the surface is:

$$f = \gamma \times 2L \qquad \qquad \text{... (1.2)}$$

Substituting equation (1.2) in equation (1.1) gives

$$W = \gamma \times 2L \times d \qquad \qquad \text{... (1.3)}$$

Since, $2L \times d$ is equal to increase in surface area 'ΔA' produced by extending the soap film, equation (1.3) changes to:

$$W = \gamma \times \Delta A$$

OR $\qquad \qquad \Delta G = \gamma \times \Delta A \qquad \qquad \text{... (1.4)}$

In which 'W' is the work done or surface free energy increase (ΔG) is expressed in ergs (or mJm^{-2}). In a thermodynamic sense, any form of energy can be divided into an intensity factor and a capacity factor. In this case, surface tension is the intensity factor and a change in area is the capacity factor.

1.3 DETERMINATION OF SURFACE TENSION AND INTERFACIAL TENSION

The methods commonly used for the determination of surface tension are:

1.3.1 Capillary Rise Method

When a capillary tube is placed in the liquid contained in a beaker, the liquid rise in the tube to a certain distance (Fig. 1.5). This is because the adhesive force between liquid molecule and gas molecule is stronger than cohesive forces between liquid molecules. The rise in the tube continue until upward force is just balanced by downward force of gravity due to the weight of the liquid.

Means at equilibrium opposing forces are equal;

i.e.   Upward force (A) = Downward force (B)   ... (1.5)

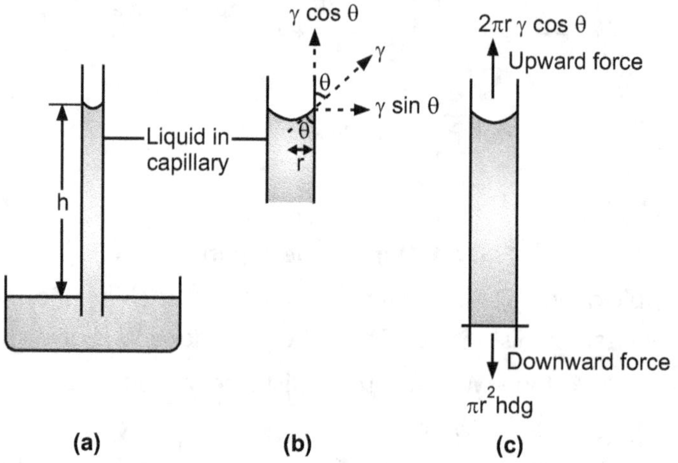

Fig. 1.5: (a) Rise of liquid in capillary tube; (b) Surface tension (γ) acts along tangent to meniscus and its vertical component is γ.Cos θ; (c) Upward force 2πrγ cos θ counterbalances the downward force due to weight of liquid in capillary and gravity πr²hρg .

Upward force (A):

This force represents the surface tension of liquid (γ) at any point on the circumference.

$$\text{Upward force (A)} = \gamma \cdot \cos\theta \cdot 2\pi r \qquad ... (1.6)$$

Where,

γ : Surface tension,

θ : Contact angle between liquid and capillary wall,

$2\pi r$: Capillary inside circumference.

But, for water, 'θ' is considered insignificant (θ = 0), because water completely wet capillary wall. The contact angle is very small for liquid used in pharmacy similar to water, Cos θ approaches 1. Then, cos θ = 1 and equation (1.6) change to

$$\text{Upward force (A)} = \gamma .2\pi r \qquad \qquad \text{... (1.7)}$$

Downward force (B):

The downward force is due to gravity and the weight of the liquid in the capillary rise.

$$
\begin{aligned}
\text{Downward force (B)} &= \text{Mass of liquid in capillary} \times \text{Acceleration} \\
&= \text{Volume} \times \text{Density} \times \text{Acceleration} \\
&= \text{Cross-sectional area} \times \text{Height} \times \text{Density} \times \text{Acceleration} \\
&= \pi r^2 \times h \times \rho \times g \qquad \qquad \text{... (1.8)}
\end{aligned}
$$

Substitute equation (1.7) and (1.8) in (1.5)

$$\gamma \times 2\pi r = \pi r^2 \times h \times \rho \times g \qquad \qquad \text{... (1.9)}$$

$$\gamma = \frac{1}{2} r \, h \rho \, g \qquad \qquad \text{... (1.10)}$$

Equation (1.10) is used to calculate surface tension.

1.3.2 Drop Formation Method

A drop of liquid is allowed to form at the lower end of a capillary tube (Fig. 1.7). The drop is supported by the upward force of surface tension acting at the outer circumference of the tube. The weight of the drop (mg) pulls it downward. When the two forces are balanced, the drop breaks. Thus at the point of breaking,

$$\text{Upward force (A)} = \text{Downward force (B)}$$

i.e. $\qquad \qquad \gamma 2\pi r = mg \qquad \qquad$ ... (1.11)

where,

γ   : Surface tension,

2πr : Outer circumference of the tube,

m   : Mass of the drop,

g   : Acceleration due to gravity.

The apparatus employed is a glass pipette with a capillary at the lower part. This is called a **Stalagmometer** or **Drop pipette** (Fig. 1.6). It is cleaned, dried and filled with the experimental liquid, say upto mark A.

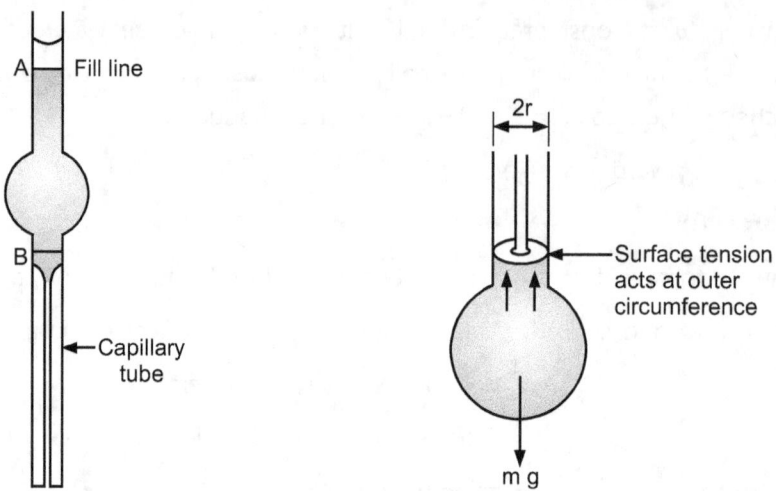

Fig. 1.6: Stalagmometer   **Fig. 1.7: A drop forming a tube having radius r**

Then the surface tension is determined by one of the two methods given below.

1.3.2.1 Drop Weight Method

About 20 drops of the given liquid are received from the drop-pipette in a weighing bottle and weighed. Thus, weight of one drop is found. The drop-pipette is again cleaned and dried. It is filled with a second reference liquid (say water) and weight of one drop is determined as before.

Then from equation (1.11)

$$m_1 g = 2\pi r\, \gamma_1 \qquad\qquad \text{... (1.12)}$$
$$m_2 g = 2\pi r\, \gamma_2 \qquad\qquad \text{... (1.13)}$$

Dividing (1.12) by (1.13)

$$\frac{m_1}{m_2} = \frac{\gamma_1}{\gamma_2} \qquad\qquad \text{... (1.14)}$$

Knowing the surface tension of reference liquid from tables, surface tension of the liquid under study, can be found.

1.3.2.2 Drop Number Method

The drop-pipette is filled upto the mark A with the experimental liquid (No. 1). The number of drops is counted as the meniscus travels from A to B. Similarly, the pipette is filled with the reference liquid (No. 2) as the meniscus passes from A to B.

Let n_1 and n_2 be the number of drops produced by the same volume V of the two liquids. Thus,

The volume of one drop of liquid 1 = V/n_1

The mass of one drop of liquid 1 = $(V/ n_1)\rho_1$

Similarly,

The mass of one drop of liquid 2 = $(V/n_2)\rho_2$

Where, ρ_1 and ρ_1 are the densities of two liquids.

Then from equation (1.14)

$$\frac{\gamma_1}{\gamma_2} = \frac{\left(\dfrac{V}{n_1}\right)\rho_1}{\left(\dfrac{V}{n_2}\right)\rho_2} = \frac{n_2\,\rho_1}{n_1\,\rho_2} \qquad \dots (1.15)$$

The value of ρ_1 is determined with a pyknometer. Knowing ρ_2 and γ_2 from reference tables, γ_1 can be calculated.

1.3.3 Ring-Detachment Method

This method is widely used to measure surface and interfacial tension. The apparatus employed is called the **du Nouy Tensiometer**.

The principle is illustrated with the help of a Fig. 1.8 and 1.9.

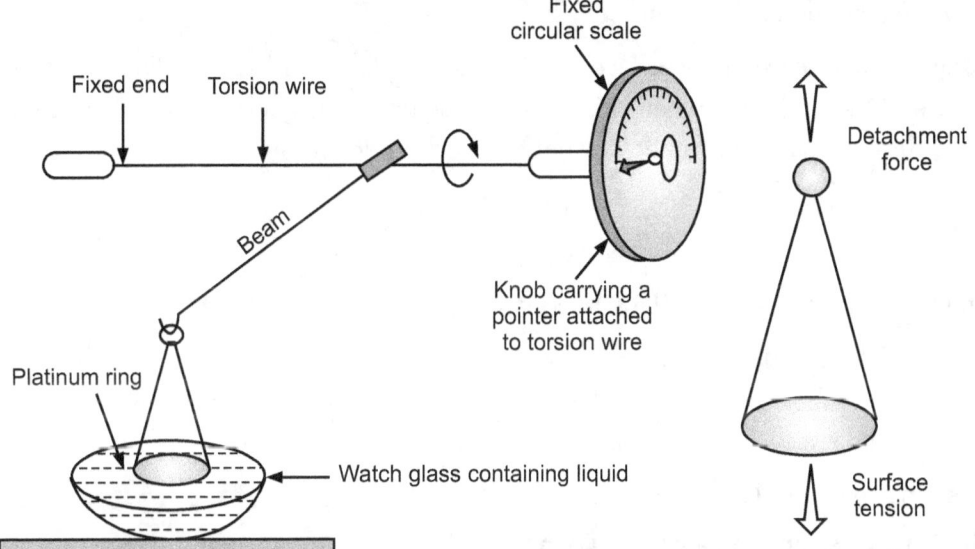

Fig. 1.8: du Nouy ring with a suspending hook   **Fig. 1.9: du Nouy tensiometer**

In this method, the force required to detach a platinum ring (du Nouy ring) from the liquid surface is measured. **This upward force (F) is exactly equal to the downward pull due to surface tension γ acting along the circumference of the ring.**

Where,

$$\text{Upward force 'F'} = \text{Downward force} \qquad \dots (1.16)$$

Upward Force:

One end of the torsion wire is fixed while the other is attached to a knob carrying a pointer (Fig. 1.8 and 1.9). The pointer moves on a fixed scale. The scale is previously calibrated by taking different weights on the beam and noting the scale reading when it is lifted from the horizontal position. The liquid whose surface tension is to be determined is placed in a watch glass so that the platinum-ring just touches its surface. The knob of the torsion wire is then slowly turned till the ring is just detached from the surface. The reading shown by the pointer on the scale gives the force 'F' in dynes.

$$\text{Upward force (F) = Dial reading in dynes} \qquad \text{... (1.17)}$$

Downward Force:

The weight of liquid that is adhered to the ring acts as downward force and try to balance the upward force. This force is equal to mg.

Where,

m : Mass of the liquid rise,

g : Acceleration due to gravity.

The downward force due to surface tension (or interfacial tension) of liquid, acts on circumference of the ring ($2\pi r\gamma$, where, r is radius of the ring). The liquid film lifted above the ring has two surfaces, outer and inner. The net force acting downward is:

$$\text{Downward force } = mg = 2\pi r \, \gamma.2$$

$$= 4\pi r \, \gamma \qquad \text{... (1.18)}$$

Substitute equation (1.17) and (1.18) in equation (1.16)

$$\text{F(dial reading in dynes) } = 4\pi r \, \gamma$$

or

$$\gamma = \frac{\text{F(dial reading in dynes)}}{4\pi r} \qquad \text{... (1.19)}$$

Surface tension is calculated from equation (1.19).

1.3.4 Maximum Bubble Pressure Method

In this method, air-pressure is applied slowly through a capillary tube dipping in the experimental liquid (Fig. 1.10). A bubble is formed at the end of the capillary. Slowly the bubble grows and becomes hemispherical. Then it breaks away when the pressure recorded by the manometer is noted. This is the maximum pressure required to make a bubble at the end of the capillary. At the moment of breaking, the forces due to maximum pressure 'P' equal to that of the opposing hydrostatic pressure 'P_h' and the surface tension 'γ' at the circumference of the capillary (Fig. 1.11).

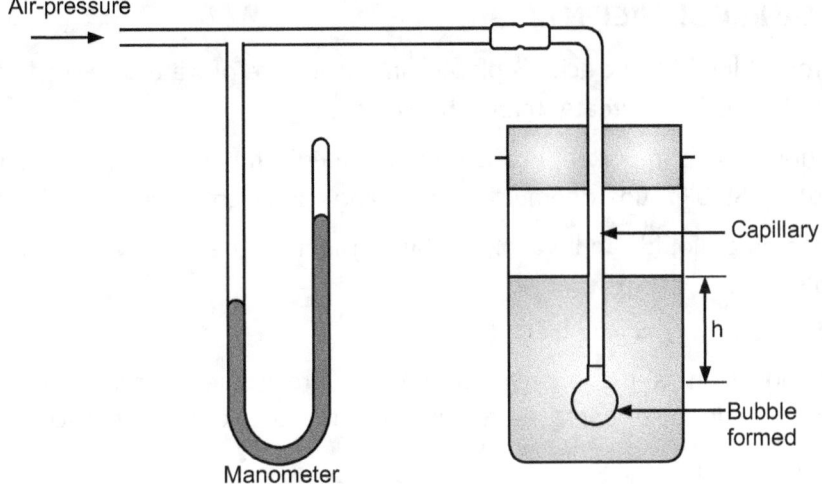

Fig. 1.10: Maximum bubble pressure apparatus

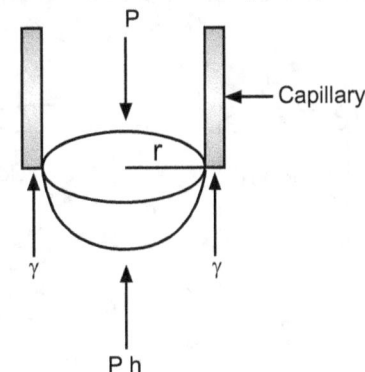

Fig. 1.11: Applied pressure on bubble is opposed by hydrostatic pressure and surface tension

Thus,
$$P \pi r^2 = P_h \pi r^2 + 2\pi r \gamma \qquad \qquad ... (1.20)$$

$$P = P_h + \frac{2\gamma}{r}$$

or
$$P = h d g + \frac{2\gamma}{r} \qquad \qquad ... (1.21)$$

Where,   r : Radius of capillary,

           d : Density of the liquid,

           h : Depth of liquid.

Knowing the value of P, h, d and r, phenomena can be found.

1.4 SPREADING COEFFICIENT

When drop of liquid (oleic acid) is placed on the surface of water, it will spread as a film and its force of adhesion is greater than cohesive force.

This phenomenon is important in adsorption of medicament from dosage form e.g. from cream and lotion. Stabilization of emulsion spreading coefficient phenomena is useful.

The spreading of liquid can be analyzed by considering the cohesive and adhesive force between molecules.

Work of Adhesion:

Work of adhesion is the energy required to break the attraction between unlike molecules. Same amount of energy is required even to break adhesive forces between the liquids.

Now, consider the hypothetical cylinder (cross-sectional area, 1 cm^2) of the sublayer liquid (water) S overlaid with a similar section of spreading liquid (Oleic acid) L, as shown in Fig. 1.12.

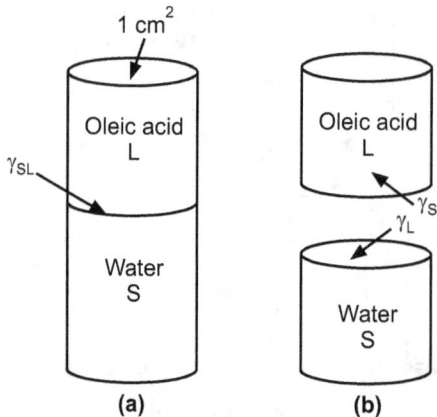

Fig. 1.12: The work of adhesion

The work of adhesion $= W_a = \gamma_L + \gamma_S - \gamma_{LS}$ ... (1.22)

Where,

γ_L : Interfacial tension of liquid,

γ_S : Interfacial tension of sublayer

γ_{LS} : Interfacial tension that has destroyed in the process.

Work of Cohesion:

The work of cohesion (Energy), required to separate the molecules of spreading liquid (oleic acid) so that it can flow over the sublayer (Water), as shown in Fig. 1.13. Here is no interfacial tension, when liquid is alone considered. Now, consider the hypothetical cylinder (cross-sectional area, 1 cm^2) is divided and two new surfaces are created (Fig. 1.13).

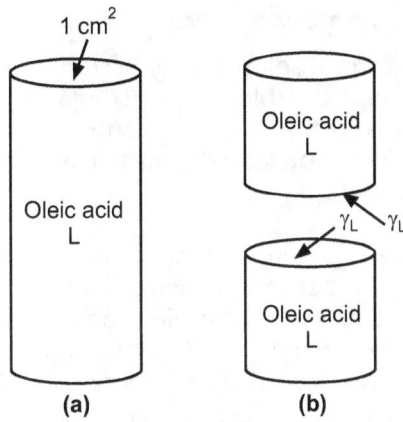

Fig. 1.13: The work of cohesion

The work of cohesion $=$ $W_c = 2\gamma_L$ ... (1.23)

Where,

γ_L : Surface tension of liquid (L)

Equation for Spreading Coefficient:

When liquid (L, oleic acid) is spreading on sublayer liquid (S, water), the work of adhesion (W_a) is greater than the work of cohesion (W_c).

The spreading coefficient is obtained by equation:

$$S = W_a - W_c = (\gamma_L + \gamma_S - \gamma_{LS}) - 2\gamma_L \qquad ... (1.24)$$

$$S = (\gamma_L + \gamma_{LS}) - \gamma_S \qquad ... (1.25)$$

If $\gamma_S > (\gamma_L + \gamma_{LS})$, then 'S' is positive, indicate spreading,

If $\gamma_S < (\gamma_L + \gamma_{LS})$, then 'S' is negative, indicate no spreading.

For the organic liquid spread on water, initial spreading coefficient may be positive or negative, but the final spreading coefficient is always negative. Some examples of substances and their spreading coefficients are given in table 1.2.

Table 1.2: Initial spreading coefficient at 20°C

Substances	S (dynes/cm)
Ethyl Alcohol	50.4
Propionic acid	45.8
Ethyl ether	45.8
Chloroform	13
Benzene	8.9
Hexane	3.4

1.5 ADSORPTION AT LIQUID INTERFACES

Adsorption to solid surfaces from solution may occur if the dissolved molecules and the solid surface have chemical groups capable of interacting. The added molecules move on to the interface, called **positive adsorption**. Example - surface active agents. Certain molecules prefer to remain in the bulk of solution, called **negative adsorption**. Example - electrolytes (sodium chloride) are added to water.

1.5.1 Surfactant

Definition: Surfactants are compounds that lower the surface tension (or interfacial tension) between two liquids or between a liquid and a solid. Surfactants may act as detergents, wetting agents, emulsifiers, foaming agents and dispersants. The name amphiphile is sometimes used synonymously with surfactant.

1.5.1.1 Structure and Orientation of Surfactant

All surfactant molecules consist of at least two parts (Fig. 1.14).

1. The hydrophilic part: It is soluble in water called as polar head.
2. The hydrophobic part: It is insoluble in water called as non-polar tail.

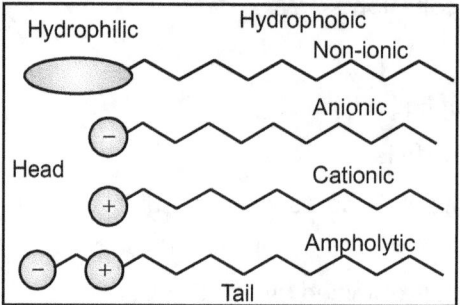

Fig. 1.14: Structure and types of surfactants according to charge

When surfactants are dissolved in water they orientate at the surface and reduce surface tension. [Fig. 1.15 (a)].

Reasons for the reduction in the surface tension:

1. When surfactant molecules are adsorbed at the water surface means that the surfactant molecules replace some of the water molecules in the surface.
2. The forces of attraction between surfactant and water molecules are less than those between two water molecules; hence the contraction force is reduced.

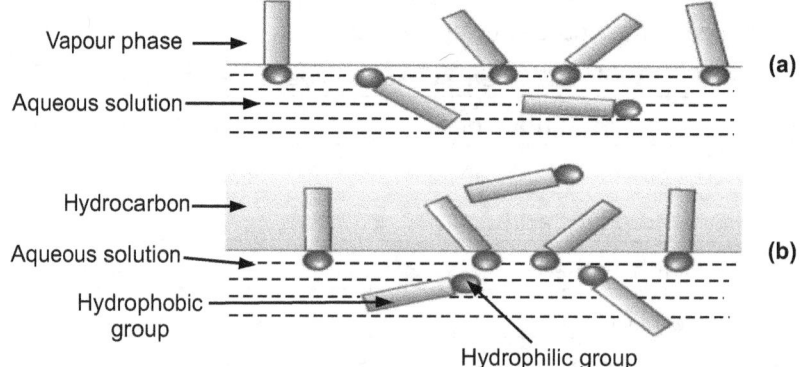

Fig. 1.15: Orientation of amphiphiles at
(a) solution–vapour interface and (b) two liquids interface

Surfactants will be also adsorbed at the interface between two immiscible liquids such as oil and water and will orientate themselves as shown in **Fig. 1.15 (b)** with their hydrophilic group in the water and their hydrophobic group in the oil. The interfacial tension at this interface, which arises because of a similar imbalance of attractive forces as at the water surface, will be reduced by this adsorption.

1.5.1.2 Types of Surfactant and Pharmaceutical Application

Depending on their charge characteristics, the surface-active molecules may be anionic, cationic, zwitterionic (ampholytic) or non-ionic **(Fig. 1.14)**. Examples of surfactants that are used in pharmaceutical formulation are as follows:

[a] Anionic Surfactants

1. A mixture of sodium alkyl sulfates, e.g. sodium dodecyl sulfate, sodium lauryl sulphate BP.

2. It is very soluble in water at room temperature, and is used pharmaceutically as a skin cleaner, having bacteriostatic action against gram-positive bacteria, and also in medicated shampoos.

3. It is a component of emulsifying wax.

[b] Cationic Surfactants

1. The quaternary ammonium and pyridinium cationic surfactants are important pharmaceutically because of their bactericidal activity against a wide range of gram-positive and some gram-negative organisms.

2. They may be used on the skin, especially in the cleaning of wounds.

3. Their aqueous solutions are used for cleaning contaminated utensils.

4. E.g. Benzolkonium chloride, cetyltrimethyl ammonium bromide.

[c] Non-ionic Surfactants

1. **Sorbitan esters** are supplied commercially as spans and are mixtures of the partial esters of sorbitol and its mono- and di-anhydrides with oleic acid. They are generally insoluble in water (low hydrophile–lipophile balance (HLB) value) and are used as water-in-oil emulsifiers and as wetting agents.

2. **Polysorbates** are complex mixtures of partial esters of sorbitol and its mono and di-anhydrides condensed with an approximate number of moles of ethylene oxide. They are supplied commercially as Tweens. The polysorbates are miscible with water, as reflected in their higher HLB values, and are used as emulsifying agents for oil-in-water emulsions.

3. **Poloxamers** are synthetic block copolymers of hydrophilic poly(oxyethylene) and hydrophobic poly(oxypropylene). Properties such as viscosity, HLB and physical state (liquid, paste or solid) are dependent on the relative chain lengths of the hydrophilic and hydrophobic blocks. They are supplied commercially as Pluronics.

1.5.1.3 Micelles Formation of Surfactant

Amphiphiles are molecules or ions which have certain affinity for both polar and nonpolar solvents. In water, at low concentration surface active agents exist individually as monomers, which are subcolloidal in size. As the concentration increases, the monomers aggregate themselves over a narrow range of concentration. These aggregates are called as micelles. Each micelle may contain around 50 monomers and size may be about 50 Å. This size falls into the colloidal range.

Critical micelle concentration, CMC, is defined as 'the concentration range of a surfactant at which micelles start forming'. CMC is a concentration range and has unit of concentration such as w/w%, w/v %, moles/litre, moles/1000 g of solvent etc.

Phenomenon of Micelle Formation:

The phenomenon of micelle formation is as follows:

Below CMC, surface active agents preferentially get adsorbed at air-water interface (Fig. 1.15). As the concentration of surfactant increases, molecules get accumulated progressively at the interface. In this process, at one particular concentration, the interface gets saturated, while the bulk phase is saturated with monomers. The formation of micelles is so spontaneous that it is difficult to differentiate the concentrations related to saturated phase and micelle phase. In the bulk of the solution, both monomers and micelles are in dynamic equilibrium (Fig. 1.16). This concentration is called as CMC. Beyond CMC, any further additional surface active agent enhances the formation of micelles only. This process is spontaneous, i.e., the free energy of the system is reduced.

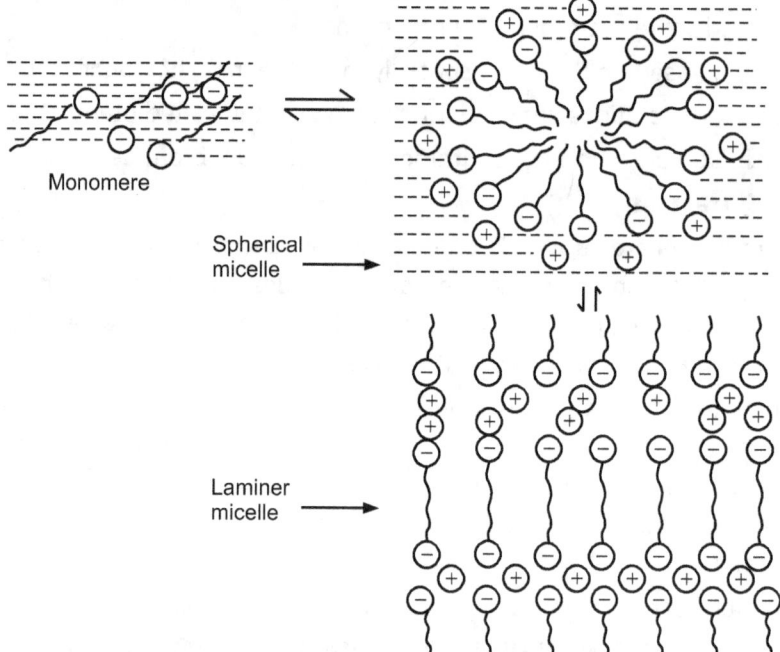

Fig. 1.16: Dynamic equilibrium of micelles in aqueous medium at high concentration of amphiphiles

Micelles assume spherical shape near CMC. In micelles, tails face toward the center and create a hydrophobic environment. The polar heads tend to associate with water molecules and form the surface of the **micelle** [Fig. 1.17 (a)]. When a non-polar dispersion medium is used, the opposite behaviour is observed called **reverse micelle** [Fig. 1.17 (b)]. Polar heads face inwards creating an aqueous pocket. The hydrocarbon portions associate with non-polar medium. At higher concentrations, laminar micelles are also formed which exist in equilibrium with spherical forms (Fig. 1.16).

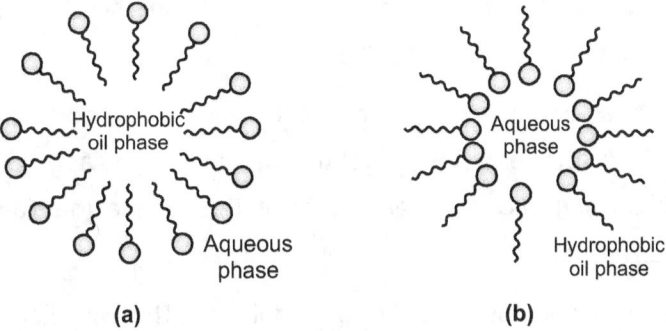

Fig. 1.17 : Structure of (a) micelle and (b) reverse micelles

1.5.2 Micellar Solubilisation

Poorly water-soluble drugs are normally solubilized in aqueous solutions by employing Micellar solubilisation. Surface active agents at and above CMC form micelles in aqueous dispersions. These micelles are spherical in shape and contain a hydrophobic interior and a hydrophilic surface. Hydrophobic pockets inside micelles offer an environment for solubilisation of poorly water soluble drugs. This phenomenon is called as **Micellar solubilisation.** (Fig. 1.18)

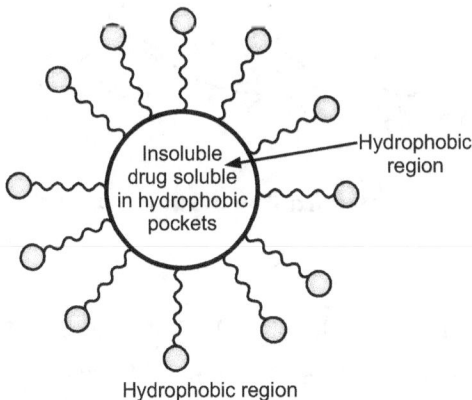

Fig 1.18: Micellar solubilisation

Examples are, solubilised systems containing volatile oils (peppermint oil), coal tar materials, phenobarbital, sulfonamides and vitamins. The hydrolytic or oxidative decomposition of drugs are reduced/prevented by using solubilised products. The process of micellar solubilisation is pictorially represented in Fig. 1.19. Here, the micelles are formed by non-ionic surfactant such as Tween 80.

The following observations are made regarding the Micellar solubilisation of drugs:

1. Benzene and toluene are non-polar molecules. So these are solubilised in the hydrocarbon interior (core) of micelles.

2. Salicylic acid is slightly polar molecule. The non-polar portion (benzene ring) is directed towards the central region of the micelles. The polar group (hydroxyl group) tends to align and accommodate itself on the surface (outside), i.e., hydrophilic (aqueous) environment.

3. p-Hydroxybenzoic acid is a highly polar molecule. This will align itself between the hydrophilic chains on the surface of the micelles.

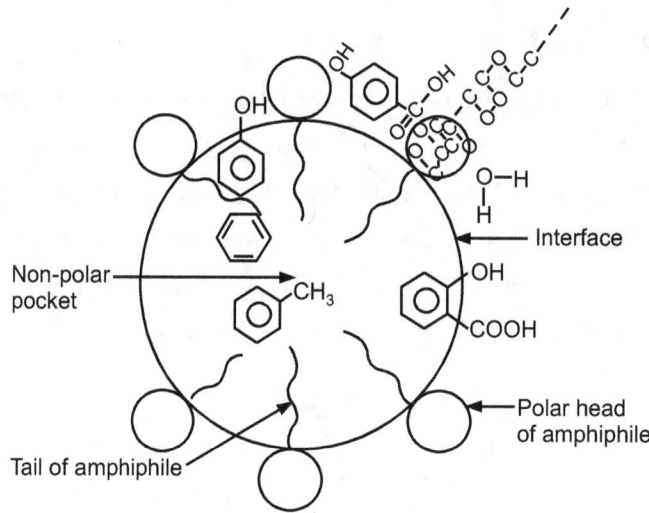

Fig. 1.19: Micellar stabilization of drugs (An artist's concept)

1.5.3 Krafft Point

Solubility of surfactant depends on the temperature of system. At low temperatures a saturated surfactant solution will be in equilibrium with solid surfactant; the temperature is too low for micelles to form and the limiting solubility will be low.

At the krafft temperature it becomes possible to form micelles and the surfactant becomes much more soluble; there is a break in the solubility curve, as shown in Fig. 1.20, example is sodium decyl sulphonate.

Below krafft point: No formation of micelle and limited solubility of surfactant.

Above krafft point: Formation micelles and the surfactant become much more soluble.

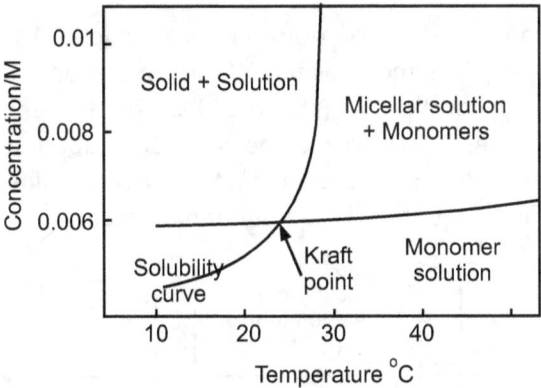

Fig. 1.20: Krafft point of surfactant

The CMC is primarily determined by the hydrophobic group of surfactant.

The Krafft temperature depends strongly on;

1. The nature of the head group and
2. The length of the hydrocarbon chain.

The hydrocarbon fragments have to be in a liquid state for micelle formation to occur. Solidification of the hydrocarbon chain is favoured by the cohesion between hydrocarbon chains, which increases with their length. Thus, the Krafft temperature increases with chain length, as shown in Table 1.3 for the Krafft temperatures of the sulphonates.

Table 1.3: Krafft temperatures of the sulphonates

$C_{10}SO_3Na$	$C_{12}SO_3Na$	$C_{14}SO_3Na$	$C_{16}SO_3Na$	$C_{18}SO_3Na$
22°C	34°C	43°C	52°C	60°C

1.5.4 Cloud Point

Cloud point is the temperature above which an aqueous solution of a water-soluble surfactant becomes turbid (Fig. 1.21).

Knowing the cloud point is important for:

1. Determining storage stability, storing formulations at temperatures significantly higher than the cloud point may result in phase separation and instability.
2. Wetting, cleaning and foaming characteristics can be different above and below the cloud point.

3. Generally, non-ionic surfactants show optimal effectiveness when used near or below their cloud point.

4. Low-foam surfactants should be used at temperatures slightly above their cloud point.

Cloud points are typically measured using 1% aqueous surfactant solutions. Cloud points range from 0° to 100°C (32 to 212°F), limited by the freezing and boiling points of water.

Cloud points are characteristics of non-ionic surfactants. An ionic surfactants (with negatively charged groups) are more water-soluble than non-ionic surfactants and will typically have much higher cloud points (above 100°C). The presence of other components in a formulation can depress or increase the solution's cloud point. For example, the addition of a coupler or hydrotrope can increase the cloud point of a solution, whereas builders or other salts will depress the cloud point temperature.

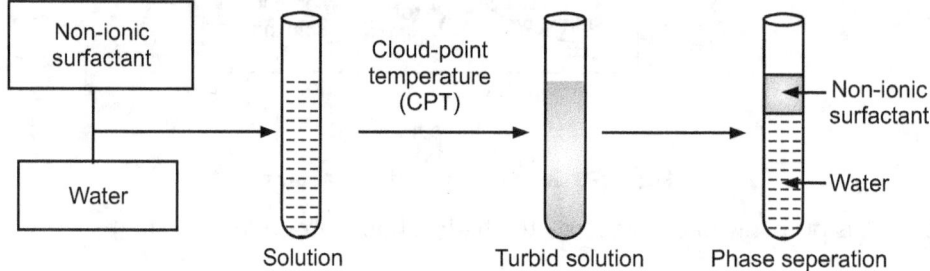

Fig. 1.21: Cloud-point non-ionic surfactant

1.5.5 The Hydrophilic-Lipophilic Balance (HLB Scale)

HLB Scale is developed by Griffin (1949), the HLB Scale ranks the tendency of a surfactant to be hydrophilic or hydrophobic (lipophilic). Since a surfactant molecule has both hydrophilic and hydrophobic portions, Griffin developed a ranking system to determine 'how hydrophilic' and 'how hydrophobic' a surfactant is. Surfactants generally have hydrophobic hydrocarbon chains with hydrophilic branches or ends (this scale is for non-ionic surfactants). The HLB scale is very relative scale; the number values of the HLB scale do not necessarily give insight into the properties of a surfactant, just their relative hydrophilicity compared to other surfactants. That said, the HLB scale is widely used in industry.

To summarize:

1. The HLB scale ranges from 1-20.

2. Surfactants with higher HLB number (greater than 10) are more hydrophilic.

3. Surfactants with lower HLB number (less than 10) are more hydrophobic (lipophilic).

4. Complete water solubility of a surfactant occurs at and above 7.3 HLB number.

Higher HLB scale valued surfactants are more hydrophilic and thus are more water soluble. Similarly, lower HLB scale valued surfactants are more lipophilic and thus more oil soluble. So, higher HLB surfactants will create oil-in-water emulsions and lower HLB surfactants will create water-in-oil emulsions.

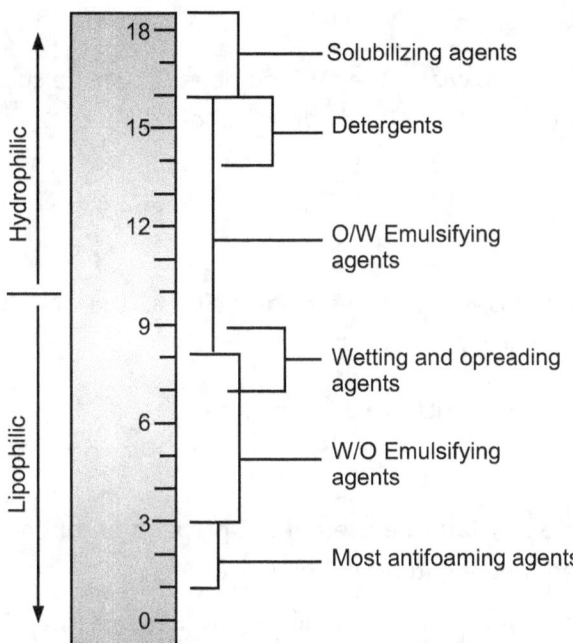

Fig. 1.22: HLB scale showing applications of surfactant and HLB requirement

Method of Estimation:

Method I:

The structure of a surfactant molecule is split into different component groups. Each group is assigned a number. The addition of these numbers for their respective groups permits the calculation of its HLB value. The equation is:

HLB = Σ(Hydrophilic group number) – Σ (Hydrophobic group number) + 7   ... (1.26)

Table 1.4: Various groups and group number

Groups	Group number
$SO_4^- Na^+$	38.7
CH_3	0.475
CH_2	0.475

Method II:

Griffin developed simple equations for calculation of the HLB number of relatively simple non-ionic surfactants. For a polyhydroxy fatty acid ester

$$HLB = 20\left(1 - \frac{S}{A}\right) \qquad ... (1.27)$$

S is the saponification number of the ester and A is the acid number. For a glyceryl monostearate, S = 161 and A = 198; the HLB is 3.8 (suitable for w/o emulsion).

Method III:

For a simple alcohol ethoxylate, the HLB number can be calculated from the weight percentage of ethylene oxide (E) and polyhydric alcohol (P).

$$HLB = \frac{E + P}{5} \hspace{4cm} \text{... (1.28)}$$

Method IV:

If the surfactant contains Polyethylene oxide (PEO) as the only hydrophilic group, the contribution from one OH group is neglected

$$HLB = \frac{E}{5} \hspace{4cm} \text{... (1.29)}$$

Required HLB (RHLB)

Normally, blends of surfactant are used in the preparation of emulsion. The HLB of the blend is estimated based on the nature of the oil phase.

Required HLB is the Hydrophilic-Lipophilic value that is desired in order to prepare a stable emulsion of w/o or o/w type.

Occasionally it is also known as **'critical HLB'**. The RHLB value is calculated based on the oil phase and the type of emulsion.

It is assumed that HLB of a mixture of two surfactants containing the fraction, f of A and (1 – f) of B is an algebraic mean of the two HLB values.

$$HLB_{mixture} = f \, HLB_A + (1 - f) \, HLB_B \hspace{3cm} \text{... (1.30)}$$

Table 1.5: A few examples with RHLBs

Oil	w/o Emulsion	o/w Emulsion
Paraffin oil	4	10
Beeswax	5	09
Anhydrous lanolin	8	12
Cyclohexane	--	15
Toluene	--	15

1.6 SOLUBLE MONOLAYER AND GIBBS ADSORPTION ISOTHERM

When a small drop of polar short chain alcohol is added in to water, it spreads on water surface. As its concentration increases, the molecules progressively get accumulated at the surface. At particular concentration, the surface is completely covered with a monomers film of added substance.

Gibbs Adsorption Isotherm

The following parameters are evaluated in this study:

1. Surface excess
2. Surface tension.
3. Concentration of amphiphiles in bulk and surface.

These parameters can be easily measured for soluble monolayers compared to insoluble films.   This study involves Gibbs adsorption isotherms.

The concentration of the surfactant in the bulk can be estimated drawing a sample from the bulk. The surface concentration can be obtained by cutting and lifting the liquid surface using a microtome blade. The collected surfactant molecules from the surface are estimated by a suitable method.

Surface excess is the difference between the surface and bulk concentration. (Fig. 1.23)

Such a direct measurement of surface excess provides number of problems.   Hence, Gibbs equation is widely used alternative method.

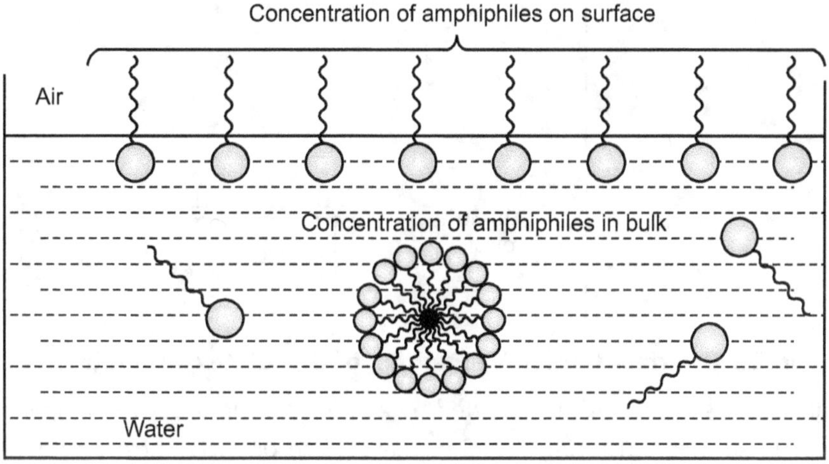

Surface excess : Concentration of amphiphiles on surface – Concentration of amphiphiles in bulk

Fig. 1.23: Soluble monolayer

The number of molecules per unit area of the surface can be estimated using Gibbs equation. The Gibbs equation may be expressed as follows:

$$\Gamma = \frac{-a_2}{RT}\left[\frac{d\gamma}{da_2}\right] \qquad\qquad \dots (1.31)$$

Where
Γ = Moles of solute adsorbed/unit area, or surface excess

R = Ideal gas constant

T = Absolute temperature

$d\gamma$ = Change in the surface tension

da_2 = Change in the solute activity at activity a_2

Surface excess is the amount of the amphiphile per unit area of surface in excess of that in the bulk liquid. For dilute solutions of non-electrolytes, activity term can be replaced by solute concentration, c.

$$\Gamma = \frac{-c_2}{RT}\left[\frac{d\gamma}{dc_2}\right] \qquad \dots (1.32)$$

Since, the term $\frac{dc}{c}$ is equal to d(ln c), the Gibbs equation can be written as

$$\Gamma = \frac{-1}{RT}\left[\frac{d\gamma}{d\,ln\,c_2}\right] \qquad \dots (1.33)$$

If graph is plotted between surface tension and the logarithm of the solute concentration from slope of the graph it is easy to determine the surface excess [Fig. 1.24].

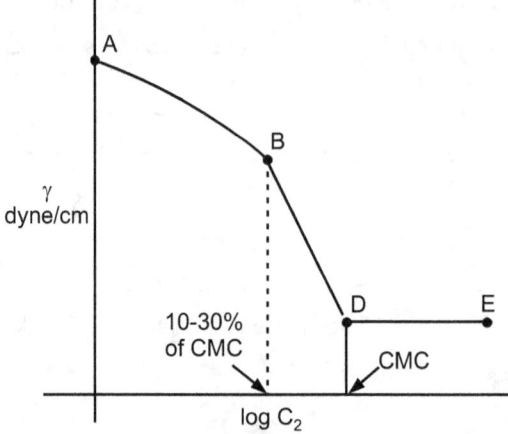

Fig. 1.24: Surface tension V logarithm of the solute concentration

The initial curved segment AB is followed by a linear segment BD, along which there is a sharp decrease in surface tension as log C increases. The point D corresponds to the CMC, the concentration at which Micelles form in the solution. Beyond the CMC the line become horizontal, further additions of surfactant no longer shows decrease in surface tension. Along the linear segment BD, the surface excess is constant. Saturation adsorption of the surfactant has been reached at point B, i.e. surface excess does not increase further as the bulk concentration increases. However, the surface tension decreases greatly until point D is reached. Within the segment BD of the curve, the surfactant molecules are closely packaged at the surface and surface area occupied per molecule is constant.

1.7 INSOLUBLE MONOLAYERS AND THE FILM BALANCE

If the non-polar groups of an amphiphilic compounds are sufficiently large so that it become almost insoluble, then compound will usually spread over a water surface to form monomolecular layer.

History:

Insoluble monolayers have a fascinating history that goes back before the American Revolution.

During a voyage to England in 1757: Benjamin Franklin observed that, Seamon when cooking grease was thrown from the ship's gallery onto the water, film is formed on the surface of the sea.

In 1765: Benjamin Franklin followed up this observation with an experiment on a half-acre pond in England and found that the application of 1 teaspoonful of oil was just sufficient to cover the pond and calm the waves.

In 1899: Lord Rayleigh showed that when small amounts of certain slightly soluble oils were placed on a clean surface of water contained in a trough, they spread to form a layer, one molecule thick (monomolecular layer). Prior to Rayleigh's work, a woman named Agnes Poekels, developed a "film balance" for studying insoluble monolayers. She earned out a series of experiments, which she summarized in a letter to Lord Rayleigh in January, 1881. In fact, she invented the film balance in 1883, over 30 years before Langmnir, whose name is normally associated with this type of apparatus.

Cross-Sectional Area of Insoluble Monolayer:

Knowing the area of the film and the volume of the spreading liquid, it should therefore be possible to compute the thickness of such films. The film thickness is equal to the length of the molecules standing in a vertical position of the surface when the molecules are packed in closest arrangement. Furthermore, if the molecular weight and the density of the spreading oil are known, the cross-sectional area available to the molecules can be easily computed.

Area of cross-section per molecule is given by

$$\text{Area of cross-section/molecule} = \frac{MS}{V\rho N} \quad\quad\quad ... (1.34)$$

Where,　M : Molecular weight of the spreading liquid,
　　　　　S : The surface area covered by the film,
　　　　　V : The volume of the spreading liquid,
　　　　　ρ : Density,
　　　　　N : Avogadro's number.

Film Balance:

1. Langmuir, Adam, Harkins, and others have made quantitative studies of the properties of films that are spread over a clear surface of the substrate liquid (usually water) contained in a trough.

2. The film can be compressed against a horizontal float by means of a movable barrier.

3. The force exerted on the float is measured by a torsion wire arrangement similar to that employed in the ring tensiometer.

4. The apparatus called film balance is shown in Fig. 1.25 and 1.26.

5. The compressive force per unit area on the float is known as the **surface pressure, π.** It is the difference in surface tension between the pure substrate, γ_o (water), and that with a film spread on it, γ, and is written as

$$\pi = (\gamma_o - \gamma) \qquad \qquad \text{... (1.35)}$$

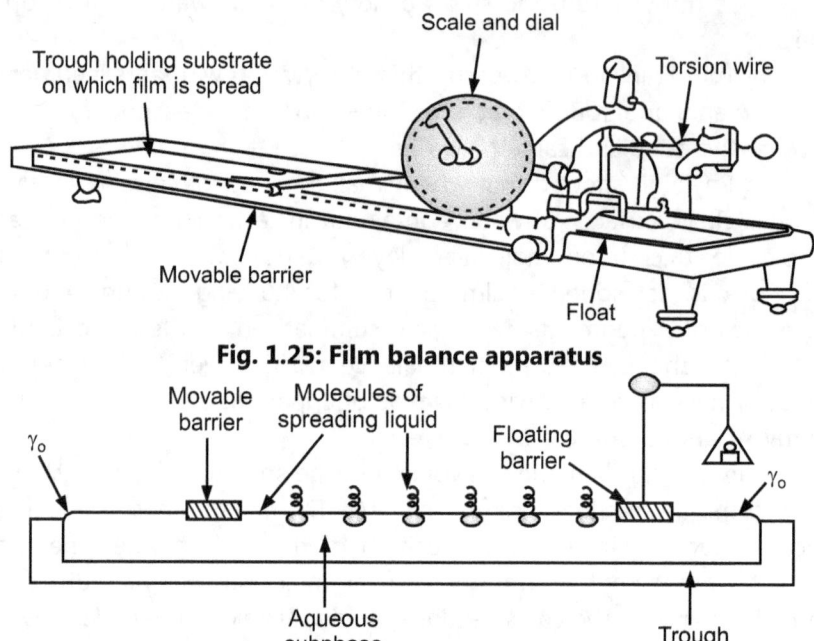

Fig. 1.25: Film balance apparatus

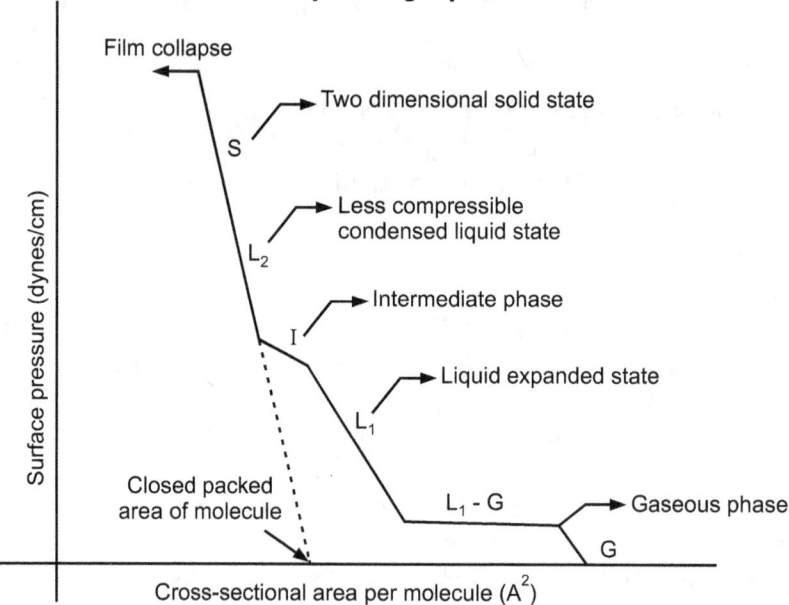

Fig. 1.26: Cross-sectional view of spreading liquid on the surface of a film balance

Fig. 1.27: Phase change that occurs when film is spread at an interface and then compressed

The film (surface) pressure is then plotted against the area of the film (Fig. 1.27).

Region G: When the film is spread over an area greater than 50 to 60 A^2/molecule, it exerts little pressure on the floating barrier. The film acts like a gas in two dimensions.

Region L_1-G: As the film begins to be compressed, a liquid phase L_1 appears that coexists in equilibrium with the gas phase. This occurs at a low surface pressure (e.g., 0.2 dynes/cm or less.)

Region L_1: The liquid expanded state may be thought of as a bulk liquid state, but in two dimensions.

Region I: Further compression of the film often leads to appearance of an intermediate phase.

Region L_2: A less compressible condensed liquid state, region L_2.

Region S: Where the film can be regarded as being in a two-dimensional solid state. Finally the molecules slip over one another and the film breaks when it is greatly compressed.

Applications:

1. **The electric potential and viscosity** of monomolecular films may be studied by means of the film balance.
2. **The molecular weight** of high polymers such as proteins can be estimated by its use.
3. **The study of biologic systems:** Some protein molecules unfold from a spherical configuration into a flat film when spread on the surface of the film in trough, and the relationship between unfolding and biologic activity can be studied.
4. **The sizes and shapes of molecules** of steroids, hormones, and enzymes and their interaction with drugs at interfaces can also be investigated by means of the film balance.

1.8 ADSORPTION AT SOLID INTERFACE

When a solid surface is exposed to a gas or a liquid, molecules from the gas or the solution phase accumulate or concentrate at the surface.

The phenomenon of concentration of molecules of a gas or liquid at a solid surface is called **adsorption.**

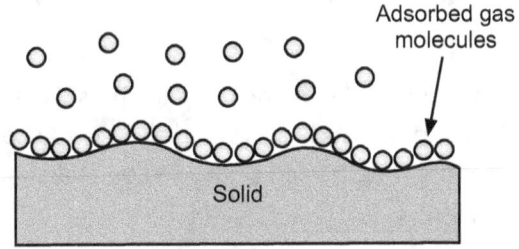

Fig. 1.28: Adsorption of a gas at a solid surface

The substance that deposits at the surface is called **Adsorbate** and the solid on whose surface the deposition occurs is called the **Adsorbent.**

Examples of Adsorption:

1. **Adsorption of a dye by a charcoal:** If finely divided charcoal is stirred into a dilute solution of methylene blue (an organic dye), the depth of colour of the solution decreases appreciably. The dye molecules have been adsorbed by charcoal particles.

2. **Adsorption of a gas by charcoal:** If a gas (SO_2, Cl_2, NH_3) is treated with powdered charcoal in a closed vessel, the gas pressure is found to decrease. The gas molecules concentrate on charcoal surface and are said to be adsorbed.

1.8.1 Adsorption versus Absorption

The term 'adsorption' must be carefully distinguished from another like-sounding term 'absorption'. **While adsorption implies deposition at the surface only, absorption implies penetration into the body of the solid** (Fig. 1.29). For illustration a chalk when dipped in ink adsorbs the latter and on breaking it is found to be white from within. On the other hand, water is absorbed by a sponge and is distributed throughout the sponge uniformly.

Both adsorption and absorption often take place side by side. It is thus difficult to distinguish between the two processes experimentally. Mc Bain introduced the general term **Sorption** which includes both the adsorption and absorption.

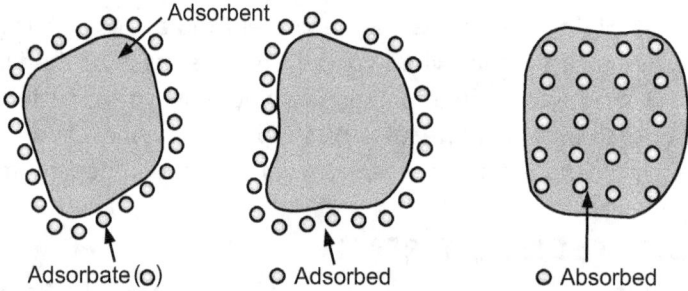

Fig. 1.29: Adsorption versus Absorption

1.8.2 Types of Adsorption

The adsorption of a gas into a solid surface is mainly of two types:

1. **Physical Adsorption**

    (i)   This is due to the gas molecules being held to the solid surface by van der Waal's attractive forces. It is also referred to as van der Waal's Adsorption.

    (ii) For example, adsorption of hydrogen or oxygen on charcoal is Physical Adsorption.

2. **Chemical Adsorption or Chemisorption**

    (i)   In this kind of adsorption, the gas molecules or atoms are held to the solid surface by chemical bonds. These bonds may be covalent or ionic in nature.

    (ii) For example, hydrogen is chemisorbed on nickel.

1.8.3 Adsorption of Gases on Solids

The adsorption of gases by solid adsorbents has certain characteristic features. Physical adsorption and chemisorption are found to differ in many respects (Table 1.6).

Table 1.6: Physical adsorption versus chemical adsorption

Physical Adsorption	Chemisorption
1. Caused by intermolecular van der Waal's forces.	1. Caused by chemical bond formation,
2. Depends on nature of gas. Easily liquefiable gases are adsorbed readily.	2. Much more specific than physical adsorption.
3. Heat of adsorption is small (about 5 kcal/mol)	3. Heat of adsorption is large (20-100 kcal/mol).
4. Reversible.	4. Irreversible.
5. Occurs rapidly at low temperature; decreases with increasing temperature.	5. Increases with increase of temperature.
6. Increase of pressure increases adsorption; decrease of pressure causes desorption.	6. Change of pressure has no such effects.
7. Forms multimolecular layers on adsorbent surface.	7. Forms unimolecular layer.

1.8.4 Adsorption Isotherms

Adsorption Isotherm is called 'the relationship between the equilibrium pressure of a gas and amount of gas adsorbed on the solid at any constant temperature'.

The adsorption of gas on a solid surface is a reversible process,

Free gas $\rightleftharpoons$ Gas adsorbed on solid

Adsorption of gas basically depends on equilibrium pressure and temperature.

1.8.4.1 Freundlich Adsorption Isotherm

Freundlich suggested relation called the Freundlich adsorption isotherm,

$$y = \frac{w}{m} = kP^{1/n} \qquad \qquad \text{... (1.36)}$$

Where, y: The mass w of gas adsorbed per unit mass m of solid adsorbent at constant pressure P.

k and n: These are constants depending on the nature of the gas and the adsorbent and on temperature.

This relation is obtained by plotting the mass of the gas adsorbed per unit mass of adsorbent (w/m) against equilibrium pressure (P) [Fig. 1.30].

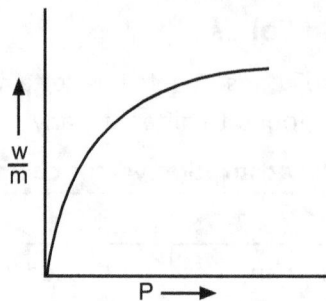

Fig. 1.30: Gas adsorbed per unit mass of adsorbent

Taking log of equation (1.36)

$$\log\left(\frac{w}{m}\right) = \log k + \frac{1}{n} \log P \qquad \ldots (1.37)$$

Thus, a plot (Fig. 1.31) of log (w/m) against log P should be a straight line with slope l/n and intercept log k.

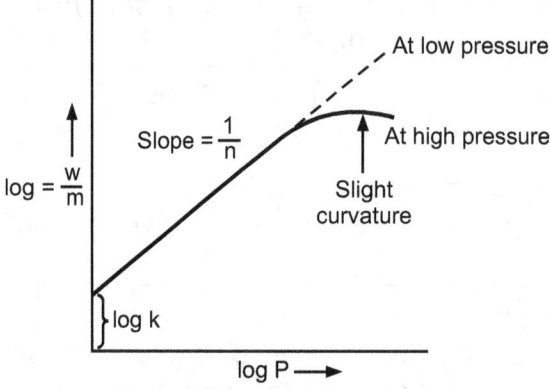

Fig. 1.31: Plot of log w/m against log P

Freundlich isotherm is not applicable at high pressures because,

(A) Low pressure: Plots were straight lines at low pressures,

(B) Higher pressure: They show a slight curvature.

This indicate that Freundlich equation is not applied to adsorption of gases by solids at higher pressures. (Fig. 1.31)

1.8.4.2 Langmuir Adsorption Isotherm

Langmuir (1916) derived a simple adsorption isotherm based on some assumptions.

Assumptions:

Langmuir made the following assumptions.

1. The layer of the gas molecule is adsorbed on active sites of the solid adsorbent.
2. It forms layer one-molecule thick (monolayer).
3. The adsorbed layer is uniform all over the adsorbent.

4. There is no interaction between the adjacent adsorbed molecules.
5. **The rate of adsorption** (condensation) is proportional to number of unoccupied sites on solid surface.
6. **The rate of desorption** (evaporation) is proportional to number of occupied sites on solid surface.

Derivation:

The amount of gas adsorbed on solid surface depends on pressure of gas on solid surface. At a particular pressure 'P':

1. θ is the fraction of the total surface covered by the gas molecules,
2. $1 - \theta$ is the fraction of the total surface uncovered by the gas molecules,
3. **The rate of adsorption**, $r_1 = k_1 (1 - \theta) P$
4. **The rate of desorption**, $r_2 = k_2 \theta$

Where, k_1 and k_2 are proportionality constants for adsorption and desorption respectively.

At equilibrium:

$$r_1 = r_2 \qquad \qquad \text{... (1.38)}$$
$$k_1 (1 - \theta) P = k_2 \theta \qquad \qquad \text{... (1.39)}$$
$$k_1 p - k_1 \theta P = k_2 \theta \qquad \qquad \text{... (1.40)}$$
$$k_1 P = k_2 \theta + k_1 \theta P \qquad \qquad \text{... (1.41)}$$
$$k_1 P = \theta (k_2 + k_1 P) \qquad \qquad \text{... (1.42)}$$
$$\theta = \frac{k_1 P}{(k_2 + k_1 P)} \qquad \qquad \text{... (1.43)}$$
$$\theta = \frac{(k_1/k_2) P}{1 + (k_1/k_2) P} \qquad \qquad \text{... (1.44)}$$

Now, assume that

$$\frac{k_1}{k_2} = b \quad \text{or} \quad \theta = \frac{y}{y_m}$$

where, $y = \dfrac{w}{m}$: The mass 'w' of gas adsorbed per gram of solid adsorbent 'm'

         y_m : The mass of gas that 1 gram of solid adsorbent can take up when monolayer is completed

$$\frac{y}{y_m} = \frac{bP}{1 + bP}$$

$$\therefore \qquad y = \frac{y_m bP}{1 + bP} \qquad \qquad \text{... (1.45)}$$

Equation (1.45) represent Langmuir isotherm. Inverting equation and multiplying by 'P', we get

$$\frac{P}{y} = \frac{1}{y_m b} + \frac{P}{y_m} \qquad \qquad \dots (1.46)$$

Now, plot of P/y against P **(Fig. 1.32)** gives a straight line and 'y_m' and 'b' can be obtained from the slope and intercept. The value of 'y_m' is used to estimate specific surface of the solids, considering that adsorption is monomolecular layer thickness.

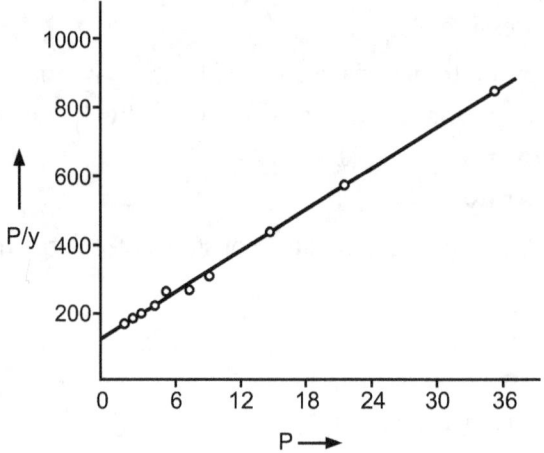

Fig. 1.32: P/y against P

Multilayer Adsorption:

Sometimes, gases are adsorbed as multi-molecular layers on solids. Braunauer, Emmette and Teller have extended equation (1.46) as:

$$\frac{P}{y(P_o - P)} = \frac{1}{y_m b} + \frac{b - P}{y_m b} \cdot \frac{P}{P_o} \qquad \qquad \dots (1.47)$$

Where,

P : Pressure of the adsorbate, in mm Hg,

y : Mass of the vapour per gram,

P_o : Vapour pressure at saturation (monolayer),

y_m : The mass of gas that 1 gram of solid adsorbent can take up when monolayer is completed,

b : Constant, proportional to heat of adsorption and latent heat of condensation of subsequent layers.

Equation (1.47) is called BET equation.

It is used to determine 'y_m', Here 'b' is greater than 2. If only monomolecular layer is formed, this plot reduces to Langmuir adsorption isotherm.

1.8.4.3 Adsorption Isotherm

Adsorption isotherms are defined as 'the plots drawn between the amount of gas adsorbed on a solid (y-axis) against the equilibrium pressure (x-axis) at constant temperature'.

There are five types of adsorption isotherms as shown in Fig. 1.33.

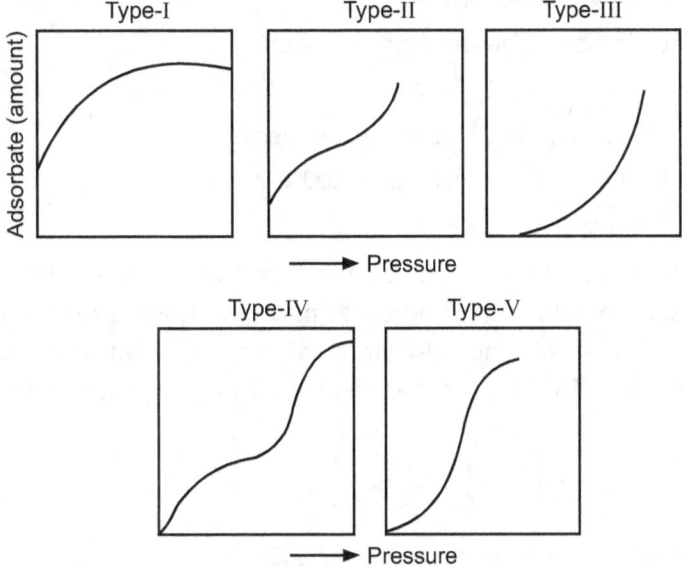

Fig. 1.33: Adsorption isotherms

Type I:

1. This represents increase in adsorption with increasing pressure and followed levelling OFF.
2. Leveling OFF: Due to saturation of gas molecule and formation of monolayer on surface of solid.
   Example: Freundlich and Langmuir adsorption isotherm.
3. Adsorption of nitrogen gas at 78 K on charcoal.

Type II:

1. This is sigmodial in shape and occur when gas undergoes physical adsorption onto non-porous solid to form a monolayer.
2. When the pressure is increased multilayer is formed.
3. Type - II is described by BET equation (b > 2) as explained earlier.
4. Example: Adsorption of nitrogen gas at 78 K on iron or platinum catalyst.

Type III:

1. It is not commonly observed.
2. The heat of adsorption of gas in the first layer is less than the latent heat of condensation of successive layers.
3. In the BET equation, the constant 'b' is smaller than 2.
4. Example: Adsorption of bromine gas on silica.

Type IV:

1. This represents the adsorption of gas on porous solids.
2. First point of inflection represents the monomolecular layer adsorption.
3. Condensation within the pores of the solid and the multimolecular layer is represented by further adsorption.
4. Example: Adsorption of benzene on silica gel.

Type V:

1. This is uncommon and shows capillary condensation.
2. Example: Water vapour on charcoal at 100°C.

1.8.5 The Solid-Liquid Interface

From the solution, the solute molecules may be adsorbed on solid. Drugs such as dyes, alkaloids, fatty acids, inorganic acids and bases may be adsorbed from solution onto solids such as alumina or charcoal. The adsorption of strychnine, atropine and quinine from aqueous solutions by different clays was expressed by Langmuir equation (1.46) in the following form.

$$\frac{c}{y} = \frac{1}{by_m} + \frac{c}{y_m} \qquad \qquad ... (1.48)$$

Where,   c is equilibrium concentration (mg / 100 ml),

   y is amount of alkaloidal base w in milligrams adsorbed per gram m of clay.

The adsorption of strychnine from aqueous solution onto three different clays such as activated attapulgite, halloysite and kaolin have been studied, and shown in Fig. 1.34.

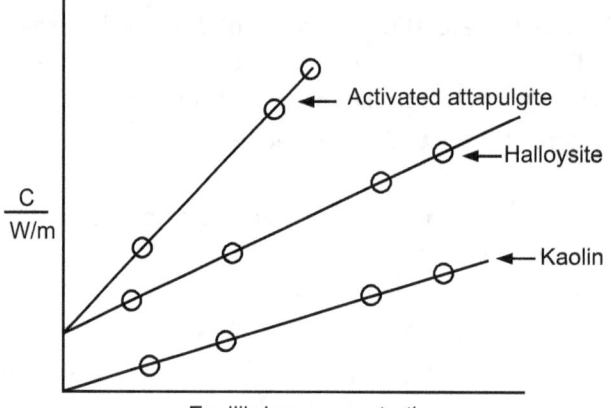

Fig. 1.34: Adsorption of strychnine onto three different clays

The smaller the slope, the better the absorption. From the Fig. 1.34 one can conclude that adsorption of Attapulgite > halloysite > kaolin.

Adsorption at solid surfaces is involved in the phenomena of **wetting and detergency.**

1.8.5.1 Wetting Phenomena

Wetting is an adsorption process in which there is an intimated contact of solid with liquid.

Pharmaceutical and medicinal importance's of wetting phenomenon:

1. **Suspension:** The displacement of air from the surface of sulfur, charcoal and other powders for the purpose of dispersing these drugs in liquid vehicles.
2. **Granulation:** In granulation process, powders are mixed with liquid binding agent. The success of process depends of good wettability of powder.
3. **Film coating:** In coating process, wetting and spreading of liquid coating mixture over tablet surface occurs.
4. The displacement of air from the matrix of cotton pads and bandages so that medicinal solutions may be absorbed for application to various body areas.
5. The displacement of dirt and debris by the use of detergents in the washing of wounds.

Surfactants are used as wetting agent because:

1. Lowering interfacial tension between solid and liquid.
2. Lowering contact angle between solid and liquid.
3. Displacement of air from solid for intimate contact of solid and liquid.

1.8.5.1.1 Contact Angle

The contact angle is 'an angle that a liquid creates with a solid surface when both come in contact together'.

Contact angle is one of the common ways to measure the wettability of a surface or material. Wetting refers to the study of how a liquid deposited on a solid. (Fig. 1.35)

Types of Contact Angles:

1. **The wetting liquid or smaller contact angle:**
    (A) The contact angle is smaller i.e. smaller than 90° with the solid.
    (B) Surface tension: Minimum surface tension between liquid and solid.
    (C) Force of attraction: Cohesive forces are weaker than adhesive forces.

2. **A non-wetting liquid or maximum contact angle:**
    (A) A contact angle between 90° and 180° with the solid.
    (B) Surface tension: Higher surface tension between liquid and solid.
    (C) Force of attraction: Cohesive forces are stronger than adhesive forces.

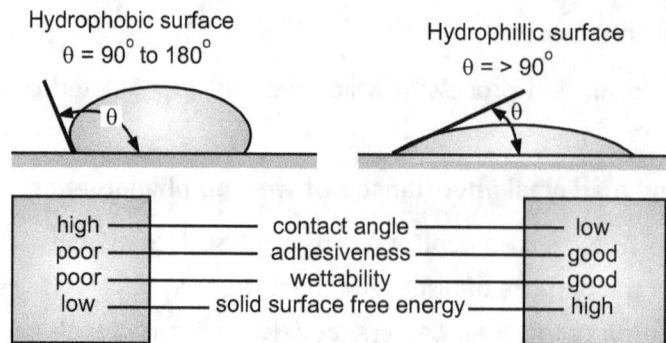

Fig. 1.35: Wetting and contact angle

1.8.5.1.2 Young's Equation

Contact angle can be conveniently estimated by placing a drop of liquid on solid surface. The force acting at equilibrium may be considered as follows (Fig. 1.36):

γ^{sv} : Interfacial tension between solid and vapour.

γ^{sl} : Interfacial tension between solid and liquid.

γ^{lv} : Interfacial tension between liquid and vapour.

At equilibrium,

$$\gamma^{sv} = \gamma^{sl} + \gamma^{lv} . \cos \theta \qquad \qquad \text{... (1.49)}$$

Where, θ is the contact angle.

Equation (1.49) is called **Young's Equation.**

The work of adhesion between the solid and liquid interface is given by Dupre's equation (1.22).

$$W^{sl} = \gamma^{sv} + \gamma^{lv} - \gamma^{sl} \qquad \qquad \text{... (1.50)}$$

By combining equation (1.49) and (1.50) we get alternative for Young's equation:

$\therefore \qquad \qquad W^{sl} = \gamma^{sl} + \gamma^{lv} . \cos \theta + \gamma^{lv} - \gamma^{sl} \qquad \qquad \text{... (1.51)}$

$\qquad \qquad W^{sl} = \gamma^{lv} (1 + \cos \theta) \qquad \qquad \text{... (1.52)}$

Wetting process improves till $\cos \theta = 1$ or $\cos \theta = 0$ and this is the ideal wetting.

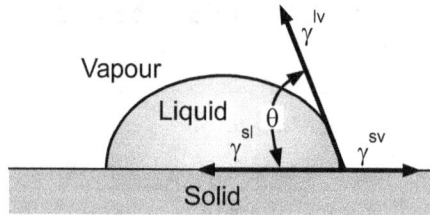

θ is the contact angle

γ^{sl} is the solid/liquid interfacial free energy

γ^{sv} is the solid surface free energy

γ^{lv} is the liquid surface free energy

Fig. 1.36: Contact angle and Young's equation

Contact angle: Range from 0° to 180° as shown in Fig. 1.37.

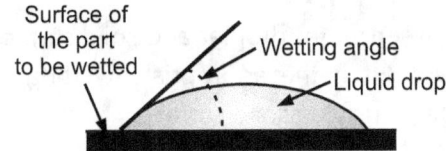

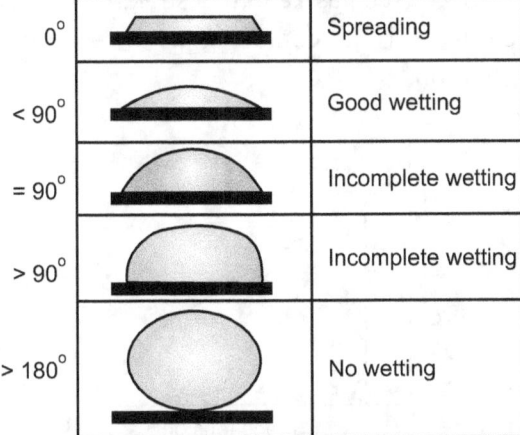

Fig. 1.37: Contact angle : Range from 0°C to 180°C

1.8.5.1.3 Wetting Process

Three types of wetting processes been identified [Fig. 1.38]:

(A) Adhesional wetting

(B) Immersional wetting and

(C) Spreading wetting.

(A) Adhesional wetting: (stage a – b)

The first step in the wetting of powder is adhesional wetting in which the surface of solid is brought into contact with the liquid surface.

(B) Immersional wetting: (stage b – c)

The particle is then forced below the surface of the liquid i.e. Immersional wetting. During this step, solid-liquid interface is formed and solid-air interface is lost.

(C) Spreading wetting: (stage c – d)

Finally, the liquid spreads over the entire surface of the solid as spreading wetting occurs. The work of spreading wetting is equal to form new solid-air and liquid-air interface and loss of the solid-air interfaces.

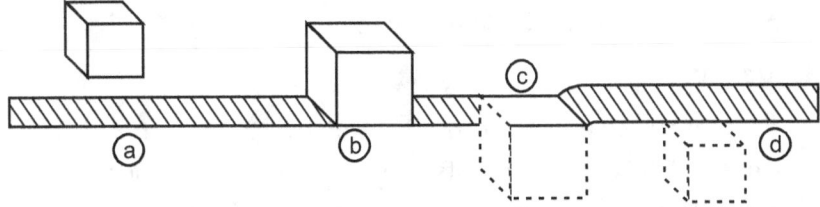

Fig. 1.38: Wetting process

1.8.5.1.4 Critical Surface Tension

The contact angle between water droplet and solid surface results when the water wets solid surface incompletely. But if the appropriate wetting agent is added to water, the solution will spread spontaneously on solid surface.

When graph of cos θ versus the surface tension was plotted, for a homologous series of liquids spread on a solid surface (such as Teflon), a straight line resulted [Fig. 1.39]. The line may be extrapolated to cos θ = 1 i.e. to contact angle of zero (i.e. complete wetting) which gives the value of surface tension.

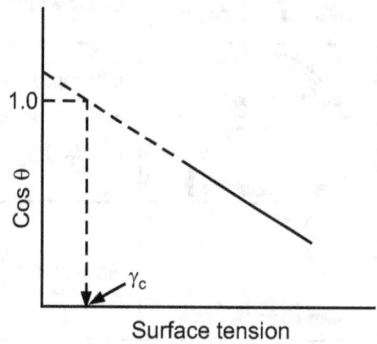

Fig. 1.39: Cos θ Vs surface tension 'γ'

The surface tension at Cos θ = 1 is called as the **critical surface tension (γ_c).** The critical surface tension was characteristic for each liquid.

1.8.5.1.5 Draws Test

The effectiveness of wetting agent depend on reduction in contact angle. But it is difficult to measure contact angle. Even no convenient method is available for direct measurement of the surface tension of a solid surface, not the value of spreading coefficient is available. As a result of these difficulties one test is used in industry for wetting and test is known as **Draws Test.**

Procedure:

1. A weighted skein of cotton yarn is allowed to sink through a wetting solution in a 500 ml graduated cylinder.
2. The time required for sinking is noted and compared.

Conclusion: Higher wetting and lower time required.

1.8.5.2 Detergency

Surfactants in aqueous solutions are used to remove the dirt from substrates such as glass, fabric, skin etc. Effective detergents are required for the cleaning of production equipment, containers for packing and also in order to maintain hygiene in the industry.

Detergency is a complex process and a number of steps are simultaneously involved (Fig. 1.40). These are:

1. Initial wetting of the dirt from the surface.
2. Solubilising of the dirt.
3. Removing the insoluble dirt as deflocculating particles.
4. Suspending the particles in the detergent solution.
5. Removing the oil soluble materials and convert into emulsion.
6. Converting the dirt into foam so as to wash easily.

The HLB requirement for the detergency is about 13 to 16.

Some examples of detergents of ionic type are:

Cationic type: Zephiran (benzyldimethylcetyl ammonium chloride), Cetrimide (cetyltrimethyl ammonium chloride).

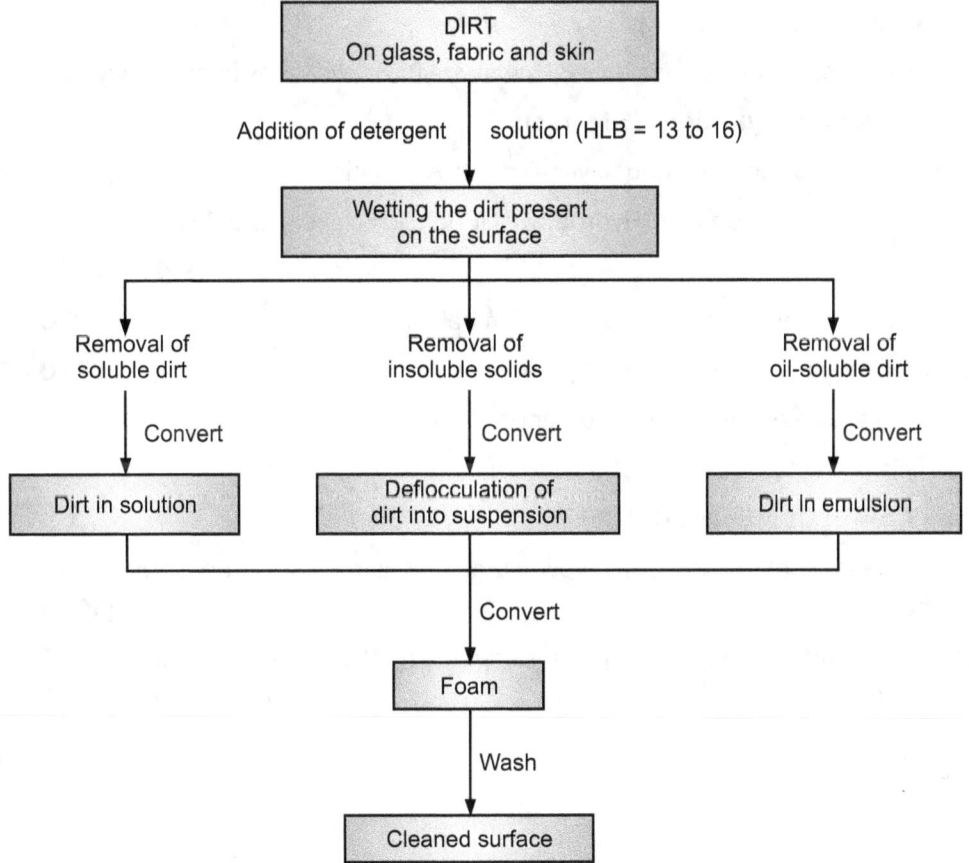

Fig. 1.40: The phenomenon of detergency

QUESTIONS

1. **Short Answer Questions (3 Marks):**

   1. What are surfactants? **[SPPU - 2014]**

   2. Derive an equation of spreading coefficient and give its significance. **[SPPU - 2014]**

   3. Discuss pharmaceutical and medicinal applications of surfactants.

   4. Justify the following statements: **[SPPU - 2014]**

      (i) Tweens are used as emulsifiers for preparing o/w emulsions.

      (ii) Water rises immediately up in the capillary tube when placed in a beaker of water.

   5. Describe the effect of temperature on the surface tension of liquids. **[SPPU - 2013]**

   6. Suggest two methods to improve the spreading of a medicament. **[SPPU - 2012]**

   7. Define and differentiate between surface and interfacial tension. **[SPPU - 2013]**

   8. Explain surface free energy.

   9. What is meant by 'surface excess? What are its applications in pharmacy?

2. **Medium Answer Questions (5 Marks):**

   1. Write note on soluble monolayer and Gibbs equation. **[SPPU - 2012]**

   2. Write short note on HLB (Hydrophilic Lipophilic Balance) and RHLB.

        [SPPU - 2011, 13, 14]

   3. Describe Insoluble monolayer and Film balance. **[SPPU - 2013]**

   4. Define contact angle. What are its applications? **[SPPU - 2014]**

   5. Write a note on wetting phenomenon.

   6. Explain Krafft point and Cloud point of surfactant.

3. **Long Answer Questions (10 Marks):**

   1. Define adsorption isotherm. Draw various types of adsorption isotherm and explain their behaviour. **[SPPU - 2012]**

   2. Define surface tension. Explain different methods of determination of surface tension. **[SPPU - 2011, 12, 13, 14, 15]**

■■■

Chapter 2...

Rheology

2.1 INTRODUCTION

Rheology (a term invented by Bingham and formally adopted in 1929) may be defined, as 'the study of the flow and deformation properties of matter under the influence of stress'. The term rheology has its origin from the Greek "rheo" means flow and "logos" means science.

These flow studies are related to pharmaceutical liquid and semisolid formulation such as suspension, emulsion, ointment, gel etc. and deformation is related to solid formulation.

These systems change their flow behaviour when exposed to different stress conditions in the following situation.

1. Mixing of formulation.
2. Pouring from a bottle.
3. Extrusion of semisolid dosage forms after squeezing the tube.
4. Rubbing the product onto and into the skin.
5. Pumping the product from mixing and storage to filling equipment.
6. Passage through syringe needle.

Thus, flow behaviour has extreme importance in both product development and quality assurance, i.e. the determination that the desired attributes of body and flow are retained for the required shelf-life of the product.

2.1.1 Importance of Rheology

1. **Hair shampoos** that need to be thick enough to pour onto the hands for transferring to the hair without flowing away through the fingers. The same is also true of skin creams and other personal products.

2. **Toothpastes** that need to be viscous enough to sit on the brush without draining into the bristles, but at the same time are easily extruded from the tube.

3. **Thixotropic or 'solid' paints** that have very special properties built into them so that they appear to be solid after storing, but on brushing out or stirring, they thin down. They will then re-thicken on standing.

4. **Printing inks** that need to spread easily when squeezed onto the type or transfer surface, but once deposited/printed onto a surface, in order to maintain a sharp edge, they must not spread by the action of surface tension or gravity.

5. **Ink** in biros and roller-ball pens that must have a low viscosity as it is being dispensed through the high-shear-rate roller-ball mechanism. However, when the ink is sitting on the writing surface, its viscosity must be high to stop it spreading far.

2.2 CONCEPT OF VISCOSITY AND NEWTONIAN'S LAW FOR FLOW

2.2.1 Viscosity

Property of a simple liquid is expressed in term of viscosity.

The **viscosity** of a fluid may be described simply as its resistance to flow or movement.

E.g. water, which is easier to flow than syrup, is said to have the lower viscosity.

Explanation:

Consider a 'bock of liquid' consisting parallel layers of molecules, (Fig. 2.1).

When pressure is applied horizontally on the top layer 'A', the liquid begins to flow. It assumes the shape shown in Fig. 2.1. Arrows indicate the magnitude of flow velocity. Since force is applied on the top layer (A), which has a surface area A [m²], it moves at greater velocity. The velocity of the second layer (B) is somewhat less than that of the first layer (A), because of the viscous drag offered by the third layer (C). Similarly, the velocity of the third layer (C) is less than that of the second layer (B), but higher than that of the fourth layer (D). These phenomenons continue and the bottom layer (N) remains stationary.

Thus, liquids resist flow when force is applied. This resistance is estimated and expressed as viscosity.

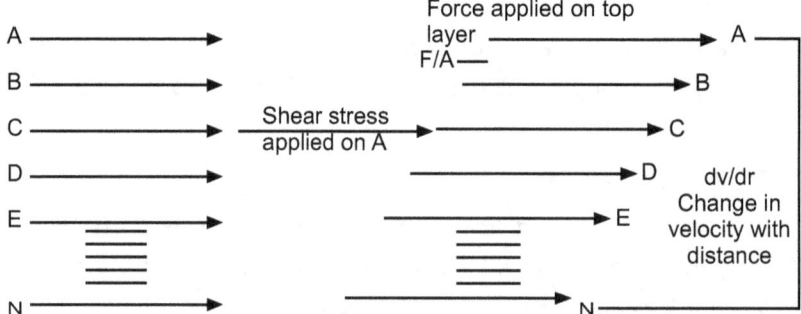

Fig. 2.1: Liquid at rest and after applied pressure

2.2.2 Newtonian's Law for Flow

Consider a "block" of liquid consisting of parallel plates of molecules, similar to a deck of cards, as shown in Fig. 2.1.

Velocity Gradient or Rate of Shear, dv/dr:

The bottom layer (N) is considered to be fixed in place. If the top plane (A) of liquid is moved at a constant velocity, each lower layer will move with a velocity directly proportional to its distance from the stationary bottom layer.

The difference of velocity dv between two planes of liquid separated by an infinitesimal distance dr is the **velocity gradient or rate of shear, $\dfrac{dv}{dr}$.**

$$\text{Rate of shear, } G = \frac{dv}{dr} \qquad\qquad \text{... (2.1)}$$

Shearing Stress (F):

The force per unit area F'/A required for flow of liquid is called the **shearing stress.**

$$\text{Shearing Stress} = F = \frac{F'}{A} \qquad\qquad \text{... (2.2)}$$

Newton was the first to study the flow properties of liquids in a quantitative way. He recognized that the higher the viscosity of a liquid, the greater the force per unit area (shearing stress) required producing a certain rate of shear.

Hence,

The rate of shear should be directly proportional to the shearing stress.

$$\text{Rate of shear} \propto \text{Shearing stress}$$

$$\frac{dv}{dr} \propto \frac{F'}{A}$$

$$\frac{dv}{dr} = \eta\,\frac{F'}{A}$$

or

$$G = \eta\, F$$

$$\eta = \frac{F}{G} \qquad\qquad \text{... (2.3)}$$

Where,

η : viscosity coefficient and also referred as **viscosity.**

A representative flow curve, or **rheogram**, obtained by plotting F versus G, for a Newtonian system is shown in Fig. 2.3. A straight line passing through the origin is obtained.

2.2.3 Unit of Viscosity

The unit of viscosity is the poise (1 centipoise = 0.01 poise).

Poise is defined as 'the shearing force required to produce a velocity of 1 cm/sec between two parallel planes of liquid each 1 cm^2 in area and separated by a distance of 1 cm.'

The cgs units for the poise are dyne sec cm^{-2} (i.e. dyne sec/cm^2) or g cm^{-1} sec^{-1} (i.e. g/cm sec).

Fluidity (ϕ), is defined as 'the reciprocal of viscosity'.

$$\phi = \frac{1}{\eta} \qquad \qquad \text{... (2.4)}$$

2.2.4 Kinematic Viscosity

The U.S. Pharmacopeia; Indian Pharmacopeia, and the National Formulary include an explanation of kinematic viscosity, which is the viscosity (η) as divided by density (ρ) of the liquid.

$$\text{Kinematic viscosity} = \frac{\eta}{\rho} \qquad \qquad \text{... (2.5)}$$

Units of kinematic viscosity are the stok (s) and the centistoke (cs).

2.2.5 Other Terms for Viscosity

Different terminologies are used to express the resistance to flow of liquids, when different substances are added to a solvent or a vehicle (Dispersion).

Most dispersions does not obey Newtonian flow;

Viscosity of polymeric dispersion increases almost many folds with concentration, i.e., the increase in viscosity with increase in concentration. Example, methylcellulose USP in the concentration of 2.0 % w/w in water shows an apparent viscosity of 80 poise at room temperature. The viscosity of water is 0.01 poise. In other words, the increase in viscosity of water is 8000 fold.

Mechanism of enhanced viscosity: Methylcellulose has three to four ether groups and one to two hydroxyl groups. When water is added to it, the groups get easily hydrated in solution. When the polymer molecule moves, the hydrated solvent sheath also moves. As a result, the size of polymer unit increases and hence, increases the resistance to flow.

Terminologies in Dispersion System:

The following terminologies are used for dispersion system:

Relative viscosity (η_r): This term is defined as 'the ratio of viscosity of the dispersion (η) to that of the solvent η_o (vehicle)'. It is mathematically expressed as:

$$\text{Relative viscosity, } \eta_r = \frac{\eta}{\eta_o} \qquad \qquad \text{... (2.6)}$$

Specific viscosity: This term is defined as 'the relative increase in the viscosity of the dispersion over that of the solvent (vehicle) alone'. It is mathematically expressed as:

$$\text{Specific viscosity, } \eta_{sp} = \frac{\eta - \eta_o}{\eta_o} \qquad \qquad \text{... (2.7)}$$

Reduced-viscosity: This term is defined as 'the ratio of specific viscosity to the concentration (c)'. It is mathematically expressed as:

$$\text{Reduced viscosity} = \frac{\eta_{sp}}{c} \qquad \qquad \text{... (2.8)}$$

Intrinsic viscosity: The reduced viscosity is determined at various concentrations of a substance and the results are plotted. The resulting line can be extrapolated to c = 0 to obtain the intercept. The intercept value is known as intrinsic viscosity. This parameter is useful to determine the molecular weight of polymers.

2.2.6 Factors Affecting the Viscosity

The flow behaviour of a material may be affected by a number of external factors. The five most important parameters are:

1. **Substance:** The viscosity of a liquid depends on its physical and chemical properties of the substances in it.
2. **Temperature:** Temperature has a major effect on the viscosity. As the temperature increases, the system acquires thermal energy which is used for braking cohesive forces. The viscosity of liquid decreases means there is increase in flow of liquid.
    The relationship between viscosity and temperature may be expressed as:
    $$\eta = Ae^{E_v/RT} \qquad \qquad \dots (2.9)$$
    Where,
    A is a constant which depends on the molecular weight and molar volume.
    E_v is an 'activation energy' required to initiate the flow between the molecules.
    For example, several mineral oils lose about 10 % of their viscosity if the temperature is only increased by 1 K.
3. **Shear rate:** The viscosity of most materials depends on the shear rate, i.e. the load.
4. **Pressure:** If great pressure is exerted on a material, its viscosity may increase as particles are organised in a more tight structure (resulting in more interaction possibilities).
5. Other influencing factors are the pH value, magnetic and electric field strength.

2.3 TYPES OF FLOW

The materials can be classified based on their flow properties.

Newtonian Systems: The systems which obey Newtonian law for flow are Newtonian systems.

Non-Newtonian Systems: The systems that do not obey Newtonian law for flow are non-newtonian systems.

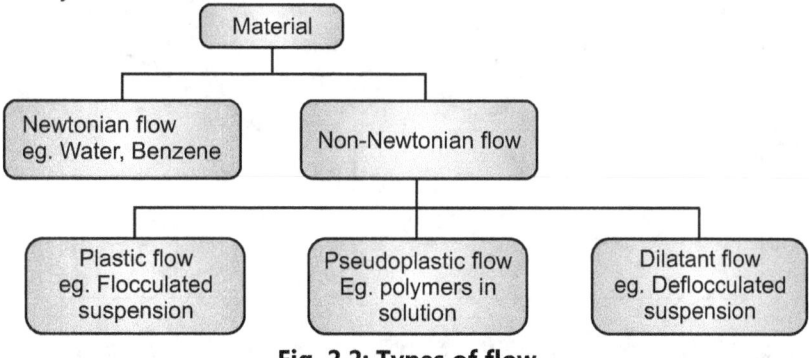

Fig. 2.2: Types of flow

2.3.1 Newtonian Flow

Liquids that obey Newton's law of flow (equation 2.3) are called as Newtonian flow. Newton's equation for the flow of a liquid is:

$$F = \eta G$$

Shear stress - Shear rate relationship is normally represented in the form of, a curve namely *rheogram or consistency curve*. When data are plotted by taking F on x axis and G on y axis, a flow curve is obtained. The rheogram passes through the origin and the slope gives the coefficient of viscosity (η). Systems that follow this linear relationship are called as Newtonian fluids. (Fig. 2.3).

Example: Water, benzene, Solutions of syrups, Glycerin

2.3.2 Non-Newtonian Flow

The most pharmaceutical fluids do not follow Newtonian law as the viscosity of many fluids varies with the rate of shear. The reason for these deviations is that the fluids concerned are not simple fluids such as water and syrup, but may be disperse or colloidal systems, including emulsions, suspensions and gels. These materials are known as non-Newtonian.

Non-Newtonian fluids are categorized as;

1.   Plastic flow
2.   Pseudoplastic flow
3.   Dilatant flow

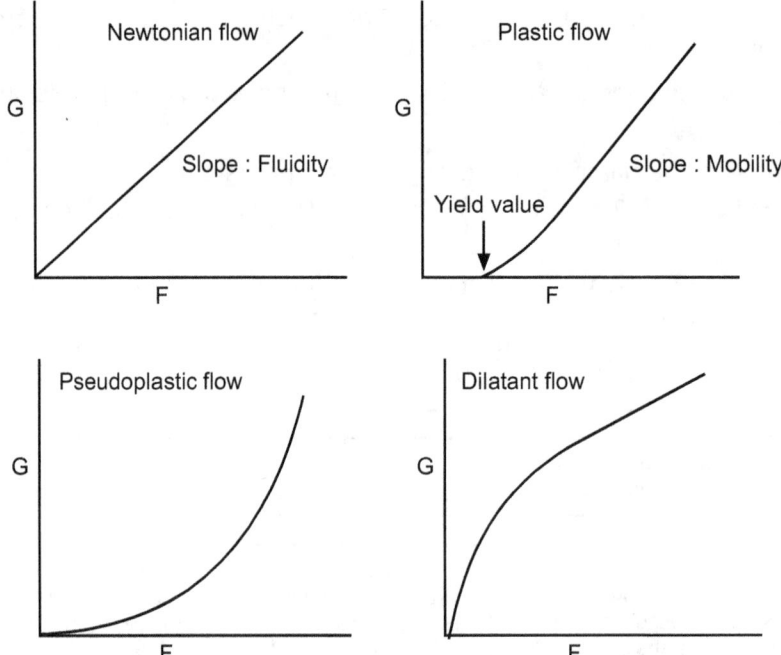

Fig. 2.3: Rheograms for Newtoian & Non-newtonian types of flow

2.3.2.1 Plastic Flow

The plastic flow curve does not pass through the origin. The substance initially behaves like an elastic material. Do not flow when small stress is applied. Further stress with increase in nonlinear portion progressively gets linearised. The straight part of the curve is extrapolated to the x axis at a particular point referred to as the **yield value.** [Fig. 2.3]

Such materials are also known as **Bingham bodies** in honor of the pioneer of modern rheology.

A Bingham body,

> **Flow:** Shearing stress above the yield value.

> **Do not flow:** Shearing stress below the yield value. The substance acts as an elastic material (Solid).

Flocculated suspension show plastic flow. [Fig. 2.4]

Bingham bodies

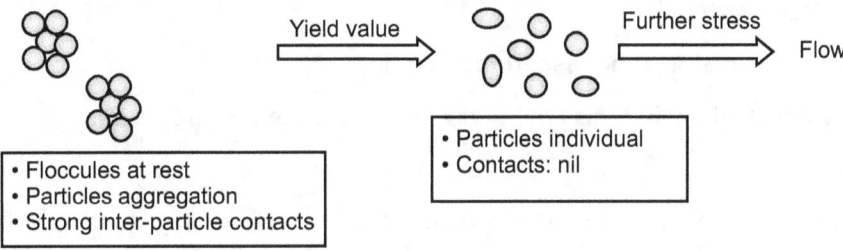

Fig. 2.4: Behaviour of plastic flow (Bingham bodies)

At rest: Floccules are the aggregation of particles with inter-particle contacts. This structure is maintained when the system is at rest.

Yield value: It represents the stress required to break the inter-particle contacts so that particles behave individually. Therefore, yield value is indicative of the **forces of flocculation**. Frictional forces between moving particles also contribute to the yield value.

Above yield value: Once the yield value exceeds, further increase in shearing stress (F – f) will bring about a proportional increase in the rate of shear.

Bingham Equation:

The slope of the rheogram in Fig. 2.3 is termed as *mobility*, analogous to fluidity in Newtonian systems, and its reciprocal is known as the *plastic viscosity*, U. The Bingham equation describing plastic flow is:

$$U = \frac{F - f}{G} \qquad \qquad ...\,(2.10)$$

Where,

> F : Shearing stress,

> f : Yield value,

> G : Rate of shear.

2.3.2.2 Pseudoplastic Flow

These are also called **shear thinning system.**

The rheogram shown in Fig. 2.3 arises at the origin and, as no yield value exists, the material will flow as soon as a shear stress is applied; but trend is not linear.

At low shear stresses; the flow curve is nonlinear, indicating that a maximum viscosity has been attained.

At higher shear stresses; the flow curve tends towards linearity, indicating that a minimum viscosity has been attained.

The slope of the curve gradually decreases with increasing rate of shear. The viscosity is derived from the slope and therefore decreases as the shear rate is increased. Materials exhibiting this behaviour are said to be **pseudoplastic**, and no single value of viscosity can be considered as characteristic. The entire curve is the most satisfactory representation of the pseudoplastic material.

Polymeric dispersion show pseudoplastic flow [Fig. 2.5].

The polymers that exhibit this type of flow include aqueous dispersions.

Example:

1. Natural and chemically modified hydrocolloids, such as tragacanth, methylcellulose and carmellose,

2. Synthetic polymers such as polyvinylpyrrolidone and polyacrylic acid.

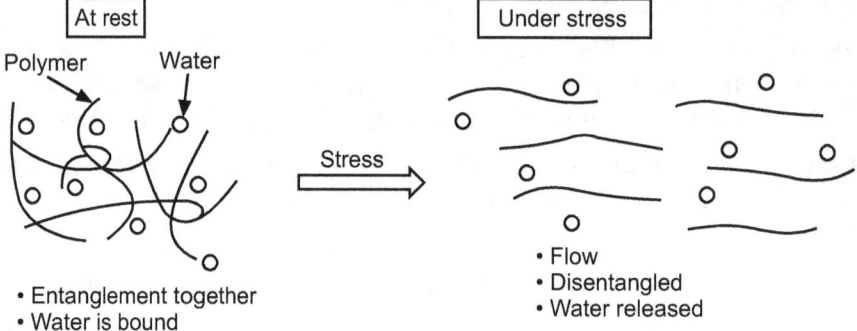

Fig. 2.5: Pseudoplastic flow of polymeric dispersion

At rest; the polymers are long, high weight molecules in solution results in entanglement together with the associate immobilized solvent.

Under stress; i.e. under the influence of shear stress, the molecules tend to become disentangled, release the entrapped water and align themselves in the direction of flow. Thus, offer less resistance to flow, and accounts for the lower viscosity.

Power Law:

There is no satisfactory quantitative explanation of pseudoplastic flow; probably the most widely used in the Power Law, which is given as;

$$F^N = \eta G \qquad \qquad \dots (2.11)$$

where, N is a number given to the exponent.

In case;

$$N = 1, \text{It is Newtonian flow.}$$
$$N > 1, \text{It is Pseudoplastic flow.}$$

Taking log of both sides, equation (2.11) can be written as

$$N \log F = \log \eta + \log G \qquad \qquad \dots (2.12)$$

On rearrangement, we get

$$\log G = N \log F - \log \eta \qquad \qquad \dots (2.13)$$

Equation (2.13) represents a straight line.

2.3.2.3 Dilatant Flow

These are also called **shear thickening system.**

The opposite type of flow to pseudoplasticity is depicted in Fig. 2.3. In that, the system exhibits enhanced resistance to flow with increase in stress. As such materials increase in volume during shearing, they are referred to as dilatant and exhibit shear thickening.

At low shear stresses; the flow curve is almost linear, indicating that a minimum viscosity has been attained.

At higher shear stresses; the flow curve tends towards non-linearity, indicating that a maximum viscosity has been attained.

When stress is removed; the system returns to its initial state i.e. fluidity.

Deflocculated suspension show dilatant flow [Fig. 2.6].

Example: The dispersion containing a high concentration (>50 %) of small, deflocculated particles.

At rest: The particles are closely packed and the interparticulate voids are minimum, which the vehicle is sufficient to fill. Consequently, at low shear rate such as those created during pouring, such fluids can adequately lubricate the relative movement of the particles.

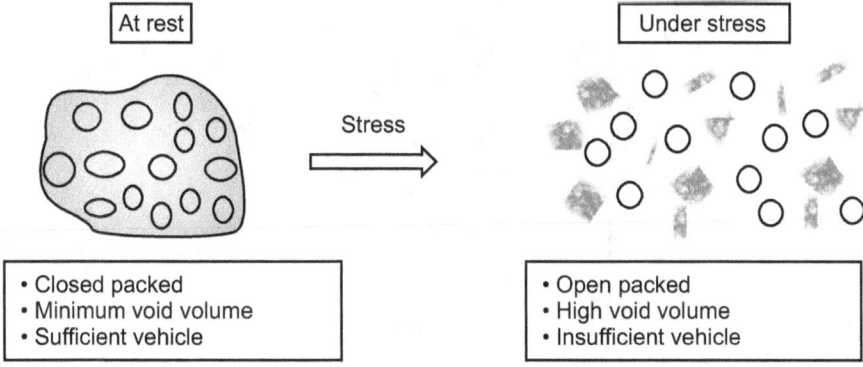

Fig. 2.6: Dilatant flow of deflocculated suspension

Under stress: As the shear rate is increased, the particles become displaced from their uniform distribution and the clumps that are produced result in the creation of larger voids, into which the vehicle drains, so that the resistance to flow is increased and viscosity rises. The effect is progressive with increase in shear rate until eventually the material may appear paste-like.

Fortunately, this effect is reversible and removal of the shear stress result in the re-establishment of the fluid nature.

An equation similar to that for pseudoplastic flow (Equation 2.13) may be used to describe dilatant behaviour, but the value of the exponent N will be greater than 1 and will increase as dilatancy increases.

2.4 THIXOTROPY

Shear thinning systems, when highly viscous system agitated, thus decreases viscosity of system (increases fluidity) and then kept aside it recover its original consistency, but it takes longer time to recover compared to the time taken for agitation. This behaviour is called thixotropy.

Thixotropy is defined as 'an isothermal and comparatively slow recovery, on standing of material, of a consistency lost through shearing'.

The phenomena of thixotropy can be observed by constructing consistency curves (Fig. 2.7). The rate of shear is progressively increased, and the corresponding stress is measured using a suitable instrument. When these readings are plotted, the up-curve, ab, is obtained. From the desired maximum, i.e. point b, if the rate of shear is reduced gradually, the down-curve, bc, is obtained. In a non-newtonian fluid, the down curve is frequently displaced to the left of the up-curve. The Fig. 2.7 shows that the material has a low consistency at any one rate of shear on the down-curve compared to that it had shown on the up-curve. Similarly, thixotropic curves can be constructed for pseudoplastic systems. In a Newtonian system, the down-curve is superimposed on the up-curve.

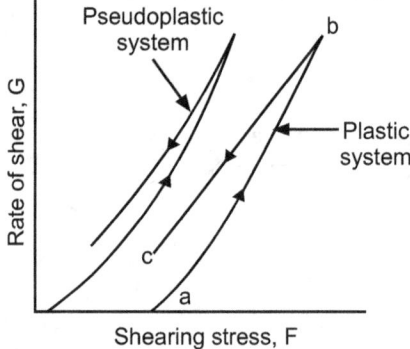

Fig. 2.7: Thixotropic behaviour of system

Particle Interaction in Thixotropic System:

The phenomenon of thixotropy is explained in terms of particle interaction (Fig. 2.8).

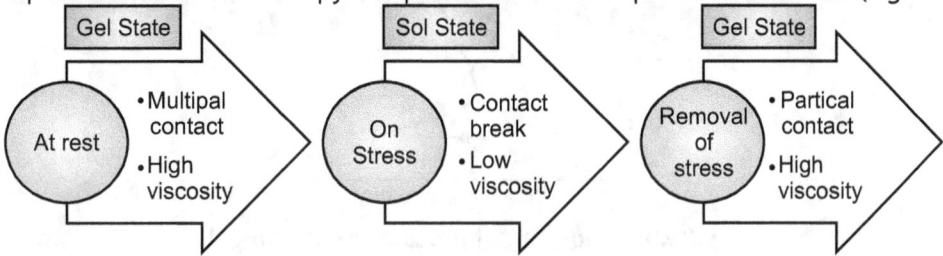

Fig. 2.8: Particle-particle interaction in a thixotropic system. (Gel-sol-Gel transformations)

At rest; particle in the dispersion impart rigidity on the system through multipoint contacts. The system behaves like a gel.

Under stress; the contacts begin to break down, the particles are aligned and the flow starts. The material undergoes a gel-to-sol transformation inducing the system to exhibit shear thinning. The system behaves like a sol.

Removal of stress; the system starts regaining its original state. This process is not instantaneous. Particles slowly come in contact with one another owing to random Brownian movement and progressively the original consistency will be restored.

2.4.1 Bulges

In case of concentrated aqueous magma (gel) of bentonite (10-15% w/w) produces a hysteresis loop with a characteristic bulge in the up-curve as shown in Fig. 2.9.

This may be due to the arrangement of crystalline plates of bentonite in the form of "house-of-cards structure" that causes the swelling of bentonite magmas. This three-dimensional structure result in a bulged hysteresis loop as observed in Fig. 2.9.

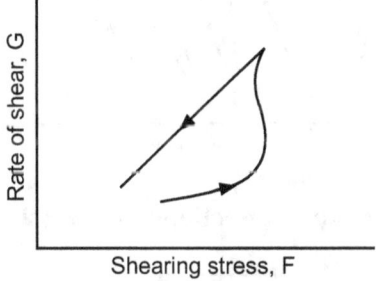

Fig. 2.9: Rheogram of aqueous magma (gel) of bentonite

2.4.2 Spurs

The gel formulations containing procaine penicillin gel shows a typical rheogram with a characteristic spur-like protrusion. The spur represents a sharp point of structural breakdown at low shear rate. The structure demonstrates high yield or spur value, y, that traces out a bowed up-curve when the three-dimensional structure breaks in the viscometer, as observed in Fig. 2.10.

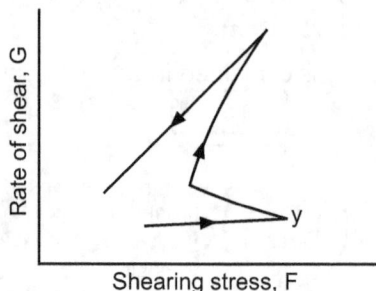

Fig. 2.10: Rheogram of procaine penicillin gel

2.5 NEGATIVE THIXOTROPY

At rest magnesia magma shows sol-like properties. On shaking, the system behaves like a gel and imparts greater suspendability. However, at equilibrium, it is readily pourable.

Anitithixotropy or negative thixotropy represents an increase in consistency on the down curve.

For example magnesia magma, exhibits an enhanced resistance to flow with increased time of shear compared to resting state. In the rheogram, the down-curve shifts to the right of the up-curve (Fig. 2.11). When magnesia magma is sheared alternatively with increasing and then decreasing rates of shear, the magma thickens. As these cycles continue, the extent of increase in the thickening reduces gradually and finally reaches equilibrium state. There will be no change in the consistency curves on further cycles of shear rate. This type of behaviour is recorded in Fig. 2.11.

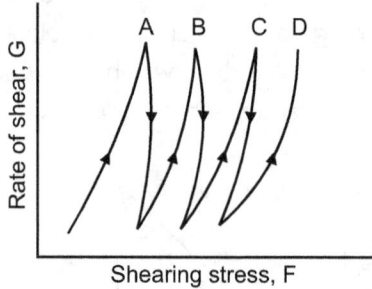

Fig. 2.11: Rheogram of antithixotropic behaviour

Following types of molecular interactions are possible in antithixotropic system shown in Fig. 2.12.

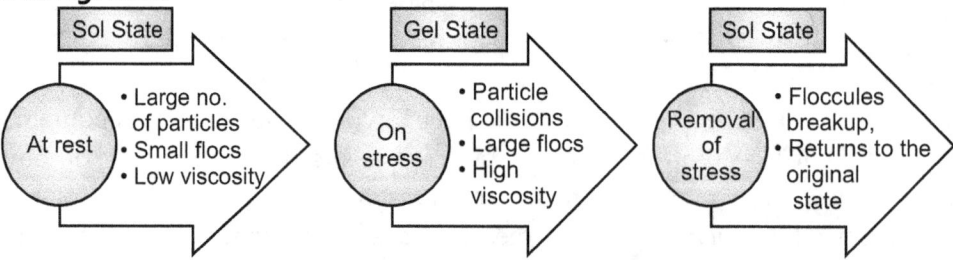

Fig. 2.12: Particle- particle interaction in an antithixotropic system (Sol-Gel-Sol transformations)

At resting state; the system consists of a large number of individual particles and small floccules. The system behaves like a sol.

Under stress; the polymer molecular collisions are increased at a greater frequency. As a result, interparticle bonding increases. At equilibrium, large floccules are available in small numbers. The system behaves like a gel.

Removal of stress; the large floccules breakup and gradually return to the original state of small floccules and individual particles. The system behaves like a sol.

Negative Thixotropy and Dilatant Flow:

1. Dilatant systems are deflocculated and the volume of solids is high (more than 50%),

2. Negative thixotropy is seen in a flocculated system containing low solid content (1 to 10%).

2.6 MEASUREMENT OF THIXOTROPY

(A) Planimeter: In a thixotropic system, the hysteresis loop is formed by the up and down curves of the rheogram. The area of hysteresis loop has been proposed as a measure of thixotropic breakdown. It can be obtained readily with the help of a planimeter.

(B) In a thixotropic system, the nature of rheogram largely depends on the rate at which shear is increased or decreased. Consider a material that follows plastic flow.

1. Suppose shear rate is increased at a constant rate on the system upto a point 'b' and then decreased.

2. When the results are plotted, 'abe' rheogram is obtained (Fig. 2.13).

3. If the shear rate is maintained at b for time t_1 seconds and then decreased, 'abce' rheogram is obtained.

4. Similarly at point 'b' if the shear rate is maintained for time t_2 seconds and then decreased, 'abde' curve is obtained.

5. The structural breakdown with respect to time at constant rate of shear gives the rheogram (Fig. 2.12).

6. Based on such rheograms, the thixotropic coefficient, B, is calculated using equation (2.14).

$$B = \frac{(U_1 - U_2)}{ln\ (t_2/\ t_1)} \qquad\qquad ...\ (2.14)$$

Where, U_1 and U_2 are the plastic viscosities of the two down curves. Thixotropic coefficient, B, represents the rate of breakdown with time at constant shear rate.

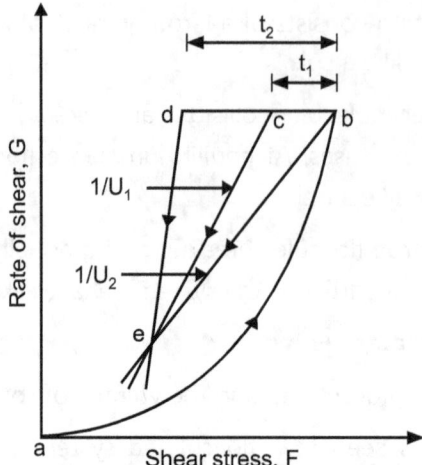

Fig. 2.13: Thixotropic behaviour of plastic system, when the material is subjected to a constant rate for t_1 and t_2

(C) In this method, the system is subjected to different rates of shear (say, v_1 and v_2) and the rheogram is obtained, which shows two hysteresis loops (Fig. 2.14). The thixotropic coefficient, M, is calculated using the equation

$$M = \frac{2(U_1 - U_2)}{\ln (v_2/v_1)^2}$$ ... (2.15)

Where, M is in dynes.sec/cm^2. U_1 and U_2 are the plastic viscosities of the down-curves having shearing rates of v_1 and v_2 respectively. Thixotropic coefficient, M, represents the loss in shearing stress per unit increase in shear rate.

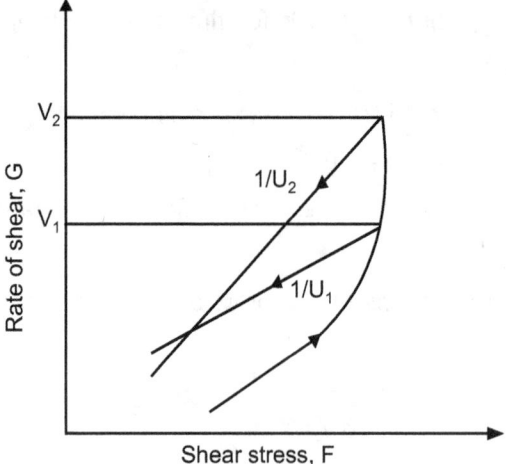

Fig. 2.14: Thixotropic behaviour of plastic system, when the material is subjected to increasing shear rates

Applications:

Thixotropy is a desirable property particularly in emulsions, suspensions and creams.

1. **Stability of suspension:** The greater the thixotropy, the higher is the physical stability of the suspension. During storage, a suspension should have high consistency (gel) in the container, so that the suspended particles do not settle rapidly.

   On moderate shaking, the suspension should become fluid (sol), so that the contents can be poured easily from the container. Thus, the principles of thixotropy are useful in dispensing and administration of a dose. At rest, the suspension regains its original consistency. These gel-sol-gel transformations improve the physical stability of dosage forms.

2. **Sustained release of drug:** The degree of thixotropy is related to the specific surface of penicillin used.

   Parenteral suspension containing 40 to 70% of procaine penicillin G in water has higher inherent thixotropy. While injecting the preparation, the structure of the suspended particles breaks down so that the product can pass through the hypodermic needle. After injection, the original structure of gel will be rebuilt. This leads to depot of the procaine penicillin G at the site of injection in the muscle, from, which it is slowly released so as to provide sustained release of drug in the body.

2.7 MEASUREMENT OF VISCOSITY

Selection of Viscometer: The classification and applications of equipment to different types of fluids are given in Fig. 2.15.

In Newtonian fluids, the rate of shear is directly proportional to the shearing stress. Therefore, **single point viscometer,** i.e., the equipment that works at a single rate of shear, is sufficient.

The following viscometers are used in this system:

1. Capillary Viscometer
2. Falling Sphere Viscometer

In Non-Newtonian fluids, multipoint viscometers are required, because the apparent viscosity is to be determined at several of rates of shear to get entire consistency curve. Multi-point viscometers can also be used to determine the viscosity of Newtonian fluids, when maintained at constant rate of shear.

The following viscometers are used in this system:

1. Cup and Bob Viscometer
2. Cone and Plate Viscometer

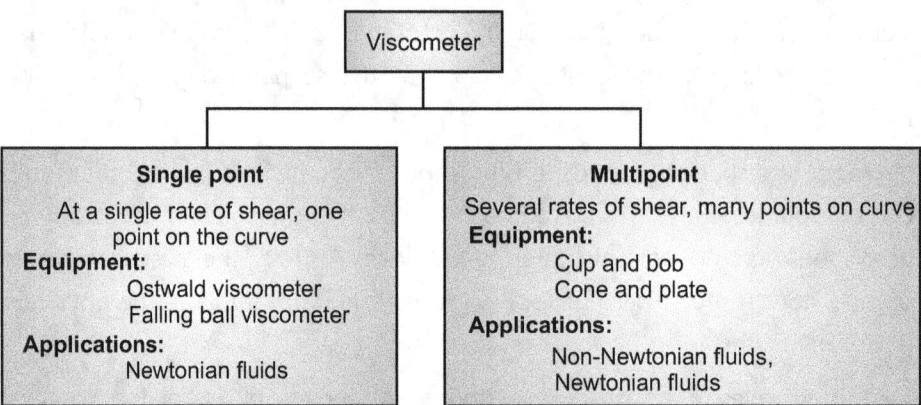

Fig. 2.15: classification and selection of viscometer

2.7.1 Capillary Viscometer (Ostwald Method)

Ostwald viscometer is used to determine the viscosity of a Newtonian liquid.

[I] Ostwald Viscometer:

The apparatus commonly used for the determination of relative viscosity of a liquid is known as Ostwald viscometer.

Working:

1. A simple form of it is shown in Fig. 2.16. The left-hand limb is essentially a pipette with two calibration marks A and B.

2. A length of capillary tube joins the pipette to a bulb C in the right-hand limb.

3. A definite volume of liquid (say 25 ml) is poured into the bulb C with a pipette.

4. The liquid is sucked up near to the top of the left-limb with the help of rubber tubing attached to it.

5. The liquid is then released to flow back into the bulb C. The time (t_1) from A to B is noted with a stopwatch.

6. Then the apparatus is cleaned and the experiment is repeated with water, taking about the same volume.

7. The time of flow of water (t_2) from A to B is recorded.

8. The density of the liquid (ρ) and water (ρ_w) are determined with the help of a pyknometer.

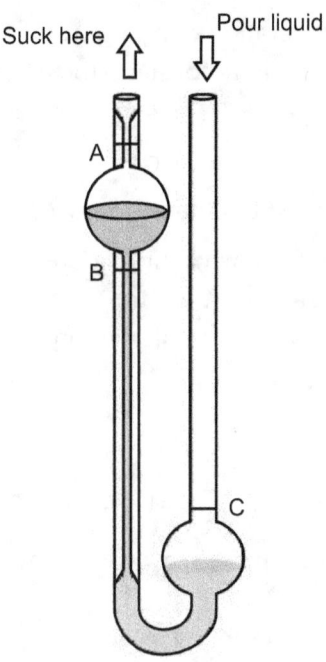

Fig. 2.16: Ostwald viscometer

[II] Pioseulle's Equation for Viscosity:

Viscosity of a liquid can be determined with the help of **Pioseulle's equation.** This expression which governs the flow of a liquid through a capillary may be written as:

$$\eta = \frac{\pi r^2 \, Pt}{8 \, lV} \qquad \qquad \ldots (2.16)$$

Where

η : Viscosity of liquid,

V : The volume of the liquid flowing through capillary in time t, (flow A to B mark),

P : The pressure-head,

r : The radius of the tube, and

l : The length between A to B mark.

The experimental measurement of r, *l* and V offers considerable difficulty, also for an Ostwald viscometer all these parameters are constant and may combine as single constant, K.

Then, equation (2.16) may be written as;

$$\eta = K P t \qquad \qquad \ldots (2.17)$$

The pressure depends on acceleration due to gravity g and density ρ of liquid (P = ρg). The acceleration due to gravity g is a constant for all capillary tubes. Then equation is written as:

$$\eta = K\,\rho\,t \qquad \qquad \text{... (2.18)}$$

Thus, equation (2.18) can be used to determine viscosity of liquid.

Ordinarily, the viscosity of an unknown liquid is determined with respect to that of water. This is called Relative Viscosity. Let t_1 and t_2 be the times of flow of a fixed volume (V) of the unknown liquid and water respectively, through the same capillary.

Viscosity for unknown liquid; $\eta_1 = K\,\rho_1\,t_1$ ... (2.19)

Viscosity for Water; $\eta_w = K\,\rho_w\,t_w$ ... (2.20)

The expression for relative viscosity $\left(\dfrac{\eta_1}{\eta_w}\right)$ can be derived as;

$$\frac{\eta_1}{\eta_w} = \frac{K\,\rho_1 t_1}{K\,\rho_w t_w} = \frac{\rho_1 t_1}{\rho_w t_w}$$

OR

$$\eta_1 = \frac{\rho_1 t_1}{\rho_w t_w}\,\eta_w \qquad \qquad \text{... (2.21)}$$

Where,

η_1 : Viscosity of unknown liquid,

η_w : Viscosity of water.

2.7.2 Rolling / Falling-Ball Viscometer

The rolling-ball principle uses gravity as the driving force. Rolling / Falling-ball viscometer is used to determine the viscosity of a Newtonian liquid.

Rolling / Falling-Ball Apparatus (Fig. 2.17)

Working:

1. It consist of a glass tube positioned at different angles.
2. A constant temperature jacket is arranged around the glass tube.
3. The test liquid is placed in sample tube.
4. A glass or still ball rolls through a closed glass which is inclined at a defined angle.
5. The time the ball takes to travel between two marks, A to B, is accurately measured.
6. The defined measuring distance is a measure for the fluid's viscosity.
7. The inclination angle of the capillary permits the user to vary the driving force. If the angle is too steep, the rolling speed causes turbulent flow.
8. For calculating the viscosity from the measured time (t), the fluid's density (ρ_f) and the ball density (ρ_b) need to be known.

According to arrangement of angle of glass tube in apparatus, it is classified as,

Rolling-ball viscometer: Angles between 10° and 80°.

Falling-ball viscometer: Angle is 80° or greater.

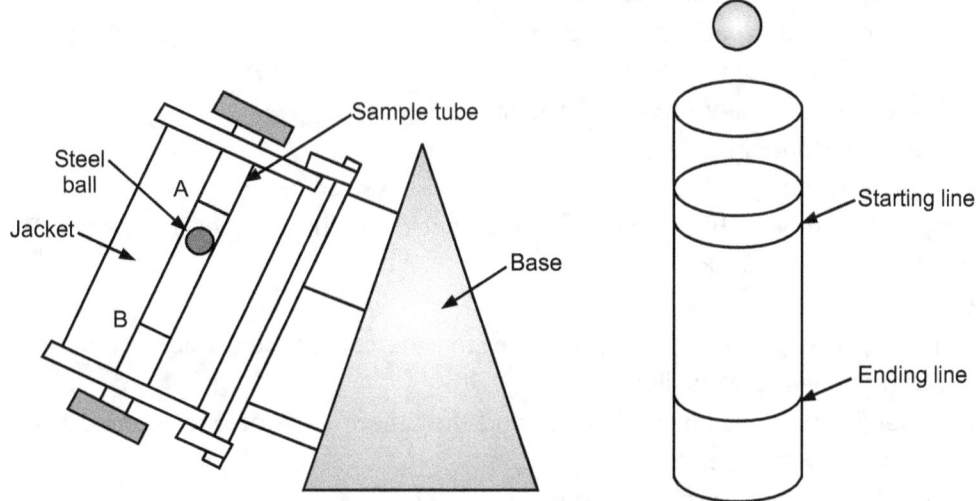

Fig. 2.17: Rolling / Falling-Ball viscometer

The viscosity of Newtonian liquid is calculated from:

$$\eta = t\,(\rho_b - \rho_f)\,B \qquad\qquad \dots (2.22)$$

Where,

    η : The viscosity of liquid

    t : The time travel in second

    ρ_b : A density of ball

    ρ_f : A density of liquid

    B : A constant for ball.

Above equation (2.22) is used for determination of viscosity of liquid.

2.7.3 Cup and Bob Viscometers

This is a multipoint viscometer and belongs to the category of rotational viscometer.

Principle:

It is explained by using Fig. 2.18.

In cup and bob viscometers, the sample is sheared in the space between the outer wall of a bob and the inner wall of a cup into which the bob fits. The torque set is attached to bob and the torque is proportional to shearing stress 'F' means, the resultant torque is proportional to the viscosity of the sample.

Classification:

According to rotation of cup and bob viscometers are classified as;

(i) The Couette type of viscometer:

The cup is rotating and bob is stationary.

Example: MacMichael viscometer.

(ii) The Searle type of viscometer:

The cup is stationary and bob is rotating.

Example: Stormer instrument

Stormer Instrument:

A popular viscometer based on the Searle principle is the Stormer instrument. This viscometer is shown in Fig. 2.18.

Working:

1. The liquid is placed in the space between the cup and the bob and is allowed to reach temperature equilibrium.
2. A weight is placed on the hanger, and the time for the bob to rotate 100 times is recorded by the operator.
3. This data is then converted to rpm.
4. The weight on torque is increased and the whole procedure repeated.
5. In this way, a rheogram can be constructed by plotting rpm versus weight added.
6. By using appropriate constant, the rpm value convert in rate of shear 'G'.
7. Similarly, weight added can be transferred to shearing stress 'F'.
8. Stromer instrument can not be used when liquid viscosity is below 20 cp.

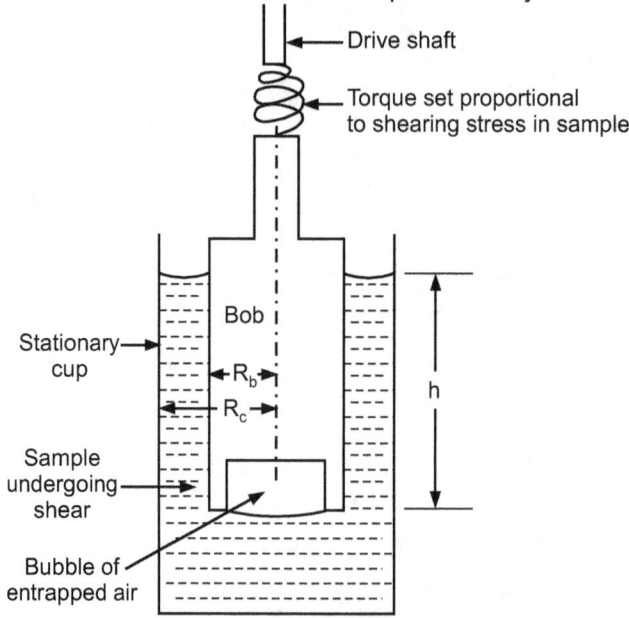

Fig. 2.18: Rotating cup and bob viscometer

Mathematical Treatment:

For a rotational viscometer, shearing stress and shearing rate relationship can be expressed;

$$\Omega = \frac{1}{\eta}\frac{T}{4\pi h}\left[\frac{1}{R_b^2} - \frac{1}{R_c^2}\right]$$ ... (2.23)

Where,

Ω : The angular velocity in radians sec^{-1} produced by T,

T : The torque in dynes cm,

h : The depth to which the bob is immersed in the liquid,

R_b : The radius of the bob,

R_c : The radius of the cup.

It is frequently more convenient to combine all the constants (h, R_b and R_c) in equation (2.23), with the result that:

$$\eta = K_v \frac{T}{\Omega}$$ ... (2.24)

In which, K_v is a constant for the instrument.

With the modified Stormer viscometer, Ω is a function of v, the rpm is generated by the weight w, in grams, that is proportional to T. Equation (2.24) may then be written as:

$$\eta = K_v \frac{w}{v}$$ ... (2.25)

K_v may be obtained by analyzing material of known viscosity in poise.

The equation for **plastic viscosity** when employing the Stormer viscometer is

$$U = K_v \frac{w - w_f}{v}$$ ... (2.26)

in which U is the plastic viscosity in poises, w_f is the yield value intercept in grams, and the other symbols have the meaning previously given.

The yield value of a Bingham body is obtained by use of the expression

$$f = K_f . w_f$$ ... (2.27)

All terms are already explained.

Plug flow:

One of the disadvantages of the cup and bob viscometer is the plug flow.

It is explained as follows:

In general, the sample is placed in the gap between the cup and bob. During evaluation, when the bob is made to rotate, the amount of stress exerted near the wall of the bob is relatively higher compared to the stress observed at the inner wall of the cup. In other words, different stresses are being exerted across the sample.

Hence, the readings may not represent the stress on the entire sample.

For example,

In plastic system, below yield value, the apparent viscosity is infinite. Above the yield value, it possesses a finite plastic plug viscosity.

When the bob is made to rotate at lower rates of shear, the stress closer to the rotating bob may be higher than yield value. But at the inner wall of the cup, the stress may be below the yield value. So the material at the zone (inner wall of the cup) remains as a solid plug.

The phenomenon of plug flow can be minimized by

1. Using the largest bob possible in order to reduce the gap.
2. Increasing the speed of rotation of the bob so that the stress at outer wall of the cup is above the yield value and the system undergoes laminar flow.

The plug flow is undesirable for the rheologic evaluation of dispersion system. On the other hand, plug flow is important in the flow of pastes. For e.g. extrusion of toothpaste and ointment from the tube. When an ointment tube is pressed, shear along the inner circumference of the tube is higher. As a result, viscosity will be lower so that ointment will be expelled easily.

2.7.4 Cone and Plate Viscometer

Principle:

The measuring unit of cone and plate viscometer is shown in Fig. 2.19. The sample is placed at the center of the plate, which is then raised into a position under the cone. The cone is driven by a variable-speed motor and the sample are sheared in the narrow gap between the stationary plate and the rotating cone. The rate of shear in rpm is increased and decreased by a selector dial and the viscous traction or torque (shearing stress) produced on the cone is read on the indicator scale. A plot of rpm (rate of snear) versus scale reading (shearing stress) may thus be constructed in the usual manner.

Working:

The instruments consist of;

1. A rotating cone with a very obtuse angle and a stationary lower flat plate.
2. The plate is raised until the apex of the cone just touches its surface.
3. The liquid fills the narrow triangular gap between cone and plate (Fig. 2.19).

4. Its surface tension prevents it from spreading on the plate. The plate is maintained at a constant temperature by circulating water.
5. The cone is driven at controlled speeds that can be varied continuously.
6. The viscous drag on the rotating cone exerts a torque on a dynamometer that is proportional to the shear stress.
7. The angle θ formed by cone and plate is usually less than 3°, and the average gap width is less than 2 mm.

Advantages:

1. The rate of shear is constant throughout the entire sample being sheared. Plug flow is not observed.

2. The sample required is small, 0.1 to 0.2 ml.

3. Cleaning and filling is easy.

4. Less time is required for temperature equilibration.

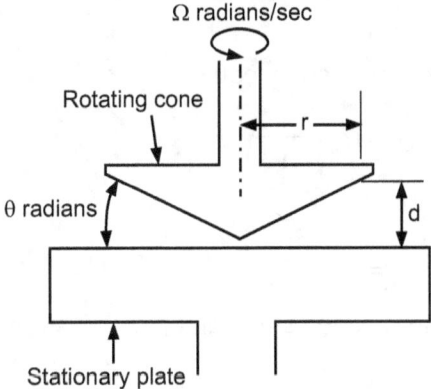

Fig. 2.19: Cone and plate viscometer

Mathematical Treatment:

For small values of θ in radians, the viscosity is determined;

$$\eta = \frac{3\theta}{2\pi R_b^2}\left(\frac{T}{\Omega}\right)$$

... (2.28)

Where,

η : The viscosity.

Ω : The angular velocity in radians sec^{-1} produced by T,

T : The torque in dynes cm.

R_b : The radius of the cone,

θ : The angle formed by cone and plate.

It is frequently more convenient to combine all the constants (θ and R_b) in equation (2.28), with the result that:

$$\eta = C\frac{T}{\Omega} \qquad \qquad ...(2.29)$$

Where, C is constant for instrument and it is obtained by analyzing material of known viscosity in poise.

Newtonian System:

The viscosity is estimated by equation

$$\eta = C\frac{T}{v} \qquad \qquad ...(2.30)$$

Where, C is constant for instrument, T is torque and Ω is a function of v, the rpm generated by the weight w, in grams, that is proportional to T.

Plastic Viscosity:

The plastic viscosity 'U' is estimated by equation

$$U = C_f . \frac{T - T_f}{v} \qquad \qquad ...(2.31)$$

and yield value

$$f = C_f \times T_f \qquad \qquad ...(2.32)$$

In which T_f is torque at the shearing stress an C_f is an instrumental constant.

2.8 VISCOELASTICITY

Viscoelastic measurements are based on the mechanical properties of materials that exhibit;

1. Viscous properties of liquids and
2. Elastic properties of solids.

Some example of viscoelastic substance;

1. In pharmacy: Creams, lotions, ointments, suppositories, suspensions, colloidal dispersing, emulsifying, and suspending agents.
2. Biologic materials: Blood, sputum and cervical fluid.

Here, rotational viscometer is not useful for determination of viscoelastic properties of substance, because rotational viscometers and similar flow instruments yield large deformations and may produce false results.

2.8.1 Behaviour of Viscoelastic Substances Under Stress

Stress for a short period: When viscoelastic materials are subjected to stress for a short period of time they undergo slight deformation under the influence of the stress but once the stress is removed, they exhibit their elastic behaviour by returning to their original shape with little permanent deformation.

Stress for a long period: If the stress is applied continuously for a long period of time, the deformation increases and becomes more permanent. When the stress is finally removed, only a small fraction of the deformation is recovered. This behaviour approaches that of a viscous liquid. [Fig. 2.20]

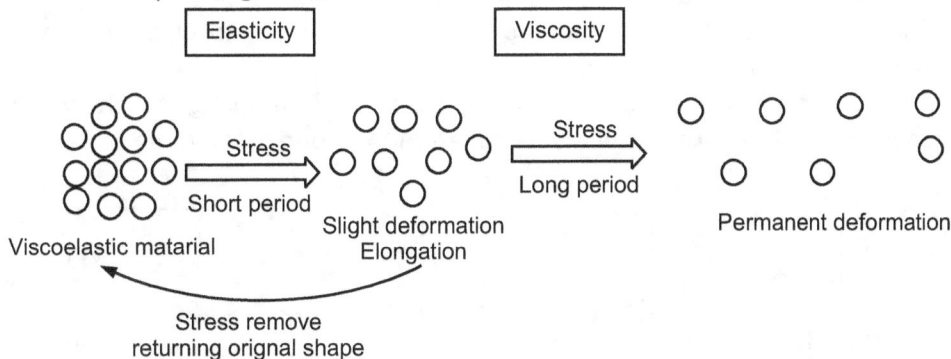

Fig. 2.20: Viscoelastic behaviour of substance under stress

A semisolid is considered to demonstrate both solid and liquid characterises. The flow of a Newtonian fluid is expressed by using equation (2.3),

$$\eta = \frac{F}{G}$$

Relating shear stress F and shear rate G.

A solid material, on the other hand, is not characterized by flow but rather by elasticity, and its behaviour is expressed by the equation for a spring (derived from Hooke's law of general physics):

$$E = \frac{F}{y} \qquad \qquad ... (2.33)$$

Where,

E is the elasticity (dyne cm^{-2}),

F is the stress,

y is the strain.

2.8.2 Mechanical Model

The viscoelastic behaviour of semisolid may be represented by using mechanical models.

Dash-pot: A viscous fluid may be represented as movement of a piston in a cylinder filled with a liquid [Fig. 2.21 (a)].

Hooke's spring: An elastic solid is modeled by the movement of a Hooke's spring [Fig. 2.21 (b)].

Maxwell element: The behaviour of a semisolid as a viscoelastic body may therefore be described by the combination of the dashpot and spring, as observed in Fig. 2.21 (c). This mechanical model of a viscoelastic material, a non-Newtonian material showing both viscosity of the liquid state and elasticity of the solid state, and combined in series is called a Maxwell element.

In a Maxwell model;

1. As a constant stress is applied to the Maxwell unit, there is a strain on the material that can be thought of as a displacement of the spring.
2. The applied stress may be thought of as also producing a movement of the piston in the dashpot due to viscous flow.
3. Removal of the stress leads to complete recovery of the spring, but the viscous flow shows no recovery, i.e., no tendency to return to its original state.

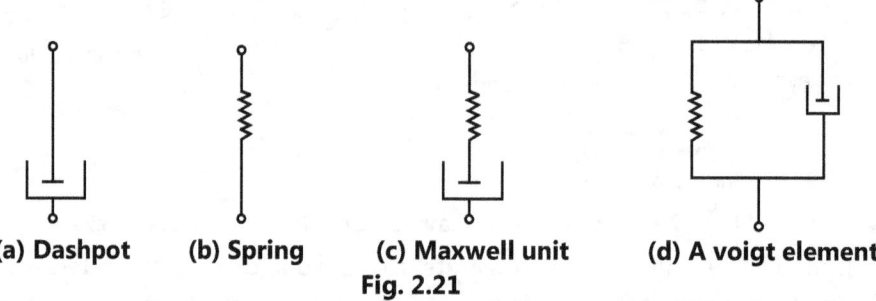

    (a) Dashpot   **(b) Spring**   **(c) Maxwell unit**   **(d) A voigt element**

Fig. 2.21

Voigt element: The spring and dashpot may also be combined in a parallel arrangement as seen in Fig. 2.21 (d), and this model for viscoelasticity is known as a Voigt element.

In the Voigt model, the spring and dashpot being attached in parallel rather than series, the drag of the viscous fluid in the dashpot simultaneously influence the extension and compression of the spring which characterizes the solid nature of the material, and the strain will vary in an exponential manner with time.

Strain is expressed as a deformation or compliance, J, of the test material in which J is strain per unit stress.

The deformation of a viscoelastic material following the Voigt model is given as a function of time t, by the expression:

$$J = J_\infty (1 - e^{-t/T}) \qquad \qquad \dots (2.34)$$

In which J_∞ is the deformation or strain per unit stress at infinite and T is viscosity per unit elasticity, η/E, which is called reiteration time.

2.8.3 Creep Curve

The mechanical models, Maxwell and Voigt, representing viscoelastic behaviour in two different ways, may be combined into a generalized model to incorporate all possibilities of flow and deformation of non-Newtonian materials.

One or several Voigt units may be combined with Maxwell elements. As observed in Fig. 2.22, two Voigt elements are combined with a Maxwell element to reproduce the behaviour of a sample of wool fat at 30° C.

The deformation J as a function of time is measured with an instrument known as a **creep viscometer** and when deformation J is plotted against time, graph obtained is called as a **creep curve.**

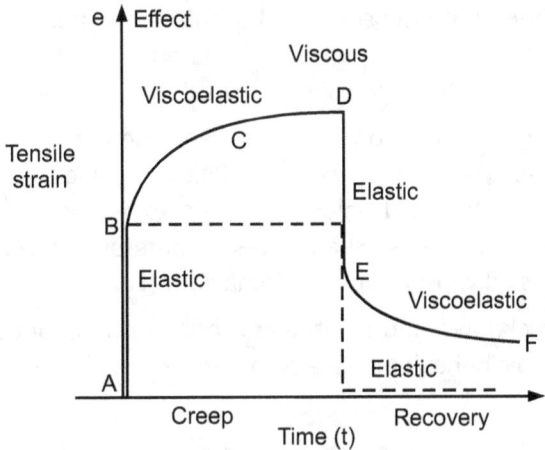

Fig. 2.22: The creep curve

The creep curve is observed to be;

Region A-B: An initial elastic jump is observed. This is elastic behaviour of the material.

Region B-C: When the material is attempting to flow as a viscous fluid but is being retarded by its solid characteristics, means this region represents viscoelastic behaviour.

Region C-D: At longer times equilibrium is established, such that for a system like this, which is ostensibly liquid, viscous flow will eventually predominate and the curve will become linear (C-D). Means this region represents viscosity behaviour.

Region DEF: When the stress is removed, only the stored energy will be recovered and this is exhibited by an initial elastic recoil (D-E) equivalent to the region A-B and the slow elastic recovery region E-F is equivalent to B-C.

2.9 RHEOLOGY FOR DISPERSION SYSTEM

The viscosity of liquid increases by the addition of a dispersion phase.

Dispersion system is classified as suspension and emulsion.

2.9.1 Suspension

Many pharmaceutical products, particularly those for children, are presented as suspensions and their rheological properties are important.

In general, these properties must be adjusted so that:

1. The product is easily administered (e.g. easily poured from a bottle or forced through a syringe needle).
2. Sedimentation is either prevented or retarded; if it does occur, redispersion is easy.
3. The product has an elegant appearance.

2.9.1.1 Non-Newtonian Behaviour of Suspension

[A] Plastic Flow:

The rheological properties of suspensions are affected by the degree of flocculation. The reason for this is that, the amount of free continuous phase is reduced, as it becomes entrapped in the floccules.

Consequently, the apparent viscosity of a flocculated suspension is normally higher. In addition, when a disperse system is highly flocculated then the possibility of interaction between floccules occurs and structured systems result.

If the forces bonding floccules together are weak then, a minimum stress required to break the floccules means, yield value will result. Below this yield value, the suspension will behave like a solid. Once the yield value has been exceeded, the amount of structural breakdown increases with increased shear stress. Therefore, flocculated suspensions will exhibit plastic or, more usually, pseudoplastic behaviour [Fig. 2.4].

Obviously, if the breakdown and reformation of the bonds between floccules are time dependent then thixotropic behaviour will also be observed.

[B] Dilatant Flow:

The formation structure does not occur in deflocculated suspension so their rheological behaviour is determined by that of the continuous phase together with the effect of distortion of the flow lines around the particles. As the suspension becomes more concentrated and the particles come into contact, then dilatancy will occur. [Fig. 2.6]

2.9.1.2 Deflocculated Articles in Newtonian Vehicles

When such sediment, a compact sediment or cake is difficult to redisperse, the rate of sedimentation can be reduced by increasing the viscosity of the continuous medium, which will remain Newtonian. However, there is a limit to which this viscosity can be increased because difficulty will be experienced, for example, in pouring the suspension from a bottle. Furthermore, if sedimentation does occur, then subsequent redispersion may be even more difficult.

2.9.1.3 Deflocculated Particles in Non-Newtonian Vehicles

Only pseudoplastic or plastic dispersion media can be used in the formulation of suspensions and both will retard the sedimentation of small particles, as their apparent viscosities will be high under the small stresses associated with sedimentation. Also, as the medium will undergo structural breakdown under the higher stresses involved in shaking and pouring, both these processes are facilitated.

The hydrocolloids used as suspending agents, such as acacia, tragacanth, methylcellulose, gelatin and sodium carboxymethylcellulos all impart Newtonian properties, normally pseudoplasticity, to the suspensions.

Thixotropy can occur and this is particularly the case with the mineral clays, such as bentonite (which must only be used in suspensions for external use). The three-dimensional gel network traps the deflocculated particles at rest and their sedimentation is retarded and may be completely prevented. The gel network is destroyed during shaking so that administration is facilitated. It is desirable that the gel network is reformed quickly so that dispersion of the particles is maintained.

2.9.1.4 Flocculated Particles in Newtonian Vehicles

Such particles will still sediment but because the aggregates are diffused, large volume sediment is produced and, as such, is easier to disperse. These systems are seldom improved by an increase in the viscosity of the continuous phase as this will only influence the rate of sedimentation. The major problem is one of pharmaceutical inelegance, in that the sediment does not fill the whole of the fluid volume.

2.9.1.5 Flocculated Particles in Non-Newtonian Vehicle

These systems combine advantages of both methods. Furthermore, variation in the properties of the raw materials to be suspended is unlikely to influence the performance of a product made on production scale. Consequently, less difference will be observed between batches made by the same method and plant.

2.9.2 Emulsions

Nearly all, but the most dilute of medicinal emulsions exhibit non-Newtonian behaviour, their rheological characteristics have a marked effect on their usefulness. The fluid emulsions are usually pseudoplastic and those approaching a semisolid nature behave plastically and exhibit marked yield values. The semisolid creams are usually viscoelastic. A considerable variety of pharmaceutical products can be formulated by altering the concentration of emulsifying agent. The latter can be used to confor viscoelastic properties on a topical cream merely by varying the ratio of surface-active agent to long-chain alcohol.

2.10 APPLICATION TO PHARMACY

The pharmaceutical applications of rheology are summarized in Table 2.1.

Table 2.1: Pharmaceutical applications of rheology

Fluids	Applications
	• Mixing.
	• Particle size reduction of disperse systems with shear.
	• Passage through orifices, including pouring, packaging in bottles, and passage through hypodermic needles.
	• Fluid transfer, including pumping and flow through pipes.
	• Physical stability of disperse systems.
Semisolids	
	• Spreading and adherence on the skin.
	• Removal from jars or extrusion from tubes.
	• Capacity of solids to mix with miscible liquids.
	• Release of the drug from the base.

contd. ...

Solids	
	• Flow of powders from hoppers and into die cavities in tabletting or into capsules during encapsulation.
	• Packagability of powdered or granular solids.
Processing	
	• Production capacity of the equipment.
	• Processing efficiency.

QUESTIONS

1. **Short Answer Questions (3 Marks):**
    1. Enlist applications of rheology.   **[SPPU - 2013, 14]**
    2. What is meant by plug flow?   **[SPPU - 2010]**
    3. How do you select a viscometer?
    4. When methylcellulose is added to water, the viscosity increases? Why?
    5. Write Newtonian law.   **[SPPU - 2010, 15]**
    6. Give advantage of cone and plate viscometer over cup and bob viscometer.
    7. Define thixotropy. Describe the role of thixotropy in formulations.   **[SPPU - 2012]**
    8. Draw the flow curve of antithixotropy flow and explain its mechanism. **[SPPU - 2012]**

2. **Medium Answer Questions (5 Marks):**
    1. Explain the shear thinning and shear thickening systems. Give one example for each type of material.   **[SPPU - 2013, 15]**
    2. Write short note on Cup and Bob viscometer.
    3. Discuss the concept of Viscoelasticity.   **[SPPU - 2013, 15]**
    4. Discuss the rheology of disperse systems.
    5. Write the principle and working of Ostwald viscometer.
    6. Write short note on Cone and Plate Viscometer.
    7. Write short note on falling ball viscometer.   **[SPPU - 2014, 15]**
    8. Write short note on Non-Newtonian types of flow.   **[SPPU - 2013, 14]**

3. **Long Answer Questions (10 Marks):**
    1. Classify rheological systems along with examples. Add note on Cup and Bob viscometer.   **[SPPU - 2013]**
    2. Explain the concept of thixotropy and the measurement of thixotropy in formulation.
                                                          [SPPU - 2010, 13, 14, 15]
    3. Write methods for determination of viscosity.   **[SPPU - 2013]**

■■■

Chapter **3**...

Chemical Kinetics and Stability

Syllabus ...

(A) Reaction Theories, Rate, Order and Molecularity, Mathematical Treatment of Zero, First and Second Order, Complex Reaction: Reversible, Parallel and Side Reactions (no derivations)

(B) Determination of Order, Effect of Temperature, Arrhenius Equation and Energy of Activation, Degradation Pathways – Physical and Chemical in Stability, Accelerated Stability Studies

(C) Problems Related to Half Life, Shelf Life, and Energy of Activation and Arrhenius Factor

3.1 INTRODUCTION

'The branch of physical chemistry which deals with the rate of reactions' is called chemical kinetics.

The study of chemical kinetics includes:

1. The rate of the reactions and rate laws.
2. The factors as temperature, pressure, concentration and catalyst, which influences the rate of a reaction.
3. The mechanism or the sequence of steps by which a reaction occurs.

The knowledge of the rate of reactions is very valuable to understand the chemistry of reactions. It is also of great importance in selecting optimum conditions for an industrial process so that it proceeds at a rate to give maximum yield.

3.1.1 Applications of Chemical Kinetics

Kinetic principles have found applications in pharmacy.

(a) Drug stability: Chemical kinetics provides the basis to predict drug stability. It is expressed as a rate process. These studies help to predict the expiry period (shelf life) of a product.

(b) Dissolution: Normally, the drug is expected to release from the solid dosage forms (tablets etc.,) and immediately go into molecular solution. This process is called dissolution. It is expressed in terms of a rate process. The greater the rate of dissolution, the faster the absorption.

(c) Drug release: Prodrugs are defined as 'those agents which do not have any therapeutic, activity as such, but are converted back *in vivo* to their parent compounds'. Prodrugs are specially designed when the parent drug is poorly soluble (for example, making a soluble derivative), or poorly bioavailable (example is, erythromycin propionate) etc. These prodrugs undergo chemical or enzymatic conversion to pharmacologically active drugs. Chemical kinetic principles are employed for predicting the release pattern of drugs from prodrugs.

(d) Pharmacokinetics: It involves the study of the transport of the drugs from the site of application to blood (absorption), from blood to tissue spaces and other body parts (distribution), and finally its removal from the body (elimination). All such processes are characterized by corresponding rate constants.

(e) Drug action: The interactions of drugs with biomembranes or receptors are being interpreted using kinetic models. Such models provide information regarding the quantitative differences in the drug action of different drugs of the same therapeutic category.

3.2 REACTION RATES

The rate of reaction tells as to what speed the reaction occurs.

Reaction Rate: Rate of reaction is defined as, 'the change in the concentration of a reactant or a product with time (M/s)'.

Let us consider a simple reaction;

$$\text{Reactant} \rightarrow \text{Products}$$

$$A \rightarrow B$$

The concentration of reactant 'A' decreases and concentration of product 'B' increases with time. [Fig. 3.1]

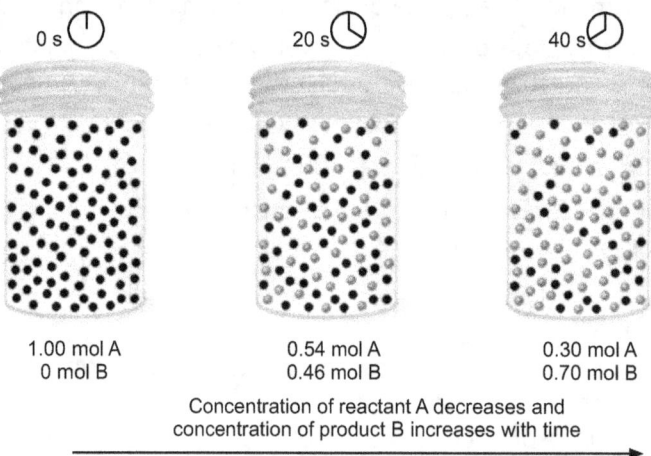

1.00 mol A   0.54 mol A   0.30 mol A
0 mol B   0.46 mol B   0.70 mol B

Concentration of reactant A decreases and
concentration of product B increases with time

Fig. 3.1: Reaction process with respect to time

From given reaction:

Rate of reaction = Rate of disappearance of A.

= Rate of appearance of B.

Now, consider rate of disappearance of reactant A;

$$Rate = \frac{\text{Change in number of moles of A}}{\text{Change in time}}$$

$$Rate = -\frac{\Delta[A]}{\Delta t} = \frac{[A]_2 - [A]_1}{t_2 - t_1} \qquad \qquad ... (3.1)$$

Where,

$[A]_1$: Concentration of reactant at time t_1.

$[A]_2$: Concentration of reactant at time t_2.

– ve sign indicates concentration of reactant A decreases.

Now, consider rate of appearance of product B;

$\therefore$
$$Rate = \frac{\text{Change in number of moles of B}}{\text{Change in time}}$$

$$Rate = \frac{\Delta[B]}{\Delta t} = \frac{[B]_2 - [B]_1}{t_2 - t_1} \qquad \qquad ... (3.2)$$

Where,

$[B]_1$: Concentration of product at time t_1

$[B]_2$: Concentration of product at time t_2

+ ve sign indicates concentration of product B increases.

A change in concentration of reactant and product with respect to time is shown graphically in Fig. 3.2.

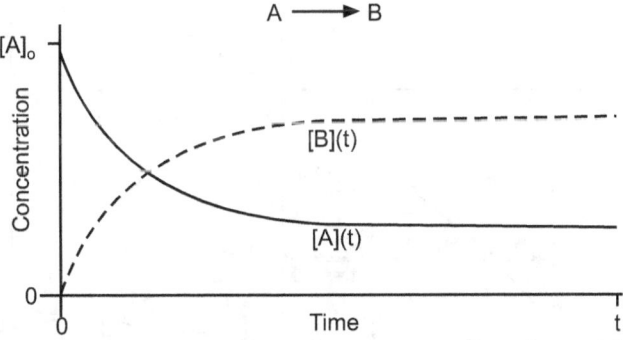

Fig. 3.2: A change in concentration of reactant and product with time

3.2.1 Unit

Reaction rate has the units if concentration divided by time.

mole/litre sec   or $mol\ l^{-1} s^{-1}$

mole/litre min   or $mol\ l^{-1} min^{-1}$

mole/litre hour   or $mol\ l^{-1} h^{-1}$

3.2.2 Example

Consider the decomposition of N_2O_5 to give NO_2 and O_2:

$$2N_2O_5 \text{ (g)} \rightarrow 4NO_2 \text{ (g)} + O_2 \text{ (g)}$$

The concentration of N_2O_5 to give NO_2 and O_2 was found experimentally every 100 seconds. The result of an experiment is listed in Table 3.1. The results are also shown graphically in Fig. 3.3.

Table 3.1: The concentration of N_2O_5 to give NO_2 and O_2

Time (s)	Concentration (M)		
	N_2O_5	NO_2	O_2
0	0.0200	0	0
100	0.0169	0.0063	0.0016
200	0.0142	0.0115	0.0029
300	0.0120	0.0160	0.0040
400	0.0101	0.0197	0.0049
500	0.0086	0.0229	0.0057
600	0.0072	0.0256	0.0064
700	0.0061	0.0278	0.0070

As the reaction process, the concentration of N_2O_5 decreases rapidly and concentration of NO_2 increases rapidly, as compared to concentration of O_2.

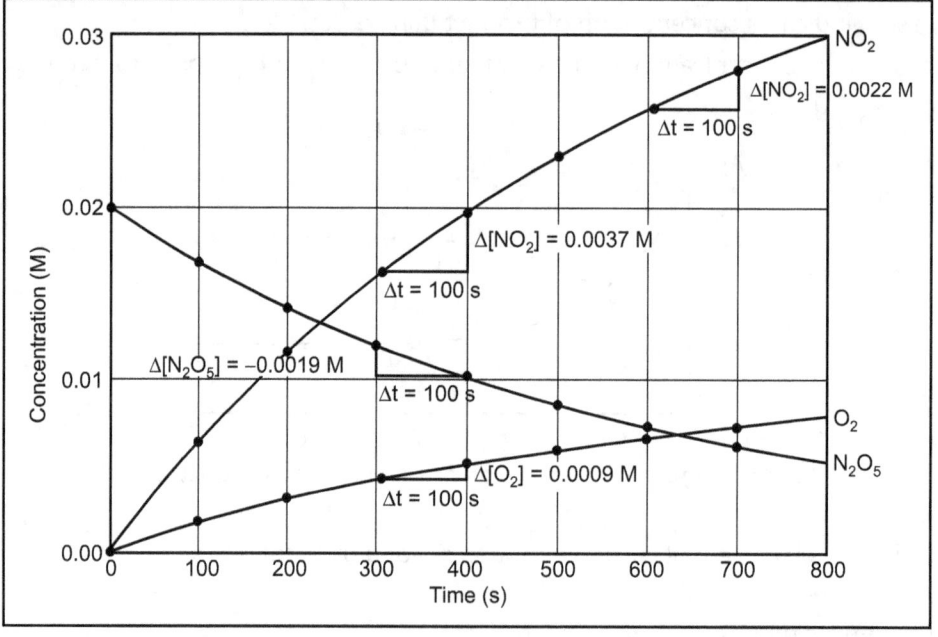

Fig. 3.3: Decomposition of N_2O_5 to give NO_2 and O_2 with function of time

From the graph looking at t = 300 to 400

$$\text{Rate } O_2 = \frac{0.0009 \text{ M}}{100 \text{ s}} = 9 \times 10^{-6} \text{ Ms}^{-1}$$

$$\text{Rate } NO_2 = \frac{0.0037 \text{ M}}{100 \text{ s}} = 3.7 \times 10^{-5} \text{ Ms}^{-1}$$

$$\text{Rate } N_2O_5 = \frac{0.0019 \text{ M}}{100 \text{ s}} = 1.9 \times 10^{-5} \text{ Ms}^{-1}$$

3.3 RATE LAWS

The rate of reaction depends on the concentration of reactant in reaction at constant temperature. The exact relation between rate and concentration is determined by measuring the reaction rate with different initial reactant concentrations.

Rate Law: The rate of a reaction is directly proportional to the reactant concentrations, each concentration being raised to some power.

Let us consider a simple reaction;

$$\text{Reactant } \rightarrow \text{ Products}$$
$$_nA \rightarrow B$$
$$\text{rate} \propto [A]^n$$
$$\text{rate} = k [A]^n \qquad \qquad \text{... (3.3)}$$

For a reaction; $_mA + _nB \rightarrow$ Products

The reaction rate with respect to A or B is determined by varying the concentration of one reactant, keeping that of the other constant. Thus, the rate of reaction may be expressed as

$$\text{Rate} = k [A]^m [B]^n \qquad \qquad \text{... (3.4)}$$

Expressions such as (3.3) and (3.4) tell the relation between the rate of a reaction and reactant concentrations.

An expression which shows how the reaction rate is related to concentrations is called the **rate law or rate equation**.

The power (exponent) of concentration n or m in the rate law is usually a small whole number integer (1, 2, 3) or fractional. The proportionality constant k is called the rate constant for the reaction.

Example:

Table 3.2: Example of rate law

	Reactions	Rate law
1.	$2N_2O_5 \rightarrow 4NO_2 + O_2$	Rate = k $[N_2O_5]$
2.	$H_2 + I_2 \rightarrow 2HI$	Rate = k $[H_2]$ $[I_2]$
3.	$2NO_2 \rightarrow 2NO + O_2$	Rate = k $[NO_2]^2$
4.	$2NO + 2H_2 \rightarrow N_2 + 2H_2O$	Rate = k $[H_2]$ $[NO]^2$

In these rate laws, where the quotient or concentration is not shown, it is understood to be 1. i.e. $[H_2]^1 = [H_2]$.

It is apparent that, the rate law for a reaction must be determined by experiment. It cannot be written by merely looking at the equation with a background of our knowledge of Law of Mass Action. However, for some elementary reactions the powers in the rate law may correspond to coefficients in the chemical equation. **But usually, the powers of concentration in the rate law are different from coefficients.** Thus, for the reaction (4. from Table 3.2) above, the rate is found to be proportional to $[H_2]$ although the quotient of H_2 in the equation is 2. For NO the rate is proportional to $[NO]^2$ and power '2' corresponds to the coefficient.

3.4 ORDER OF A REACTION

The order of a reaction is defined as 'the sum of the powers of concentrations in the rate law'.

Let us consider the example of a reaction which has the rate law (equation 3.4);

$$Rate = k\,[A]^m\,[B]^n$$

The order of such a reaction = m + n.

The order of a reaction can also be defined with respect to a single reactant. Thus, the reaction order with respect to A is m and with respect to B it is n.

The overall order of reaction (m + n) may range from 1 to 3 and can be fractional.

Classification of Reaction According to the Order:

Zero Order: m + n = 0

First order: m + n = 1

Second order: m + n = 2

Third order: m + n = 3

In case of zero order reaction: A reactant whose concentration does not affect the reaction rate is not included in the rate law. In effect, the concentration of such a reactant has the power 0. Thus, $[A]^\circ = 1$.

A zero order reaction is one whose rate is independent of concentration.

For example, the rate law for the reaction

$$NO_2 + CO \rightarrow NO + CO_2 \quad \text{at } 200° \text{ C is}$$

$$Rate = k[NO_2]^2$$

Here the rate does not depend on [CO], so this is not included in the rate law and the power of [CO] is understood to be zero. The reaction is **zero order** with respect to CO. The reaction is second order with respect to $[NO_2]$. The overall reaction order is 2 + 0 = 2.

3.5 MOLECULARITY OF REACTION

Chemical reactions are classified into two types:

1. Elementary Reactions: Simple reaction which occurs in single step.
2. Complex reactions: Reactions which occurs in two or more steps.

3.5.1 Molecularity of Elementary Reaction

Molecularity of an Elementary Reaction is defined as 'total number of reactant molecules involved in a reaction'.

An elementary reaction is classified according to number of reactant molecules in the reaction (Fig. 3.4).

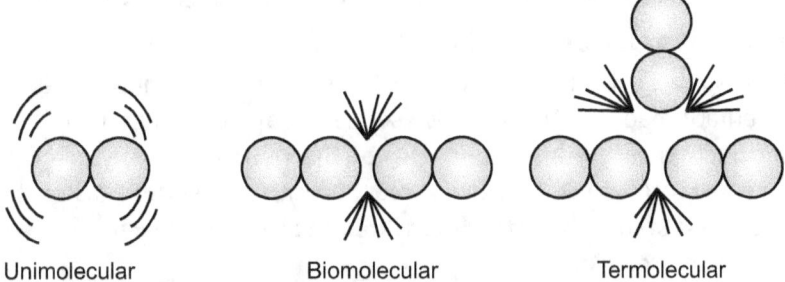

Unimolecular   Biomolecular   Termolecular

Fig. 3.4: A classification of elementary reaction

1. **Unimolecular (Molecularity = 1)**
    Example: $Br_2 \rightarrow 2\ Br$.
2. **Bimolecular (Molecularity = 2)**
    Example: $2H_2O_2 \rightarrow 2H_2O + O_2$
3. **Termolecular (Molecularity = 3)**
    Example: $2NO + O_2 \rightarrow 2NO_2$

Why High Molecularity Reactions are Rare?

Most of the reactions involve one, two or at the most three molecules. The reactions involving four or more molecules are very rare (Fig. 3.5).

The rarity of reactions with high molecularity can be explained on the basis of the **kinetic molecular theory.**

1. According to this theory, the rate of a chemical reaction is proportional to the number of collisions taking place between the reacting molecules.
2. The chances of simultaneous collision of reacting molecules will go on decreasing with increase in number of molecules.
3. Thus, the possibility of three molecules colliding together is much less than in case of bimolecular collision.
4. For a reaction of molecularity 4, the four molecules must come close and collide with one another at the same time. The possibility of their doing so is much less than even in the case of termolecular reaction.

Hence, the reactions involving many molecules proceed through a series of steps, each involving two or three or less number of molecules. Such a reaction is called a **complex reaction** and the slowest step determines the overall rate of the reactions.

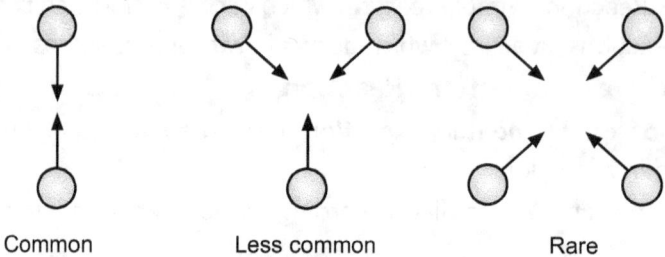

Common   Less common   Rare

Fig. 3.5: Collision between reaction molecules

3.5.2 Molecularity of a Complex Reaction

Most chemical reactions are complex reactions. These occur in a series of steps. Each step is an elementary reaction. The stepwise sequence of elementary reactions that convert reactions to products is called the **mechanism of the reaction.** In any mechanism, some of the steps will be fast, others will be slow. A reaction can proceed no faster than its slowest step. Thus, the slowest step is the **rate–determining step** of the reaction.

The decomposition reaction of N_2O_5

i.e., $\qquad\qquad 2N_2O_5 \;\rightarrow\; 4NO_2 + O_2$

is an example of a complex reaction. It occurs by the following steps:

Step 1: $\qquad\quad 2N_2O_5 \;\rightarrow\; 2NO_2 + 2NO_3 \qquad$ (slow)

Step 2: $\qquad NO_2 + NO_3 \;\rightarrow\; NO + NO_2 + O_2 \quad$ (slow)

Step 3: $\qquad NO + NO_3 \;\rightarrow\; 2NO_2 \qquad\qquad$ (fast)

Each elementary reaction has its own molecularity equal to the number of molecules or atoms participating in it. It is meaningless to give the molecularity of the overall reaction because it is made of several elementary reactions, each, perhaps with a different molecularity. At best could be thought of as: **the number of molecules or atoms taking part in the rate–determining step.**

Thus, step 2 in the above mechanism is rate-determining and has molecularity '2' which could be considered as the molecularity of the decomposition reaction of N_2O_5.

3.5.3 Molecularity versus Order of Reaction

The term molecularity is often confused with order of a reaction.

Thus for a reaction,

$$2A + B \rightarrow \text{Products}$$

$$\text{Rate} = k\,[A]^2\,[B]$$

Two molecules of A and one molecule of B are participating in the reaction.

Therefore, **molecularity of the reaction** is, 2 + 1 = 3.

The sum of powers in the rate law is 2 + 1 and hence the **reaction order is also 3.**

Thus, the molecularity and order for an elementary reaction are equal.

Table 3.3: Differences between order and molecular of reaction

	Order of Reaction	Molecularity of Reaction
1.	It is the sum of powers of the concentration terms in the rate law expression.	It is number of reacting species undergoing simultaneous collision in the elementary or simple reaction.
2.	It is an experimentally determined value.	It is a theoretical concept.
3.	It can have fractional value.	It is always a whole number.
4.	It can assume zero value.	It cannot have zero value.
5.	Order of a reaction can change with the conditions such as pressure, temperature, concentration.	Molecularity is invariant for a chemical equation.

3.6 INTEGRATED RATE LAW

1. Zero order reaction
2. Pseudo order reaction
3. First order reaction
4. Second order reaction

3.6.1 Zero Order Reaction

Very rare reactions follow zero order kinetics.

The zero order reaction means that, the rate of the reaction is proportional to the concentration of reactant raised to the **power zero**. In other words, the rate of zero order reaction is independent of the reactant concentration. This implies that the rate of the reaction remains constant until the reactant has completely converted into the products.

Therefore, **zero order reaction** is defined as 'the reaction whose rate is independent of the reactant concentration and remains constant throughout the course of the reaction'.

3.6.1.1 Rate Law for Zero Order Reactions

Consider a zero order reaction,

$$A \rightarrow \text{Products}$$

The rate law of the reaction is given by

$$\text{Rate} = \frac{d[A]}{dt} = k[A]^\circ = k \qquad \qquad \text{... (3.5)}$$

On rearrangement it becomes:

$$d[A] = -k.dt \qquad \qquad \text{... (3.6)}$$

On integration of the equation between limits [A] = [A]$_0$ at t = 0 and [A] = [A]$_t$ at t = t we get

$$\int_{[A]_0}^{[A]_t} d[A] = -k \int_{t}^{0} dt \qquad \qquad \text{... (3.7)}$$

Hence,

$$[A]_t - [A]_0 = -kt \qquad \qquad \text{... (3.8)}$$

$$[A]_t = -kt + [A]_0 \qquad \qquad \text{... (3.9)}$$

$$k = \frac{[A]_0 - [A]_t}{t} \qquad \qquad \text{... (3.10)}$$

The equations (3.9) and (3.10) are the forms of integrated rate law of zero order reactions.

3.6.1.2 Unit of K of Zero Order Reactions

According to equation (3.10), the units of k are given by

$$k = \frac{[A]_t - [A]_0}{t} = \frac{\Delta[A]}{t} = \frac{mol}{lit} \times \frac{1}{Time}$$

Thus, the unit of k is: **mol lit^{-1} time $^{-1}$.**

3.6.1.3 Graphical Representation

The integrated rate law for zero order reactions is given by equation (3.9).

$$[A]_t = -kt + [A]_0$$
$$\downarrow \qquad \downarrow \qquad \downarrow$$
$$y = \quad mx + c$$

The equation (3.9) has the form of linear equation y = mx + c. The plot of [A], versus t is a straight line as shown in Fig. 3.6. The slope of the straight line is equal to – k, and intercept on [A]$_t$ axis is [A]$_0$.

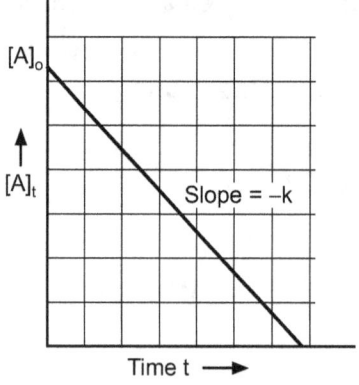

Fig. 3.6: Variation [A]$_t$ with time

3.6.1.4 Half Life of Zero Order Reaction

Half life is defined as 'the time required for concentration of reactant to reduce to half of its initial concentration'. Half life is represented as $t_{1/2}$.

The integrated rate law for zero order reactions is given by equation (3.9).

$$[A]_t = -k t + [A]_0$$

Where;

     $[A]_t$: The concentration of A that remains unreacted at time t.

     $[A]_0$ is initial concentration at t = 0.

As per the definition; $\dfrac{[A]_0}{2}$ at $t = t_{1/2}$

Hence we can write; $[A]_t = \dfrac{[A]_0}{2}$ at $t = t_{1/2}$.

With this condition, equation (3.9) become,

$$\frac{[A]_0}{2} = -kt_{1/2} + [A]_0$$

$$kt_{1/2} = [A]_0 - \frac{[A]_0}{2} = \frac{[A]_0}{2}$$

$$t_{1/2} = \frac{[A]_0}{2k} \qquad \qquad \dots (3.11)$$

The unit for half life of reaction is time scale, i.e. sec/conc, min/conc, etc.

According to equation (3.11), the half life of zero order reaction is directly proportional to initial concentration of reactant.

3.6.1.5 Shelf Life of Zero Order Reaction

Shelf Life is defined as 'the time required for the concentration of the reactant to reduce to 90% of its initial concentration'.

Shelf life is represented as t_{90} and has the unit time/conc. The shelf life equation can be derived as follows:

As per the definition; $\dfrac{90\,[A]_0}{100}$ or $0.9\,[A]_0$ at $t = t_{90}$

Hence, we can write; $[A]_t = 0.9\,[A]_0$ at $t = t_{90}$

With this condition equation (3.9) become,

$$0.9\,[A]_0 = -k\,t_{90} + [A]_0$$

$$k\,t_{90} = [A]_0 - 0.9\,[A]_0$$

$$t_{90} = \frac{[A]_0 - 0.9\,[A]_0}{k} = \frac{0.1\,[A]_0}{k} \qquad \qquad \dots (3.12)$$

Equation (3.12) uses to determine shelf life of zero order reaction.

3.6.1.6 Examples of Zero Order Reaction

Zero order reactions are not common. They occur only under some special circumstances. Most of the zero order reactions take place on a metal surface. For example,

1. The decomposition of NH_3 (g) on a hot platinum surface:

$$2NH_3 \text{ (g)} \xrightarrow[\text{Pt}]{\Delta} N_2(g) + 3H_2(g)$$

The platinum surface gets completely covered by a layer of NH_3 molecules. The number of NH_3 molecules, attached on the surface of platinum is very small compared to the total number of NH_3 molecules. Most of the NH_3 molecules remain in the gas phase and these do not react. The molecules present on the metal surface can only react. Consequently, the rate of the reaction is independent of the total concentration of NH_3 and hence remains constant.

2. The decomposition of nitrous oxide to nitrogen and oxygen in the presence of platinum catalyst:

$$2N_2O \xrightarrow{\text{Platinum}} 2N_2(g) + O_2(g)$$

Similar to decomposition of NH_3 on platinum surface, when all the active sites on the metal surface are occupied by N_2O molecules, most of the molecules remain in the gas phase. Because only the N_2O molecules on the surface react. The reaction rate is independent of the total concentration of N_2O. The reaction then follows zero order kinetics.

3.6.1.7 Solved Problems on Zero Order Reaction

Problem 3.1: A drug is exposed to 40°C and the intensity of colour was measured. The initial absorbance of the solution at 500 nm was 1.245. After 90 days, the absorbance was decreased to 1.235. Estimate the reaction rate assuming that the colour fading follows zero order.

Solution: Reaction rate is mathematically expressed in terms of rate constant.

Data: $A_0 = 1.245$; $A_t = 1.235$; t = 90 days; k =?, $t_{1/2}$ =?; t_{90} =?

Calculation of k: From rate of law of zero order reaction,

$$k = \frac{[A]_0 - [A]_t}{t}$$

Adding values in equation, we get

$$k = \frac{1.245 - 1.235}{90}$$

$$= 1.11 \times 10^{-4} \text{ days}^{-1} \quad \text{or} \quad 0.00011 \text{ days}^{-1}$$

Problem 3.2: The decomposition of H_2O_2 in the presence of platinum as catalyst is a zero order reaction. Initial concentration of H_2O_2 is 23.8 ml and after 10 min concentration decreases upto 14.7 ml. calculate half life and shelf life of reaction.

Given: Rate constant of reaction is 0.91 min^{-1}.

Solution: Given data: $A_0 = 23.8$; $A_t = 14.7$; $t = 10$ min; $k = 0.91$, $t_{1/2} = ?$; $t_{90} = ?$

Calculation of $t_{1/2}$: From equation of Half life of zero order reaction,

$$t_{1/2} = \frac{[A]_0}{2K}$$

Addition of values in equation:

$$t_{1/2} = \frac{23.8}{2 \times 0.91} = 13.07 \text{ min}$$

Calculation of t_{90}: From equation of shelf life of zero order.

$$t_{90} = \frac{0.1 \, [A]_0}{k} = \frac{0.1 \times 23.8}{0.91} = 2.615 \text{ min.}$$

3.6.2 Pseudo Order Reaction

A reaction in which one of the reactants is present in a large excess shows an order different from the actual order. The experimental order which is not the actual one is referred to as the pseudo order. Since for elementary reactions molecularity and order are identical, pseudo–order reactions may also be called pseudo molecular reactions. Let us consider a reaction

$$A + B \rightarrow \text{Products}$$

In which, the reactant **B is present in a large excess**. Since it is an elementary reaction, its rate law can be written as

$$\text{Rate} = k\,[A][B]$$

As B is present in large excess, its concentration remains practically constant in the course of reaction. Thus, the rate law can be written as

$$\text{Rate} = k\,[A]$$

Where the new rate constant $k' = k\,[B]$. Thus, the actual order of the reaction is second–order but in practice it will be first–order. Therefore, the reaction is said to have a **Pseudo–First Order.**

Example of Pseudo order reaction:

Hydrolysis of Sucrose: Sucrose upon hydrolysis in the presence of a dilute mineral acid gives glucose and fructose.

$$C_{12}H_{22}O_{11} \quad + \quad H_2O \rightarrow \quad C_6H_{12}O_6 \quad + \quad C_6H_{12}O_6$$

| Sucrose (excess) | | Glucose | Fructose |

If a large excess of water is present, $[H_2O]$ is practically constant and the rate law may be written

$$\text{Rate} = k\,[C_{12}H_{22}O_{11}]\,[H_2O]$$
$$= k'\,[C_{12}H_{22}O_{11}]$$

The reaction though of second order is experimentally found to be of first order. Thus, it is a pseudo–first–order reaction.

3.6.3 First Order Reaction

A reaction whose rate depends on the single reactant concentration raised to a first power is called the **first order reaction**.

3.6.3.1 Rate Law for First Order Reactions

Consider a simple general first order reaction

$$A \;\rightarrow\; \text{Products}$$

The differential rate law for this first order reaction is

$$-\frac{d[A]}{dt} = k[A] \qquad\qquad \ldots (3.13)$$

Where

[A] : The concentration of the reactant A that remains unreacted at time t.

$\dfrac{-d[A]}{dt}$: The rate of reaction measured at time t at which A is convened to the products.

By rearranging and integrating the equation (3.13) between the limits $[A] = [A]_0$ at $t = 0$ and $[A] = [A]_t$ at $t = t$, we write,

$$\int_{[A]_0}^{[A]_t} \frac{d[A]}{[A]} = -k \int_0^t dt \qquad\qquad \ldots (3.14)$$

Where,

$[A]_0$: The initial concentration of A at $t = 0$

$[A]_t$: The concentration of A that remains unreacted at $t = t$.

On performing the integration, we get;

$$ln\,[A]_t - ln\,[A]_0 = -kt \qquad \text{or} \quad ln\,\frac{[A]_t}{[A]_0} = -kt \qquad\qquad \ldots (3.15)$$

Hence, $$kt = ln\,\frac{[A]_0}{[A]_t} \qquad\qquad \ldots (3.16)$$

$\therefore$ $$k = \frac{1}{t}\,ln\,\frac{[A]_0}{[A]_t} \qquad\qquad \ldots (3.17)$$

Converting into $\log_{10}$ the integrated rate law becomes

$$k = \frac{2.303}{t} \log_{10} \frac{[A]_0}{[A]_t}$$ ... (3.18)

If we let

'a' mol lit^{-1} (that is M) as the initial concentration of A at t = 0

'x' as the concentration of A that decreases during time t from the beginning of the reaction. Also x means concentration of product at time t.

Then the concentration of A that remains unreacted at time t is given by;

$$[A]_t = [A]_0 - x = a - x$$

Where, $[A]_0 = a$ mol lit^{-1}.

With these values the equation (3.18) can be written as:

$$k = \frac{2.303}{t} \log_{10} \left(\frac{a}{a-x}\right)$$ ... (3.19)

The equations (3.18) and (3.19) are the various forms of the integrated rate law for the first order reactions.

3.6.3.2 Units of k

The integrated rate law for the first order reaction is given by equation (3.18).

$$k = \frac{2.303}{t} \log_{10} \frac{[A]_0}{[A]_t}$$

Because, $\log_{10} \frac{[A]_0}{[A]_t}$ is a unitless quantity. The unit of k will be given by reciprocal of time.

For example, t is expressed in s and k will have the unit s^{-1}.

3.6.3.3 Graphical Representation

1. The differential rate law for first order reaction,

$$A \rightarrow \text{Products}$$

$$\text{Rate} = -\frac{d[A]}{dt} = k[A]_t + 0$$

$$\downarrow \qquad \downarrow \qquad \downarrow$$

$$y \quad = mx \quad + \quad c$$

The equation is of the form y = mx+c, the equation of a straight line. Hence, the graph of rate versus $[A]_t$ is a straight line passing through origin as shown in Fig. 3.7. The slope of the straight line is k.

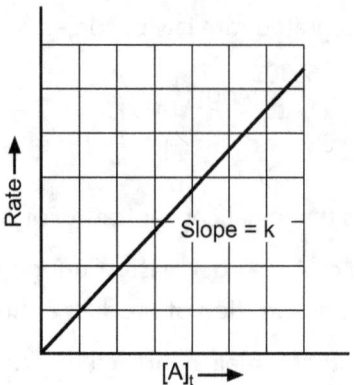

Fig. 3.7: Variation of rate with [A]$_t$

2. The integrated rate law given by equation (3.18) is,

$$k = \frac{2.303}{t} \log_{10} \frac{[A]_0}{[A]_t}$$

On rearrangement, equation (3.18) can be written as,

$$k = \frac{kt}{2.303} = \log_{10} [A]_0 - \log_{10} [A]_t \qquad \ldots (3.20)$$

$$\log_{10} [A]_t = -\frac{k}{2.303} t + \log_{10} [A]$$

$$\downarrow \qquad \downarrow \qquad \downarrow \qquad\qquad\qquad \ldots (3.21)$$

$$y = mx + c$$

Equation (3.21) has the form of linear equation y = mx + c. Hence, the graph of $\log_{10} [A]_t$ versus t is straight line as shown in Fig. 3.8. The slope of the straight line is equal to $\frac{-k}{2.303}$ from which k can be calculated,

$$k = -2.303 \times \text{Slope}$$

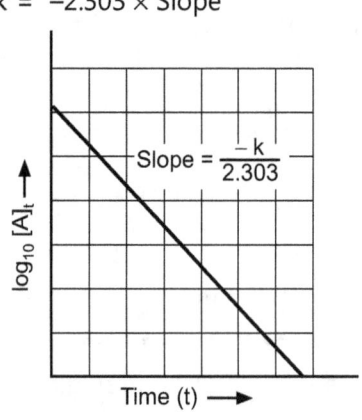

Fig. 3.8: Variation of $\log_{10} [A]_t$ with time

3. The equation (3.19) on rearrangement gives

$$k = \frac{2.303}{t} \log_{10} \left(\frac{a}{a - x} \right)$$

Rearranging, $\log_{10} \left(\frac{a}{a - x} \right) = \frac{kt}{2.303} t + 0$

$$\downarrow \qquad\qquad \downarrow \qquad \downarrow$$

$$y \quad = \quad mx \quad + c$$ ... (3.22)

The equation (3.22) has the straight line form $y = mx + c$. The graph of $\log_{10} \left(\frac{a}{a - x} \right)$ versus t is a straight line passing through origin as shown in Fig. 3.9. The slope of the graph is $\frac{k}{2.303}$.

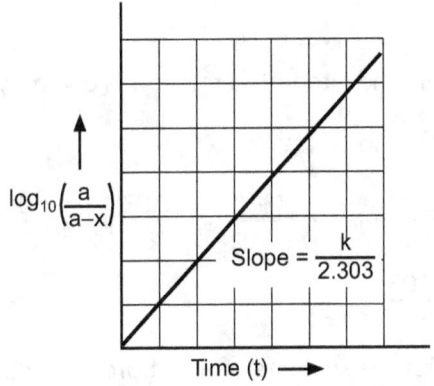

Fig. 3.9: Variation of $\log_{10} \left(\frac{a}{a - x} \right)$ with time

3.6.3.4 Half Life of First Order Reactions ($t_{1/2}$)

The half life of a reaction is defined as, 'the time needed for the reactant concentration to fall to one half of its initial value'.

Where,

As per the definition; $\frac{[A]_0}{2}$ at $t = t_{1/2}$

Hence we can write; $[A]_t = \frac{[A]_0}{2}$ at $t = t_{1/2}$.

For the first order reaction the integrated rate law is given by the equation (3.18).

$$k = \frac{2.303}{t} \log_{10} \frac{[A]_0}{[A]_t}$$

$$k = \frac{2.303}{t_{1/2}} \log_{10} \frac{[A]_0}{[A]_0/2}$$

$$t_{1/2} = \frac{2.303}{k} \log_{10} 2 = \frac{2.303}{k} \times 0.301$$

$\therefore$ $$t_{1/2} = \frac{0.693}{k}$$ ... (3.23)

The equation (3.23) implies that the half life of a first order reaction is constant and is independent of the reactant concentration.

3.6.3.5 Shelf Life of First Order Reaction

As per the discussion in section 3.6.1.5.

The shelf life equation can be derived as follows:

As per the definition; $\frac{90 \, [A]_0}{100}$ or $0.9 \, [A]_0$ at $t = t_{90}$

Hence we can write; $[A]_t = 0.9 \, [A]_0$ at $t = t_{90}$

For the first order reaction, the integrated rate law is given by the equation (3.18).

$$k = \frac{2.303}{t} \log_{10} \frac{[A]_0}{[A]_t}$$

$$k = \frac{2.303}{t_{90}} \log_{10} \frac{[A]_0}{0.9 \, [A]_0} = \frac{2.303}{k} \log_{10} \left(\frac{1}{0.9}\right) = \frac{2.303}{k} \log_{10} (1.11)$$

$$t_{90} = \frac{0.105}{k}$$ ... (3.24)

The equation (3.24) implies the shelf life of a first order reaction.

3.6.3.6 Examples of First Order Reactions

The following reactions are found to have first order:

1. Decomposition of H_2O_2:

   $2H_2O_2 \longrightarrow 2H_2O + O_2$; Rate $= k \, [H_2O_2]$

2. Decomposition of N_2O_5:

   $2N_2O_5 \longrightarrow 4NO_2 + O_2$; Rate $= k \, [N_2O_5]$

3.6.3.7 Solved Problem of First Order Reaction

Problem 3.3: A solution of drug contained 50,000 unit/ml when prepared. It was analysed after a period of 60 and 120 days and was found to contain 35,000 and 25,000 unit/ml respectively. Calculate rate constant of reaction.

Solution: Given data: $A_0 = 50000$; $A_t = 35000$ after 60 days; $A_t = 25000$ after 120 days; $k = ?$

Consider equation of Rate law of first order reactions,

$$k = \frac{2.303}{t} \log_{10} \frac{[A]_0}{[A]_t}$$

Calculation of k for 60 days

$$k_{60} = \frac{2.303}{60} \log_{10} \left(\frac{50000}{35000}\right) = \frac{2.303 \times 0.154}{60} = 0.0059 \ days^{-1}$$

Calculation of k for 120 days

$$k_{120} = \frac{2.303}{120} \log_{10} \left(\frac{50000}{25000}\right) = \frac{2.303 \times 0.301}{120} = 0.0057 \ days^{-1}$$

Problem 3.4: When drug A is exposed under sunlight it gets degraded to convert into product B by first order. It was analysed after a period of 10 hr and concentration of product B was found to contain 120 gm/ml. Initial concentration of A in formulation was 500 gm/ml. Calculate rate constant of reaction, half life and self life of reaction.

Solution: Given data: a = 500; x = 120; t = 10; k =?; $t_{1/2}$ =?; t_{90} =?;

Calculation of k:

Consider equation of Rate law of first order reactions,

$$k = \frac{2.303}{t} \log_{10} \left(\frac{a}{a - x}\right)$$

$$k = \frac{2.303}{10} \log_{10} \left(\frac{500}{500 - 120}\right) = \frac{2.303 \times 0.119}{10} = 0.02/hr^{-1}$$

Calculation of $t_{1/2}$: Consider equation for half-cycle of first order reactions,

$$t_{1/2} = \frac{0.693}{k} = \frac{0.693}{0.027} = 25.66 \ hr$$

Calculation of t_{90}: Consider equation for shelf life of first order reactions,

$$t_{90} = \frac{0.105}{k} = \frac{0.105}{0.027} = 3.8 \ hr.$$

Problem 3.5: The half life of a drug that decomposed by first order is 50 days. Calculate k and t_{90}.

Solution: Given data: $t_{1/2}$ =50; k =?; t_{90} =?

Calculation of $t_{1/2}$: Consider equation for half life of first order reactions,

$$t_{1/2} = \frac{0.693}{k} \quad or \quad 50 = \frac{0.693}{k} \quad k = \frac{0.693}{50} = 0.0138 \ days^{-1}$$

Calculation of t_{90}: Consider equation for shelf life of first order reactions,

$$t_{90} = \frac{0.105}{k} = \frac{0.105}{0.0138}$$

$$= 7.60 \ days$$

3.6.4 Second Order Reaction

Second order reaction is defined as 'a reaction in which the rate depends on the concentration terms of two reactants each raised to the power one'.

Consider the following reaction:

$\quad$ A + B $\longrightarrow$ Products

3.6.4.1 Rate Law for Second Order Reactions

The rate equation can be written as:

$$-\frac{dA}{dt} = -\frac{dB}{dt} = k_2 \, [A]^1 \, [B]^1 \qquad \ldots (3.25)$$

Where [A] and [B] are the concentrations of A and B, respectively, and k_2 is the specific rate constant for second order.

In other words, the rate of reaction is first order with respect to A, and again first order with respect to B. So the overall order of this reaction is second order.

As per the definition, the rate equation for second order is,

$$-\frac{dA}{dt} = -\frac{dB}{dt} = k_2 \, [A] \, [B] \qquad \ldots (3.26)$$

Let us consider,

'a' and 'b' be the initial concentrations of A and B, respectively,

'x' be the concentration of each species reacting in t.

Substituting these terms in equation (3.26)

$$\frac{dx}{dt} = k_2 \, (a - x) \, (b - x) \qquad \ldots (3.27)$$

Now, consider a case where a = b (both A and B have the same concentration).

Then the above equation changes to equation (3.28)

$$\frac{dx}{dt} = k_2 \, (a - x)^2 \qquad \ldots (3.28)$$

Integrate equation (3.28) employing the conditions x = 0 at t = 0 and x = x at t = t.

$$\int_0^x \frac{dx}{(a - x)^2} = k_2 \int_0^t dt \qquad \ldots (3.29)$$

On performing the integration, we get;

$$\frac{1}{(a - x)} - \frac{1}{(a - 0)} = k_2 \, (t - 0) \qquad \ldots (3.30)$$

$$\frac{a - a + x}{a(a - x)} = k_2 t \qquad \ldots (3.31)$$

$$k_2 = \frac{1}{at} \cdot \frac{x}{(a - x)} \qquad \ldots (3.32)$$

Equation (3.32) is the integral equation for second order reaction, where a = b.

3.6.4.2 Unit of k_2

The units for k_2 are $conc^{-1}$ $time^{-1}$. When the concentration of reactants is expressed as moles/litre, then k_2 has units litre/mol. time (min).

3.6.4.3 Graphical Representation

The integrated rate law given by equation (3.30) is,

$$\frac{1}{(a-x)} - \frac{1}{(a-0)} = k_2(t-0)$$

On rearrangement, equation (3.30) can be written as,

$$\underset{\downarrow}{\frac{1}{(a-x)}} = \underset{\downarrow}{k_2 t} + \underset{\downarrow}{\frac{1}{a}}$$
$$y = mx + c$$

... (3.33)

If $1/(a-x)$ is plotted against time, t (on x axis), a straight line with a positive slope is obtained (Fig. 3.10). Intercept will be $1/a$. This graph permits the estimation of k_2. The slope is equal to k_2.

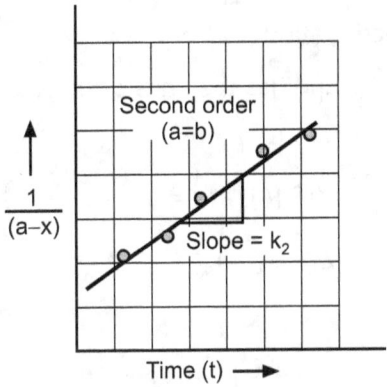

Fig. 3.10: plot 1/(a–x) against time (t)

3.6.4.4 Half Life of Second Order Reactions ($t_{1/2}$)

The half life of a reaction is defined as 'the time needed for the reactant concentration to fall to one half of its initial value'.

As per the definition; $\frac{[A]_0}{2}$ at t $= t_{1/2}$

Hence we can write; $[A]_t = \frac{[A]_0}{2}$ at t $= t_{1/2}$.

Where,

$[A]_0$: Initial concentration 'a'

$[A]_t$: Concentration when time t has elapsed $(a-x)$

For the second order reaction, the integrated rate law is given by the equation (3.30).

$$k_2 t = \frac{1}{(a-x)} - \frac{1}{a}$$

$$\therefore \qquad k_2 t = \frac{1}{[A]_t} - \frac{1}{[A]_0} \qquad \qquad \dots (3.34)$$

At $t_{1/2}$;

$$k_2 t_{1/2} = \frac{1}{1/2\,[A]_0} - \frac{1}{[A]_0} = \frac{2}{[A]_0} - \frac{1}{[A]_0} \qquad \dots (3.35)$$

$$t_{1/2} = \frac{1}{k_2\,[A]_0} \qquad \qquad \dots (3.36)$$

It is clear from equation that:

1. Half life depends on initial concentration.

2. Half life is inversely proportional to rate constant.

3.6.4.5 Shelf Life of Second Order Reaction

Shelf Life is defined as 'the time required for the concentration of the reactant to reduce to 90% of its initial concentration'.

Shelf life is represented as t_{90} and has the units of time/cone. The shelf life equation can be derived as follows:

As per the definition; $90\,\dfrac{[A]_0}{100}$ or $0.9\,[A]_0$ at $t = t_{90}$

Hence we can write; $[A]_t = 0.9\,[A]_0$ at $t = t_{90}$

Where,

$$[A]_0 \ : \ \text{Initial concentration 'a'}$$

$$[A]_t \ : \ \text{Concentration when time t has elapsed '}(a-x)\text{'}$$

For the second order reaction, the integrated rate law is given by the equation (3.30)

$$k_2 t = \frac{1}{(a-x)} - \frac{1}{a}$$

$$\therefore \qquad k_2 t = \frac{1}{[A]_t} - \frac{1}{[A]_0}$$

At t_{90};

$$k_2 t_{90} = \frac{1}{0.9\,[A]_0} - \frac{1}{[A]_0} = \frac{[A]_0 - 0.9\,[A]_0}{0.9\,[A]_0 \cdot [A]_0} = \frac{0.1\,[A]_0}{0.9\,[A]_0^{\,2}} \qquad \dots (3.37)$$

$$t_{90} = \frac{0.11}{[A]_0\,k_2} \qquad \qquad \dots (3.38)$$

3.6.4.6 Examples

(a) Alkaline hydrolysis of esters such as methylacetate or ethyl acetate.

(b) Hydrolysis of chlorbutanol in presence of sodium hydroxide.

3.6.4.7 Solved Problems on Second Order Reaction

Problem 3.6: In the saponification of methyl acetate at 25°C, the concentration of sodium hydroxide remaining after 75 minutes was 0.00552 M. The initial concentration of ester and the base was 0.01 molar. Calculate the second order rate constant and half life of the reaction.

Solution: Given data: a = 0.01M; a − x = 0.00552 M; t = 75 min; k=?; $t_{1/2}$ =?

x = a − (a − x) = 0.01 − 0.00552 = 0.00448

Calculation of k:

$$k = \frac{1}{at} \cdot \frac{x}{(a-x)} = \frac{1}{0.01 \times 75} \cdot \frac{0.00448}{0.00552} = 1.082 \text{ lit./mol.min}$$

Calculation of $t_{1/2}$:

$$t_{1/2} = \frac{1}{k[A]_0} = \frac{1}{1.082 \times 0.01} = 92.42 \text{ min.}$$

Problem 3.7: Hydrolysis of ethyl acetate by NaOH using equal concentration of the reactants was studied by titrating 25 ml of the reaction mixture at different time intervals against standard acid. From the data given below, determine reaction rate constant and half life of second order reaction.

Time (min)	0	25
ml acid used	16.00	4.32

Solution: Given data: a = 16; a − x = 4.32, x = a − (a − x) = 11.68

Calculation of k:

$$k_2 = \frac{1}{at} \cdot \frac{x}{(a-x)}$$

$$= \frac{1}{16 \times 25} \cdot \frac{11.68}{4.32}$$

$$= 0.00675$$

Calculation of $t_{1/2}$:

$$t_{1/2} = \frac{1}{k_2 [A]_0} = \frac{1}{0.00675 \times 16}$$

$$= 2370 \text{ mins.}$$

Problem 3.8: Drug 'A' decomposed in air and product 'C' is formed by second order reaction. Reaction rate constant was 0.25 after 30 min and initial concentration of A was 0.23 M. Calculate half life of reaction.

Solution: Given data: $k_2 = 0.25$, $A_0 = 0.23$; $t_{1/2} = ?$

Formula:
$$t_{1/2} = \frac{1}{k_2 [A]_0}$$

$$= \frac{1}{0.25 \times 0.23}$$

$$= 17.39 \text{ min.}$$

Table 3.4: Summarised data of integrated rate equation

	Zero order	First order	Second order
Rate Law	$-\dfrac{d[A]}{dt} = k$	$-\dfrac{d[A]}{dt} = k[A]$	$-\dfrac{d[A]}{dt} = k[A]^2$
Integrated Rate Law	$k = \dfrac{[A]_0 - [A]_t}{t}$	$k = \dfrac{2.303}{t} \log_{10} \dfrac{[A]_0}{[A]_t}$	$k_2 t = \dfrac{1}{[A]_t} - \dfrac{1}{[A]_0}$
Units of k	$\text{mol lit}^{-1} \text{time}^{-1}$	s^{-1}	$\text{conc}^{-1} \text{time}^{-1}$
Half life	$t_{1/2} = \dfrac{[A]_0}{2k}$	$t_{1/2} = \dfrac{0.693}{k}$	$t_{1/2} = \dfrac{1}{k_2 [A]_0}$
Shelf life	$t_{90} = \dfrac{0.1 [A]_0}{k}$	$t_{90} = \dfrac{0.105}{k}$	$t_{90} = \dfrac{0.11}{[A]_0 k_2}$

3.7 DETERMINATION OF ORDER OF REACTION

There are at least four different methods to determine the order of a reaction.

3.7.1 Using Integrated Rate Equations

The reaction under study is performed by taking different initial concentrations of the reactant (a) and noting the concentration (a − x) after regular time intervals (t). The experimental values of a, (a − x) and t are then substituted into the integrated rate equations for the zero, first and second order reactions (Described in section 3.6.1.1, 3.6.3.1 and 3.6.4.1). **The rate equation which yields a constant value of k corresponds to the correct order of the reaction.** This method of ascertaining the order of a reaction is essentially a method of hit–and–trial but was the first to be employed. It is still used extensively to find the order of simple reactions.

Example: Decomposition of H_2O_2 in aqueous solution. The decomposition of H_2O_2 in the presence of platinum as catalyst.

$$H_2O_2 \xrightarrow{\text{Pt}} H_2O + O$$

A solution of H_2O_2 when titrated against $KMnO_4$ solution at different time intervals gave the following results:

Time (minutes)	0	10	20
Volume of $KMnO_4$ used for 10 ml H_2SO_4	23.8 ml	14.7 ml	9.1 ml

Show that the decomposition of H_2O_2 is a first order reaction.

Solution: The integrated rate equation for first order reaction is

$$k = \frac{2.303}{t} \log \left(\frac{a}{a-x} \right)$$

Since volume of $KMnO_4$ used in the titration is measure of concentration of H_2O_2 in solution,

$\therefore$

$$a = 23.8 \text{ ml}$$
$$(a - x) = 14.7 \qquad \text{when } t = 10 \text{ min.}$$
$$(a - x) = 9.1 \qquad \text{when } t = 20 \text{ min.}$$

Substituting these values in the rate equation above, we have

$$k = \frac{2.303}{10} \log \left(\frac{23.8}{14.7} \right)$$
$$= 0.2303 \, (\log 23.8 - \log 14.7)$$
$$= 0.2303 \, (1.3766 - 1.1673) = 0.04820$$

and

$$k = \frac{2.303}{20} \log \left(\frac{23.8}{9.1} \right)$$
$$= 0.10165 \, (\log 23.8 - \log 9.1)$$
$$= 0.10165 \, (1.3766 - 0.9595) = 0.04810$$

Since the value of k is almost constant, the decomposition of H_2O_2 is a **first order reaction.**

3.7.2 Graphical Method

This part is already discussed in section 3.6.1.3, 3.6.3.3 and 3.6.4.3.

3.7.3 Using Half–Life Period

Two separate experiments are performed by taking different initial concentrations of a reactant. The progress of the reaction in each case is recorded by analysis. When the initial concentration is reduced to one-half, the time is noted. Let the initial concentrations in the two experiments be $[A_1]$ and $[A_2]$, while times for completion of half change are t_1 and t_2 respectively.

Calculation of Order of Reaction:

We know that, half–life period for a first order reaction is independent of the initial concentration, [A]. We also know:

$$\text{half-life} \propto \frac{1}{[A]} \text{ for 2}^{nd} \text{ order reaction}$$

$$\text{half-life} \propto \frac{1}{[A]^2} \text{ for 3}^{rd} \text{ order reaction}$$

$$\text{half-life} \propto \frac{1}{[A]^{n-1}} \text{ for n}^{th} \text{ order reaction}$$

Substituting values of initial concentrations and half–life periods from the two experiments, we have

$$t_1 \propto \frac{1}{[A_1]^{n-1}}$$

$$t_2 \propto \frac{1}{[A_2]^{n-1}} \quad \text{... (3.39)}$$

and

$$\frac{t_2}{t_1} = \left[\frac{A_1}{A_2}\right]^{n-1} \quad \text{... (3.40)}$$

$$(n-1) \log\left[\frac{A_2}{A_1}\right] = \log\left[\frac{t_1}{t_2}\right] \quad \text{... (3.41)}$$

Solving for n, the order of reaction

$$n = 1 + \frac{\log\left[\dfrac{t_1}{t_2}\right]}{\log\left[\dfrac{A_2}{A_1}\right]} \quad \text{... (3.42)}$$

3.7.4 The Differential Method

This method was suggested by Van't Hoff and, therefore, it is also called **Van't Hoff's differential method.** According to it, the rate of a reaction of the nth order is proportional to the nth power of concentration.

$$-\frac{dC}{dt} = k\, C^n \quad \text{... (3.43)}$$

Where C = concentration at any instant. In two experiments performed with different initial concentrations, we can write

$$-\frac{dC_1}{dt} = k\, C_1^n \quad \text{... (3.44)}$$

$$-\frac{dC_2}{dt} = k\, C_2^n \quad \text{... (3.45)}$$

Taking logs of the equation (3.44) and (3.45)

$$\log\left(-\frac{dC_1}{dt}\right) = \log k + n \log C_1 \qquad \qquad \text{... (3.46)}$$

$$\log\left(-\frac{dC_2}{dt}\right) = \log k + n \log C_2 \qquad \qquad \text{... (3.47)}$$

On substracting equation (3.47) from (3.46), we get

$$n = \frac{\log\left(-\frac{dC_1}{dt}\right) - \left(-\frac{dC_2}{dt}\right)}{\log C_1 - \log C_2} \qquad \qquad \text{... (3.48)}$$

To find n, [– dc/dt] in the two experiments is determined by plotting concentrations against time (t). The slope, [– dc/dt] at a given time interval is measured by drawing tangents. Using the values of slopes [– dc_1/dt] and [– dc_2/dt] in the equation (3.48), n can be calculated.

3.7.5 Ostwald's Isolation Method

This method is employed in determining the order of complicated reactions by 'isolating' one of the reactants so far as its influence on the rate of reaction is **concerned.** Suppose the reaction under consideration is:

$$A + B + C \longrightarrow \text{Products}$$

The order of the reaction with respect to A, B and C is determined. For the determination of the order of reaction with respect to A, B and C, they are taken in a large excess so that their concentrations are not affected during the reaction. The order of the reaction is then determined by using any of the methods described earlier. Likewise, the order of the reaction with respect to B and C is determined. If n_A, n_B and n_C are the orders of the reaction with respect to A, B and C respectively, the order of the reaction n is given by the expression.

$$n = n_A + n_B + n_C \qquad \qquad \text{... (3.49)}$$

3.8 SIMULTANEOUS REACTIONS/COMPLEX REACTIONS

Sometimes there are some side reactions accompanying the main chemical reaction. Such reactions are known as **complex reactions** as these do not take place in a single step. In other words, such complex reactions proceed in a series of steps instead of a single step and the rate of overall reaction is in accordance with the stoichiometric equation for that reaction. Generally, following types of complications occur.

1. **Consecutive reactions**

2. **Parallel reactions**

3. **Reversible or opposing reactions**

These are discussed as follows:

3.8.1 Consecutive Reactions

The reactions in which the final product is formed through one or more intermediate steps are called **consecutive reactions.** These are also known as **sequential** reactions. In such reactions, the product formed in one of the elementary reactions acts as the reactant for some other elementary reaction. Various step reactions can be written for the overall reaction as shown below:

$$A \xrightarrow{k_1} B \xrightarrow{k_2} C$$

	A	B	C
Initial concentration:	$[A]_0$	0	0
Conc. after time t:	$[A]$	$[B]$	$[C]$

In the above reaction, the product C is formed from the reactant A through intermediate B. In this reaction, each stage has its own different rate constants k_1 for the first step and k_2 for the second step. The net or overall rate of reaction depends upon the magnitude of these two rate constants. The initial concentration and concentration after time t are shown below each species in above reaction under consideration.

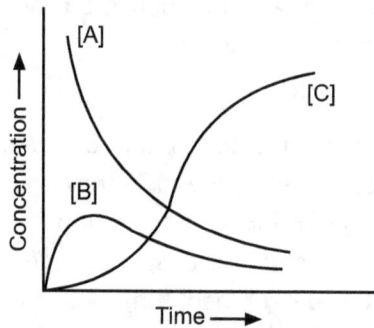

Fig. 3.11: Variation of concentration of reactants and products in a consecutive reaction

From the Fig. 3.11 it is clear that the concentration of A decreases exponentially, the concentration of B first increases and then decreases and that of C increases (from zero) with time and finally attains the value equal to $[A]_0$ (initial concentration A) when all A has changed into the final product C.

Examples of First Order Consecutive Reactions:

(a) Decomposition of dimethyl ether in gaseous phase

$$CH_3COCH_3 \xrightarrow{k_1} CH_4 + HCHO \xrightarrow{k_2} H_2 + CO$$

(b) Decomposition of ethylene oxide

$$CH_2\text{——}CH_2 \text{ (over O)} \xrightarrow{k_1} (CH_3CHO) \xrightarrow{k_2} CH_4 + CO$$

3.8.2 Parallel or Side Reactions

In these reactions, the reacting substance follows two or more paths to give two or more products. The preferential rate of such may be changed by varying the conditions like pressure, temperature or catalyst. The reaction in which the maximum yield of the products is obtained is called the **main or major reaction** while the other reaction (or reactions) is called **side or parallel reactions**.

For example,

$$A \begin{cases} \xrightarrow{k_1} B \\ \xrightarrow{k_2} C \end{cases}$$

In the above reaction, the reactant A gives two products B and C separately in two different reactions with rate constants k_1 and k_2 respectively.

If $k_1 > k_2$ the reaction A → B will be the major reaction and A → C will be the side or parallel reaction.

Examples of Parallel or Side Reactions

(a) Reaction of ethyl bromide with potassium hydroxide

$$CH_3CH_2Br + KOH \begin{cases} \rightarrow CH_2{=}CH_2 + KBr + H_2O \quad (\text{Ethylene}) \\ \rightarrow CH_3CH_2OH + KBr \quad (\text{Ethyl alcohol}) \end{cases}$$

Ethyl bromide

(b) Dehydration of 2–methyl—2—butanol

$$CH_3{-}\underset{\underset{OH}{|}}{\overset{\overset{CH_3}{|}}{C}}{-}CH_2{-}CH_3 \begin{cases} \rightarrow CH_3{-}\underset{}{\overset{\overset{CH_3}{|}}{C}}{=}CH{-}CH_3 \quad (\text{2-methyl-2-butene}) \\ \rightarrow CH_2{=}\underset{}{\overset{\overset{CH_3}{|}}{C}}{-}CH_2{-}CH_3 \quad (\text{2-methyl-1-butene}) \end{cases}$$

2-methyl-2-butanol

3.8.3 Reversible or Opposing Reactions

In reversible or opposing reactions, the products formed also react to give back the reactants. Initially, the rate of forward reaction is very large which decreases with passage of time and the rate of backward or reverse reaction is zero which increases with passage of time. A stage is reached when two rates become equal. This situation is called the **chemical**

equilibrium. It is dynamic in nature i.e., all the species are reaching at the rate at which they are being formed. A reaction of this type may be represented as:

$$A \underset{k_b}{\overset{k_f}{\rightleftharpoons}} B$$

Initial concentration	$[A]_0$	0
Conc. after time t	$[A]$	$[B]$

where k_f and k_b are the rate constants of the forward and backward reactions respectively.

The overall rate of reaction is given by:

Rate of Reaction = Rate of Forward Reaction – Rate of Backward Reaction

Examples of Opposing Reactions:

(a) Dissociation of hydrogen iodides

$$2HI \underset{k_b}{\overset{k_f}{\rightleftharpoons}} H_2 + I_2$$

(b) Isomerisation of cyclopropane into propene

$$\underset{\text{cyclopropane}}{\Delta} \underset{k_b}{\overset{k_f}{\rightleftharpoons}} \underset{\text{Propene}}{CH_3 - CH = CH_2}$$

(c) Isomerisation of ammonium cyanate into urea in aqueous solution.

$$\underset{\text{Ammonium cyanate}}{NH_4CNO} \underset{k_b}{\overset{k_f}{\rightleftharpoons}} \underset{\text{Urea}}{NH_2 - \overset{\overset{O}{\|}}{C} - NH_2}$$

3.9 THEORY OF REACTION RATES

There are two types of reaction rates theory:

1. Collision Theory
2. Transition State Theory

3.9.1 Collision Theory of Reaction Rates

According to this theory, a chemical reaction takes place only by collisions between the reacting molecules. But not all collisions are effective. Only a small fraction of the collisions produce a reaction.

The main conditions for collision between the reactive molecules to be productive are:

1. Reacting substance (atom, ions or molecules) must collide.
2. The reacting molecules must collide with proper orientation.
3. The colliding molecules must possess sufficient kinetic energy to cause a reaction.

Now, let us have a closer look at these two postulates of the collision theory.

3.9.1.1 The Reacting Molecules must Collide with Correct Orientation

The reactant molecules must collide with favourable orientation (relative position). The correct orientation is that which ensure direct contact between the atoms involved in the breaking and forming of bonds.

Example: Consider a simple reaction involving a collision between two molecules – ethene, $CH_2 = CH_2$, and hydrogen chloride (HCl), for example: these react to give chloroethane.

$$CH_2 = CH_2 + HCl \longrightarrow CH_3CH_2Cl$$

As a result of the collision between the two molecules;

(a) The double bond between the two carbons is converted into a single bond.

(b) Also bond between hydrogen and chlorine was broken.

(c) A hydrogen atom gets attached to one of the carbons and a chlorine atom to the other.

Effective collision: The reaction can only happen if the hydrogen end of the H–Cl bond approaches the carbon–carbon double bond. Any other collision between the two molecules does not work. The two, simply bounce off each other. (See Fig. 3.12 [a]).

Ineffective collision: The double bond has a high concentration of negative charge around it due to the electrons in the bonds. The approaching chlorine atom is also slightly negative because it is more electronegative than hydrogen. The repulsion simply causes the molecules to bounce off each other. (See Fig. 3.12 [b])

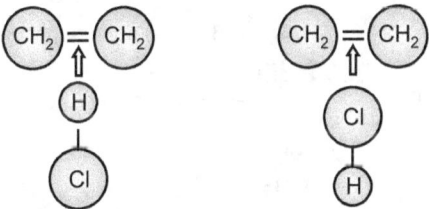

(a) Effective collision (b) Ineffective collision

Fig. 3.12: Effective and ineffective collision of reacting molecule

3.9.1.2 The Energy of the Collision

Activation Energy (E_a):

Even if the species are orientated properly, we still cannot get a reaction unless the particles collide with a certain minimum energy called the **activation energy of the reaction.**

Activation energy is the 'minimum energy required before a reaction can occur'.

If the particles collide with;

If Energy < E_a:

(a) The energy is less than the activation energy, nothing important happens. They bounce apart. The energy of activation is barrier into the reaction.

(b) Where collisions are relatively gentle, there is not enough energy available to start the bond–breaking process, and so the particles do not react.

If energy = & > E_a:

(a) Only those collisions which have energies equal to or greater than the activation energy result in a reaction.

(b) Any chemical reaction results in the breaking of some bonds (needing energy) and the making of new ones (releasing energy). Obviously some bonds have to be broken before new ones can be made. Activation energy is involved in breaking some of the original bonds.

Example: Lets us consider reaction;

$$CH_2 = CH_2 + H - Cl \longrightarrow CH_3CH_2Cl$$

A chemical reaction occurs by breaking bonds between $CH_2=CH_2$ to form CH_2-CH_2, therefore energy is required for conversion of double bond to single bond. The energy for the breaking of bonds comes from the kinetic energy possessed by the reacting molecules before the collision. Fig. 3.13 shows the energy of molecules $CH_2=CH_2$ and H–Cl as the reaction progresses.

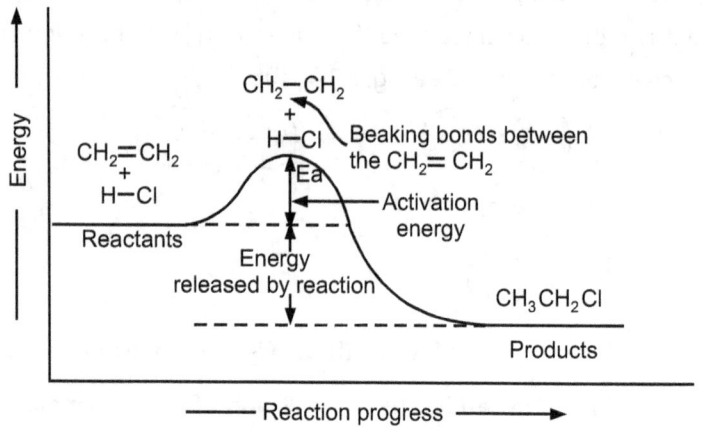

Fig. 3.13: The energy of molecules $CH_2=CH_2$ and H–Cl as the reaction progresses

Fig. 3.13 also shows the activation energy, E_a, which is the minimum energy necessary to cause a reaction between the colliding molecules. Only the molecules that collide with a kinetic energy greater than E_a are able to get over the barrier and react. The molecules colliding with kinetic energies less than E_a fail to surmount the barrier. The collisions between them are unproductive and the molecules simply bounce off one another.

3.9.1.3 Collision Theory and Reaction Rate Expression

Taking into account the two postulates of the collision theory, the reaction rate for the elementary process.

$$A + B \longrightarrow C + D$$

is given by the expression

$$\textbf{Rate} = \textbf{k} = \textbf{f P z} \qquad \qquad ... (3.50)$$

Where

Energy factor, f = Fraction of molecules which possess sufficient energy (E_a) to react.

This factor exists because in most reactions, before new bonds can form, old bonds must be at least partially broken. Breaking bonds requires energy, and one way to inject sufficient energy into a molecule to break a bond is to collide it with another molecule at high enough speed. The minimum speed required depends on the strength of the bond.

This factor, called the **energy factor,** changes with the temperature: higher temperature results in faster motion and, on the average, more violent collisions, so the fraction of collisions with the minimum energy needed to react also increases.

Therefore, A correlation between f and temperature is

$$f = e^{-E_a/RT} \qquad \qquad ... (3.51)$$

Where,

$- E_a$: Activation energy,

R : Gas constant,

T : Absolute temperature.

Probability Factor, p = Probable fraction of collisions with effective orientations.

Often a reaction cannot take place unless the colliding molecules have the correct orientation, that is, they are turned in the right direction as they collide. The fraction of collisions that have the proper orientation is called the **probability factor.**

Frequency Factor, z = Collision frequency.

Since, in order to react, molecules must collide, this factor that determines reaction rate is the number of collisions that occur per second. This is called the **frequency factor.**

Also,

$$p z = A \qquad \qquad ... (3.52)$$

Where, A is Arrhenius factor.

Therefore, substituting equation (3.51) and (3.52) in (3.50) we get,

$$k = A e^{-E_a/RT} \qquad \qquad ... (3.53)$$

This is Arrhenius equation.

3.9.1.4 Limitations of the Collision Theory

The collision theory of reaction rates is logical and correct. However, it has been oversimplified and suffers from the following weaknesses.

1. The theory applies to simple **gaseous reactions only**. It is also valid for solutions in which the reacting species exist as simple molecules.

2. The values of rate constant calculated from the collision theory expression (Arrhenius equation) are in agreement with the experimental values only for simple bimolecular reactions. **For reactions involving complex molecules**, the experimental rate constants are quite different from the calculated values.

3. There is no method for determining the steric effect (p) for a reaction whose rate constant has not been determined experimentally.

4. In the collision theory it is supposed that only the kinetic energy of the colliding molecules contributes to the energy required for surmounting the energy barrier. There is no reason why the rotational and vibrational energies of molecules should be ignored.

5. **The collision theory is silent on the cleavage and formation of bonds involved in the reaction.** The various drawbacks in the simple collision theory do not appear in the modern transition state theory.

3.9.2 Transition State Theory

The transition state or activated complex theory was developed by Henry Erying (1935). This theory is also called the **absolute rate theory** because with its help it is possible to get the absolute value of the rate constant. The transition state theory assumes that simply a collision between the reactant molecules does not really causes a reaction. During the collision, **the reactant molecules form a transition state or activated complex which decomposes to give the products.**

Thus,

$$\underbrace{A + B{-}C}_{\text{Reactants}} \longrightarrow \underbrace{ABC\,\#}_{\substack{\text{Active}\\\text{complex}}} \longrightarrow \underbrace{A{-}B + C}_{\text{Products}}$$

The double dagger superscript (+) is used to identify the activated complex. The transition state theory may be summarised as follows:

1. **In a collision,** the fast approaching reactant molecules (A and BC) slow down due to gradual repulsion between their electron clouds. In the process, **the kinetic energy of the two molecules is converted into potential energy.**

2. As the molecules come close, **the interpenetration of their electron clouds occurs. This allows the rearrangement of valence electrons.**

3. A partial bond is formed between the atoms A and B with corresponding weakening of B – C bond. This leads to formation of an **activated complex or transition state.** The activated complex is momentary and decomposes to give the products (A – B + C).

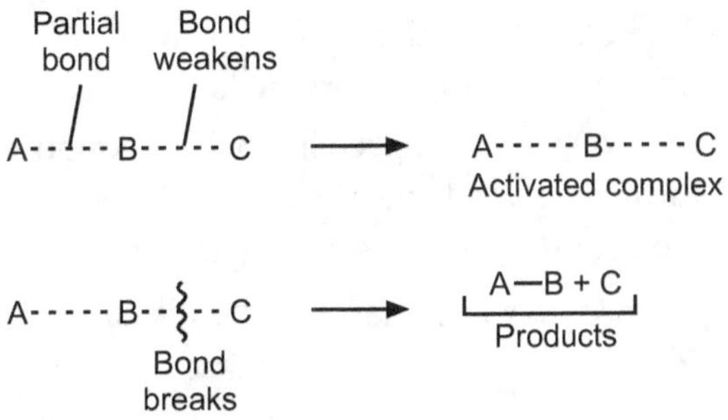

Fig. 3.14: Process of transition state theory

3.9.2.1 Example

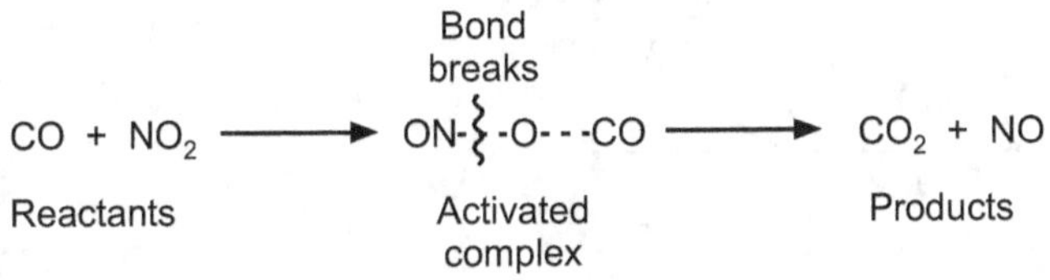

Now look at the reaction between carbon monoxide (CO) gas and nitrogen dioxide (NO_2) gas at a temperature above 500 K. The reaction was completed by following steps.

1. **Collision of reactants:** The reactant CO and NO_2 required to colloid in proper orientation.

2. **Formation of Activated Complex:** The carbon atom in a CO molecule must contact an oxygen atom in an NO_2 molecule at the instant of impact and temporary bond between the carbon atom and an oxygen atom form.

    The intermediate substance, in this case NO–O–CO, is called an **activated complex.**

3. **Formation of Product:** An activated complex is a temporary, unstable arrangement of atoms that may form products or may break apart to re–form the reactants. Because the activated complex is as likely to form reactants as it is to form products, it is sometimes referred to as the **transition state**.

    In this case, bond between NO–O was broken forming products carbon dioxide (CO_2) gas and nitrogen monoxide (NO) gas.

3.9.2.2 Types of Reaction According To Potential Energy of Reactant and Product

The reaction is classified according to potential energy as follows:

[I] Exothermic reaction

[II] Endothermic reaction

[I] Exothermic Reaction

Fig. 3.15 shows the energy diagram for the progress of the reaction between carbon monoxide and nitrogen dioxide.

In addition to the energies of the reactants and products, this diagram shows the activation energy of the reaction. Activation energy can be thought of as a barrier the reactants must overcome, in order to form the products.

In this case, the CO and NO_2 molecules collide with enough energy to overcome the barrier, and the products formed lie at a lower energy level. Therefore, energy releases in the process of reaction and yield product have less energy than reactant.

The potential energy of product less than reactant is called as exothermic reaction.

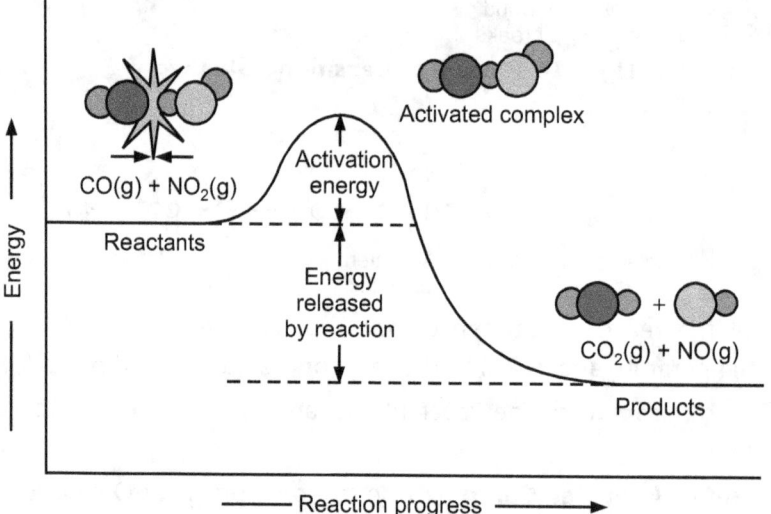

Fig. 3.15: In an exothermic reaction, molecules collide with enough energy to overcome the activation energy barrier, form an activated complex, then release energy and form products at a lower energy level.

[II] Endothermic Reaction

Fig. 3.16 shows the reverse endothermic reaction between CO_2 and NO to reform CO and NO_2.

$$CO_2 + NO \longrightarrow CO + NO_2$$

Reactants   Products

In this reverse reaction, the reactants, which are the molecules that were formed in the exothermic forward reaction, lie at a low energy level and must overcome significant activation energy to reform CO and NO_2. This requires an input of energy. If this reverse reaction is achieved, CO and NO_2 again lie at a high energy level.

Therefore, energy absorbed in the process of reaction and yield products have high energy than reactants.

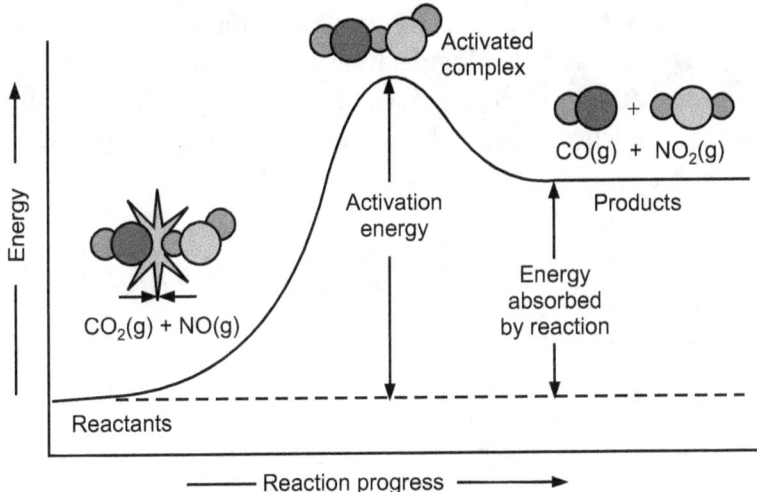

Fig. 3.16: In the reverse endothermic reaction, the reactant molecules lying at a low energy level must absorb energy to overcome the activation energy barrier and form high–energy products

3.10 TEMPERATURE DEPENDENCE OF REACTION RATES (ARRHENIUS EQUATION)

It has been found that the rates of most of the chemical reactions increase with temperature, e.g.

1. In everyday life we see that the fuels such as oil, coal etc. are inert at room temperature but burn rapidly at higher temperatures.
2. Many foods spoil rapidly at room temperature but last longer in freezer.

Average kinetic energy of molecules is proportional to temperature. As temperature increases, the kinetic energy of molecules increases.

The collision theory tells us that a bimolecular reaction occurs when two properly oriented molecules with sufficient kinetic energy (at least E_a) collide. At any temperature a definite fraction of molecules has the kinetic energy equal to or greater than E_a to form the product molecules upon collision.

As temperature increases the fraction of the colliding molecules that possesses minimum kinetic energy (E_a) also increases and hence the rate of the reaction increases.

Explanation:

1. Fig. 3.17 shows the fraction of molecules with given kinetic energy as a function of kinetic energy at two different temperatures T_1 and T_2, ($T_2 > T_1$).
2. The area between the curve and the horizontal axis is proportional to the total number of molecules. The total area is the same at T_1 and T_2.

3. However, the area that represents the fraction of molecules with kinetic energy that exceeds E_a is greater at higher temperature T_2 than at lower temperature T_1.

4. This indicates that the fraction of molecules with energy larger than E_a increases with temperature and hence the rate of the reaction correspondingly increases.

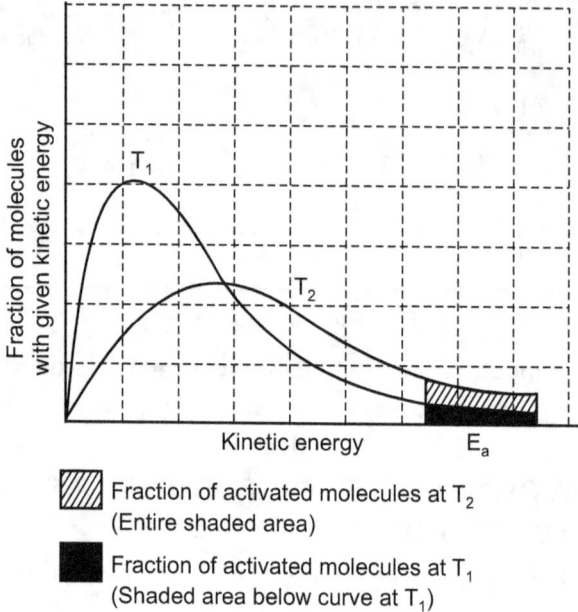

Fraction of activated molecules at T_2
(Entire shaded area)

Fraction of activated molecules at T_1
(Shaded area below curve at T_1)

Fig. 3.17: Comparison of fraction of molecules activated at T_1 and T_2

It has been found that generally an increase of temperature increases the rate of reaction. As a rule, an increase of temperature by 10°C doubles the reaction rate.

3.10.1 Arrhenius Equation

In 1889, Arrhenius suggested as simple relationship between the rate constant, k, for a reaction and the temperature of the system.

As per discussion in Article (3.9.1.3) Arrhenius equation (3.53) is

$$k = A\,e^{-E_a/RT}$$

Here e is an experimentally determined quantity, E_a is the activation energy, R is the gas constant, A is Arrhenius factor and T is Kelvin temperature.

Taking natural logs of each side of the Arrhenius equation, it can be put in a more useful form:

$$\ln k = -\frac{E_a}{RT} + \ln A \qquad\qquad \dots (3.54)$$

$\therefore$
$$\log k = \frac{-E_a}{2.303\ RT} + \log A \qquad\qquad \dots (3.55)$$

Arrhenius equation is valuable because it can be used to calculate the activation energy, E_a if the experimental value of the rate constant, k, is known.

Calculation of E_a Using Arrhenius Equation

1. Graphical method:

In slightly rearranged form Arrhenius equation (3.54) can be written as:

$$\ln k = -\frac{E_a}{R}\left(\frac{1}{T}\right) + \ln A$$

$$\underset{y}{\uparrow} \quad = \quad \underset{mx}{\uparrow} \quad + \quad \underset{b}{\uparrow}$$

We can see that, the equation (3.54) is that of a straight line, y = mx + b. The two variables in this equation are $\ln k$ and $1/T$.

Thus, if we plot the natural logarithm of k against $1/T$, we get a straight line (Fig. 3.18). From the slope of the line, we can calculate the value of E_a.

$$\text{Slope} = -\frac{E_a}{R}$$

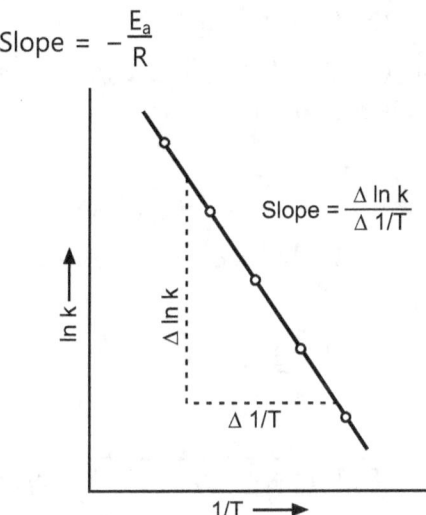

Fig. 3.18: The plot of $\ln k$ versus $1/T$ gives a straight line

2. Calculation of E_a from the values of k at two temperatures:

The rate constant, k, is measured at two temperatures. E_a, is then calculated using the formula that can be derived as follows from equation (3.54) above.

At temperature T_1 where the rate constant is k_1,

$$\ln k_1 = -\frac{E_a}{RT_1} + \ln A \qquad \qquad \text{... (3.56)}$$

At temperature T_2 where the rate constant is k_2,

$$\ln k_2 = -\frac{E_a}{RT_2} + \ln A \qquad \qquad \text{... (3.57)}$$

Subtracting the equation (3.56) from the equation (3.57), we have

$$\ln k_2 - \ln k_1 = \left(-\frac{E_a}{RT_2} + \ln A\right) - \left(-\frac{E_a}{RT_1} + \ln A\right)$$

$$\ln\left(\frac{k_2}{k_1}\right) = \frac{E_a}{R}\left(\frac{1}{T_1} - \frac{1}{T_2}\right)$$

or

$$\log\frac{k_2}{k_1} = \frac{E_a}{2.303\ R}\left[\frac{T_2 - T_1}{T_1 T_2}\right] \qquad \qquad \dots (3.58)$$

Thus, the values of k_1 and k_2, measured at T_1 and T_2 can be used to find E_a.

3.10.2 Solved Problem of Energy of Activation

Problem 3.9: The gas–phase reaction between methane (CH_4) and diatomic sulphur (S_2) is given by the equation

$$CH_4\ (g) + 2S_2\ (g) \longrightarrow CS_2\ (g) + 2H_2S\ (g)$$

At 550°C the rate constant for this reaction is 1.1 l/mol^{-1} sec and at 625°C the rate constant is 6.4 l/ mol^{-1} sec. Calculate E_a for this reaction.

Solution: Given Data:

$$K_1 = 1.1 / mol^{-1}\ sec\ \ at\ t_1 = 550 + 273 = 823\ k$$

$$K_2 = 6.4 / mol^{-1}\ sec\ \ at\ t_2 = 625 + 273 = 898\ k$$

Substitute values in equation:

$$\ln\left(\frac{k_2}{k_1}\right) = \frac{E_a}{R}\left(\frac{1}{T_1} - \frac{1}{T_2}\right)$$

$$\ln\left(\frac{6.4}{1.1}\right) = \frac{E_a}{8.3145\ J\ K^{-1}\ mol^{-1}}\left(\frac{1}{823\ K} - \frac{1}{898\ K}\right)$$

Solving for E_a, we get

$$E_a = \frac{(8.3145\ J\ K^{-1}\ mol^{-1})\ \ln\left(\frac{6.4}{1.1}\right)}{\left(\frac{1}{823\ K} - \frac{1}{898\ K}\right)}$$

$$= 1.4 \times 10^5\ J/mol$$

3.11 TYPES OF DEGRADATION PATHWAY

Basically degradation pathway is classified as;

1. Physical degradation
2. Chemical degradation
3. Microbial degradation

3.11.1 Physical Degradation

Components of pharmaceuticals (drug substances and excipients) exist in various microscopic physical states with differing degrees of order. Examples are amorphous and various crystalline, hydrated and solvated states. With time, the drug or the excipient may change from one state, usually unstable or metastable, to a more thermodynamically stable state. The rate of conversion will depend on the chemical potential corresponding to the free–energy difference between the states and the energy barrier (like that for chemical reactions) that must be overcome for the conversion to take place.

1. Crystallization of Amorphous Drugs:

Attempts are often made to formulate poorly water–soluble drugs in their amorphous state. This is because, the solubility of amorphous materials is generally higher than that of the same substances in their crystalline state. However, because of the lower free energy of the crystalline state, amorphous substances tend to change to their more thermo-dynamically stable crystalline state with time. Therefore, crystallization of amorphous drug substances may occur during long–term storage and may lead to drastic changes in the release characteristics of the drug and, hence, changes in its clinical and toxicological behaviour. Changes in crystal habit during storage have been reported for many drug substances.

Some examples are discussed below.

(a) Amorphous nifedipine, coprecipitated with polyvinylpyrrolidone, undergoes partial crystallization during storage under high–humidity conditions. This change from a largely amorphous state to a partially crystalline state resulted in altered dissolution and solubility behaviour.

(b) Oxyphenbutazone, which can exist in an amorphous state and three different crystalline states (anhydrous, monohydrate and hemihydrate), exhibits crystallization and polymorphic transitions during storage depending on humidity, as illustrated in Fig. 3.19.

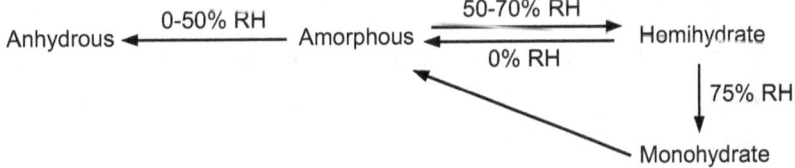

Fig. 3.19: Schematic representation of the polymorphic transitions of oxyphenbutazone

2. Polymorphism:

Polymorphs are different crystalline forms of the same drug. Because these forms have different free energy or chemical potentials, depending on temperature conditions, transitions between polymorphs occur. Polymorphic transitions during storage may alter critical properties of drugs because the solubility and dissolution rate of drug substances generally vary with changes in their crystalline form. From a storage perspective, temperature and humidity affect polymorphic transitions.

Transitions between anhydrous and hydrated forms have been reported for many drug substances such as raclopride, theophylline, nitrofurantoin, sulfaguanidine and phenobarbital. Again, significant differences in solubility can exist between the anhydrous and hydrated forms of the same drug.

3. Formation and Growth of Crystals:

Molecules in a crystal, and the crystals themselves, should not be considered static.

Crystals can grow or decrease in size provided that there is a medium across which the molecules can travel. This could be a liquid phase or a gaseous phase into which the molecules can sublime. For example, drug substances and excipients in solid dosage forms, such as tablets and granules, may recrystallize or sublime onto the surface of the dosage form during storage. So–called **whisker crystallization** was observed in tablets of ethenzamide and caffeine anhydride. This crystallization was enhanced in porous tablets and at higher temperatures.

The effect of humidity on whisker crystallization was complex. In that, crystallization of ethenzamide and caffeine anhydride tablets was enhanced at higher and lower humidity, respectively.

Aspirin tablets exhibited whisker crystallization of salicylic acid, a degradation product. This was found to change the tablet strength and to be dependent on tablet pore size.

4. Sublimation:

Pharmaceuticals containing components that sublime easily may undergo changes in drug content owing to the sublimation of the drug substances or excipients.

In the case of nitroglycerin, which is a liquid with a significant vapour pressure, sublingual tablets exhibit significant variations in drug content during storage owing to inter-tablet migration through the vapour phase.

This transfer was inhibited by adding water–soluble, non–volatile fixing agents such as polyethylene glycol.

5. Moisture Adsorption:

Moisture adsorption is generally observed with solid pharmaceuticals. Moisture adsorption during storage can also affect the physical stability of pharmaceuticals, leading to changes in such properties as appearance and dissolution rate. Adsorption of moisture is governed by the physical properties of the drug substance and excipients.

For example, the adsorption of moisture by aspirin crystals was enhanced by adding hydrophilic excipients.

6. Loss of Volatile Constituents:

Medicinal agents such as iodine, camphor, menthol, ethyl alcohol, anesthetic ether, chloroform have a tendency to evaporate from the product during storage. Similarly, nitroglycerine tablets may lose its potency owing to volatilisation of the medicament. The preventive measures include keeping the product in well–closed containers, and storing it in cool place.

7. Loss of Water:

Loss of vehicle (water) from the product leads to decrease in weight, rises in concentration of drug and increases potency. Efflorescent substances, such as borax, caffeine and quinidine sulphate, have a natural tendency to lose water. Products such as emulsions and semisolids exhibit cracking. Loss of water depends on temperature and humidity. Preventive measures include preserving the product in a well–closed container and storing it in a cool place.

3.11.2 Chemical Degradation and Preventive Measures

'Change in the physical nature of the drug' is called as **chemical degradation**.

1. Hydrolysis:

The principles that generally govern hydrolysis reactions may be listed as follows:

   (a) **Ester and amide groups drugs:** They are reacting with one molecule of water and undergo hydrolysis. Ester groups break faster than amide groups.
   (b) **Weak acids or bases:** Therefore, these may be available as ionic forms or neutral molecules. Hydrolysis reaction between ionic species proceeds faster than with neutral molecules (to a large extent it is solubility related phenomenon).
   (c) **Hydrolysis reactions are catalysed by $(H)^+$ and $(OH)^-$ ions:** Hydroxyl ions catalyse hydrolysis by about 100 to 1000 times more actively than hydrogen ions.

These principles help in rationalising the design of formulations from stability point of view.

Table 3.5: Example of drugs which decompose by hydrolysis

Esters	Amides
1. Aspirin	1. Chloramphenicol
2. Procaine	2. Ampicillin
3. Atropine	3. Cephalosporins

Example:

Drugs that contain ester groups, such as aspirin,

Aspirin undergo hydrolysis reaction and formation of salicylic acid and acetic acid but this decamped product, salicylic acid shows gastric irritation.

Drugs that contain amide groups, such as Chloramphenicol,

Amides undergo hydrolysis, though at a slower rate than esters. Chloramphenicol belongs to the category of amides. Its decomposition is influenced by acids, bases, phosphate ions, acidic and citrate buffers.

$$O_2N\text{—}\bigcirc\text{—}CHOH\text{—}\underset{\underset{NHCOCHCl_2}{|}}{CH}\text{—}CH_2OH \quad \xrightarrow[\substack{HPO_4^- \\ \text{Acetic acid} \\ \text{citrates}}]{H. (OH)^-}$$

Chloramphenicol

$$O_2N\text{—}\bigcirc\text{—}CHOH\text{—}\underset{\underset{NH_2}{|}}{CH}\text{—}CH_2OH \quad + \quad Cl_2CHCOOH$$

Dichloro acetic acid

Protection against Hydrolysis:

Hydrolysis reactions are known to occur in presence of moisture, catalytic species H^+ and $(OH)^-$. Protective measures should aim at eliminating the influence of these factors on the drug.

Removal of water: As the presence of water is responsible for hydrolysis, it is better to avoid its contact with the drug in the preparation.

Example:

(a) Storing the drug in dry form. When desired, reconstitute the product. Example is streptomycin dry powder for injection.

(b) Using water–immiscible vehicle for the dispersion of drug. Example is aspirin in silicone fluid.

Buffers: Drug may be stabilized by the use of buffers. The pH of the solution should be adjusted so that the drug will have maximum stability and therapeutic activity.

Example: Pilocarpine is highly active in alkaline pH, because it exists in the unionized (free base) form. But at alkaline pH, it is highly irritating to the eye and also decomposes rapidly. Therefore, to prevent hydrolysis, acidic pH has to be selected. Select a buffer with low buffer capacity so that when administered in the eye, the pH gradually rises and releases the free base for drug action. For this reason, boric acid buffer of a pH 5.0 with low buffer capacity is selected.

Complexation: Drug may be stabilized by the complexation of drug with complexing agent.

Example: Hydrolysis of benzocaine in aqueous solution can be inhibited by the addition of caffeine which forms a complex. As a result of complexation, the attack of catalytic species on benzocaine may be reduced. Now, the rate of hydrolysis depends on the amount of free uncomplexed benzocaine present in solution. As the amount of caffeine increases, more and more amount of benzocaine will be complexed. This leads to decreased hydrolysis. Thus, the shelf life of the product can be prolonged. Other drugs which may be stabilized by complexation are procaine, tetracaine etc.

Suppression of solubility: When the solubility of a drug decreases, the concentration of drug in solution phase will be decreased. Hence, the rate of hydrolysis is reduced.

Example:

(a) Citrates, dextrose, sorbitol and gluconates, when combined with drugs, the solubility of drugs will be suppressed, probably because of decreased hydration of drug molecules.

(b) **Salts:** The degradation of penicillin can be prevented by using poorly soluble salt of procaine penicillin in the dosage form.

(c) **Derivatives:** Poorly water soluble derivatives such as esters (higher fatty acids) of drugs can be used to reduce the tendency of hydrolysis. Examples are erythromycin propionate, erythromycin stearate, chloramphenicol palmitate etc.

2. Oxidation:

Oxidation involves the removal of electrons from a molecule. The reaction between the compounds and molecular oxygen is called **autooxidation.** In fats and oils, autooxidation of unsaturated fatty acids proceeds in the presence of atmospheric oxygen, light and traces of heavy metals or organic peroxides. For example, the rate of oxidation of ascorbic acid is increased by a factor of 10^5, when copper ions are present in the concentration of 0.002 M.

The general principles that govern an oxidation reaction may be listed as follows:

(a) The presence of atomospheric oxygen (also air) promotes the rate of oxidation.

(b) Since oxidation frequently involves free radicals, chain reactions occur. Light provides the necessary energy to initiate the oxidation process.

(c) The presence of trace metals also accelerates the rate of oxidation.

(d) Organic peroxides promote the chain initiation and propagate the oxidation reaction.

(e) Drugs are either weak acids or bases. Therefore, these may be available as ionic forms or neutral molecules. Oxidation reaction between ionic species proceeds faster than with neutral molecules (to a large extent it is solubility related phenomenon).

(f) Oxidation reactions are catalysed by H^+ and OH^- ions. Hydroxyl ions catalyse oxidation faster than hydrogen ions. Alkaline solutions are known to react with atmospheric oxygen and form oxides.

Drugs which decompose by oxidation pathways are given below:

Arachis oil, Vitamin A, Ethyl oleate, Riboflavin, Clove oil, Vitamin B_{12}, Cinnamon oil Ascorbic acid, Promethazine, Morphine etc.

Example: The autooxidation kinetics of ascorbic acid has been extensively studied. The overall reaction may be represented as:

Ascorbic acid   Dehydro ascorbic acid

Influence of Trace Metal:

When solutions are free from traces of copper, ascorbic acid is not oxidized by molecular oxygen to a measurable extent, except in alkaline solutions. However, even traces of copper lead to the rapid oxidation of ascorbic acid. When CO and KCN are added to the above reaction mixture, they form complexes with metal ions, and therefore, oxidation of ascorbic acid is inhibited. These reactions demonstrate the influence of cupric ion on the oxidation of ascorbic acid.

$$\text{Ascorbate ion in solution} \xrightarrow[\text{Slow oxidation}]{Cu^{2+}} \text{Semi quinone} \xrightarrow[\text{Rapid oxidation}]{O_2} \text{Dehydro ascorbic acid}$$

Influence of air on oxidation:

The rate of decomposition decreases when higher concentration of ascorbic acid is used. It is presumed that a part of the ascorbic acid reacts with oxygen and thus depletes free oxygen. When air is bubbled through the reaction mixture, the rate of oxidation is enhanced. When dissolved oxygen is maintained at saturation level, the reaction rate remains constant. Therefore, oxygen is responsible for the autooxidation reactions.

Protection against Oxidation:

Oxidation reactions are known to occur in presence of oxygen, trace metals, H^+ and $(OH)^-$ ions. Protective measures should aim at eliminating the influence of these factors on the drug.

Antioxidants: Antioxidants mean this excipient inhibit the oxidation reaction.

Oil soluble antioxidant: These agents act by breaking the free radical chain reactions at the step of chain propagation.

Tocopherols are the naturally occurring antioxidants. Other examples are butylated hydroxy anisole (BHA), butylated hydroxy toluene (BHT), propyl gallate etc. These are widely used in foods, cosmetics and drugs.

Water–soluble antioxidants: They act by preferentially undergoing oxidation instead of the drug itself.

Example is ascorbic acid, cysteine, acetylcysteine, thioglycolic acid etc.

Chelating agents: Addition of a chelating agent to a product will be useful when traces of heavy metals catalyse the oxidation. Substances such as EDTA (ethylerrediamine tetraacetic acid) citric acid and tartaric acid, form complexes with heavy metals. Thus, metal ions are not available to catalyse the oxidation. For example, addition of EDTA to the buffer system prevents the degradation of drugs such as prednisolone and ascorbic acid.

Vehicles: Usually water is used as a solvent for most products. The replacement of water by other solvents is often employed as a means of stabilizing drugs. But, other solvents when used in combination with water, they have catalyzing effect on oxidation.

Therefore careful consideration should be given while attempting to use solvents for stabilizing drugs.

Micellar solubilisation: Surfactants such as polysorbate 80 enhance the rate of oxidation of ascorbic acid at low concentration, but protect above its critical micelle concentration (cmc), presumably by entrapping the drugs in the spherical micelles. Sometimes, spherical micelles offer a site for surface adsorption of catalytic ions and enhance rate of reaction.

Buffers: Buffer system imparts stability when oxidation is catalysed by H^+ or $(OH)^-$ ions. Choose a buffer with appropriate pH to maintain maximum stability of the product.

Prevent the exposure to light: Light is responsible for oxidation. The preparation is protected from light by employing amber coloured bottles or using appropriate packaging material.

Oxygen free environment: Oxygen enhances oxidative degradation. Therefore, air is replaced with inert gases such as nitrogen or carbon dioxide.

Low temperature storage: Since high temperature enhances the rate of reaction, the product is stored in a cool place.

3. Isomerism:

Some drugs often have same structural formula, but possess different stereochemical configurations. Interconversion of one stereochemical form into another leads to inactive or less active drugs.

[I] Optical Isomerisation:

In solutions, the optically active form (+ve or –ve form) of a drug gets converted into its enantiomorph (+ve and –ve form). This process continues until the two forms are equal in concentration. The optical activity at equilibrium will be zero, i.e., optically inactive.

A few examples are:

$$(-) \text{ Adrenaline} \xrightarrow{\hspace{3cm}} (\pm) \text{ Adrenaline}$$

(–) Adrenaline — greater biological activity → (±) Adrenaline — (+ and – is 50 : 50) less potent

(–) Hyocyamine — more intense mydriatic $\xrightarrow[\text{light}]{\text{Heat or alkali}}$ (±) Hyocyamine — less potent

Preventive measures: The product is protected from light and heat. Optimum pH has to be maintained for maximum activity.

[II] Geometric Isomerisation:

In this case, the compounds exist as trans and cis isomers, based on their relative spatial configuration of groups around a double bond (s). These changes may bring about corresponding changes in its biological activity.

For example:

Vitamin A palmitate (all trans) — More active $\xrightarrow{\hspace{2cm}}$ 6-mono-cis derivative + 2, 6-di-cis derivative — Less active

4. Absorption of carbon dioxide:

Solutions absorb carbon dioxide from the atmosphere. For example:

Sodium hexobarbitone (IV injection) $\xrightarrow[\text{hydrolysis}]{\text{salt}}$ Solution (Basic pH) $\xrightarrow[CO_2]{\text{absorb}}$ Hexobarbitone precipitate (Acidic pH)

Preventive measures: The product is stored in well–filled and well–closed containers. Manufacturers supply the product as a dry sterile powder. The instruction should be — to dissolve the drug before use in CO_2 free sterile water for injection.

5. Decarboxylation:

These types of reactions are normally observed when a parenteral solution contains sodium carbonate. During autoclaving (for sterilisation), the carboxylic acid groups will be knocked off.

Examples: Sodium p–aminosalicylic acid (PAS, anti–TB drug) Procaine hydrochloride (local anesthetic)

Procain (clear solution) $\xrightarrow{\text{hydrolysis}}$ p-amino benzoic acid $\xrightarrow{- CO_2}$ Aniline liquid $\xrightarrow{\text{light}}$ Dark coloured liquid

Preventive measures: Carbon dioxide gas is passed into the solution for one minute. The container is sealed so as to be air–tight prior to autoclaving.

3.12 STABILITY TESTING

Stability testing of pharmaceutical products is a complex set of procedures involving considerable cost, time consumption and scientific expertise in order to build in quality, efficacy and safety in a drug formulation.

The most important steps during the developmental stages include pharmaceutical analysis and stability studies that are required to determine and assure the identity, potency and purity of ingredients, as well as those of the formulated products.

Definitions:

1. **Stability of a pharmaceutical product** may be defined as 'the capability of a particular formulation in a specific container/closure system to remain within its physical, chemical, microbiological, toxicological, protective and informational specifications'.

2. In other words, it is the extent to which a product retains, within the specified limits, throughout its period of storage and use, the same properties and characteristics possessed at the time of its packaging.

3.12.1 Reasons to Study Stability of Pharmaceutical Product

1. The stability of the active ingredient(s); interaction between active ingredients and excipients.

2. The effect of light, heat and moisture conditions encountered during shipment, storage and handling.

3. In addition, degradation reactions like oxidation, reduction, hydrolysis or racemization, which can play vital role in stability of a pharmaceutical product.

4. Stability depends on such conditions like concentration of reactants, pH, radiation, catalysts etc.

5. A pharmaceutical product may undergo change in appearance, consistency, content uniformity, clarity (solution), moisture contents, particle size and shape, pH, package integrity thereby affecting its stability.

6. Such physical changes may be because of impact, vibration, abrasion, and temperature fluctuations such as freezing, thawing or shearing etc.

7. Stability of a pharmaceutical product can also be affected because of microbiological changes like growth of microorganisms in non-sterile products and changes in preservative efficacy.

3.12.2 Importance of Stability Testing

The primary reason for stability testing is the concern for the well–being of the patient suffering from the disease for which the product is designed. Apart from degradation of the unstable product into toxic decomposition products, loss of activity upto a level of 90% of that claimed on the label may lead to failure of the therapy resulting in death e.g. nitroglycerine tablets for angina and cardiac arrest. Also,

1. Provide evidence as to how the quality of the drug product varies with time.
2. Establish shelf life for the drug product.
3. Determine recommended proper storage conditions and suggest labelling instructions.
4. Determine container closure system suitability.
5. To establish a re–test period for the drug substance

3.12.3 Climatic Zones for Stability Testing

For the purpose of stability testing, the whole world has been divided into four zones (I – IV) depending upon the environmental conditions, the pharmaceutical products are likely to be subjected to during their storage. These conditions have been derived on the basis of the mean annual temperature and relative humidity data in these regions. Based upon this data, long–term or real–time stability testing conditions and accelerated stability testing conditions have been derived. The standard climatic zones for use in pharmaceutical product stability studies have been presented in the Table 3.6.

The break–up of the environmental conditions in each zone and also the derived long–term stability test storage conditions, as given by WHO have also been presented.

Table 3.6: ICH climatic zones and long term stability conditions

Climatic zone	Climate/ Definition	Major countries/ Regions	MAT*/ Mean Annual Partial Water Vapour Pressure	Long-term testing conditions
(I)	Temperate	United Kingdom, Northern Europe, Russia, United States	≤15°C ≤11 hPa	21°C/45% RH
(II)	Subtropical and Mediterranean	Japan, Southern Europe	> 15-22°C />11-18 hPa	25°C/60% RH
(III)	Hot and Dry	Iraq, India	>22°C/≤15 hPa	30°C/35% RH
(IV) (a)	Hot and humid	Iran, Egypt	>22°C/>15-27 hPa	30°C/65% RH
(IV) (b)	Hot and very humid	Brazil, Singapore	>22°C/>27 hPa	30°C/75% RH

* MAT - Mean annual temperature measured in open air.

3.12.4 Stability Testing

This guideline was published by WHO (Word Health Organization) for Stability testing of active pharmaceutical ingredients and finished pharmaceutical products for **Climatic zone III and IV**.

Also, The ICH (International Conference of Harmonization) Q 1 A guideline for Stability testing of active pharmaceutical ingredients and finished pharmaceutical products for **Climatic zone I and II**.

In this section, discussion on stability study for pharmaceutical ingredients and finished pharmaceutical products for Climatic zone III and IV.

3.12.4.1 Principles

The purpose of stability testing is to provide evidence of how the quality of drugs and products varies with time under the influence of a variety of environmental factors such as temperature, humidity and light.

The stability programme also includes the study of product–related factors that influence its quality. For example, interaction of drug with excipients, container closure systems and packaging materials. In fixed dose combination drugs, the interaction between two or more drugs also has to be considered.

As a result of stability testing a re–test period for the API (in exceptional cases, e.g. for unstable drugs, a shelf–life is given) or a shelf–life for the products can be established and storage conditions can be recommended.

3.12.4.2 Points in Stability Testing

In stability testing following points are considered:

(a) Selection of batches
(b) Container closure system
(c) Specification
(d) Testing frequency
(e) Storage conditions

(a) Selection of batches: Least three primary batches of the drug should normally be provided. The batches should be manufactured to a minimum of pilot scale by the same synthesis route as production batches.

(b) Container Closure System: The stability studies should be conducted on the drug substance packaged in a container closure system.

(c) Testing Frequency: For long–term studies, frequency of testing should be sufficient to establish the stability profile of the API.

   (i) For long term studies: The frequency of testing at the long term storage condition should normally be every 3 months over the first year (e.g. 0, 3, 6, 9 and 12 months), every 6 months over the second year.

(ii) **For accelerated storage condition:** A minimum of three time points, including the initial and final time points (e.g., 0, 3 and 6 months) from a 6 month study is recommended.

(iii) **For intermediate term studies:** When testing at the intermediate storage condition is called for as a result of significant change at the accelerated storage condition, a minimum of four time points, including the initial and final time points (e.g., 0, 6, 9, 12 months), from a 12 month study is recommended.

(d) **Storage Conditions:** In general, a drug substance should be evaluated under storage conditions (with appropriate tolerances) that test its thermal stability and, if applicable, its sensitivity to moisture. The storage conditions and the lengths of studies chosen should be sufficient to cover storage, shipment and subsequent use.

(A) General Case:

Study	Storage condition	Minimum time period covered by data at submission
Long-term[a]	25°C ± 2°C/60% RH ± 5% RH or 30°C ± 2°C/65% RH ± 5% RH or 30°C ± 2°C/75% RH ± 5% RH	12 months or 6 months
Intermediate[b]	30°C ± 2°C/65% RH ± 5% RH	6 months
Accelerated	40°C ± 2°C/75% RH ± 5% RH	6 months

a   Whether long–term stability studies are performed at 25°C ± 2°C/60% RH ± 5% RH or 30°C ± 2°C/65% RH ± 5% RH or 30°C ± 2°C/75% RH ± 5% RH is determined by the climatic condition under which the API is intended to be stored. Testing at a more severe long–term condition can be an alternative to testing condition, i.e. 25°C/60% RH or 30°C/65% RH.

b   If 30°C ± 2°C/65% RH ± 5% RH or 30°C ± 2°C/75% RH ± 5% RH is the long–term condition. There is no intermediate condition.

If long–term studies are conducted at 25 °C ± 2 °C/60% RH ± 5% RH and "significant change" occurs at any time during six months' testing at the accelerated storage condition, additional testing at the intermediate storage condition should be conducted and evaluated against significant change criteria. In this case, testing at the intermediate storage condition should include all long–term tests, unless otherwise justified, and the initial application should include a minimum of six months' data from a 12–month study at the intermediate storage condition.

"Significant change" for an API is defined as 'failure to meet its specification'.

(B) Storage in a Refrigerator:

Study	Storage condition	Minimum time period covered by data at submission
Long-term	5°C ± 3°C	12 months
Accelerated[a]	25°C ± 2°C/60% RH ± 5% RH or 30°C ± 2°C/65% RH ± 5% RH or 30°C ± 2°C/75% RH ± 5% RH	6 months

a   Whether accelerated stability studies are performed at 25 ± 2°C/60% RH ± 5% RH or 30°C ± 2°C/65% RH ± 5% RH or 30°C ± 2°C/75% RH ± 5% RH is based on a risk–based evaluation. Testing at a more severe long term condition can be an alternative to storage testing at 25°C/60%RH or 30°C/65%RH.

If significant change occurs between three and six months testing at the accelerated storage condition, the proposed re–test period should be based on the data available at the long–term storage condition.

If significant change occurs within the first three months testing at the accelerated storage condition, a discussion should be provided to address the effect of short–term excursions outside the label storage condition, e.g. during shipping or handling. This discussion can be supported, if appropriate, by further testing on a single batch of the drug for a period shorter than three months but with more frequent testing than usual. It is considered unnecessary to continue to test a drug for the whole six months when a significant change has occurred within the first three months.

(C) For Storage in a Freezer:

Study	Storage condition	Minimum time period covered by data at submission
Long-term	– 20°C ± 5°C	12 months

In the rare case of any API of non–biological origin being intended for storage in a freezer, the re–test period or shelf–life should be based on the long–term data obtained at the long–term storage condition. In the absence of an accelerated storage condition for APIs intended to be stored in a freezer, testing on a single batch at an elevated temperature (e.g. 5°C ± 3°C or 25°C ± 2°C or 30°C ± 2°C) for an appropriate time period should be conducted to address the effect of short–term excursions outside the proposed label storage condition, e.g. during shipping or handling.

(D) For Storage below –20°C:

APIs intended for storage below –20°C should be treated on a case–by–case basis.

3.13 ACCELERATED STRESS TESTING

The objective of accelerated stability studies is to predict the shelf of a product by accelerating the rate of decomposition, preferably by increasing the temperature. Accelerated stability studies are experiment designs.

Stress testing performs following way:

1. Drug liquid preparations (solution dosage forms) are stored at elevated temperatures, viz., 50, 60, 70, 85, 100 and 121°C.

2. In addition, the samples should be studied at 40°C, 75% RH and incubator temperature (35–37°C).

3. To confirm the results obtained from accelerated stability studies, it is necessary to simultaneously conduct experiments at room temperature (i.e., 30°C, 70% RH) and/or refrigerator temperature (4–5°C).

4. During different time intervals, samples are withdrawn. The sampling may be done at:

   A minimum of three time points, including the initial and final time points (e.g., 0, 3, and 6 months), from a 6–month study is recommended.

5. For drug products which may degrade rapidly (examples are certain radiopharmaceuticals) more frequent sampling is necessary.

6. The drug content is estimated using a stability indicating assay method.

3.13.1 Graphical Representation for Determination of Degradation Constant k and Self Life of Drug

An analytic data obtained during accelerated stress testing was used for determination of degradation rate constant k and self life of drug.

Method I:

The method of accelerated testing of pharmaceutical products is based on the principles of chemical kinetics.

In this method;

1. The specific rates of decomposition k values for the decomposition of a drug in solution at various elevated temperatures are obtained by plotting some function of concentration against time, as seen in Fig. 3.20.

Then,

2. The logarithms of the specific rates of decomposition k are then plotted against the reciprocals of the absolute temperatures as shown in Fig. 3.21.

3. The resulting line is extrapolated to room temperature.

4. The k_{25} is used to obtain a measure of the stability of the drug under ordinary shelf conditions.

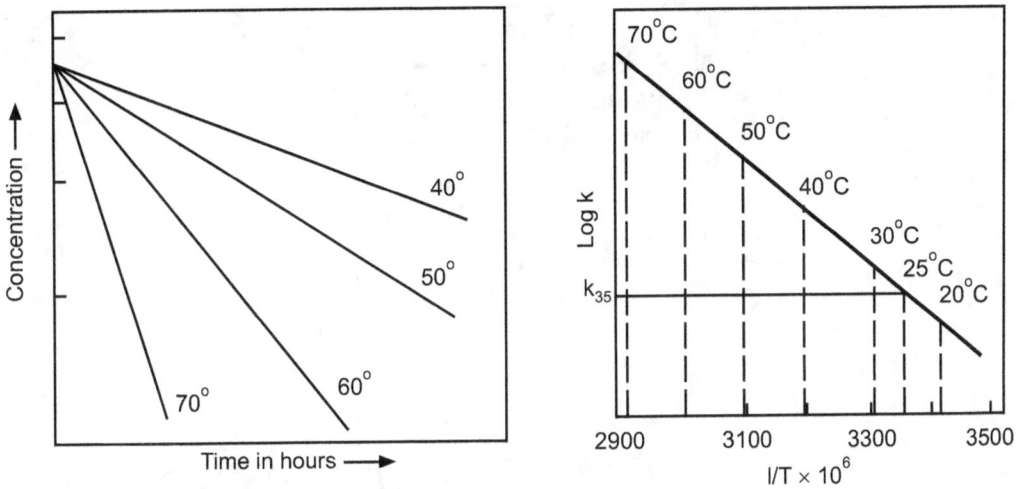

Fig. 3.20: Accelerated breakdown at elevated temperature

Fig. 3.21: Arrhenius plot for predicting stability

Method II:

1. The log per cent of drug remaining is plotted against time in days.
2. The time for the potency to fall to 90% of the original value, i.e., t_{90}, is read from the graph. (Fig. 3.22).

Then,

3. The log time to 90% is then plotted against l/T, (Fig. 3.23).
4. The time at 25° C gives the shelf–life of the product in days.
5. The decomposition data illustrated in Fig. 3.23 result in a t_{90} value of 199 days. Shelf–life and expiration dates are estimated in this way.

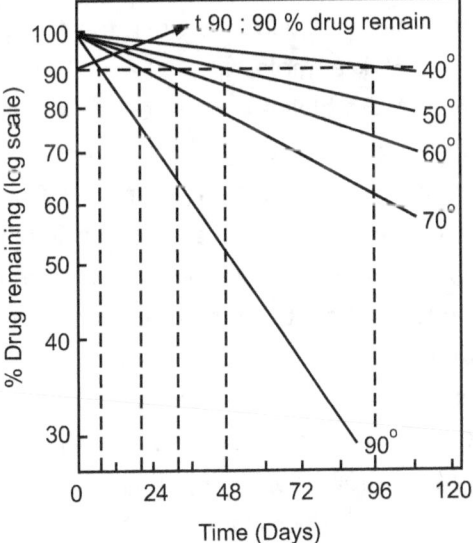

Fig. 3.22: Time in day required for drug fall to 90%

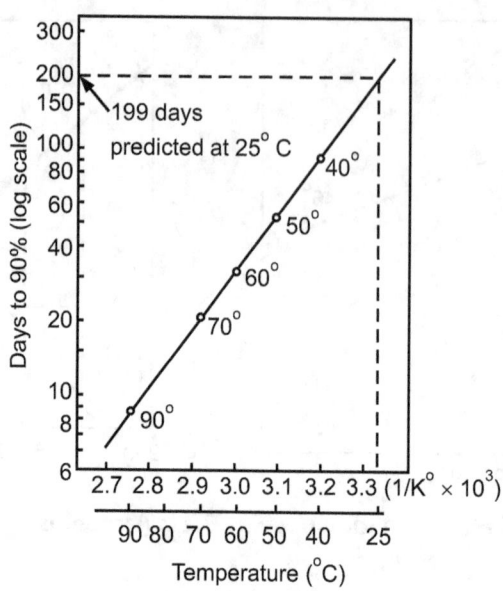

Fig. 3.23: A log t$_{90}$ vs temperature

3.13.2 Limitations

Though accelerated stability studies have several advantages and are widely used in pharmacy, it have a few limitations.

The following aspects have to be considered in this study design:

1. Accelerated stability studies are valid only when the breakdown depends on temperature.

2. Accelerated stability studies are valid only when the energy of activation obtained in the study is about 10 to 30 kcal/mole.

3. The results (shelf life etc.,) obtained for one set of conditions for a preparation cannot be applied to other preparations of the same drug.

4. Whenever slight changes in the formula is made, kinetic study at one elevated temperature will be sufficient (helpful) to predict the stability

5. Stability predictions at elevated temperatures are of little use when the degradation is due to diffusion, microbial contamination and photochemical reactions (E$_a$ range from 2 to 3 kcal/mole).

6. Stability studies are meaningless, when the product loses its physical integrity at higher temperatures. For example, coagulation of suspending agent (Methylcellulose), denaturation of proteins, breaking of an emulsion or change in the distribution coefficient of emulsifier at the high temperatures and loss of consistency of ointments.

QUESTIONS

1. **Short Answer Questions (3 Marks):**

   1. Write applications of chemical kinetics.   **[SPPU - 2012, 13]**

   2. Define and differentiate between order and molecularity.   **[SPPU - 2013]**

   3. Define pseudo order and give two examples.   **[SPPU - 2014]**

   4. Define the term 'stability' of a pharmaceutical. How is it quantified? Write the equation for the same.   **[SPPU - 2014]**

   5. Describe the influence of temperature on the rate of reaction.   **[SPPU - 2014]**

   6. Define rate determining step, order of reaction and molecularity of reaction.

          [SPPU - 2013]

   7. Discuss apparent zero order reaction.   **[SPPU - 2013]**

   8. Differentiate between shelf life and half life for a first order reaction.

   9. Define and differentiate between first order and pseudo first order reaction with example.   **[SPPU - 2011]**

   10. Calculate reaction rate and shelf life of the product that decomposes by first order. The half life of drug is 65 days.

   11. A solution of drug contained 1200 units/ml when prepared. After 60 days, it was analyzed and found to have 400 units/ml. Assuming the decomposition is first order; calculate half life, shelf life and rate of reaction.

   12. The reaction between methane A and B and formation of C. At 400°C the rate constant for this reaction is 2.1 l mol^{-1} sec and at 556°C the rate constant is 6.1 l mol^{-1} sec. Calculate E_a for this reaction.

2. **Medium Answer Questions (5 Marks):**

   1. Write short note on Accelerated stability studies.   **[SPPU - 2013, 14]**

   2. Explain degradation pathway of drugs.   **[SPPU - 2013, 14]**

   3. Define energy of activation. Give its significance.

   4. Write Complex reactions with suitable example.

3. Long Answer Questions (10 Marks):

1. Compare first and second order reactions with respect to the rates and explain the mechanism for their behaviour.   **[SPPU - 2012]**

2. Explain effect of temperature on rate of reaction.   **[SPPU - 2013]**

3. Define and explain 'order of reaction'. Discuss different methods used for determining the order of reaction.   **[SPPU - 2014]**

4. Explain integrated rate law equation.

■■■

Chapter 4...

Micromeritics

4.1 INTRODUCTION

4.1.1 Definition

Micromeritics is defined as 'the science and technology of small particles'.

Colloidal dispersions are characterized by particles which are too small to be seen in the ordinary microscope. The particles of pharmaceutical emulsions and suspensions and the "fines" of powders fall in the range of the optical microscope. Particles having the size of coarser powders, tablet granulations, and granular salts fall within the sieve range.

The approximate size ranges of particles in pharmaceutical dispersions are listed in Table 4.1.

Table 4.1: Particle dimension in Pharmaceutical Dispersion System

Particle size (μm)	Approximate sieve size	Example
0.5-10	--	Suspension and fine emulsions.
10-50	--	Flocculated suspension and coarse emulsion.
50-100	325-140	Fine powder.
150-1000	100-18	Coarse powder.
1000-3360	18-6	Average granule size.

4.1.2 Unit

The unit of particle size used most frequently in micromeritics is the micrometer, μm, also called the micron, μ,

$$1 \ \mu m = 10^{-6} \ m$$

$$1 \ m\mu \ or \ nm = 10^{-9} \ m$$

One must not confuse μm with mμ (millimicron). The millimicron now is most commonly referred to as the nanometer (nm).

4.1.3 Pharmaceutical Importance

Knowledge and control of the size, and the size range of particles is of profound importance in pharmacy. Thus, size and hence surface area, of a particle can be related in a significant way to the physical, chemical and pharmacologic properties of a drug.

1. **Drug release and dissolution:** Clinically, the particle size of a drug can affect its release from dosage forms that are administered orally, parenterally, rectally and topically. Particle size is inversely proportional to surface area of particles. High surface area (small size particle) brings about intimate contact of the drug with the dissolution fluid. Hence, increase dissolution and drug release rate.

2. **Absorption and drug action:** Particle size and surface area influence the drug absorption and drug action. As discussed earlier, smaller particle size increase dissolution rate and as dissolution rate increases rate of absorption also increases. Hence, quicker and greater is the drug action.

3. **Stability:** The successful formulation of suspensions and emulsions and tablets, from the viewpoints of both physical stability and pharmacologic response, also depends on the particle size achieved in the product. Smaller particle size in suspension and emulsion show better physical stability.

4. **Dose uniformity:** In the area of tablet and capsule manufacture, control of the particle size is essential in achieving the necessary flow properties and proper mixing of granules and powders. The flow of granules should be uniform in order to ensure precise weight of the tablet and drug content.

4.2 PARTICLE SIZE

In collection of particles there is uneven distribution of particles size means more than one size of particles i.e. **polydisperse sample** and same size of particles in collection of particles is termed as **mono-size or monodisperse.**

Also shapes of particles in collection are non-uniform. Some particle is spherical in shape and some are asymmetric as shown in Fig. 4.1.

The size of a sphere is readily expressed in terms of its **diameter.**

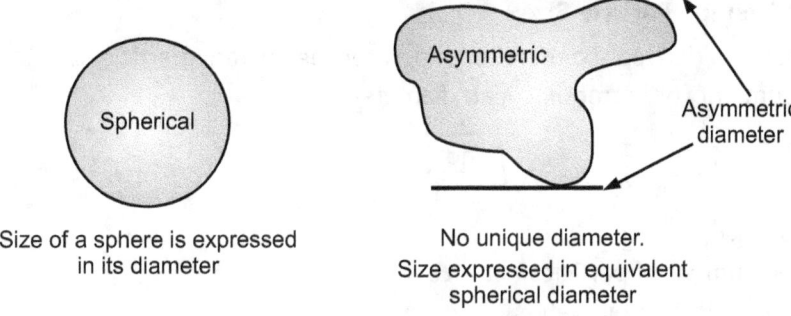

Fig. 4.1: Spherical and asymmetric particle

4.2.1 Equivalent Spherical Diameter for Asymmetric Particles

As the degree of asymmetry of particles increases, however, so does the difficulty of expressing size in terms of a meaningful diameter. Under these conditions there is no one unique diameter for a particle. Therefore, asymmetric particles size is expressed in **equivalent spherical diameter.**

Size of particles is expressed as follows:

1. **Surface diameter, (d_s)** is the diameter of a sphere having the same surface area as that of the asymmetric particle.

2. **Volume diameter, (d_v)** is the diameter of a sphere having the same volume as that of the asymmetric particle.

3. **Projected diameter, (d_p)** is the diameter of a sphere having the same area as of the asymmetric particle when viewed under a microscope.

4. **Stokes diameter, (d_{st})** which describes an equivalent sphere undergoing sedimentation at the same rate as the asymmetric particle. Stokes' diameter is determined from sedimentation studies on the suspended particles.

Any collection of particles is usually polydisperse. It is therefore necessary to know not only the size of a certain particle, but also how many particles of the same size exist in the sample. Thus, we need an estimate of the size range present and the number or weight fraction of each particle size. This is the particle size distribution, and from this we may calculate an average particle size for the sample.

4.2.2 Average Particle Size

Most of the pharmaceutical powders are polydisperse, i.e. they contain particles of different sizes. There is no universal way of defining size of a powder. However, it is necessary to assign powder with a characteristic value.

Equation for Average Particle Size:

Edmundson has derived a general equation for the average particle size, whether it is an arithmetic, geometric, or harmonic mean diameter.

$$d_{mean} = \sqrt[p]{\frac{\Sigma nd^{p+f}}{\Sigma nd^f}}$$ ... (4.1)

In equation (4.1),

n : The number of particles in a size range,

d : The equivalent diameters,

p : An index related to the size of an individual particle, since d raised to the power p = 1, p = 2 or p = 3 is an expression of the particle length, surface or volume, respectively.

The value of the index p also decides whether;

(a) arithmetic mean: p is positive

(b) geometric mean: p is zero or

(c) harmonic mean: p is negative.

f : The frequency index, has values of 0, 1, 2 or 3, then the size frequency distribution is expressed in terms of the total number, length, surface or volume of the particles, respectively.

4.2.3 Arithmetic Mean Diameters

Arithmetic mean diameter is defined as 'sum of particles size divided by number of particles'.

Types of Arithmetic Mean Size: These are based on the value of p and f used in equation (4.1)

1. **Length number mean (d_{ln}):**

   When, p = 1 and f = 0

   In this case, equation (4.1) is expressed as follows:

   $$d_{ln} = \frac{\Sigma nd}{\Sigma n}$$ ... (4.2)

   This mean is satisfactory if size range is narrow and distribution is normal. These conditions are rarely found in pharmaceutical powders.

2. **Surface-number mean (d_{sn}):**

   When, p = 2 and f = 0

   In this case, equation (4.1) is expressed as follows:

   $$d_{sn} = \sqrt{\frac{\Sigma nd^2}{\Sigma n}}$$ ... (4.3)

   It refers to particles having average surface area.

3. **Volume-numbers mean (d_{vn}):**

   When, $p = 3$ and $f = 0$

   In this case, equation (4.1) is expressed as follows:

   $$d_{vn} = \sqrt[3]{\frac{\Sigma nd^3}{\Sigma n}} \qquad \qquad \text{... (4.4)}$$

   Refers to particle having average weight and is related inversely to N, the number of particles per gram of material.

4. **Surface-Length or Length-Weight Mean (d_{vs}):**

   When, $p = 1$ and $f = 1$

   In this case, equation (4.1) is expressed as follows:

   $$d_{sl} = \frac{\Sigma nd^2}{\Sigma nd} \qquad \qquad \text{... (4.5)}$$

   This is not practical significant.

5. **Volume-Surface or Surface-Weight Mean (d_{vs})**

   When, $p = 1$ and $f = 2$

   In this case, equation (4.1) is expressed as follows

   $$d_{vs} = \frac{\Sigma nd^3}{\Sigma nd^2} \qquad \qquad \text{... (4.6)}$$

   Important pharmaceutically, because inversely related to the specific surface area S_w.

6. **Weight-moment or volume-weighted mean (d_{wm}):**

   When, $p = 1$ and $f = 3$

   In this case, equation (4.1) is expressed as follows

   $$d_{wm} = \frac{\Sigma nd^4}{\Sigma nd^3} \qquad \qquad \text{... (4.7)}$$

   This diameter has limited pharmaceutical significances.

4.3 PARTICLE SIZE DETERMINATION

Determination of particle size is very important in pharmaceutical consideration. In manufacturing process of tablet, capsule, suspension etc. there will be required desired size of particle. Also solubility and dissolution is depending on particle size.

Particle size of drugs in pharmaceutical products can affect:

1. The release of drugs from dosage forms that are administered orally, parenterally, rectally and topically.

2. The physical stability and pharmacologic response of suspensions, emulsions and tablets.

3. Flow properties and mixing of granules and powders in tablet and capsule manufacture.

Methods to estimate particle size are:

1. Sieve method

2. Optical microscopy

3. Sedimentation method

4. Coulter counter method

4.3.1 Sieve Method

This method is directly given weight distribution of powder.

Equivalent Diameter:

Sieve diameter, d_{sieve}, is defined as 'the width of the minimum square aperture through which the particle will pass' and shown diagrammatically in Fig. 4.2 for different-shaped particles.

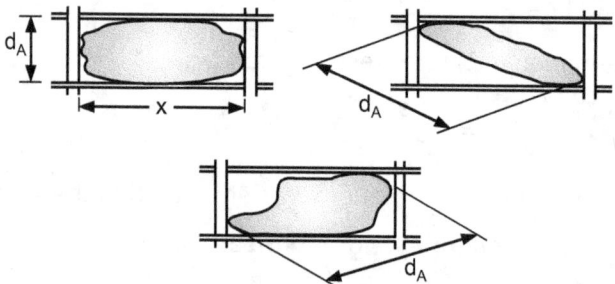

Fig. 4.2: Sieve diameter (d_{sieve}) is the size of the aperture for various shaped particles

Range of Analysis:

The International Standards Organization (ISO) sets a lowest sieve diameter of 45 μm and, as powders are usually defined as having a maximum diameter of 1000 μm, this could be considered to be the upper limit.

In practice, sieves can be obtained for size analysis over a range from 5 to 1,25,000 μm.

Sieve:

Sieves for pharmaceutical testing are constructed from wire cloth with square meshes, woven from wire of brass, bronze, stainless steel or any other suitable material. Sieves should not be coated or plated. There must be no reaction between the material of the sieve and the substance to be sieved. Standard sieves and their dimensions as per IP are given in Table 4.2.

Table 4.2: Designation and dimension of IP specification sieves

Sieve number	Aperture size micrometer	Sieve number	Aperture size micrometer
10	1700	44	325
12	1400	60	250
16	1000	85	35
22	710	100	36
25	600	120	34
30	500	150	36
36	425	170	35

Sample Preparation and Analysis Conditions:

Sieve analysis is usually carried out using dry powders, although for powders in liquid suspension or which agglomerate during dry sieving, a process of wet sieving can be used.

Method:

1. Arrange the set of sieves in descending order. (Place sieve number 10 at top, below which place sieve numbers 20, 40, 60, 80, 100 respectively and 120 at the bottom).
2. Weigh, accurately, the given sample (100 g) and pour on the top sieve. Place the lid to avoid loss during shaking.
3. This sieve set is fixed to the mechanical shaker apparatus [Fig. 4.3] and shaken for a certain period of time (5 minutes).
4. The powder retained on each sieve is weighed.
5. Frequently, the powder is assigned the mesh number of the screen through which it passes or on which it is retained.
6. It is expressed in terms of arithmetic or geometric mean of the two sieves.
7. For example, a powder passing through a 36 mesh and retained on 44 mesh sieve is assigned an arithmetic mean diameter of (425+ 325)/2 or 375 µm. This is reported as undersize.
8. Data are analyzed for normal, log-normal, cumulative per cent frequency distribution and probability curves.
9. The relevant diameters such as geometric mean weight diameter and standard deviation can be obtained.

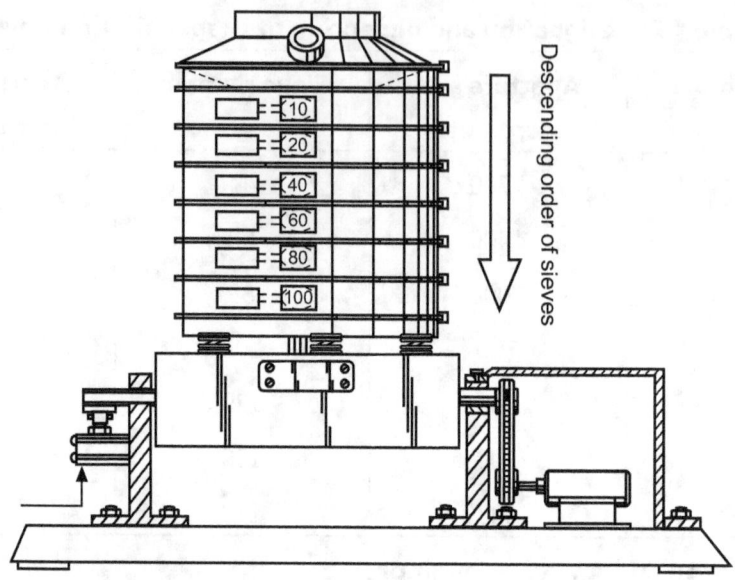

Fig. 4.3: Mechanical sieve shaker

Advantages of Sieve Method:

1. It is inexpensive, simple and rapid with reproducible result.

Disadvantages of Sieve Method:

1. Lower limit of the particle size is 45 μm.
2. If powder is not dry, apertures become clogged with particles, leading to improper sieving.
3. During shaking, attrition (particles colliding with each other) occurs causing size reduction of particles. This leads to errors in estimation.

Alternative Techniques:

1. Another form of sieve analysis is called **air-jet sieving**.
2. It uses individual sieve rather than a complete nest of sieves.
3. Starting with the finest aperture sieve and progressively removing undersize particle fraction by sequentially increasing the apertures of each sieve, particles are encouraged to pass through each aperture under the influence of a partial vacuum applied below the sieve mesh.
4. A reverse air jet is circulated beneath the sieve mesh blowing oversize particles away to prevent blocking.
5. Air-jet sieving is often more efficient and reproducible than using mechanically vibrated sieve analysis, although with finer particle agglomeration can become a problem.

4.3.2 Optical Microscopy

This method directly gives number distribution, which can be further converted to weight distribution. This method is widely used for analysis of particles size in suspension and globule size in emulsion.

Equivalent Diameter:

In this method, the size is expressed as projected diameter (d_p) which describes the diameter of a sphere having the same area as the asymmetric particle when observed under a microscope.

Range of Analysis:

Particles size measurement is in the range of 0.2 µm to 100 µm.

Sample Preparation and Analysis Conditions:

Specimens prepared for optical microscopy must be adequately dispersed on microscope slide to avoid agglomeration of particles and also direct sprinkling of powder on slide.

Method:

1. Eye-piece of the microscope is fitted with a micrometer and calibrated using a standard stage micrometer.
2. Take the powder sample and prepare a suspension with a suitable vehicle such as paraffin oil. When water is used as a vehicle, verify the aspects of hydration (swelling) of the particles. The sample of suspension is mounted on a slide or a ruled cell and placed on the mechanical stage.
3. The size of the particle is estimated with the help of the eye-piece micrometer.
4. Around 625 particles must be counted in order to estimate the true mean. This is necessary because particles are not spherical and assessment will be subjective and inaccurate unless a large sample is measured.
5. The size frequency distribution curves such as normal, log-normal, cumulative, frequency and probability curves are plotted. Finally, the statistical diameters for the powder are estimated.

Other Diameters:

1. **Projected area diameter:** Diameter of circle having same area as the projected area of the particle resting in stable position. [Fig. 4.4 (a)]
2. **Feret's diameter:** The mean value of the distance between pairs of parallel tangents to the projected outline of the particle. This can be considered as the boundary separating equal particle areas. [Fig. 4.4 (b)]
3. **Martin's diameter:** The mean chord length of the projected outline of particle. [Fig. 4.4 (b)]

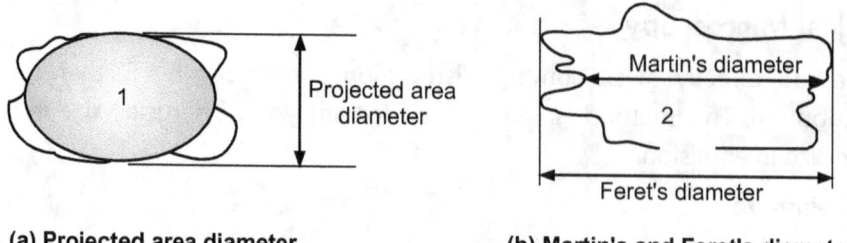

(a) Projected area diameter   (b) Martin's and Feret's diameter

Fig. 4.4: Other diameters

Advantages of Optical Microscopy:
1. Easy and simple.
2. Contamination and aggregation of particles can be detected.
3. Small quantity of sample required.

Disadvantages of Optical Microscopy:
1. This method is time consumable and tedious.
2. Result is not reproducible.

Alternative Methods:

Alternatives to light microscopy include scanning electron microscopy (SEM) and transmission electron microscopy (TEM). Scanning electron microscopy is particularly appropriate when a three-dimensional particle image is required; in addition, the very much greater depth of field of an SEM compared to a light microscope may also be beneficial. Both SEM and TEM analysis allow the lower particle sizing limit to be greatly extended over that possible with a light microscope.

4.3.3 Sedimentation Methods

Sedimentation means settling of disperse particles. Study of sedimentation of particles is evaluation parameter of suspension and emulsion. The stability of suspension depends on the sedimentation rate of dispersed phase.

Equivalent Diameters:

In this method, size is expressed as Stoke's diameter, d_{st}, which describe the diameter of an equivalent sphere having the same rate of sedimentation as that of the asymmetric particle.

Range of Analysis:

Particles size measurement is in the range of 1 μm to 200 μm.

Sample Preparation and Analysis Conditions:

Particle size distributions can be determined by examining the powder as it sediments out. In cases where the powder is not uniformly dispersed in a fluid, it can be introduced as a thin layer on the surface of the liquid. If the powder is hydrophobic, it may be necessary to add a dispersing agent to aid wetting. In cases where the powder is soluble in water, it will be necessary to use non-aqueous liquids.

Method:

Andreasen pipette: One of the most popular of the pipette methods was that developed by Andreasen and Lundberg and commonly called the **Andreasen pipette** (Fig. 4.5).

1. The Andreasen fixed-position pipette consists of a 200 mm tall graduated cylinder which can hold about 500 ml of suspension fluid.
2. A pipette (10 ml) is located centrally in the cylinder and held in position by a ground-glass stopper and its tip coincides with the zero level.

The procedure is as follows:

1. Transfer the suspension into the Andreasen vessel. Place the stopper and shake the vessel to distribute the suspension uniformly.
2. Remove the stopper and place the pipette and securely suspend the vessel in a constant temperature water bath.
3. At different time intervals, 10 ml samples are withdrawn using three way tap and collected in a watch-glass.
4. Samples are evaporated and weighed.
5. The weight or the amount of particles obtained in each time interval is referred to as weight undersize. The weights are converted into cumulative weight undersize.
6. The largest size present in each sample is then calculated from Stokes' equation.

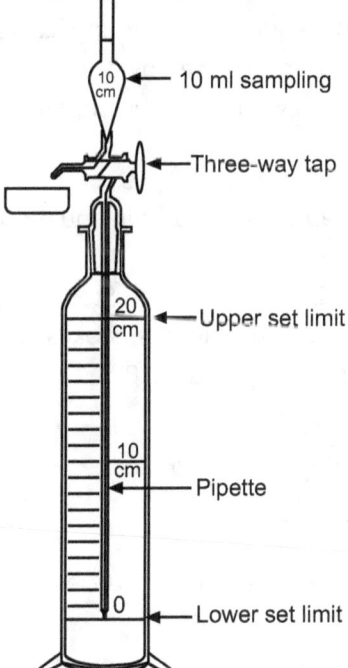

Fig. 4.5: Diagram of Andreasen pipette

Stokes' Equation for Determination of Particles Size:

The rate of sedimentation of particles in a suspension or emulsion is obtained by Stokes' law.

$$v = \frac{h}{t} = \frac{d_{st}^2 (\rho_s - \rho_o) g}{18 \eta} \qquad \text{... (4.8)}$$

Where,

v : Rate of sedimentation,

h : Distance of fall in time, t (Height of liquid above the lower end of the pipette at the time of sampling),

η : Viscosity of the medium,

ρ_s : Density of the particles,

ρ_0 : Density of the dispersion medium,

g : Acceleration due to gravity,

d_{st} : Stokes diameter of particle.

The equation (4.8) is rearranged to get the Stokes' diameter, d_{st} of particles.

$$d_{st} = \sqrt{\frac{18 \eta h}{(\rho_s - \rho_o) g t}} \qquad \text{... (4.9)}$$

Limitation for Stokes' equation:
Flow should be laminar:

Stokes' equation is applicable when flow of sediment particles is laminar. In the condition of turbulences flow this equation is not applicable, because turbulences flow will affect the sedimentation of other particles thereby causing error in the estimation.

Type of flow is determined by Reynolds number, R_e, which is defined as follows:

$$R_e = \frac{v \, d \, \rho_o}{\eta} \qquad \text{... (4.10)}$$

Where all symbols have the same meaning as in equation (4.8).

In case,

R_e = or < 0.2, flow is laminar, Stokes' equation is applicable, but

R_e > 0.2, flow is turbulences, Stokes' equation is not applicable

Therefore, combining equations (4.8) and (4.10), we get

$$v = \frac{d_{st}^2 (\rho_s - \rho_o) g}{18 \eta} = \frac{R_e \eta}{d_{st} \rho_o} \qquad \text{... (4.11)}$$

$$d_{st}^3 = \frac{18 \eta^2 R_e}{(\rho_s - \rho_o) g \rho_o} \qquad \text{... (4.12)}$$

Equation (4.12) allows calculating maximum particle diameter when R_e > 0.2.

Advantages of Sedimentation:

1. Easy and simple.
2. Applicable in determination of stability of suspension and emulsion.

Disadvantages of Sedimentation:
1. One of the limitations of gravitational sedimentation is that below a diameter of approximately 5 µm, particle settling becomes prolonged because of diffusion and Brownian motion of particle.
2. Time consuming.
3. Large sample is required.
4. In case of turbulences flow, incorrect result.

4.3.4 Particle Volume Measurement (Coulter Counter Method)

In 1953, engineer Wallace H. Coulter submitted a patent that proposed a deceptively simple method to measure the volume of particles and size of particles. This method is also called as the **"electric sensing zone"** method.

The method is measurement of difference in resistance between a particle and surrounding fluid. The Coulter counter uses the concept of the resistivity to count particles.

Equivalent diameters:

Size is expressed as volume diameter, d_v, which describe the diameter of the sphere having the same volume as that of the asymmetric particles.

Range of analysis:

Partial size ranging from 0.5 µm to 500 µm is measured by this method.

Principle and Method:

Fig. 4.6 shows a Coulter counter apparatus.

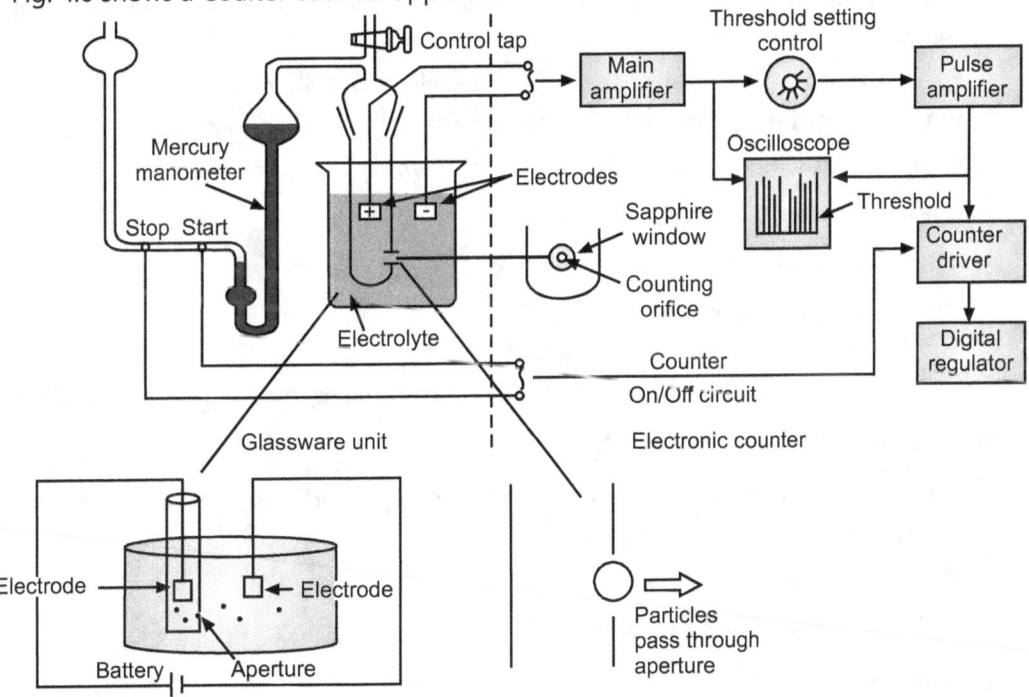

Fig. 4.6: A voltage is applied between the two electrodes over the aperture. When a particle travels through the aperture, the resistance in the aperture increases. The resulting current drop can be measured

1. For experimental purpose two solutions will be prepared:
   (a) Conducting electrolyte solution (NaCl solution).
   (b) Non-conducting particles suspended in conducting electrolyte solution.
2. Then, test tube containing a second solution (particles + electrolyte solution) is placed in a beaker and beaker is already filled by conducting electrolyte solution.
3. A small aperture in the test tube connects the two.
4. Electrodes are placed in the beaker and in the test tube.
5. A voltage is applied between them through the aperture.
6. The resistance between the two electrodes increases every time when a non-conducting particle passes through the aperture.

   There will be two possibilities;
   (a) **If the conduction particle passes through aperture,** it will be more conductive than the fluid, then the resistance decreases.
   (b) **If the particle passes through aperture,** it will be less conductive than the fluid, the resistance increases.
7. This change in electric resistance is termed as voltage pulse, which is related to the particle volume. This voltage pulse is amplified and fed to a pulse height analyzer. This analyzer is previously calibrated in terms of particle size for different threshold settings.
8. For a given threshold value, the pulses are electronically counted. By changing the threshold settings gradually, number of particles of each size range is obtained. Thus, the particle size distribution can be obtained.

Advantages of Coutler Counter Method:

1. 4000 particle per second can be counted.
2. Highly accurate method.
3. Short period required to determination of size.
4. It can be useful for determination of particle contamination in parenteral solution.

Disadvantages of Coutler Counter Method:

1. Unsuitable for water soluble drug, if hydrophilic drug disperse in non-polar solvent, it may produce adequate conductance.
2. It is expensive method.

4.4 PARTICLE NUMBER AND WEIGHT

Particle Number:

The number of particles per unit weight, N, is expressed in terms of volume number mean diameter, d_{vn}.

Assuming particles are spherical in shape following relation may be obtained.

$$\text{Volume of a single particle} = \frac{1}{6} \pi d_{vn}^3 \qquad \text{... (4.13)}$$

$$\text{Mass of single particle} = \text{Volume} \times \text{Density}$$

$$\text{Mass of single particle} = \frac{1}{6} \pi d_{vn}^3 \rho \qquad \text{... (4.14)}$$

The following relation may be obtained.

$$\frac{\text{Weight of single particle}}{1 \text{ particle}} = \frac{\text{Weight of powder (1 g)}}{\text{Number of particles, N}}$$

$$\frac{\frac{1}{6} \pi d_{vn}^3 \rho}{1} = \frac{1 \text{ g}}{N}$$

$$N = \frac{6}{\pi d_{vn}^3 \rho} \qquad \text{... (4.15)}$$

Powder Weight:

$$\text{Mass of powder} = \text{Number of particles} \times \text{Volume} \times \text{Density}$$

$$\text{Mass of powder} = N \frac{1}{6} \pi d_{vn}^3 \rho \qquad \text{... (4.16)}$$

The shape of the particle and density are independent of particle size. Considering the constant, π and ρ in equation (4.16), the relationship can be written as;

$$\text{Mass of powder} \propto N \, d_{vn}^3 \qquad \text{... (4.17)}$$

4.5 PARTICLE SIZE DISTRIBUTION

When the number, or weight, of particles lying within a certain size range is plotted against the size range or mean particle size, a so-called frequency distribution curve is obtained.

4.5.1 Number of Particles Versus Particle Size (Fig. 4.7)

Number of particles lying within a particular size range is plotted against the mean particle size. The obtained normal distribution curve is symmetrical around the mean size (Fig. 4.7 based on Table 4.3). Obtained curve was bell shaped.

Table 4.3: Data is expressed as number of particles. (Microscopic method)

Size range (μm)	Mean size range D (μm)	Number of particles (n)
0.50 - 1.00	0.75	2
1.00 - 1.50	1.25	10
1.50 - 2.00	1.75	22
2.00 - 2.50	2.25	54
2.50 - 3.00	2.75	17
3.00 - 3.50	3.25	8
3.50 - 4.00	3.75	5
		$\Sigma n = 118$

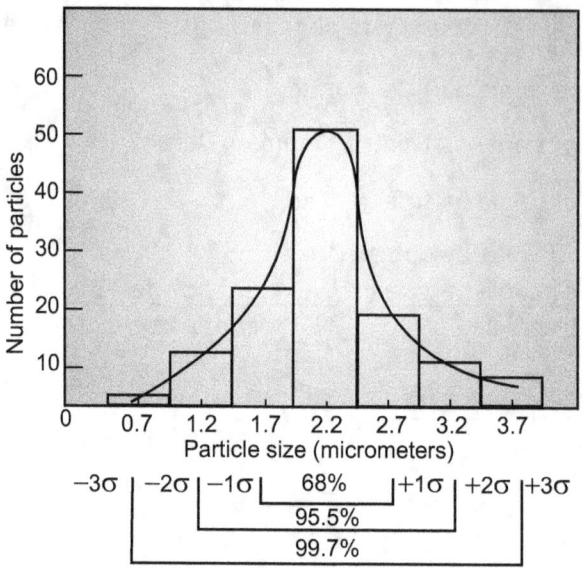

Fig. 4.7: Normal distribution curve

Note: The peak is the mean and mode.

Such plots give a visible representation of the distribution that an average diameter cannot achieve. This is important, for it is possible to have two samples with the same average diameter but different distributions. Also, it is immediately apparent from a frequency distribution curve what particle size occurs most frequently within the sample. This is termed as the mode.

The standard deviation, σ, is an indication of the distribution about the mean. In a normal distribution,

- 68% of the population lie ± 1σ from the mean,
- 95.5% lie within the mean ± 2σ and
- 99.7% lie within the mean ± 3σ.

It is not commonly found in pharmaceutical powders, which are frequently processed by milling or precipitation.

4.5.2 % Distribution Versus Particle Size (Fig. 4.8)

The systems tend to have an unsymmetric, or skewed, i.e. uneven around mean, distribution of the type depicted in Fig. 4.8 (based on Table 4.4, column 5 and 7). It is normally a long tail of larger particle size.

Table 4.4: Size distribution data (Microscopic method)

Size range (µm)	Mean size range, D (µm)	Log of mean size range, D (µm)	Number of particles, (n)	% n	Cumulative % frequency undersize (n)	% Weight (nd³)	Cumulative % frequency undersize (Weight)
2 - 4	3	0.477	2	1	1	0.03	0.03
4 - 6	5	0.698	32	16	17	2.31	2.34
6 - 8	7	0.845	64	32	49	12.65	14.99
8 - 10	9	0.954	48	24	73	2.16	35.15
10 - 12	11	1.041	30	15	88	23.01	58.16
12 - 14	13	1.113	14	7	95	17.72	75.88
14 - 16	15	1.176	6	3	98	11.67	87.55
16 - 18	17	1.230	3	1.5	99.5	8.49	96.04
18 - 20	19	1.278	1	0.5	100	3.95	99.99
			Σn = 200				

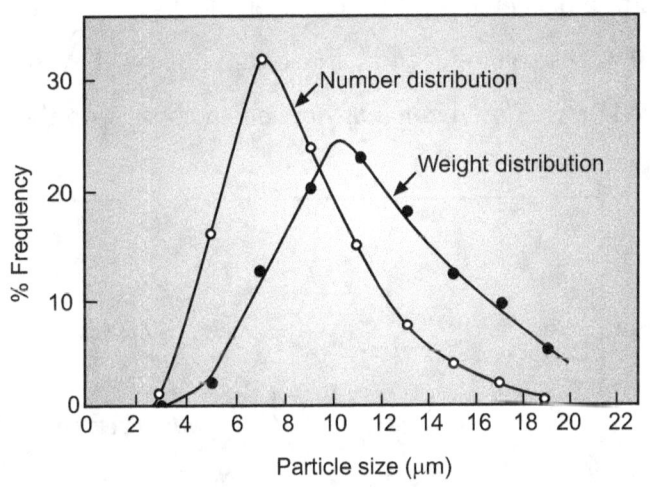

Fig. 4.8: Normal distribution curve for a powder. Data are taken from Table 4.4 column 5 and 7

4.5.3 Cumulative Percentage over or under a Particular Size Versus Particle Size (Fig. 4.9)

An alternative method of representing the data is to plot either the cumulative percentage over or under a particular size versus particle size. This has been done in Fig. 4.9 (based on Table 4.4, column 6 and 8) using the cumulative per cent undersize. A sigmodial curve results, with the mode being that particle size at the greatest slope.

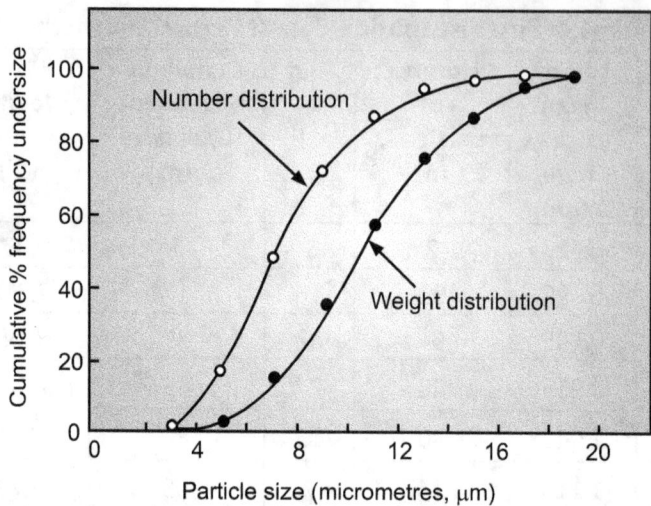

Fig. 4.9: Cumulative frequency plot of data in Table 4.4

4.5.4 Log-Normal Distribution

When the data in Fig. 4.8 (taken from Table 4.4) are plotted as frequency versus the logarithm of the particle diameter, a typical bell-shaped curve is frequently obtained. This is depicted in Fig. 4.10 [x axis-column 3 and y axis-column 5 and 7]. A size distribution, fitting this pattern is spoken of as a *log-normal distribution*, in contrast to the normal distribution shown in Fig. 4.7.

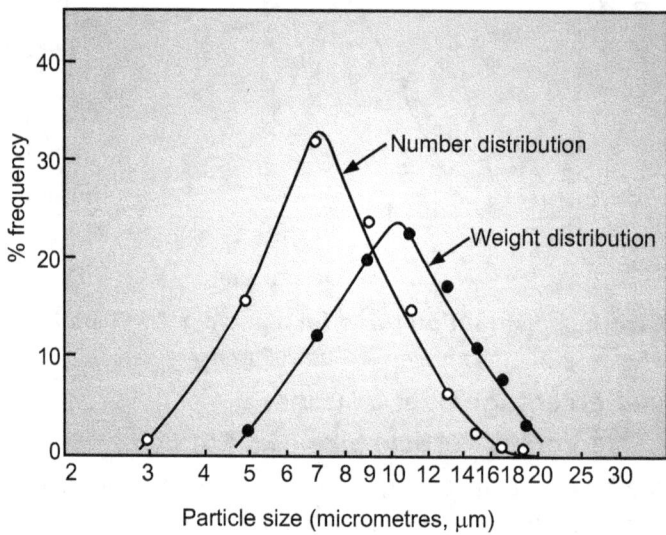

Fig. 4.10: Frequency distribution plot of data in Table 4.3 showing log-normal relation

4.5.5 Log-Probability Curve

When the logarithm of the particle size is plotted against the cumulative percent frequency on a probability scale, a linear relationship is observed (Fig. 4.11). Such a linear plot has the distinct advantage that we can now characterize a log-normal distribution curve by means of two parameters;

- Slope of the line and
- Reference point.

The reference point used is the logarithm of the particle size equivalent to 50% on the probability scale, i.e., the 50% size. This is known as the geometric mean diameter and is given the symbol d_g.

The slope is given by the geometric standard deviation, σ_g, which is the quotient of the ratio (84% undersize or 16% oversize)/(50% size) or (50% size)/(16% undersize or 84% oversize). This is simply the slope of the straight line in Fig. 4.11, for the number distribution data i.e. 7.1 µm and σ_g = 1.43.

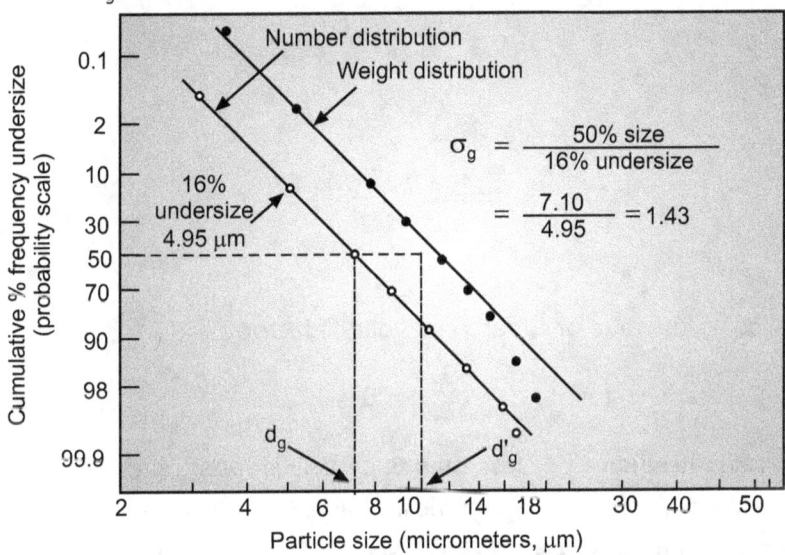

Fig. 4.11: Log Probability plot

4.6 PARTICLE SHAPE

Particle shape will influence the surface area, flow property, packing and compaction properties of the particles.

Shape of the particle is either spherical or asymmetric,

- A sphere has minimum surface area per unit volume.
- An asymmetric particle has greater surface area per unit volume.

The surface area or volume of a sphere and asymmetric particle can be written as:

Table 4.5: Surface area and volume of a sphere and asymmetric particle

	Surface area	Volume
Sphere	πd_s^2	$\dfrac{\pi d_s^3}{6}$
Asymmetric particle	$\alpha_s\, d_p^2$	$\alpha_v\, d_p^3$

Where, d_s and d_p are diameters of sphere and asymmetric particle respectively, α_s is surface area factor and α_v volume factor.

Solving for α_s and α_v by equating the appropriate properties (surface area and volume) provides:

$$\alpha_s = \frac{\pi d_s^2}{d_p^2} \quad \text{and} \quad \alpha_v = \frac{\pi d_s^3}{6 d_p^3} \qquad \text{... (4.18)}$$

When $d_s = d_p$

$$\alpha_s = \pi = 3.124$$

and

$$\alpha_v = \frac{\pi}{6} = \frac{3.124}{6} = 0.524 \qquad \text{... (4.19)}$$

Shape factor:

It is expressed as 'the ratio of surface and volume factor'.

$$\text{Shape factor} = \frac{\alpha_s}{\alpha_v} = \frac{3.124}{0.524} = 6 \qquad \text{... (4.20)}$$

If shape factors is equal to or less than 6; particle is spherical in shape, is and **If shape factor is more than 6**; particle is asymmetric in shape.

4.7 PARTICLE SURFACE AREA – METHOD

Surface area of a powder can be determined from particle size data.

Pharmaceutical Importance:

1. Particle size is inversely proportional to surface area.
2. The surface area of a particle plays an important role in flow and packaging properties of a powder.
3. Also dissolution and solubility of drug depend on the particle surface area. In this case, increase in surface area, increases the solubility of drugs.

Example:

(a) Bephenium hydroxynaphthoaie (an anthelmintic) is administered as a suspension. The I.P. prescribes the specific surface area limit of not less than 7000 cm^2/g. As the specific surface is reduced, the activity of the drug also falls because dissolution rate decreases.

(b) Griseofulvin, an antifungal antibiotic, should have the surface area of not less than 13000 to 17000 cm^2/g. If it is less, the absorption of the drug will fall.

Specific Surface Area:

Specific surface is defined as 'the surface area per unit weight (S_w) or unit volume (S_v) of the material'.

Determination of S_v:

$$S_v = \frac{\text{Surface area of particles}}{\text{Volume of particles}} = \frac{\text{No. of particles} \times \text{Surface area of each particle}}{\text{No. of particles} \times \text{Volume of each particle}} \quad \text{... (4.21)}$$

Substitute values from Table 4.5.

$$\therefore \qquad S_v = \frac{n\,\alpha_s\,d^2}{n\,\alpha_v\,d^3} = \frac{\alpha_s}{\alpha_v\,d} \quad \text{... (4.22)}$$

According to equation (4.20), $\dfrac{\alpha_s}{\alpha_v}$ = 6, therefore equation (4.22) can be written as,

$$S_v = \frac{6}{d} \quad \text{... (4.23)}$$

Determination of S_w:

$$S_w = \frac{\text{Surface area of particles}}{\text{Weight of particles}} = \frac{\text{No. of particles} \times \text{Surface area of each particle}}{\text{No. of particles} \times \text{Weight of each particle}}$$

$$= \frac{n\,\alpha_s\,d^2}{\text{No. of particles} \times \text{Density} \times \text{Volume}} \quad \text{... (4.24)}$$

Substitute values from Table 4.5.

$$\therefore \qquad S_w = \frac{n\,\alpha_s\,d_{vs}^2}{n\,\alpha_v\,d_{vs}^3\,\rho} = \frac{\alpha_s}{\alpha_v\,d_{vs}\,\rho} \quad \text{... (4.25)}$$

According to equation (4.20), α_s/α_v = 6, therefore equation (4.25) can be written as,

$$\therefore \qquad S_w = \frac{6}{d_{vs}\,\rho} \quad \text{... (4.26)}$$

Equations (4.23) and (4.26) accurately determine the surface area of nonporous particle. But these equations have certain limitations. This equation is not applicable for porous particles, because surface area of porous particle is greater than nonporous particle, when projected diameter is same.

Therefore alternative methods can be used for determination of surface area, these are following:

1. Air Adsorption method
2. Air Permeability method.

[I] Air Adsorption Method

This method is depending on adsorption of gas on particle surface.

Principle:

The gas adsorption method is a method for measuring the amount of gas adsorbed on the surface of a powder sample as a function of the pressure of the adsorbate gas, and is used to determine the specific surface area of a powder sample. Measurements are usually performed at the boiling point of liquid nitrogen (– 196°C).

When the gas is physically adsorbed by the powder sample, the following relationship holds; [This equation is already discussed in chapter 1, equation (1.46)].

$$\frac{P}{y(P_o - P)} = \frac{1}{y_m b} + \frac{b - P}{y_m b} \cdot \frac{P}{P_o} \qquad \dots (4.27)$$

Where,

P   :   Partial vapour pressure of adsorbate gas in equilibrium (kPa),

P_0 :   Saturated pressure of the adsorbate gas at – 196°C (kPa),

y   :   Volume of gas adsorbed at equilibrium (ml),

y_m :   The mass of gas that 1 gram of solid adsorbent can take up when monolayer is completed,

b   :   Constant, proportional to heat of adsorption and latent heat of condensation of subsequent layers.

This equation is called BET equation.

The specific surface area, S, is determined from y_m, the volume of gas adsorbed in a monolayer on the sample.

$$S = \frac{y_m \times N \times a}{m \times 22400} \qquad \dots (4.28)$$

Where,

S   :   Specific surface area (m²/g),

N   :   Avogadro constant,

a   :   Effective cross-sectional area of one adsorbate molecule (m²),

m   :   Mass of the test powder (g),

Specific surface area is generally expressed in units of m²/ g.

Either of the methods described below can be used to measure the gas adsorption.

Method:

In the volumetric method, the test powder is placed in a sample container with a known volume and the volume of gas adsorbed is determined from the change in pressure associated with the adsorption of gas on the surface of sample powder. Nitrogen is typically used as the adsorbate gas, and a gas such as krypton is preferred for samples with a small specific surface area.

Equipment:

The test equipment typically comprises a sample container, a gas supply unit, a gas mixing unit, a gas flow regulator, a gas concentration detector, and a Dewar vessel. The sample container is made from glass and is formed in a U-shape to allow smooth gas flow. The gas flow path can be sealed to form an airtight passage. There are two gas supply units; one for the adsorbate gas, and one for the diluent gas.

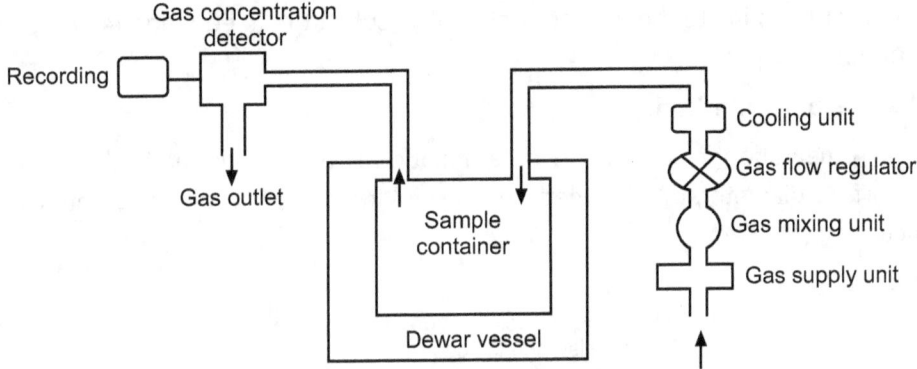

Fig. 4.12: Apparatus used for determination of specific surface area by air adsorption method

Procedure:

1. Precisely weigh the tared sample container.
2. Place a quantity of the test powder having a total surface area of at least 1 m³ in the sample container.
3. Perform pretreatment to remove any gases and vapours that have been physically adsorbed onto the sample surface, by outgassing the sample under reduced pressure. Heating may also be employed as long as there is no effect on the physical or chemical properties of the sample.
4. After the pretreatment is completed, precisely weigh the sample container with the sample and subtract the mass of the tared container measured previously, to obtain the mass of the test powder.
5. Take a fixed quantity of the adsorbate gas and introduce it into the sample container that has been chilled by immersion in liquid nitrogen.

6. The adsorbate gas is adsorbed on the powder sample.

7. The pressure decreases until gas/solid adsorption reaches to a new equilibrium.

8. The volume of gas adsorbed is calculated from the difference between the volume of adsorbate gas that was introduced and the volume of un-adsorbed gas remaining in the void volume.

9. The void volume is measured by using helium either before or after the adsorption measurements are performed.

10. For the multiple-point BET method, calculate the specific surface area by repeating 3 measurements or more of the volume adsorbed, under a relative equilibrium pressure of the adsorbate gas in the range from 0.05 to 0.30. For the single-point method, make one measurement of the volume adsorbed, under a relative pressure close to 0.30.

11. P, P_o and y can be obtained from the experiment and substituted in equation (4.27) in order to estimate the y_m. Then value of y_m substitute in equation (4.28) to estimate surface area.

[II] Air Permeability Method:

The instrumentation is simple and determination is quick. This method is also used to estimate surface diameter, d_s. This method is useful in controlling batch to batch variations in production of powders.

Principle:

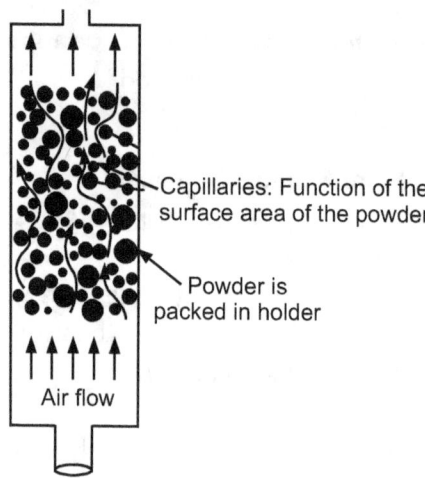

Fig. 4.13: Structural illustration of principle of air adsorption method

Powder is packed in the sample holder (see Fig. 4.13). In this packing, surface-surface contacts between particles appear as a series of capillaries. The surface of these capillaries is a function of the surface area of the powder. The air, when allowed to pass, travel through these capillaries and thus this method is related to surface area of powder. When air is allowed to pass through the powder bed at a constant pressure, the bed resists the flow of air. This results in a pressure drop. The greater the surface area per gram of the powder, S_w the greater the resistance to flow. The permeability of air for a given pressure drop is inversely proportional to specific surface.

The Kozeny-Carman equation is used to estimate the surface area by this method.

$$S_w^2 = \frac{A}{\eta V} \frac{\Delta Pt}{Kl} \frac{\varepsilon}{(1-\varepsilon)^2} \qquad \qquad ... (4.29)$$

Where

       A : Cross-sectional area of the bed (pack), cm^2

       ΔP : Pressure difference of the plug,

       t : Time of flow (seconds),

       l : Length of the sample holder, (cm)

       ε : Porosity of the powder,

       S_w : Surface area per gram of the powder (cm/g),

       η : Viscosity of the air (poise),

       K : Constant (5.0±0.5) that accounts the irregular capillaries,

       V : Volume of air flowing through the bed (cm^3).

Method:

Fisher subsieve size instrument is commercially available. Assembling of the apparatus is shown in Fig. 4.14. It consists of a sample tube containing the packed powder sample with one end connected to an air pump through a constant pressure regulator. The other end is attached to a calibrated manometer containing a suitable liquid of low viscosity and negligible vapour pressure.

The air pump builds up air pressure and allowed to flow through the packed powder in the sample tube. The flow of air is measured by the manometer. The level of the fluid in the manometer indicates the average diameter of the particles. Commercial equipment is standardized to eliminate the mathematical computation. Average particle diameter can be read from the calculator charts supplied with the equipment.

The porosity of the powder (ε) and viscosity of air (η) are estimated separately. A and l are constants represent sample holder. ΔP and V can be obtained from the experiment and substituted in equation (4.29) in order to estimate the surface area.

Following points are considered for accuracy in result:

1. Compression of powder in tube:

- When powder is loosely packed, there is less resistance to air and get accurate result.
- When powder is highly compress show great resistance to flow of air and can't get accurate result.

2. Irregularity of the capillaries:

Capillaries are not circular and are longer than the length of the bed.

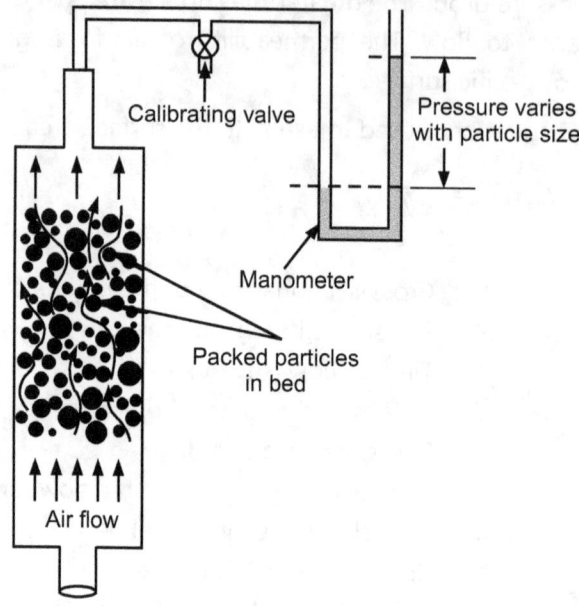

Fig. 4.14: Fisher subsieve size instrument

4.8 DERIVED PROPERTIES OF POWDERS

Size distribution and surface areas are the two fundamental properties of powders, there are, in addition to these, numerous derived properties that are based upon these fundamental properties.

Derived properties of powder enlist follow:

1. Porosity
2. Packing arrangement
3. Density
   (a) Bulk density
   (b) Tapped density
   (c) True density
   (d) Granule density
4. Bulkiness
5. Flow properties
6. Compaction

4.8.1 Porosity (Voids)

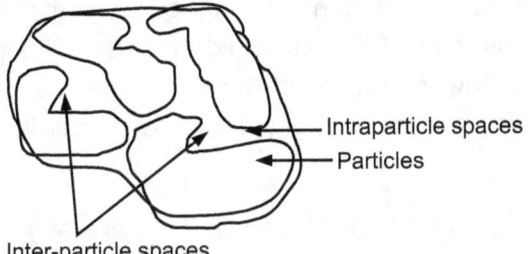

Bulk volume, V_b = Particles volume + Intraparticles spaces volume + Inter-particle spaces
True volume, V_p = Particles volume
Void volume, ε = Intraparticles spaces volume + Inter-particle spaces

Fig. 4.15: Particles arrangement

Bulk volume, V_b:

Suppose a powder is placed in a graduated cylinder and the total volume is noted. The volume occupied is known as the bulk volume, V_b.

V_b = Particles volume + Intraparticles space + Interparticles space

If the powder is non-porous, i.e., has no internal pores or capillary spaces, the bulk volume of the powder consists of the true volume of the solid particles plus the volume of the spaces between the particles.

True volume, V_p = Volume of particles itself (means excluding volume of pores and capillary).

Void volume, v:

The volume of the spaces, known as the void volume, v, is given by the equation,

$$v = V_b - V_p \qquad \qquad \text{... (4.30)}$$

The porosity or voids ε of the powder is defined as 'the ratio of the void volume to the bulk volume of the packing'.

$$\therefore \qquad \varepsilon = \frac{V_b - V_p}{V_b} = 1 - \frac{V_p}{V_b} \qquad \qquad \text{... (4.31)}$$

Porosity is frequently expressed in per cent,

$$\varepsilon = \frac{V_b - V_p}{V_b} \times 100 \qquad \qquad \text{... (4.32)}$$

Applications:

1. **Dissolution:** The surface area of porous particles is high. Dissolution rate of drug depend on the surface area. As surface area means porosity increases dissolution rate increases.

2. **Disintegration rate:** Drug is classified as porous and non-porous. Rate of disintegration of porous drug is high as compared to non-porous drug.

3. **Adsorption:** Charcoal is highly porous solid. Because of its porosity, it is used in poison treatment. It shows maximum adsorption of poison in GIT.

4. **Diffusion:** As porosity increases rate of diffusion also increases.

4.8.2 Packing Arrangements

The study of packing arrangement of particles is necessary in disintegration and dissolution of tablet.

The particles are in uniform sized spheres. Then one of the following packing arrangements is possible.

1. Closest or rhombohedral, and
2. Most open, loosest or cubic packing.

ε = 26 %   ε = 48 %

Particles closest packing   **Particles loose packing**

Fig. 4.16: Packing arrangement of powder

The theoretic porosity of a powder consisting of uniform spheres in closest packing is 26% and for loosest packing is 48%. The arrangements of spherical particles in closest and loosest packing are shown in Fig. 4.16.

There are three possibilities of particles arrangement according to shape and size distribution.

1. **Real powders: neither spherical in shape nor uniform in size.**
   - It is to be expected that the particles of ordinary powders may have any arrangement intermediate between closest and loose.
   - Porosities are in between 30 and 50%.

2. **If the particles are of greatly different sizes:**
   - The smaller particles sift between the larger particles means filling gap between particles. In preparation of tablet, granules are compressed with fine powder minimizes the voids spaces between particles.
   - Porosities are below 26%.

3. **In powders containing flocculates or aggregates:**
   - The formation of bridges and arches in the packing.
   - The porosity may be above the theoretic maximum of 48%.

4.8.3 Density of Powder

Since particles may be hard and smooth in one case and rough and spongy in another, one must express densities with great care.

Density is universally defined as 'weight per unit volume'.

The difficulty arises when one attempts to determine the volume of particles containing microscopic cracks, internal pores and capillary spaces.

The methods of determining the various densities are now discussed.

4.8.3.1 Bulk Density

The bulk density of a powder is the ratio of the mass of an untapped powder sample and its volume [Fig. 4.15].

$$\text{Bulk density, } \rho = \frac{\text{Mass of powder}}{\text{Bulk volume}}$$

Bulk volume V_b is already discussed in section porosity.

Unit: The bulk density is expressed in grams per millilitre (g/ml) although the international unit is kilogram per cubic metre (1 g/ml = 1000 kg/m^3). It may also be expressed in grams per cubic centimetre (g/cm^3).

The bulking properties of a powder are dependent upon the preparation, treatment and storage of the sample, i.e. how it was handled. The particles can be packed to have a range of bulk densities and, moreover, the slightest disturbance of the powder bed may result in a changed bulk density.

The bulk density depends on particle on particle size distribution, shape and cohesiveness of particles.

Procedure:

1. Pass a quantity of powder sufficient to complete the test through a sieve with apertures greater than or equal to 1.0 mm, if necessary, to break up agglomerates that may have formed during storage. This must be done gently to avoid changing the nature of the material.
2. Into a dry graduated cylinder of 250 ml (readable to 2 ml), gently introduce, without compacting, approximately 100 g of the test sample (m) weighed with 0.1% accuracy.
3. Carefully level the powder without compacting, if necessary, and read the unsettled bulk volume (V_b) to the nearest graduated unit.
4. Calculate the bulk density in (g/ml) using the formula m/V_b.
5. Generally, replicated determinations are desirable for the determination of this property.

Applications:

1. Bulk density helps in selection of proper size of a container, packing material and mixing apparatus.
2. According to bulk density, size of capsule determines lower bulk density, therefore big size capsule is required.
3. Bulk density is used to check uniformity of drug.

4.8.3.2 Tapped Density

The Tapped density of a powder is 'the ratio of the mass of a tapped powder sample and its volume including the contribution of the interparticulate void volume' [Fig. 4.15].

$$\text{Tapped density, } \rho = \frac{\text{Mass of powder}}{\text{Tapped volume}}$$

Tap volume, V_t = Particles Volume + Inter-Particles Volume

The tapped density is increased after mechanically tapping a container containing the powder sample as compared to bulk density.

The tapped density is obtained by mechanically tapping a graduated measuring cylinder or vessel containing the powder sample. After observing the initial powder volume or mass, the measuring cylinder or vessel is mechanically tapped, and volume or mass readings are taken until little further volume or mass change is observed.

Apparatus:

The apparatus (Fig. 4.17) consists of the following:

(a) 250 ml graduated cylinder (readable to 2 ml) with a mass of 220 ± 44 g; and a settling apparatus capable of producing, in 1 minute, either nominally 250 ± 15 taps from a height of 3 ± 0.2 mm, or nominally 300 ± 15 taps from a height of 14 ± 2 mm. The support for the graduated cylinder, with its holder, has a mass of 450 ± 10 g.

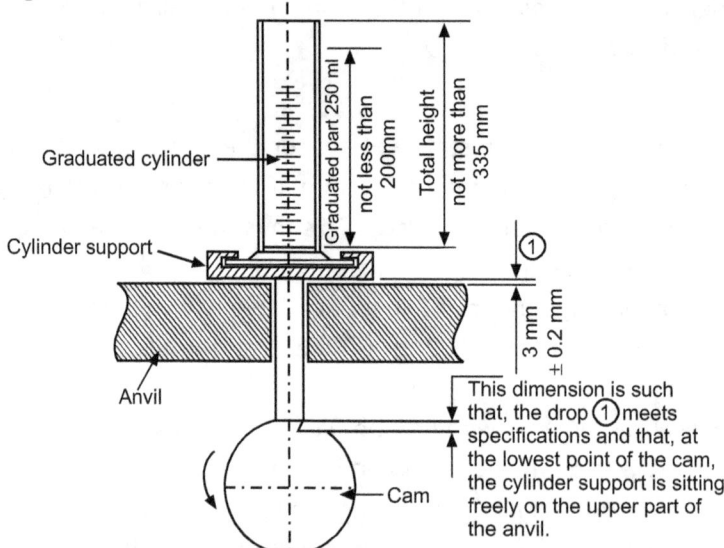

Fig. 4.17: Tapping apparatus

Procedure:

1. Proceed as described above for the determination of the bulk volume (V_b).
2. Secure the cylinder in the holder.
3. Carry out 10, 500 and 1250 taps on the same powder sample and read the corresponding volumes V_{10}, V_{500} and V_{1250} to the nearest graduated unit. If the difference between V_{500} and V_{1250} is less than or equal to 2 ml, V_{1250} is the tapped volume.
4. If the difference between V_{500} and V_{1250} exceeds 2 ml, repeat in increments such as 1250 taps, until the difference between succeeding measurements is less than or equal to 2 ml.
5. Fewer taps may be appropriate for some powders, when validated.
6. Calculate the tapped density (g/ml) using the formula m/V_t in which V_t is the final tapped volume.
7. If it is not possible to use a 100 g test sample, use a reduced amount and a suitable 100 ml graduated cylinder (readable to 1 ml) weighing 130 ± 16 g and mounted on a holder weighing 240 ± 12 g. The modified test conditions are specified in the expression of the results.

4.8.3.3 True Density

True density, ρ_p, is the density of the actual solid material.

True volume, V_p = Particle volume itself. (Excluded volume of pores and intra-particles space)

Determination of True Density:

1. Helium densitometer: For porous and non-porous solid.
2. Liquid displacement method: For non-porous solid.

1. Helium densitometer:

This method is used to determine the true volume of porous and non-porous solid.

Helium gas is selected for this method because:

- It cannot be adsorbed on surface of solid.
- It can be easily penetrated into void of particles.

Method:

1. The volume of the empty apparatus (dead space) is first determined by introducing a known quantity of helium.

    V_1 = Volume of empty apparatus (Bulk volume of powder)
2. A weighed amount of powder (M) is then introduced into the sample tube.
3. Adsorbed gases are removed from the powder by an out-gassing procedure.

4. Helium is again introduced.

5. The pressure is read on a mercury manometer, and by application of the gas laws, the volume of helium surrounding the particles and penetrating into the small cracks and pores is calculated.

V_2 = Volume occupied by helium in pores and intra-particle space between particles (volume of voids)

6. The difference between the volume of helium filling the empty apparatus and the volume of helium in the presence of the powder sample yields the volume occupied by the powder.

$V_p = V_1 - V_2$

7. Knowing the weight of the powder, one is then able to calculate the true density.

2. Liquid Displacement Method:

This method is used to determine the true volume of non-porous solid.

Obtained density by this method is lower than the helium displacement method, because liquid such as water and ethanol cannot occupy the pores of particles.

Select the liquid in which powder is insoluble and heavy.

Method: Pycnometer or specific gravity bottle may be used:

1. Weigh the empty pycnometer, W_1
2. Then fill solid in pycnometer and weigh the pycnometer, W_2
3. ∴ Weight of solid, $W_3 = W_2 - W_1$
4. Then weight of pycnometer with solid and filled with liquid, W_4
5. Weight of liquid displaced by solid = $W_4 - W_2$
6. True density is the weight of the powder divided by the weight of the liquid it displaces,

$$V_t = \frac{W_2 - W_1,}{W_4 - W_2} \qquad \text{... (4.33)}$$

For example, if the weight of a sample of glass beads is 5.0 grams and the weight of water required to fill a pycnometer is 50.0 grams, then the total weight would be 55.0 grams. When the beads are immersed in the water and the weight is 53.0 grams or a displacement is of 2.0 grams of water, the density is 5.0 /2.0 = 2.5.

4.8.3.4 Granular Density (ρ_g)

The volume of the particles together with their intra-particle spaces then gives the granule volume, and from knowledge of the powder weight, the granular density is obtained.

$$\rho_g = \frac{\text{Granule weight}}{\text{Granule volume}}$$

Granular density may be determined by a method similar to the liquid displacement method. Mercury is employed since it fills the void spaces but fails to penetrate into the internal pores of the particles.

A measure of **true density** was obtained by highly compressing the powders. The samples were compressed to 100,000 lb/sq. inch, and the resulting tablets were weighed. The volumes of the tablets were computed after measuring the tablet dimensions with calipers. The weight of the tablet divided by the volume then gave the "true" or high-compression density.

Intra-particles porosity of granules:

It is determined by using values of granular volume and true volume.

$$\varepsilon_{\text{intra-particle}} = \frac{V_g - V_p}{V_g} = 1 - \frac{V_p}{V_g} \qquad \text{... (4.34)}$$

Therefore,

$$\varepsilon_{\text{intra-particle}} = 1 - \frac{W/\rho_p}{W/\rho_g} = 1 - \frac{\rho_g}{\rho_p} \qquad \text{... (4.35)}$$

4.8.4 Bulkiness

Bulk volume of powder is the reciprocal of bulk density, often called as bulkiness or bulk.

It is an important consideration in the packaging of powders. The bulk density of calcium carbonate may vary from 0.1 to 1.3, and the lightest or bulkiest type would require a container about 13 times larger than that needed for the heaviest variety.

Bulkiness increases with a decrease in particle size. In a mixture of materials of different sizes, however, the smaller particles sift between the larger ones and tend to reduce the bulkiness.

4.8.5 Flow Properties

The flow properties of powder play an important role in the manufacturing of tablet or capsules. Weight variation of tablets is common problem in tablet manufacturing and is mainly due to poor or irregular flow of powder from the hopper to the die. A flow property depends on particle size, shape, porosity and density, and surface texture.

Following methods are used to measure the flow of powder material.

4.8.5.1 Angle of Repose

Angle of repose (θ) is a characteristic related to inter-particulate friction or resistance to movement between particles.

Angle of repose is the maximum angle possible between the surface of a pile of powder and the horizontal plane.

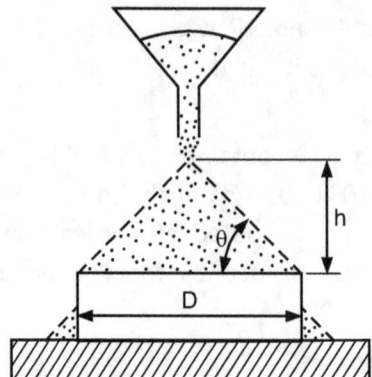

Fig. 4.18: Determination of angle of repose

Method (Fixed funnel, standing cone method)

1. A homogenous sample; representative of the bulk powder is used for the study.
2. The ring stand with funnel is placed on a sheet of plane paper as shown in Fig. 4.18.
3. The height (h) of the tip of the funnel is adjusted to 2-4 cm above the plane paper.
4. The sample powder is fed into the funnel slowly.
5. A pile of the powder will be formed on the paper. When the tip of the powder cone formed on the paper enters the funnel nozzle, the feeding of powder in the funnel is stopped.
6. A circle is drawn on the paper around the boundaries of the cone formed on the paper.
7. The powder is removed from the paper.
8. Using the calipers or ruler, the diameter of the cone is measured at four different points. The average of these values is recorded as diameter of the cone (d). The radius (r) is calculated by dividing the diameter by 2.
9. The angle of repose is calculated using formula,

$$\tan \theta = \frac{h}{r}$$

$$\theta = \tan^{-1}\frac{h}{r} \qquad\qquad \dots (4.36)$$

One can determine the flow property of any powder sample using corresponding values of angle of repose given in Table 4.6.

Table 4.6: Flow properties and corresponding angle of repose

Flow property	Angle of repose (°)
Excellent	25-30
Good	31-35
Fair: Aid not needed	36-40
Passable: may hang-up	41-45
Poor: must agitate and vibrate	46-55
Very poor	56-65
Very, very poor	More than 66

4.8.5.2 Compressibility Index and Hausner Ratio

1. Because the interparticulate interactions influencing the bulking properties of a powder are also the interactions that interfere with powder flow, a comparison of the bulk and tapped densities can give a measure of the relative importance of these interactions in a given powder.

2. Such a comparison is often used as an index of the ability of the powder to flow. For example, the Compressibility Index or the Hausner Ratio.

3. **In a free-flowing powder,** such interactions are less significant, and the bulk and tapped densities will be closer in value.

4. **For poorer flowing materials,** there are frequently greater interparticulate interactions, and a greater difference between the bulk and tapped densities will be observed.

5. These differences are reflected in the Compressibility Index and the Hausner Ratio. Compressibility Index is also called as Carr's Index.

$$\text{Compressibility index} = \frac{V_b - V_t}{V_t} \times 100$$

V_b = Bulk volume

V_t = Tapped volume

Hausner Ratio:

$$\text{Hausner Ratio} = \frac{V_b}{V_t}$$

The Carr's index and Hausner ratios with the corresponding flow properties are given in Table 4.7.

Table 4.7: Flow properties and corresponding compressibility index and Hausner ratio

Compressibility Index (%)	Flow Character	Hausner Ratio
10	Excellent	1.00 – 1.11
11-15	Good	1.12 – 1.18
16-20	Fair	1.19 – 1.25
21-25	Passable	1.26 – 1.34
26-31	Poor	1.35 – 1.45
32-37	Very poor	1.46 – 1.59
>38	Very, very poor	> 1.60

4.8.5.3 Factors Affecting and Improvement of Flowability

1. **Alteration of particle size and size distribution:**

   Factor:

   - Coarse particles are generally less cohesive than fine particles, means fine particles affect the flowability of powder.
   - Also ununiform size distribution affects flowability of powder.

Improvement:
- The size distribution can also be altered to improve flowability by removing a proportion of the fine particle fraction.
- Increasing the proportion of coarser particles, such as through granulation.

2. **Alteration of particle shape or texture:**

   Factor:
   - In general, for a given particle size, more spherical particles have better flow properties than more irregular particles.
   - The surface texture of particles may also influence powder flowability, as particles with very rough surfaces will be more cohesive and have a greater tendency to interlock than smooth-surfaced particles.

   Improvement:
   - The process of spray-drying can be used to produce near-spherical excipients. For example, spray-dried lactose.
   - The shape and texture of particles can also be altered by control of production methods, such as crystallization conditions.

3. **Alteration of surface forces:**

   Factor:
   - Electrostatic charge affects flowability of powder.

   Improvement:
   - Reduction of electrostatic charge can improve powder flowability and this can be achieved by altering process conditions to reduce friction contact. For example, Electrostatic charges in powder containers can be prevented or discharged by efficient earth connections.

4. **Moisture content:**

   Factor:
   - The moisture content of particles is of so importance to powder flowability, as adsorbed surface moisture films tend to reduces flowability.

   Improvement:
   - In cases where moisture content is excessive, powders should be dried and, if hygroscopic, stored and processed under low-humidity conditions.
   - A small proportion of very fine magnesium oxide may be used as a flow activator. Used in this way, magnesium oxide appears to disrupt the continuous film of adsorbed water surrounding the moist particles.
   - The use of silicone-treated powder, such as silicone-coated talc or sodium bicarbonate, may also be beneficial in improving the flowability of moist or hygroscopic powder.

5. **Use vibration-assisted hopper:**

   Factor:
   - In cases where the powder arch strength within a hopper is greater than the stress due to gravitational effects, powder flow will be interrupted or prevented.

Improvement:

- Use vibrating hopper, where arching or bridging occur within hopper. Both the amplitude and the frequency of vibration can be altered to produce the desired effect.

6. Use force feeder

Factor:

- The flow of powders that discharge irregularly or flood out of hoppers.

Improvement:

- It can be improved by fitting vibrating baffles, known as live-bottom feeders, at the base of the conical section within a hopper,

Other Flow Improvement techniques (Formulation additive)

Flow activators are commonly referred to pharmaceutical as *'glidants'* although some also have lubricant or antiadherent properties. Flow activators improve the flowability of powders by reducing adhesion and cohesion.

A flow activator with an exceptionally high specific surface area is colloidal silicon dioxide, which may act by reducing the bulk density of tightly packed powders.

Colloidal silicon dioxide also improve a flowability of formulations, even those containing glidants, although in some cases it can causes flooding.

Commonly used glidants are; Magnesium stearate, talc, starch etc.

4.8.6 Compaction: Compressed Tablets

The behaviour of powders under compression is significant in pharmaceutical tableting.

There are examples of behaviour of powder after compression, these are:

- **Closest packing:** When powders were compacted under a pressure of about 5 kg/cm^2, the porosities of the powders composed of rigid particles (For example, sodium carbonate).
- **Dilatant effect:** Hence, these powders were dilatant, i.e., they showed an unexpected expansion, rather than contraction, under the influence of stress.
- **Deformation effect:** In the case of soft and spongy particles (e.g. kaolin), however, the particles are deformed on compression, and the porosities were lower than after tapping the powder down to its condition of closest packing.

Effect of compression force on sulfathiazole tablets

1. The effect of compression force on specific surface area, granule density, porosity, tablet hardness, and disintegration time of sulfathiazole tablets is shown in Fig. 4.19.
2. The specific surface of a sulfathiazole tablet granulation, determined by the BET method, increased to a maximum and then decreased.
3. The initial increase in surface area can be attributed to the formation of new surfaces as the primary crystalline material is fragmented.
4. While the decrease in specific surface beyond a compression force of 2500 pounds is presumably due to cold bonding between the unit particles.
5. It was also observed that porosity decreased and density increased as a linear function of the logarithm of the compression force, except at the higher force levels.

6. As the compression is increased, so the tablet hardness and fracture resistance also rise.

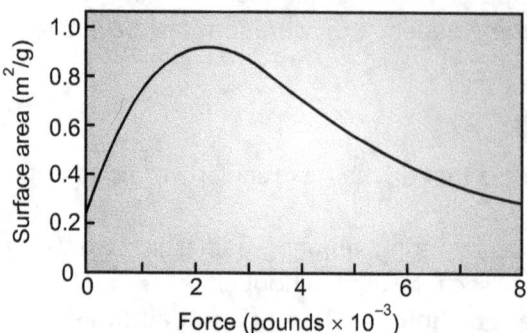

Fig. 4.19: The influence of compressional force on the specific surface of sulfathiazole granulation

QUESTIONS

1. **Short Answer Questions (3 Marks):**
   1. Define true density, granular density, bulk density of powder.   **[SPPU-2015]**
   2. List four methods to improve flow properties of granules and powders. **[SPPU-2015]**
   3. Explain method of contact angle and what is its application.
      [SPPU-2015, 2013 and 2012]
   4. Describe optical microscopy for particle size determination.   **[SPPU-2015]**
   5. Explain pharmaceutical importance of particle size and size distribution.**[SPPU-2013]**
   6. Define and differentiate between fundamental and derived properties. **[SPPU-2013]**
   7. Write application of coulter-counter apparatus.   **[SPPU-2012]**
   8. Write application of micromeritics.   **[SPPU-2011]**
   9. Write various types of equivalent spherical diameter.
   10. What is particle number and weight?
   11. What is specific surface area? What it is importance in pharmacy?
   12. Define porosity. What are its applications in pharmacy?

2. **Medium Answer Questions (5 Marks):**
   1. Explain determination of true density and granular density.   **[SPPU-2015]**
   2. Write factors affecting flow.   **[SPPU-2012]**
   3. Explain particle size distribution.   **[SPPU-2012]**
   4. Write methods for determining surface area.   **[SPPU-2010]**
   5. Write note on coulter-counter apparatus.

3. **Long Answer Questions (10 Marks):**
   1. Enlist and explain various methods for particle size determination. Give the significance of micromeritics studies in pharmacy.   **[SPPU-2015, 2013 and 2011]**
   2. Enumerate the derived properties of powders and how they are evaluated?
      [SPPU-2014, 2013 and 2011]
   3. What is specific surface of particle? How is surface area of a powder sample determined? What are its applications?   **[SPPU-2011 and 2012]**

■■■

Chapter **5**...

Colloids

Syllabus ...

(A) Introduction and Types, Optical, Kinetic and Electrical Properties of Colloids, Electrical Double Layer, Nernst and Zeta potential, Donnan Membrane Equilibrium.

(B) Protective Colloids, Stabilization of Colloidal System, DLVO Theory, Schulz Hardy Rule, Hoffmeister Series, Applications in Pharmacy.

5.1 INTRODUCTION

Solutions play an important role in our life. A large number of substances such as milk, butter, cheese, cream, coloured gems, boot polish, rubber and ink also play an important role in our daily life. They are also solutions of another kind. They are colloidal solutions.

Thomas Graham (1861) studied the ability of dissolved substances to diffuse into water across a permeable membrane. He observed that crystalline substances such as sugar, urea, and sodium chloride passed through the membrane, while others like glue, gelatin and gum arabic did not. The former he called **crystalloids** and the latter **colloids.**

The term colloid has been derived from two terms, namely *kolla* and *eidos*. '*kolla*' means glue and '*eidos*' means like i.e. glue-like. The size of the particles in colloidal solutions is bigger than the size of particles present in crystalloid solutions such as sugar or salt in water.

5.2 DISTINCTION BETWEEN A TRUE SOLUTION, COLLOIDAL SOLUTION AND COARSE DISPERSION

Solution of sugar in water is homogeneous but in milk it is not homogeneous. When closely looked at milk, oil droplets floating in it are seen. Thus, although it appears to be homogenous it is actually heterogeneous in nature. The nature of the solution formed depends upon the size of the solute particles.

(a) **True solution:** If the size of the solute particles is less than 1 nm. E.g. Sugar solution.

(b) **Colloidal solution:** The size is between 1 to 1000 nm. E.g. Milk.

(c) **Coarse dispersion:** When the size of solute particles is greater than 1000 nm. E.g. Suspension and emulsion.

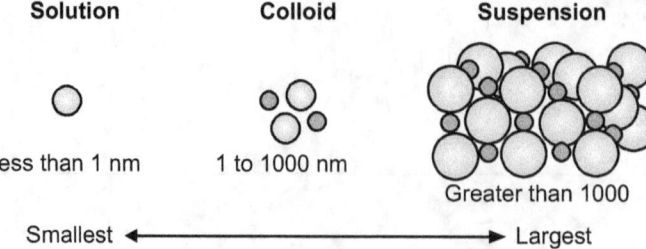

Fig. 5.1: Partials size in various system

Therefore we may conclude that colloidal solution is an intermediate state between true solution and coarse dispersion (Table 5.1).

Table 5.1: Some important properties of true solutions, colloid and suspensions

Sr. No.	Name of Property	True Solution	Colloid Solution	Suspension
1.	Size	Size of properties is less than 1 nm.	Size of particles is between 1 nm and 1000 nm.	Size of particles is greater than 1000 nm.
2.	Filterability	Pass through ordinary filter paper and also through animal membrane.	Pass through ordinary filter paper but not through animal membrane.	Do not pass through filter paper or animal membrane.
3.	Settling	Particles do not settle down on keeping.	Particles do not settle down on their own but can be made to settle down by centrifugation.	Particles settle down on their own under gravity.
4.	Visibility	Particles are invisible to the naked eye as well as under a microscope.	Particles are invisible to the naked eye but their scattering effect can be observed with the help of a microscope.	Particles are visible to the naked eye.
5.	Separation	The solute and solvent cannot be separated by ordinary filteration or by ultra filteration.	The solute and solvent cannot be separated by ordinary filteration but can be separated by ultra-filteration.	The solute and solvent can be separated by ordinary filteration.
6.	Diffusion	Diffuse quickly.	Diffuse slowly.	Do not diffuse.

5.3 PHASES OF COLLOIDAL SOLUTION

Colloidal solutions are heterogeneous in nature and always consist of at least two phases: the **dispersed phase** and the **dispersion medium**.

1. **Dispersed Phase:** It is the substance present in small proportion and consists of colloidal size particles (1 to 1000 nm).

2. **Dispersion Medium:** It is the medium in which the colloidal particles are dispersed.

For example, in a colloidal solution of sulphur in water, sulphur particles constitute the 'dispersed phase' and water is the 'dispersion medium'.

Each of the two phases namely, dispersed phase and dispersion medium can be solid, liquid or gas. Thus, different types of colloidal solutions are possible depending upon the physical state of the two phases. Different types of colloidal solutions and their examples are shown in Table 5.2. Gases cannot form a colloidal solution between themselves, because they form homogenous mixtures.

Table 5.2: Types of colloidal solutions

Sr. No.	Dispersed Phase	Dispersion Medium	Type of Colloidal Solution	Examples
1.	Solid	Solid	Solid solution	Gemstones
2.	Solid	Liquid	Sol	Paints, muddy water, gold sol, starch sol, arsenious sulphide sol.
3.	Solid	Gas	Aerosol of solids	Smoke, dust in air
4.	Liquid	Solid	Gel	Jellies, Cheese
5.	Liquid	Liquid	Emulsion	Milk, Cream
6.	Liquid	Gas	Aerosol	Mist, fog, cloud
7.	Gas	Solid	Solid foam	Foam rubber, pumice stone
8.	Gas	Liquid	Foam	Forth, whipped cream

Out of the various types of colloidal solutions listed above, the most common are **sols** (solid in liquid type), **gels** (liquid in solid type) and **emulsions** (liquid in liquid type). If the dispersion medium is water then the 'sol' is called a **hydrosol**; and if the dispersion medium is alcohol then the 'sol' is called an **alcosol**.

5.4 CLASSIFICATION OF COLLOIDS

Colloidal solutions can be classified depending upon the interaction between dispersed phase and the dispersion medium. Colloidal solutions are classified into three categories:

   (a) Lyophilic colloids
   (b) Lyophobic colloids
   (c) Associated colloids

5.4.1 Lyophilic Colloids

1. The word Lyophilic means solvent lover. Lyophilic colloidal solutions are those in which the dispersed phases have a great affinity (or love) for the dispersion medium.
2. The dispersion media forms a sheath around the colloidal particles and solvates. This makes the dispersion thermodynamically stable.
3. Therefore, such solutions are easily formed simply by bringing dispersed phase and dispersion medium in direct contact with each other.
4. However, these colloidal solutions have an important property i.e. they are reversible in nature. This means that once lyophilic colloidal solution has been formed then dispersed phase and dispersion medium can be separated easily. Once separated, these can again be formed by remixing the two phases. These sols are quite stable.
5. If water is used as dispersion medium then it is termed as hydrophilic colloid.
6. Substances like gum, gelatin, starch etc. when mixed with suitable dispersion medium, directly pass into colloidal state and form colloidal solution.

5.4.2 Lyophobic Colloids

1. The word Lyophobic means solvent hating. Lyophobic colloidal solutions are those in which the dispersed phase has no affinity for the dispersion medium.
2. These are stable because of the presence of charge on particles. The like charge on partials keeps them away from each other and are distributed uniformly on account of repulsive force.
3. However, solvent sheath surrounding the particle is absent. Therefore, this dispersion is thermodynamically unstable.
4. These sols can be readily precipitated and once precipitated they have little tendency to go back into the colloidal state. Thus, these sols are irreversible in nature.
5. Also they are not very stable and require a stabilizing agent to remain in the colloidal form.
6. In case water is used as dispersion medium it is called as hydrophobic sol.
7. These sols have to be prepared by special methods.
8. Metals like Au, Ag and their hydroxides or sulphides etc., when simply mixed with dispersion medium do not pass directly into colloidal state.

5.4.3 Associated Colloids

Associated or amphiphilic colloids form the third group in this classification. Associated colloids is the solution of surfactant or amphiphilic molecules. As we have seen in Chapter 1, in Article Surfactant (Refer Article 1.5.1, from Chapter 1). In this it includes structure of surfactant, CMC and micelle formation.

Example:

Soap is an example. Soap is sodium salt of long chain fatty acid RCOONa. When put in water, soap forms $RCOO^-$ (insoluble tail) and Na^+ (hydrophilic head). These $RCOO^-$ ions associate themselves around dirt particles as shown below forming a micelle (Fig. 5.2).

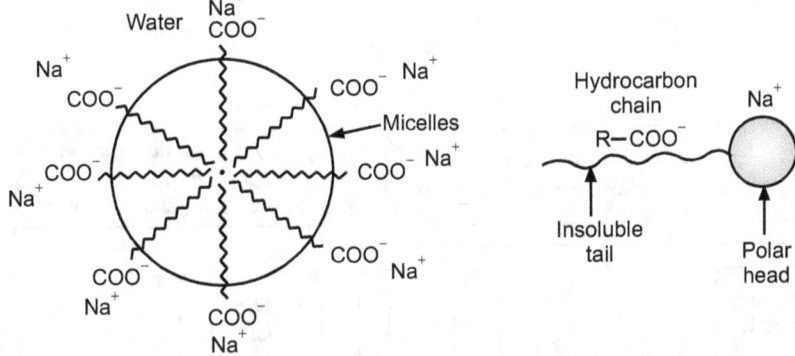

Fig. 5.2: Aggregation of RCOO⁻ ions to from micelles

Table 5.3: Distinguish between types of colloidal dispersion

Property	Lyophilic Colloids	Lyophobic Colloids	Association Colloids
Dispersed phase	Mostly organic molecules	Largely inorganic particles	Aggregation of surface active agents
Nature of interaction	Stronger, solvent sheath around particle	Little interaction	Aggregates are solvated
Presence of charge	Less charged, but solvated	High charged	Charged micelles, but solvated
Method of preparation	Readily form sol	Special methods are required	Readily form when concentration is equal to CMC
Viscosity of the dispersion	Higher than that of medium alone	Nearly same as the dispersion medium	Viscosity increases, but not appreciably
Presence of electrolytes			
Low concen-trations	Stable	Unstable (coagulation) stable	Stable precipitates
High concen-trations	Coacervation precipitates		
Reversibility	Reversible	Irreversible	Reversible

5.5 METHODS OF PREPARATION

As discussed earlier, the lyophilic sols can be prepared directly by mixing the dispersed phase with the dispersion medium. For example, colloidal solutions of starch, gelatine, gum etc. are prepared by simply dissolving these substances in hot water. Similarly, a colloidal sol of cellulose nitrate is obtained by dissolving it in alcohol.

However, lyophobic colloids cannot be prepared by **direct method**.

Hence, two types of methods are used for preparing lyophobic colloids. These are;

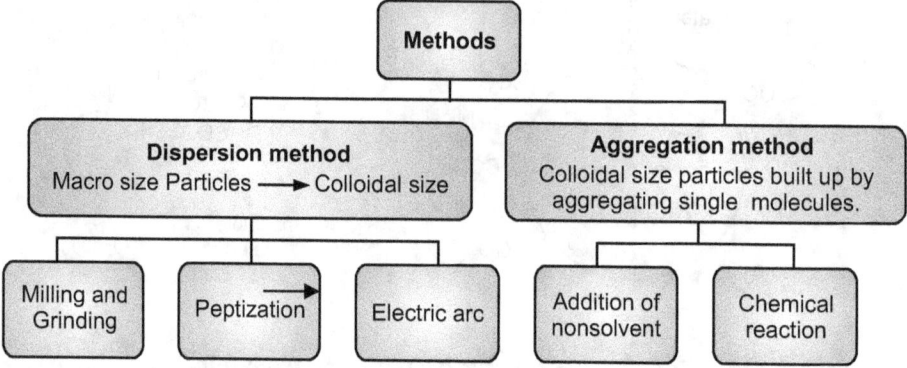

5.5.1 Dispersion Method

The general principle involved in mechanical dispersion is conversion of macro size particles in colloidal size.

5.5.1.1 Milling and Grinding (Colloidal Mill)

The substance to be dispersed is finely ground by usual methods. It is then shaken with the dispersion medium which gives a coarse suspension. Further size reduction is achieved by a colloidal mill.

Colloidal mill: The mill consists of two steel discs having a very small clearance between them. These discs are rotated at high speeds in opposite directions. When a suspension is allowed to pass through these discs, the coarse particles are broken down into smaller particles. This process is repeated until the desired size of dispersion is obtained. Examples are colloidal kaolin and zinc oxide. (Fig. 5.3)

Sometimes, grinding the substance preferably in the presence of some stabilizers facilitates the formation of a fine state of subdivision. For example, colloidal sulfur is made by grinding sulfur with sucrose or lactose. Other stabilizing agents are gums, gelatin, soaps etc.

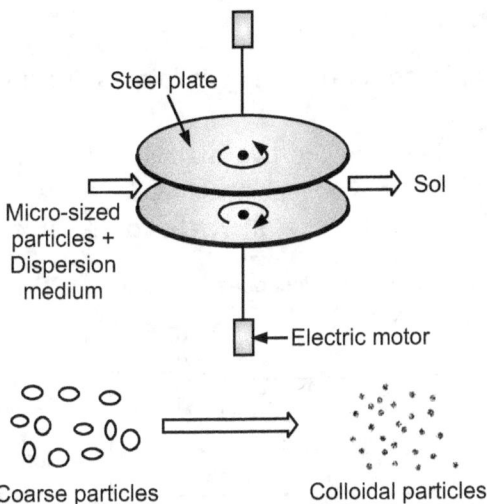

Fig. 5.3: Colloidal mill

5.5.1.2 Peptization

Peptization is the process of converting a freshly prepared precipitate into colloidal form by the addition of a suitable electrolyte. The electrolyte is called **peptising agent.**

For example; when ferric chloride is added to a precipitate of ferric hydroxide, ferric hydroxide gets converted into reddish brown coloured colloidal solution.

This is due to preferential adsorption of cations of the electrolyte by the precipitate. When $FeCl_3$ is added to $Fe(OH)_3$, Fe^{3+} ions from $FeCl_3$ are adsorbed by $Fe(OH)_3$ particles. Thus, the $Fe(OH)_3$ particles acquire + ve charge and they start repelling each other forming a colloidal solution. [Fig. 5.4]

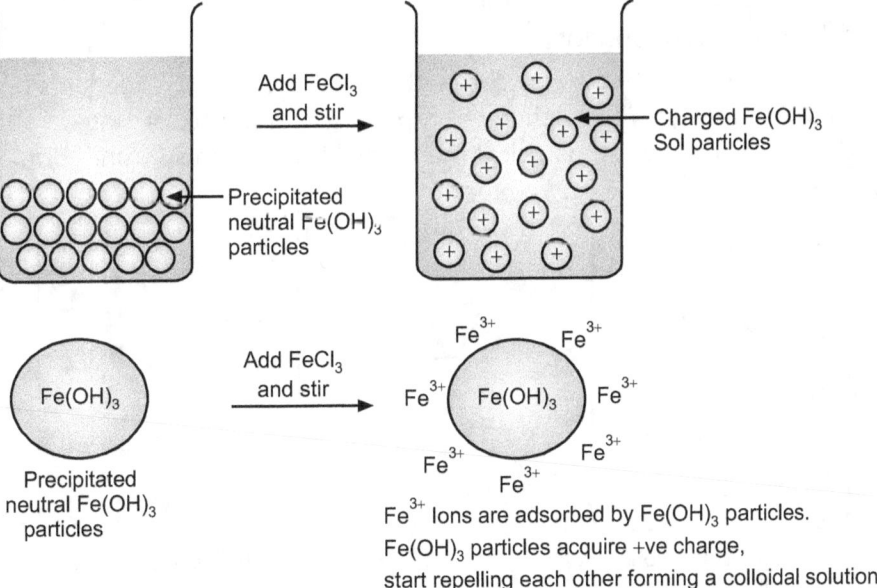

Fig. 5.4: Peptization process

5.5.1.3 Electric Arc

These methods are employed for obtaining colloidal solutions of metals like gold, silver, platinum etc. (Fig. 5.5)

An electric arc is struck between the two metallic electrodes placed in a container of water. The intense heat of the arc converts the metal into vapours, which are condensed immediately in the cold water bath. This results in the formation of particles of colloidal size.

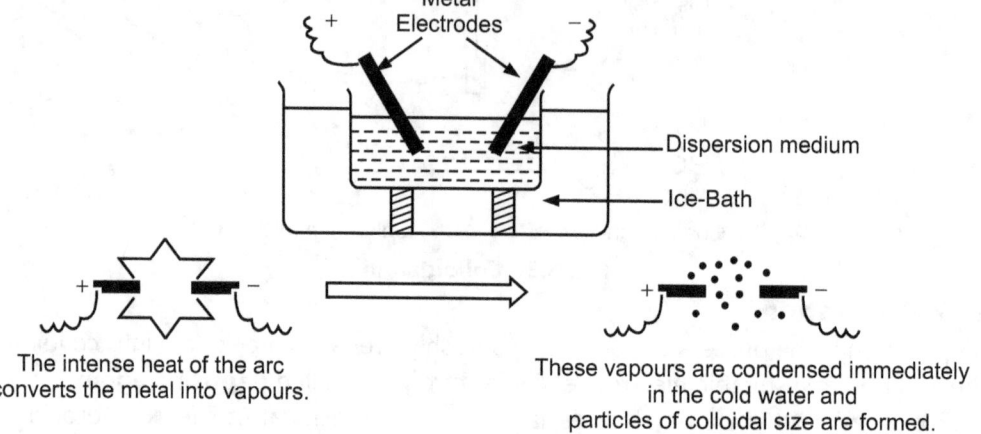

The intense heat of the arc converts the metal into vapours.

These vapours are condensed immediately in the cold water and particles of colloidal size are formed.

Fig. 5.5: Electric arc method

5.5.2 Aggregation Method

These methods consist of **chemical reactions or change of solvent** whereby the atoms or molecules of the dispersed phase appearing first, coalesce or aggregate to form colloidal particles.

5.5.2.1 Addition of Nonsolvent

Sulphur is soluble in alcohol. A concentrated alcoholic solution of sulphur is poured into an excess amount of water. The sulphur which present in a molecular state in alcohol gets precipitated out as finely divided particles. These particles grow rapidly and form a colloidal dispersion.

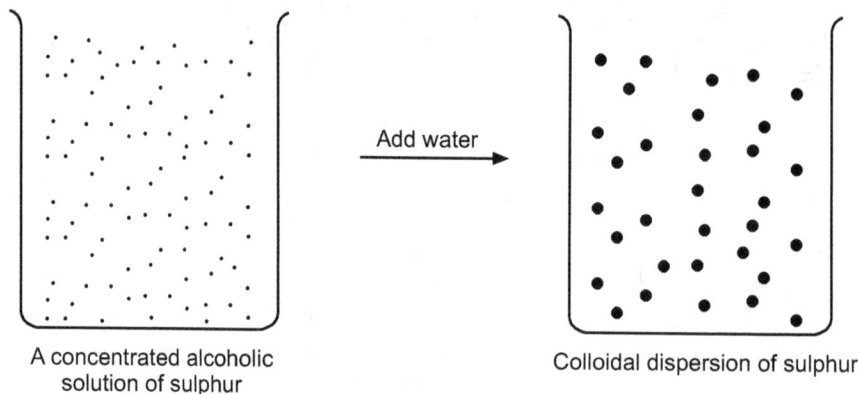

A concentrated alcoholic solution of sulphur

Add water

Colloidal dispersion of sulphur

Fig. 5.6: Preparation of sulphur solution

5.5.2.2 Chemical Reaction

(a) **Double Decomposition:** An arsenic sulphide (As_2S_3) sol is prepared by passing a slow stream of hydrogen sulphide gas through a cold solution of arsenious oxide (As_2O_3). This is continued till the yellow colour of the sol attains maximum intensity.

$$As_2O_3 + 3H_2S \longrightarrow As_2S_3 \text{ (sol)} + 3H_2O$$

Excess hydrogen sulphide (electrolyte) is removed by passing in a stream of hydrogen.

(b) **Reduction:** Silver sols and gold sols can be obtained by treating dilute solutions of silver nitrate or gold chloride with organic reducing agents like tannic acid or methanal (HCHO).

$$AgNO_3 + \text{Tannic acid} \longrightarrow \text{Ag sol}$$

$$AuCl_3 + \text{Tannic acid} \longrightarrow \text{Au sol}$$

(c) **Oxidation:** A sol of sulphur is produced by passing hydrogen sulphide into a solution of sulphur dioxide.

$$2H_2S + SO_2 \longrightarrow 2H_2O + S \downarrow$$

(d) **Hydrolysis:** Sols of the hydroxides of iron, chromium and aluminium are readily prepared by the hydrolysis of salts of the respective metals. In order to obtain a red sol of ferric hydroxide, a few drops of 30% ferric chloride solution is added to a large volume of almost boiling water and stirred with a glass rod.

$$FeCl_3 + 3H_2O \longrightarrow Fe(OH)_3 + 3HCl$$
$$\text{Red sol}$$

5.6 PURIFICATION OF COLLOIDAL SOLUTION

When a colloidal solution is prepared, it contains certain impurities. These impurities are mainly electrolytic in nature and they tend to destabilise the colloidal solutions. Therefore colloidal solutions are purified by the following methods:

1. Dialysis
2. Electrodialysis
3. Ultrafiltration

5.6.1 Dialysis

The process of dialysis is based on the fact that colloidal particles cannot pass through semipermeable membrane such as parchment paper or cellophane membrane while the ions of the electrolyte and small molecules can pass through semipermeable membrane. The colloidal solution is taken in a bag of cellophane which is suspended in a tub full of fresh water. The impurities diffuse out leaving pure colloidal solution in the bag (Fig. 5.7).

The process of removing ions (or molecules) from a sol by diffusion through a permeable membrane is called **Dialysis.** The apparatus used for dialysis is called a **Dialyser.**

Example: A ferric hydroxide sol (red) made by the hydrolysis of ferric chloride will be mixed with some hydrochloric acid. If the impure sol is placed in the dialysis bag for some time, the outside water will give a white precipitate. After a pretty long time, it will be found that almost the whole of hydrochloric acid has been removed and the pure red sol is left in the dialyser bag.

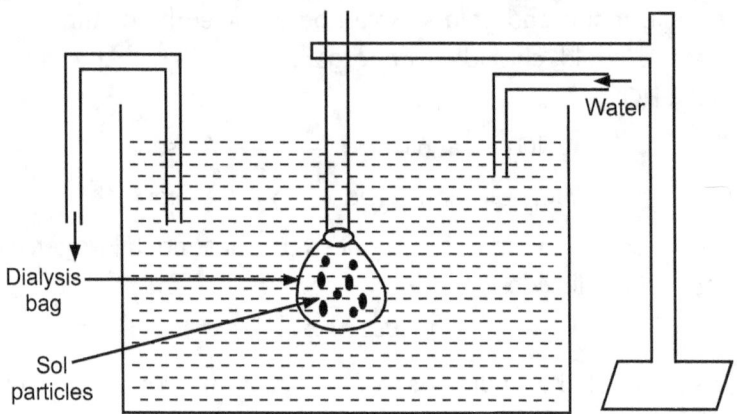

Fig. 5.7: A dialyser

5.6.2 Electrodialysis

The dialysis process is slow and to speed up its rate, it is carried out in the presence of an electrical field. When the electric field is applied through the electrodes, the ions of the electrolyte present as impurity diffuse towards oppositely charged electrodes at a fast rate. The dialysis carried out in the presence of electric field is known as **electrodialysis** (Fig. 5.8).

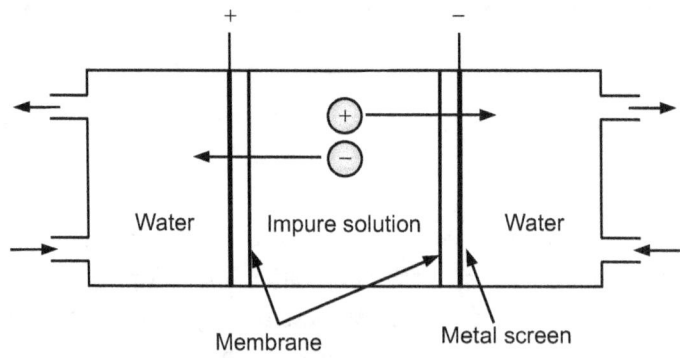

Fig. 5.8: Electrodialysis

5.6.3 Ultrafiltration

Sols pass through an ordinary filter paper. Its pores are too large to retain the colloidal particles. However, if the filter paper is impregnated with collodion or regenerated cellulose such as cellophane or risking, the pore size is much reduced. Such a modified filter paper is called an **ultrafilter**.

The separation of the colloidal particles from the liquid medium and electrolytes by filtration through an ultrafilter is called **Ultrafiltration.**

Ultrafiltration is a slow process. Gas pressure (or suction) has to be applied to speed it up. The colloidal particles are left on the ultrafilter in the form of slime. The slime may be stirred into fresh medium to get back the pure sol. By using graded ultrafilters, the technique of ultrafiltration can be employed to separate colloidal particles of different sizes.

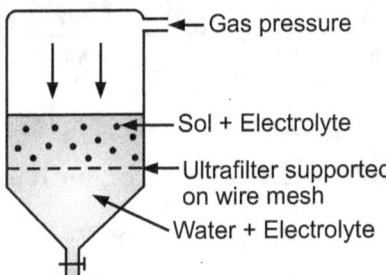

Fig. 5.9: Ultrafiltration

5.7 OPTICAL PROPERTIES OF COLLOIDAL SOLUTION

5.7.1 Tyndall Effect

Tyndall in 1869, observed that if a strong beam of light is passed through a colloidal solution placed in a dark place and viewed at right angles to the direction of light beam, the path of light shows up as a hazy beam or cone. This is due to the fact that sol particles absorb light energy and then emit it in all directions in space. This emission of light is known as **Scattering of Light.**

"The phenomenon of scattering of light by the sol particles is called **Tyndall Effect**".

The illuminated beam or cone formed by the scattering of light by the sol particles is often referred as **Tyndall Beam or Tyndall Cone**.

True solutions do not show Tyndall effect. Since ions or solute molecules are too small to scatter light, the beam of light passing through a true solution is not visible when viewed from the side. Thus, Tyndall effect can be used to distinguish a colloidal solution from a true solution.

Explanation:

The Tyndall effect is due to scattering of light by colloidal particles. The colloidal particles first absorb light and then a part of absorbed light is scattered from the surface of the colloidal particles. Maximum scattering intensity being in a plane at right angles to plane of incident light, the path becomes visible when seen from that direction. The particles of pure solvents or true solution are too small to scatter light.

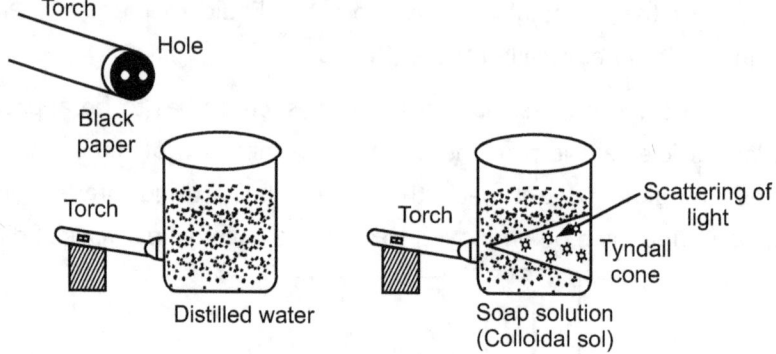

Fig. 5.10: Scattering of light

5.7.2 Ultramicroscope Shows the Presence of Individual Particles

Colloidal particles cannot be seen with a microscope.

Zsigmondy (1903) used the Tyndall phenomenon to set up an apparatus named as the **ultramicroscope.** An intense beam of light is focused on a sol contained in a glass vessel. The focus of light is then observed with a microscope at right angles to the beam. Individual sol particles appear as bright specks of light against a dark background (dispersion medium). It may be noted that under the ultramicroscope, the actual particles are not visible. These are the larger halos of scattered light around the particles that are visible. **Thus, an ultramicroscope does not give any information regarding the shape and size of the sol particles.**

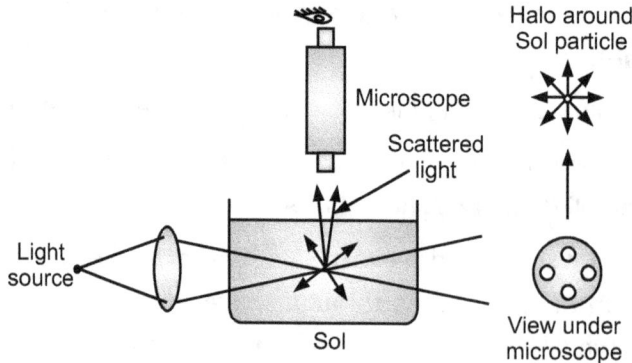

Fig. 5.11: Ultramicroscope

5.7.3 Solution Particles can be seen with an Electron Microscope

In an electron microscope, beam of electrons is focused by electric and magnetic fields on to a photographic plate. This focused beam is allowed to pass through a film of sol particles. Thus, it is possible to get a picture of the individual particles showing a magnification of the order of 10,000. With the help of this instrument, we can have an idea of the size and shape of several sol particles including paint pigments, viruses and bacteria. These particles have been found to be spheriod, rod-like, disc-like or long filaments.

5.7.4 Turbidity

This method is used to estimate the concentration of dispersed particles and molecular weight of the solute. The instruments used to measure turbidity are given below.

Spectrophotometer: It measures the intensity of the transmitted light in the direction of the incident light. The principle is shown in Fig. 5.12. The relationship between turbidity and relative intensity of the transmitted light can be expressed as:

$$\frac{I}{I_0} = e^{\tau l} \qquad \qquad \dots (5.1)$$

Where,

I_0 : Intensity of incidence light

I : Intensity of transmitted light

l : Length of the sample (path), 1 cm

τ : Turbidity

If the amount of dispersed solid is high, more light is scattered and the transmitted light will have less intensity. This method is useful to study lyophobic sols. In case of hydrophilic sols such as gums, proteins and other polymers, these effects are weaker. If the colloids show very low turbidities, it is more convenient to measure the scattered light instead of measuring the transmitted light.

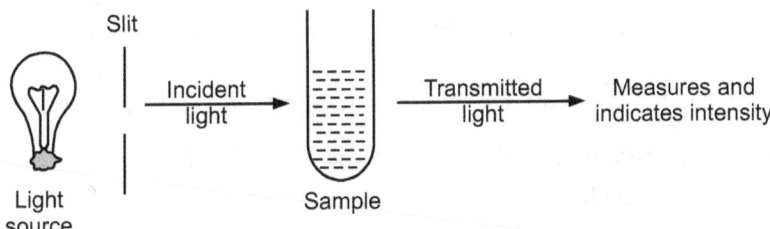

Fig. 5.12: Turbidity measurement by spectrophometer

5.7.5 Light Scattering

This method is used to study proteins, polymers, association colloids and lyophobic sols. Molecular weight of polymers and micelles can be measured by this method. If the particles are spherical, the scattering of light will be same in all directions. If particles are rod-shaped, these tend to orient themselves in a flow of liquid and give different effects along and at right angles to the direction of flow.

Principle: Light source having a wavelength higher than the dimensions of the particles is used here. The turbidity is measured from the scattered light by viewing at a particular angle.

$$\tau = \frac{16\pi}{3} R_{90} \qquad \qquad \text{... (5.2)}$$

$$R_{90} = \frac{Ir^2}{I_0} \qquad \qquad \text{... (5.3)}$$

where;

I_0 : Intensity of the scattered light,

I : Intensity of the incidence light,

r : Distance from the scattered particle to the point of observation,

τ : Turbidity,

R_{90} : Rayleigh ratio.

When light scattering is treated as a consequence of random, non-uniformities of concentrations (due to difference in refractive indices), the relationship between turbidity and molecular weight was also derived by Debye. The expression is:

$$\frac{Hc}{\tau} = \frac{1}{M} + 2Bc \qquad \qquad \text{... (5.4)}$$

c : Concentration of solute g/cm^3,

M : Average molecular weight of the colloid,

B : Interaction constant of the solvent-solute system,

H : A constant for a particular system,

A plot of $\frac{Hc}{\tau}$ against concentration gives a straight line. The slope is 2B and intercept is $\frac{1}{M}$. Thus, the molecular weight of the colloid is estimated. The constant, H is an optical constant for a particular system. It depends on the refractive index. This constant, changes with concentration and wavelength of light used.

5.8 KINETIC PROPERTIES OF COLLOIDS

5.8.1 Brownian Movement

The continuous rapid zig-zag movement executed by a colloidal particle in the dispersion medium is called **Brownian movement or motion.**

This phenomenon is so named after **Sir Robert Brown** who discovered it in 1827. He was observed this phenomenon with pollen grains suspended in water.

When a sol is examined with an ultramicroscope, the suspended particles are seen as shining specks of light. By following an individual particle it is observed that the particle is undergoing a constant rapid motion. It moves in a series of short straight-line paths in the medium, changing directions abruptly.

Brownian movement may be exhibited by particle as large as about 5 nm. They bombard with each other and collide with the wall of the container. Also, colloidal particles cannot sediment. Brownian movement works against the gravitational force.

The motion of the molecules cannot be observed, of course, since the molecules are too small to see.

The velocity of the particles increases with decreasing particle size. Increasing the viscosity of the medium, which may be accomplished by the addition of glycerin or a similar agent, decreases and finally stops the Brownian movement.

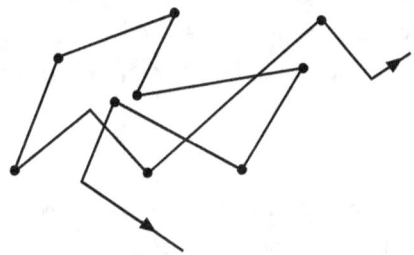

Fig. 5.13: Brownian movement or motion of colloidal particles

5.8.2 Diffusion

Since size of colloidal particles is small, these diffuse through permeable membrane. Particles diffuse spontaneously from a region of higher concentration to one of lower concentration until the concentration of the system is uniform throughout. Diffusion is a direct result of Brownian movement.

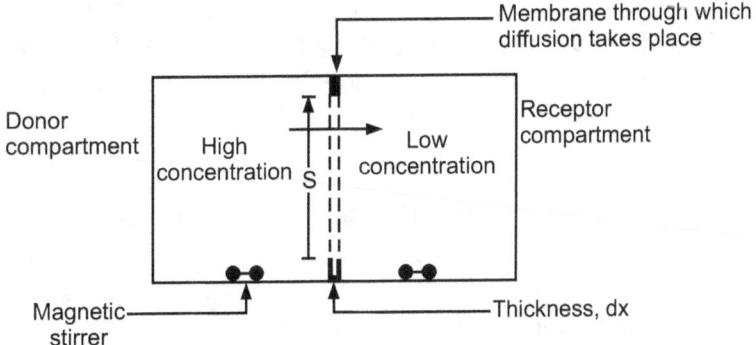

Fig. 5.14: Diffusion of colloids in high concentration to low concentration

According to **Fick's first law,** the amount d_q of substance diffusing in time dt across a plane of area S is directly proportional to the change of concentration dc with distance travelled dx.

Fick's law is written as,

$$d_q = -DS \frac{dc}{dx} \, dt \qquad \qquad \text{... (5.5)}$$

Where,

D : The diffusion coefficient,

$\dfrac{dc}{dx}$: The amount of material diffusing per unit time across a unit area, called the concentration gradient.

D, thus has the dimensions of area per unit time. The coefficient may be obtained in colloidal chemistry by diffusion experiments in which the material is allowed to pass through a porous disc and samples are removed and analyzed periodically. Another method involves measuring the change in the concentration or refractive index gradient of the free boundary that is formed when the solvent and colloidal solution are brought together and allowed to diffuse.

5.8.3 Osmotic Pressure

The determination of molecular weights of dissolved substances from colligative proper-ties such as the depression of freezing point or the elevation of boiling point is a standard procedure. However, of the available methods, only osmotic pressure has a practical value in the study of colloidal particles because of the magnitude of the changes in the properties.

For example, the depression of freezing point of a 1% w/v solution of a macromolecule of molecular weight 70000 Da is only 0.0026 K, far too small to be measured with sufficient accuracy by conventional methods and also very sensitive to the presence of low molecular weight impurities.

In contrast, the osmotic pressure of this solution at 20°C would be 350 Nm^{-2} or about 35 mm of water. Not only does the osmotic pressure provide an effect that is measurable, but also the effect of any low molecular weight material, which can pass through the membrane, is virtually eliminated.

Osmosis:

If a solution and solvent are separated by a semi-permeable membrane, the tendency to equalize chemical potentials (and hence concentrations) on either side of the membrane. The results in a net diffusion of solvent from low concentration to high concentration across the membrane is called as **osmosis.**

The pressure necessary to balance this osmotic flow is termed as **osmotic pressure.**

For a colloidal solution, the osmotic pressure can be described by:

$$\frac{\pi}{C} = \frac{RT}{M} + BC \qquad \qquad \dots (5.6)$$

Where,

π : Osmotic pressure,

C : The concentration of the solution,

M : The molecular weight of the solute,

R : Gas constant,

T : Absolute temperature,

B : A constant depending on the degree of interaction between the solvent and solute molecules.

Thus, a plot of $\frac{\pi}{C}$ versus C is linear with the value of the intercept at C = 0 giving $\frac{RT}{M}$ enabling the molecular weight of the colloid to be calculated.

5.8.4 Sedimentation

The velocity v of sedimentation of spherical particles having a density ρ in a medium of density ρ_0 and a viscosity η_0 is given by Stoke's law:

$$v = \frac{2r^2 (\rho - \rho_0) g}{9 \eta_0} \qquad \qquad \dots (5.7)$$

In which, g is the acceleration due to gravity.

If the particles are subjected only to the force of gravity, then the lower size limit of particles obeying Stokes' equation is about 0.5 μm. This is because, Brownian movement becomes significant and tends to offset sedimentation due to gravity and promotes mixing.

Ultra-centrifuge: Consequently, a stronger force must be applied to bring about the sedimentation of colloidal particles in a quantitative and measurable manner. This is accomplished by use of the ultra-centrifuge, developed by Svedberg in 1925, which can produce a force a million times than that of gravity.

In a centrifuge, the acceleration of gravity is replaced by $\omega^2 x$ in which ω is the angular velocity and x is the distance of the particle from the center of rotation. Equation (5.7) is accordingly modified to

$$v = \frac{dx}{dt} = \frac{2r^2 (\rho - \rho_0) \omega^2 x}{9 \eta_0} \qquad \qquad \dots (5.8)$$

The speed at which a centrifuge is operated is commonly expressed in terms of the number of revolutions per minute (rpm) of the rotor. It is frequently more desirable to express the rpm as angular acceleration ($\omega^2 x$) or the number of times that the force of gravity is exceeded.

The instantaneous velocity $v = \dfrac{dx}{dt}$ of a particle in a unit centrifugal field is expressed in terms of the Svedberg sedimentation coefficients,

$$S = \frac{\left(\dfrac{dx}{dt}\right)}{\omega^2 x} \qquad \text{... (5.9)}$$

Owing to the centrifugal force, particles having a high molecular weight pass from position x_1 at time t_1 to position x_2 at time t_2, and the sedimentation coefficient is obtained by integrating equation (5.8) to give

$$s = \frac{\ln\left(\dfrac{x_2}{x_1}\right)}{\omega^2(t_2 - t_1)} \qquad \text{... (5.10)}$$

The distances x_1 and x_2 refer to positions of the boundary between the solvent and the high-molecular weight component in the centrifuge cell.

The boundary is located by the change of refractive index, which may be attained at any time during the run and translated into a peak on a photographic plate. Photographs are taken at definite intervals, and the peaks of the **schlieren patterns**, as they are called, give the position x of the boundary at each time, t. If the sample consists of a component of a definite molecular weight, the schlieren pattern will have a single sharp peak at any moment during the run. If components with different molecular weights are present in the sample, the particles of greater weight will settle faster, and several peaks will appear on the schlieren patterns.

Therefore, ultracentrifugation is useful not only for determining the molecular weight of polymers, particularly proteins, but also may be used to ascertain the degree of homogeneity of the sample. Gelatin, for example, is found to be a polydisperse protein with fractions of molecular weight 10,000 to 100,000. (This accounts in part for the fact that gelatin from various sources is observed to have variable properties when used in pharmaceutical preparations.)

The sedimentation coefficients may be computed from equation (5.10) after the two distances x_1 and x_2 are measured on the schlieren photographs obtained at times t_1 and t_2; the angular velocity so is equal to 2π times the speed of the rotor in revolutions per second. Knowing s and obtaining D from diffusion data, it is possible to determine the molecular weight of a polymer, such as a protein, by use of the expression

$$M = \frac{RTs}{D(1 - \bar{v}\rho_0)} \qquad \text{... (5.11)}$$

where

R : The molar gas constant,

T : The absolute temperature,

v : The partial specific volume of the protein, and

ρ_0 : The density of the solvent.

Both s and D must be obtained at, or corrected to, 20° C for use in equation (5.11).

5.8.5 Viscosity

The viscosity of a colloidal dispersion is affected by a variety of factors;

(a) **Shape of the dispersed particles:** Spherical particles impart relatively low viscosity to dispersion, while particles of linear shape yield more viscous systems.

(b) **Affinity of particles to the medium:** If linear particles are placed in a medium having low affinity for particles, these tend to assume spherical shape and the viscosity falls.

(c) **Type of colloids:** In general, lyophilic colloids have viscosities greater than that of the dispersion medium. Lyophobic colloids have viscosities almost equal to the dispersion medium.

(d) **Molecular weight of the particles:** Higher the molecular weight of the material, greater will be the viscosity.

Therefore, by measuring the viscosity, molecular weight of the polymers can be determined.   Examples: dextran (plasma expanders), gelatin etc.

Viscosity is an expression of the resistance to flow of a system under an applied stress. The flow of a dilute colloidal system (having spherical particles) is expressed by an equation developed by Einstein.

$$\eta = \eta_0 (1 + 2.5 \, \phi) \qquad \qquad \dots (5.12)$$

where

η : Viscosity of the dispersion medium,

η_0 : Viscosity of the dispersion,

ϕ : Volume fraction of particles.

Rearranging equation (5.12) gives

$$\frac{\eta}{\eta_0} = 1 + 2.5 \, \phi = \eta_{rel} \text{ i.e., relative viscosity}$$

$$\frac{\eta}{\eta_0} - 1 = 2.5 \, \phi = \eta_{sp} \text{ i.e., specific viscosity}$$

$$\frac{\eta_{sp}}{\phi} = 2.5$$

The volume fraction is estimated as the volume of particles per total volume of dispersion. The volume fraction, ϕ, represent concentration term since ϕ is related to c,

$$\frac{\eta_{sp}}{c} = 2.5 \text{ or k} \qquad \qquad \dots (5.13)$$

Where,

c : Particles in grams per 100 ml of dispersion,

k : Intrinsic viscosity.

By determining the η_o $\eta_{rel,}$ and η_{sp} can be estimated. When $\frac{\eta_{sp}}{c}$ is plotted against c, a straight line may be obtained. Extrapolating this line to infinite dilution (y-axis) gives the intercept, which is k value. (Fig. 5.15). This constant, k, is the intrinsic viscosity $[\eta]$.

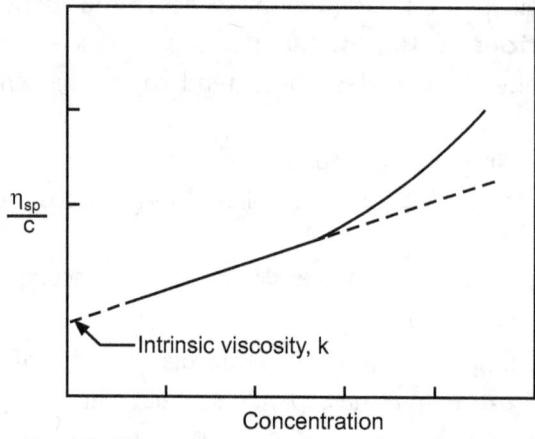

Fig. 5.15: Viscosity-concentration plot used for the determination of molecular weight of polymers

The approximate molecular weight of the dispersed phase can be estimated using intrinsic viscosity. According to Mark-Hownink equation

$$[\eta] = KM^a \qquad \qquad \dots (5.14)$$

where,   K : Constant,

a : Constant,

$[\eta]$: Intrinsic viscosity.

Constants K and a are characteristics of a particular polymer-solvent system. These constants are obtained by calibrating with a colloidal dispersion of known characteristics and molecular weight (M).

Once K and a are known, molecular weight, M can be calculated by experimentally determining the intrinsic viscosity (Fig. 5.15). A capillary viscometer (Ostwald viscometer) can be used for this purpose.

5.9 ELECTRIC PROPERTIES

5.9.1 The Sol Particles carry an Electric Charge

The most important property of colloidal dispersions is that, all the suspended particles possess either a positive or a negative charge. The mutual forces of repulsion between similarly charged particles prevent them from aggregating and settling under the action of gravity. This gives stability to the sol.

The sol particles acquire positive or negative charge by preferential adsorption of positive or negative ions from the dispersion medium. For example, ferric hydroxide sol particles are positively charged because these adsorb Fe^{3+} ions from ferric chloride ($FeCl_3$) used in the preparation of the sol. Since the sol as a whole is neutral, the charge on the particle is counterbalanced by oppositely charged ions termed as counterfoils (in this case Cl^-) furnished by the electrolyte in medium. (Fig. 5.16)

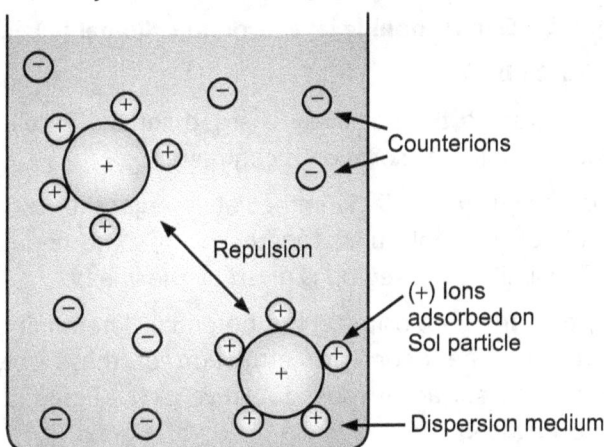

Fig. 5.16: Adsorption of ions from dispersion medium gives charge to sol and start repulsion

5.9.2 Electric Double Layer

The concept of the electrical double layer at the interface can be illustrated with the help of Fig. 5.17.

At Interface of Solid/Liquid:

Consider a solid surface in contact with a polar solution containing ions, e.g., an aqueous solution of an electrolyte (Cations and anion).

Let us assume that some of the cations are adsorbed onto the surface, giving it a positive charge. Remaining in solution is the rest of the cations plus the total number of anions added.

Such a situation is shown in Fig. 5.17, where aa' is the surface of the solid. The adsorbed ions that gave the surface its positive charge are referred to as the **potential determining ions.**

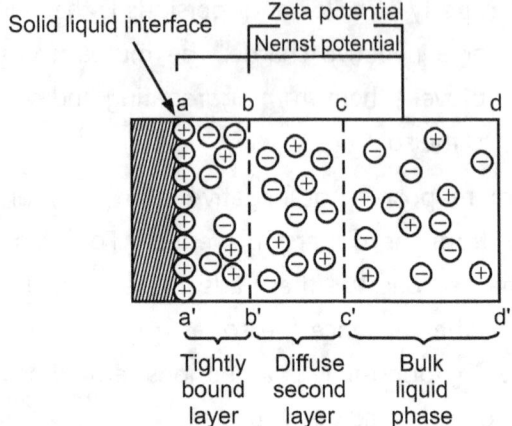

Fig. 5.17: Electric double layer around colloidal particle

Tightly bound layer (aa' to bb'):

Then anions are attracted to the positively charged surface by electric forces. But also some cations repel, once the initial absorption is complete.

Such a situation is shown in Fig. 5.17, immediately adjacent to this surface layer is a region of tightly bound solvent molecules, together with some negative ions, also tightly bound to the surface. The limit of this region is given by the line bb'.

These ions having a charge opposite to the potential determining ions are known as **counterions or gegenions.** The degree of attraction of these solvent molecules and counterions is such that if the surface is moved relative to the liquid, the shear plane is bb' rather than aa', the **true surface.**

The potential at bb' is still positive, since, there are fewer anions in the tightly bound layer than cations adsorbed onto the surface of the solid.

This is first layer (extending from aa' to bb') called as tightly bound layer.

Diffuse layer (bb' to cc'):

In addition to these electric forces, thermal motion tends to produce an equal distribution of all the ions in solution. As a result, an equilibrium situation is set up, in which, some of the excess anions approach the surface, while the remainders are distributed in decreasing amounts as one proceeds away from the charged surface.

In the region (Fig. 5.17) bounded by the lines bb' and cc', there is an excess of negative ions.

This is a second layer (from bb' to cc) that is more diffuse. The so-called **diffuse double layer** therefore extends from aa' to cc'.

Bulk liquid phase (Beyond cc'):

At a particular distance from the surface, the concentration of anions and cations are equal, i.e., conditions of electric neutrality prevail. It is important to remember that the system as a whole is electrically neutral, even though there are regions of unequal distribution of anions and cations.

Beyond cc', the distribution of ions is uniform and electric neutrality is obtained (Fig. 5.17).

Two situations other than that represented by Fig. 5.17 are possible.

1. If the counterions in the tightly bound, solvated layer equal the positive charge on the solid surface, then electric neutrality occurs at the plane bb' rather than cc'.

2. Should the total charge of the counterions in the region aa'-bb' exceed the charge due to the potential determining ions, then the net charge at bb' will be negative, rather than less positive as shown in Fig. 5.17.

This means that, in this instance, for electric neutrality to be obtained at cc', an excess of positive ions must be present in the region bb'-cc'.

If the potential determining ion is negative, the arguments just given still apply, although positive ions will be present in the tightly bound layer.

Nernst potential:

It is the potential of the solid surface itself, aa' owing to the presence of potential determining ions.

Nernst potential, E, or electrothermodynamic potential is defined as 'the difference in potential between the actual surface and the electroneutral region of the solution'.

Zeta potential:

It is the potential observed at the shear plane i.e. bb' line (Fig. 5.17).

Zeta potential, ζ, or electrokinetic potential is defined as 'the difference in the potential between the surface of the tightly bound layer and the electroneutral region of the solution'.

Zeta potential can also be defined as 'the work required bringing a unit charge from infinity to the surface of the particles'.

The potential energy decreases rapidly in the initial stage, followed by a gradual decrease towards the boundary cc'. The counterions, which are present close to the surface bb' and in the region of bb' to cc', may reduce the particle-particle interactions. Hence, the potential energy decreases more gradually in this region. In general, zeta potential is more important in the field of pharmacy compared to Nernst potential, because the electrical double layer also moves, when the particle is under motion.

Applications: Zeta potential governs the degree of repulsions between the adjacent ions of like-charges. Hence, it is used to predict particle-particle interaction. Such information provides insights about the stability of systems containing dispersed particles. An optimum zeta potential is desirable for the maximum stability.

If zeta potential falls below a particular value, the attractive forces exceed the repulsive forces. This result in the aggregation of particles. This phenomenon is observed in colloids. Zeta potential decreases more rapidly when the concentration of electrolytes is increased or the valency of counter ions is higher.

5.9.3 Electrophoresis

When a potential difference (electric field) is applied across two platinum electrodes immersed in a colloidal solution, the particles of dispersed phase move towards either the positive or negative electrode. This observation was first discovered by **Rauss** in **1807** and was investigated later by **Linder** and **Picton**.

The movement of colloidal particles under the action of electric field is known as **Electrophoresis**. If the colloidal particles move towards the positive electrode (Anode) they carry negative charge. On the other hand, if the sol particles migrate towards negative electrode (Cathode), they are positively charged. From the direction of movement of colloidal particles it is possible to find out the charge on colloidals.

Demonstration of Electrophoresis:

The demonstration of electrophoresis is as follows:

Take a colloidal sol say AS_2S_3 sol in a U tube. Place an electrolyte, having density less than that of solution (say distilled water). The electrolyte provides distinct boundary between electrolyte and colloidal sol. Place two platinum electrodes in two arms of U tube such that they dip in the colloidal sol. When a high potential difference of about 100 volts is applied across the two platinum electrodes, it is observed that the level or Boundary of colloidal solution falls on the negative electrode side and rises up on positive electrode side. On reaching the positive electrode, the colloidal particles get discharged. As a result of neutralisation of charge, the colloidal particles aggregate and settle down at the bottom.

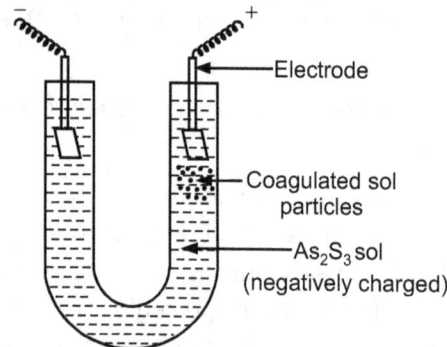

Fig. 5.18: Demonstration of electrophoresis

5.9.4 Electro-Osmosis

A colloidal solution as a whole is electrically neutral in nature i.e., dispersion medium carries an equal and opposite charge to that of the particles of dispersed phase. When the movement of dispersed phase of colloidal solution is prevented by suitable means, the dispersion medium can be made to move under the influence of an applied electric field or potential. This phenomenon is referred to as **Electro-Osmosis**. Thus, electro-osmosis may be defined as 'the movement of the dispersion medium under the influence of an applied electric field when the particles of dispersed phase are prevented from moving'.

Demonstration of Electro-Osmosis:

The phenomenon of electro-osmosis can be demonstrated experimentally as follows: The demonstration of electro-osmosis is carried out in a specially designed apparatus. The apparatus consists of a bigger tube having two side tubes **T** and **T'** attached to its ends. The bigger tube is divided into three compartments **A, B** and **C** by means of two semi-permeable membranes. A tube carrying a stop-cock is attached to the central compartment **A**. Two platinum electrodes are inserted in the outer compartments **B** and **C**. A colloidal dispersion is placed in the central compartment **A** and the outer compartments **B** and **C** are filled with water. The water in compartments **B** and **C** also extend to the side tube **T** and **T'**. The function of membrane is to prevent the movement of colloidal particles. Therefore, when a potential difference is applied across the electrodes held close to the membranes in the compartment **B** and **C**, dispersion medium begins to move.

If the particles carry positive charge, the dispersion medium would start moving towards the anode and the level of water in the side tube **T** would be seen to rise, indicating the presence of negative charge on the dispersion medium. If the particles carry negative charge, the dispersion medium would be seen to move towards cathode and water in the side tube **T** would start rising.

Electro-osmosis is utilized for dewatering moist clay and drying of dye pastes.

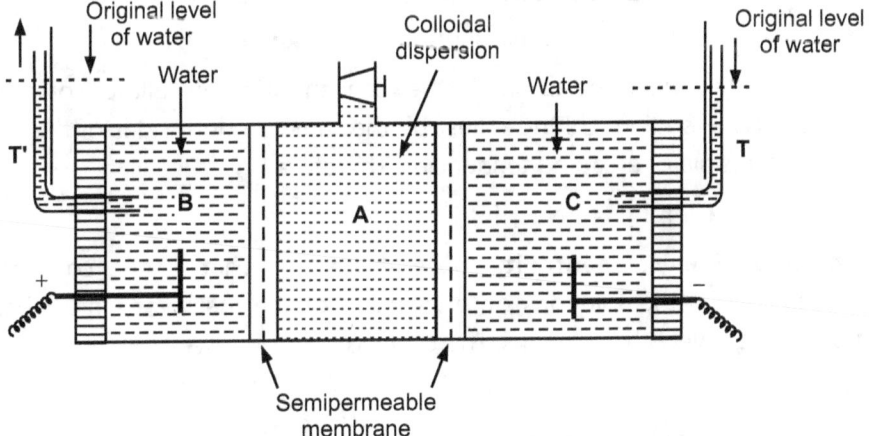

Fig. 5.19: Demonstration of electro-osmosis

5.10 DONNAN MEMBRANE EQUILIBRIUM

Donnan membrane equilibrium principle is used to enhance the absorption drug.

Explanation:

Initial state:

The glass chamber; it was divided into two parts by semipermeable membrane i.e. inside and outside.

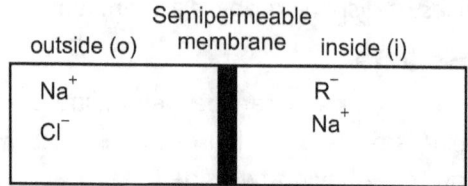

Fig. 5.20: Glass chamber containing Na⁺ Cl⁻ and R⁻ Na⁺ solution

Inside: Contain sodium chloride solution (Na^+ Cl^-).

Outside: Contain negatively charged colloid, together with its counter ions (R^-Na^+)

The volumes of solution on the two sides of the membrane are considered to be equal.

Movement through semipermeable membrane: The sodium and chloride ions can pass freely across the barrier but colloidal anionic particles cannot pass across the barrier. Soon equilibrium is attained.

After equilibrium:

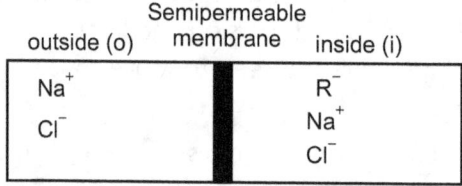

Fig. 5.21: After equilibrium movement of ions

After equilibrium has been established, the concentration in dilute solutions (more correctly the activity) of sodium chloride must be the same on both sides of the membrane, according to the principle of escaping tendencies. Therefore,

$$[Na^+]_0 \, [Cl^-]_0 = [Na^+]_i \, [Cl^-]_i \qquad \qquad \text{... (5.15)}$$

The condition of electroneutrality must also apply. That is, the concentration of positive charged ions in the solutions on either side of the membrane must balance the concentration of negatively charged ions. Therefore, on the outside:

Outside:

$$[Na^+]_0 = [Cl^-]_0 \qquad \qquad \text{... (5.16)}$$

Inside:

$$[Na^+]_i = [Cl^-]_i + [R^-]_i \qquad\qquad ...(5.17)$$

Equations (5.16) and (5.17) may be substituted into (5.15) to give

$$[Cl^-]_0\,[Cl^-]_0 = [Cl^-]_i\,([Cl^-]_i + [R^-]_i)$$

$$[Cl^-]_0^2 = [Cl^-]_i^2 + ([Cl^-]_i\,[R^-]_i)$$

$$[Cl^-]_0^2 = [Cl^-]_i^2 \left(1 + \frac{[R^-]_i}{[Cl^-]_i}\right)$$

$$\frac{[Cl^-]_0^2}{[Cl^-]_i^2} = 1 + \frac{[R^-]_i}{[Cl^-]_i}$$

$$\frac{[Cl^-]_0}{[Cl^-]_i} = \sqrt{1 + \frac{[R^-]_i}{[Cl^-]_i}} \qquad\qquad ...(5.18)$$

Equation (5.18) gives the ratio of concentrations of the diffusible anion outside and inside the membrane at equilibrium.

The equation shows that a negatively charged polyelectrolyte inside a semipermeable sac would influence the equilibrium concentration ratio of a diffusible anion. It tends to drive the ion of like charge out through the membrane.

When $[R^-]_i$ is large compared to $[Cl^-]_i$, the ratio roughly equals $\sqrt{[R^-]_i}$.

If, on the other hand, $[Cl^-]_i$ is quite large with respect to $[R^-]_i$. The ratio in equation (5.18) becomes equal to unity, and the concentration of the salt is thus equal on both sides of the membrane.

Example: The sodium carboxymethylcellulose is used as anionic colloid ($Na^+\,cmc^-$), for enhancing the absorption of drugs such as sodium salicylate and potassium benzylpenicillin.

At initial:

Assume as drug absorbed through GIT.

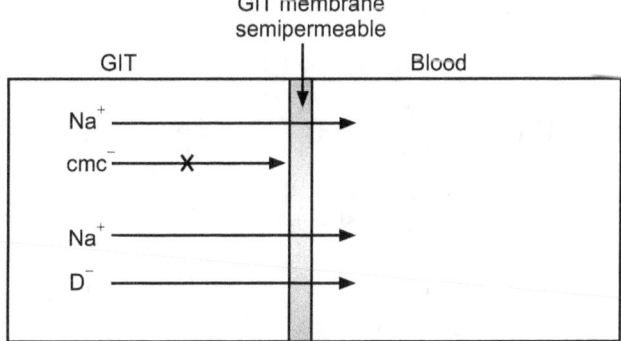

(Na^+cmc^-) : Anionic colloid

(Na^+D^-) : Anionic diffusible drug

Fig. 5.22: At initial stage movements of ions

If [Cl⁻] in equation (5.18) is replaced by the concentration of the diffusible drug, anion [D⁻] and [R⁻] is replaced by the concentration of the anion colloid [cmc⁻].

The sodium and drug ions can pass freely across the barrier but colloidal anionic particles cannot pass across the barrier. Soon equilibrium is attained.

At equilibrium,

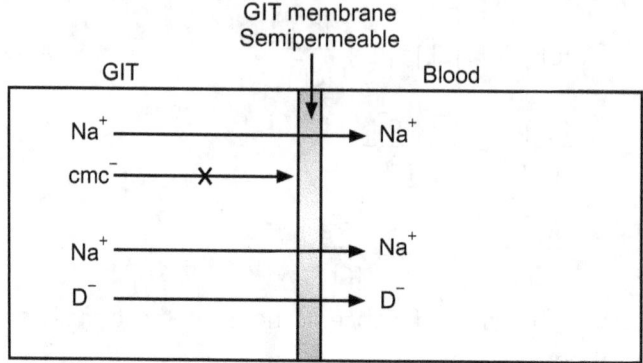

(Na⁺cmc⁻) : Anionic colloid

(Na⁺D⁻) : Anionic diffusible drug

Fig. 5.23: At equilibrium movements of ions

At equilibrium Na^+ and D^- ions diffuse into blood, but cmc^- ions cannot diffuse through membrane. Means –ve charge in GIT increases and +ve charge decreases, therefore for mataining charge on both sides, diffusion of D^- ions increases into the blood.

Diffusion of anionic drug molecules was increased because of non-diffusible anionic colloidal molecules.

Therefore equation (5.18) becomes:

$$\frac{[D^-]_0}{[D^-]_i} = \sqrt{1 + \frac{[cmc^-]_i}{[D^-]_i}} \qquad \ldots (5.19)$$

It will be observed that

when, $\dfrac{[cmc^-]_i}{[D^-]_i} = 8$ the ratio $\dfrac{[D^-]_0}{[D^-]_i} = 3$ and

when, $\dfrac{[cmc^-]_i}{[D^-]_i} = 99$ the ratio $\dfrac{[D^-]_0}{[D^-]_i} = 10$ and

Therefore, the addition of an anionic colloid to a diffusible drug anion should enhance the diffusion of the drug.

Applications:

1. Because of the presence of sodium carboxymethylcellulose more than doubled the rate of transfer of the negatively charged dye, scarlet red sulfonate increases.

2. By *in vivo* experiments that ion-exchange resins and even sulfate and phosphate ions that do not diffuse readily through the intestinal wall tend to drive anions from the intestinal tract into the bloodstream.

Limitation:

The opposite effect, that of retardation of drug absorption, may occur if the drug complexes with the macromolecule.

5.11 STABILIZATION OF COLLOIDS

Good colloidal stability means that little or no particle aggregation has occurred in the dispersions between preparation and use. Stability studies include chemical and physical stability of dispersion. The manufacturing pharmacist is expected to understand the following aspects,

1. Reasons for the instability of dispersions,
2. Suitable measures to stabilise the dispersions.

The physical stability can be achieved by maintaining the particles in Brownian motion. The ways to achieve this property are:

(a) **Provide electric charge on the surface of the dispersed particle:** The like charges on the particles will prevent these coming closer together and thus maintaining a Brownian movement; this factor plays a significant role in case of lyophobic colloids.

(b) **Maintain a solvent sheath around the particle:** This solvent layer prevents the particles coming closer and also maintain Brownian movement. This factor plays an important role in case of lyophilic colloids.

As long as the sol maintains the above mentioned environment, its stability is not a problem. This delicate balance may be disturbed due to variety of reasons.

The following factors sensitize the dispersed phase, which results in precipitation (coagulation or flocculation) of the particles. Lyophobic colloids are more prone to precipitation.

Formulation: Ingredients, electrolytes etc.

Environmental: Temperature, agitation during handling etc.

5.11.1 DLVO Theory: (Derjaguin, Landau, Verway and Overbeek Theory)

Lyophobic colloids are thermodynamically unstable and tend to form aggregates, dispersed particles are highly charged. Stability of the dispersion is explained on the basis of DLVO theory.

According to this theory, the distance between two dispersed particles mainly influences particle-particle interaction. Using this theory, one can approximately determine the amount of electrolyte (of a particular valency type) required to precipitate or stabilize a colloid.

In a colloidal dispersion, the Brownian motion results in frequent collisions between particles. Such interactions are mainly responsible for the stability of colloids.

There are two types of interactions, namely attractions and repulsions.

1. When attractions predominate, the particles adhere after collision and aggregate.
2. When repulsions predominate, the particles rebound after collisions and remain individually dispersed.

The potential energy versus interparticle distance for particles in dispersion is given in Fig. 5.24. These are described as follows.

The interactions between particles are described as follows:

Van der Waals attraction forces:

This force depend mainly on chemical nature and size of the particle. These forces are London-type and cannot be altered readily. The potential energy of attraction is represented by V_A (Fig. 5.24).

Electrostatic repulsive forces:

The electrostatic repulsive forces depend mainly on the density, surface charge, and thickness of the double layer. These indicate the magnitude of zeta potential. The potential energy representing repulsions is denoted by V_R (Fig. 5.24).

Net energy of interaction:

An algebraic addition of the above two curves gives the net energy of interaction. The potential energy is represented by V_T (Fig. 5.24).

$$V_T = V_A + V_R$$

                 ... (5.20)

The following conclusions may be drawn from the energy curves:

Primary minimum (sign of precipitation):

When particles are very close to each other, atomic orbitals overlap and penetrate each other. This is indicated by a rapid rise in potential energy. The net result is a stronger attraction which leads to precipitation.

Net energy peak (sign of better stability):

At intermediate distances, appreciable repulsive force operates (positive zeta potential energy). This potential barrier keeps the particles in Brownian movement and imparts stability to the dispersion.

At this peak, the maximum potential is designated by V_m.

The stability of a colloidal system is defined by the height of the maximum point in the potential energy curve.

This value of V_m is about 10 to 20 kt, which corresponds to a zeta potential of about 50 mV. Such a system is considered kinetically stable. The potential energy barrier must be surmounted, if the colloidal particles approach each other sufficiently close to fall into the deep primary minimum of reversible coagulation.

Secondary minimum (sign of aggregation):

This is observed when the particles are separated by long distances, about 1000 to 2000Å. Particles experience attraction forces and form aggregated or coacervates. The presence of a secondary minimum is taken advantageously in the controlled flocculation of a coarse dispersion.

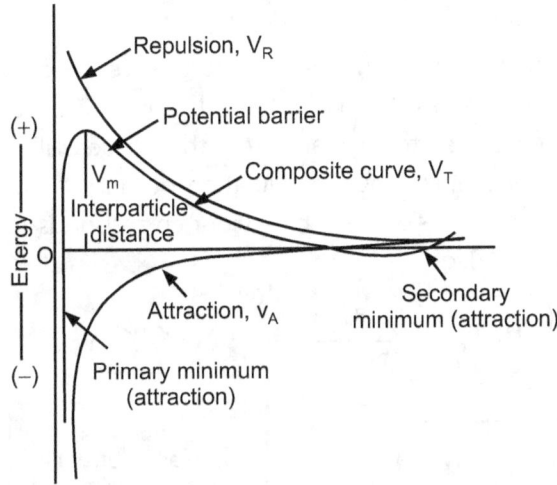

Fig. 5.24: Potential energy vs interparticle distance

In summary, according to DLVO theory, colloidal particles coagulate whenever their kinetic energy is sufficient to surmount the potential energy barrier, V_m. Thus, the coagulation colloidal particle may be accelerated by two ways;

1. By reducing the height of the potential barrier.
2. By increasing kinetic energy of particles.

5.11.2 Factors Affecting Stability of Colloidal Dispersion

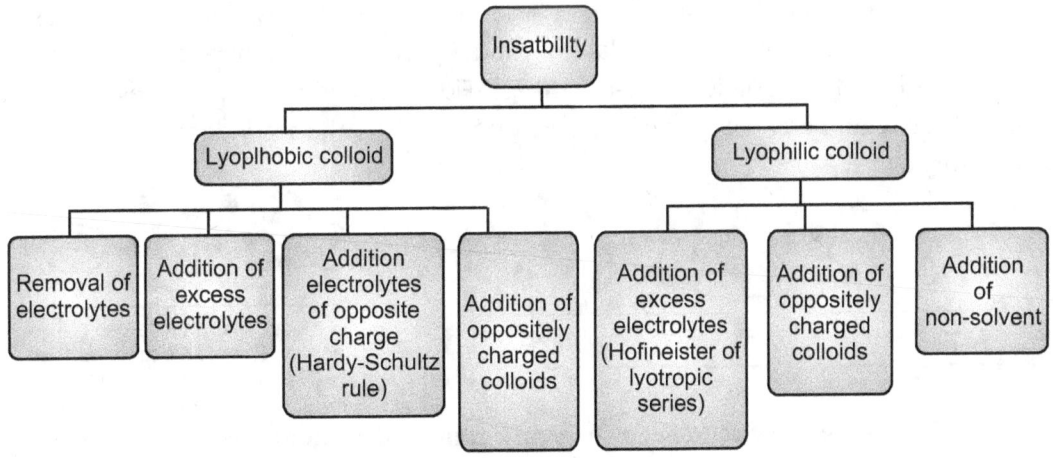

5.11.2.1 Instability of Lyophobic Colloids

Coagulation or precipitation of the sol is defined as 'a state in which flocculation (aggregation) and settling of the dispersed particles is observed'. Coagulation or flocculation indicates the instability of the dispersion.

Reasons for coagulation of lyophobic particles are:

(A) Removal of Electrolytes:

When electrolytes are present in traces, interparticle repulsion decreases. The electric double layer potential decreases below a critical value. The repulsions between the approaching particles are reduced to such an extent that those colliding with certain velocity can join together as shown below. Thus, coagulation occurs. The dispersed solids tend to settle at the bottom of the dispersion. This behaviour corresponds to the primary minimum in the DLVO of energy curve. (Fig. 5.24).

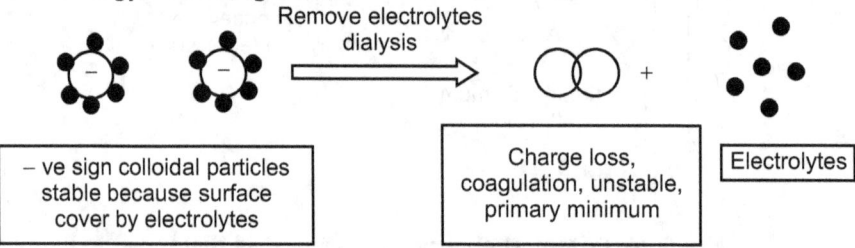

Fig. 5.25: Instability of colloidal dispersion because removal of electrolytes

Lyophobic colloidal particles are stable because electrolytes are adsorbed on surface and proved charge. Because of same charge, particle shows electrostatic repulsion, inhibit the coagulation of particles. In purification process of colloid, there is chances of loss of electrolyses. Therefore colloidal particles loss charge, show coagulation of colloidal particle, means instability (Fig. 5.25).

(B) Addition of excess electrolytes:

For the stabilization of sol, a minute charge on particles is desirable. When excess of electrolytes are added, particles coagulate beyond a particular concentration. This is due to the accumulation of oppositely charged particles (Fig. 5.26) and consequent deviation from critical value of zeta potential. This behaviour corresponds to the secondary minimum in the DLVO theory (Fig. 5.24).

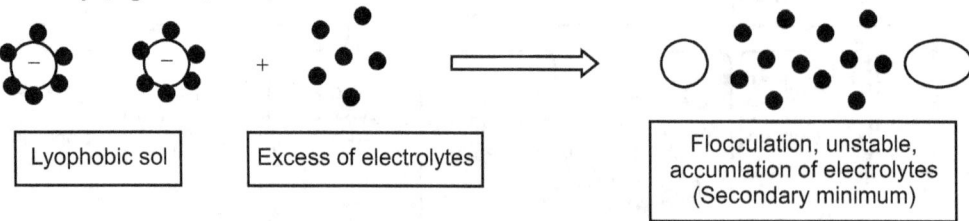

Fig. 5.26: Instability of colloidal dispersion because addition of excess electrolytes

(C) Addition of opposite charge Electrolytes (Hardy-Schultz Rule):

The coagulation of a colloidal solution by an electrolyte does not take place until the added electrolyte has certain minimum concentration in the solution. The minimum amount of an electrolyte (millimoles) that must be added to one litre of a colloidal solution so as to bring about complete coagulation or flocculation is called the **Coagulation or Flocculation Value of the Electrolyte.** [Fig. 5.27]

Thus, smaller is the flocculation value of electrolyte, greater is its coagulation or precipitating power. Different electrolytes have different coagulation values. The coagulation behaviour of various electrolytes was studied by **Hardy and Schultz.**

They gave a generalisation known as Hardy – Schultz Law, which states, **"Greater the valency of oppositely charged ions of the electrolyte being added, the faster is coagulation".**

So, for coagulation of sols carrying negative charge Al^{3+} ion is more effective than Ba^{2+} ions or Na^+ ions.

Thus in case of positively charged sol, the coagulating power of anions is in the order of

$$[Fe(CN)_4]^{4-} > PO_4^{3-} > SO_4^{2-} > Cl^-$$

and in case of negatively charged sols, the coagulating power of cations is in the order of

$$Al^{3+} > Ba^{2+} > Na^+$$

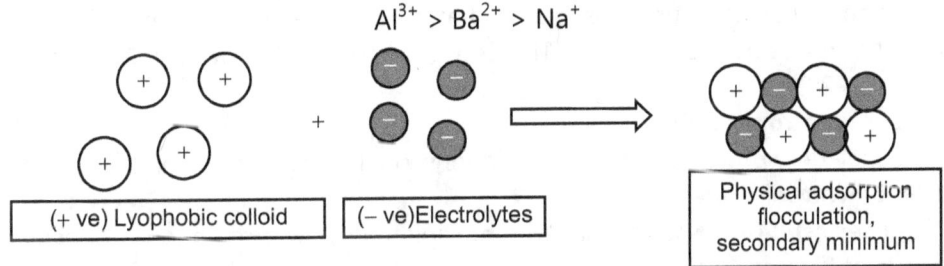

| (+ ve) Lyophobic colloid | (– ve) Electrolytes | Physical adsorption flocculation, secondary minimum |

Fig. 5.27: Instability of colloidal dispersion because Addition of opposite charge Electrolytes

(D) Addition of oppositely charged colloids:

When a hydrophilic or a hydrophobic colloid, with an opposite charge is mixed with a hydrophobic colloid, coagulation of colloidal particles will be observed (Fig. 5.28).

The reason may be the reduction of zeta potential below a critical value (20 to 50 volts). Physical adsorption of oppositely charged particles neutralizes the ionic surface and decreases coulombic repulsion forces as shown above. This behaviour corresponds to the secondary minimum in the DVLO theory of energy curves (Fig. 5.24).

For example; Bismuth subnitrate undergoes dissociation in dispersion. When tragacanth (anionic colloid) is added, the anions combine with bismuth ions and the salt precipitates out.

In summary, the concentration of electrolytes is critical to maintain the stability of lyophobic colloids. This critical value is characterized by the optimum zeta potential of dispersed particles. Very low or very high zeta potentials indicate instability. A highly stable gold sol exhibits nearly a zero potential. Boiling of sols also lead to coagulation.

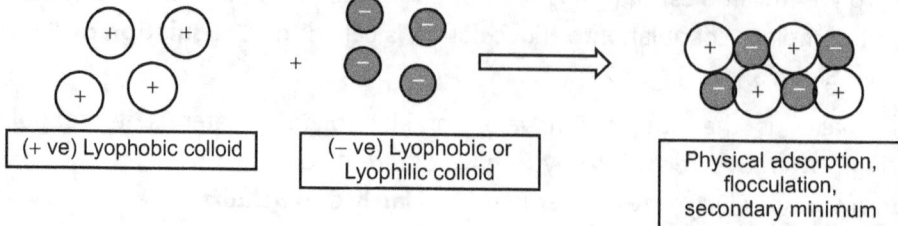

Fig. 5.28: Instability of colloidal dispersion because of a addition of opposite charge colloids

5.11.2.2 Instability of Lyophilic Colloids

Normally, lyophilic colloids are thermodynamically stable systems. The stability of a lyophilic colloid in water is determined both by the electrical charge and by hydration. However, particles may also undergo aggregation, coagulation or precipitation.

Reasons for coagulation of lyophilic dispersed phase:

(A) Addition of excess electrolytes (Hofineister of lyotropic series):

When electrolytes are added in moderate quantities, the zeta potential diminishes and coagulation does not result. But at higher quantities, electrolytes do bring about coagulation. In general, lyophilic colloids are stable because of the solvent sheath around the particles. In hydrophilic colloids, hydration of particles is observed. When electrolytes are added at high concentrations, ions get hydrated, and water is no more, available for hydration of particles as shown above. This results in flocculation or salting out of colloidal particles. [Fig. 5.29]

Hofineister of lyotropic series:

The coagulating power of anions or cations on hydrophilic colloids is arranged by Hofineister of lyotropic series.

Hofmeister rank order states that "the precipitating power of an ion is directly related to the ability of that ion to separate water molecules from the colloidal particles".

According to this statement, anions or cations are arranged in a series listed as follows:

Anions:

citrates > tartrates > sulfates > acetates > chlorides > nitrates > bromides > iodides

Cations:

$Mg^{2+} > Ca^{2+} > Ba^{2+} > Na^+ > K^+$

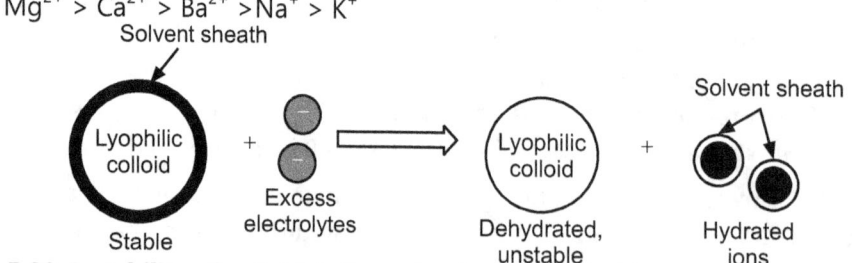

Fig. 5.29: Instability of colloidal dispersion because of addition of excess electrolytes

(B) Addition of oppositely charged colloids:

Mixing of lyophilic colloid with oppositely charged colloids results in flocculation. It is believed that the shells of tightly bound water molecules surrounding the particles prevent them from coalescing, but the electrostatic attractions of their opposite charges hold a number of particles together (i.e., flocculation). In this case, the dispersion contains colloid-rich aggregates which settle at the bottom imparting greater viscosity. The upper layer is poor in colloid. An example of this type is mixing of acacia and gelatin. Acacia carries negative charge and gelatin possesses positive charge below its isoelectric point (below pH 4.7). When these dispersions are mixed, coacervates form as shown in Fig. 5.30.

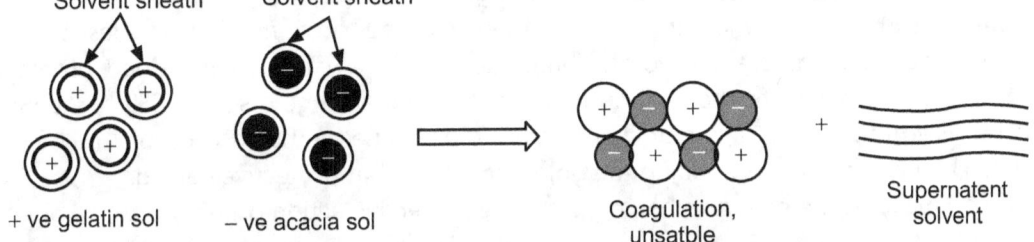

Fig. 5.30: Instability of colloidal dispersion because addition of oppositely charged colloids

(C) Addition of Nonsolvent

Less polar solvents such as alcohol and acetone have greater affinity to water. When these are added to hydrophilic colloids, dehydration of particles will be observed as shown below. Now the stability of the particles depends on the charge they possess. Addition of even a small amount of electrolytes leads to flocculation. Thus, a lyophilic colloid is converted into lyophobic colloid. (Fig. 5.31)

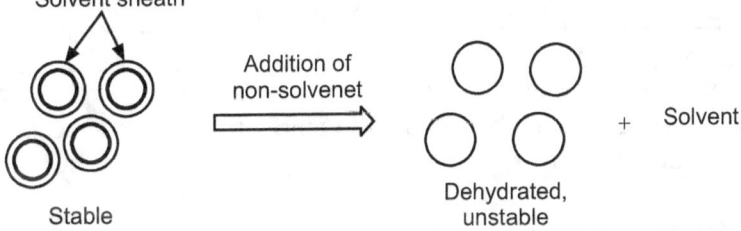

Fig. 5.31: Instability of colloidal dispersion because addition of non-solvent

5.12 SENSITIZATION OF COLLOIDS

If a very small amount of hydrophilic colloid is added to a hydrophobic sol, it is sometimes observed that the latter has become more sensitive to precipitation on subsequent addition of electrolytes. This sensitization may be partly due to adsorption of the oppositely charged hydrophilic sol on hydrophobic particles as shown Fig. 5.32.

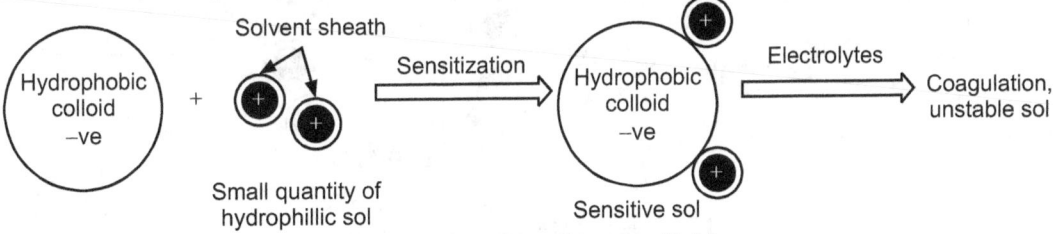

Fig. 5.32: Sensitization of colloids

5.13 GOLD NUMBER AND PROTECTION OF COLLOIDS

Lyophilic sols are more stable than lyophobic sols. Lyophobic sols can be easily coagulated by the addition of small quantity of an electrolyte. When a lyophilic sol is added to any lyophobic sol, it becomes less sensitive towards electrolytes. Thus, lyophilic colloids can prevent the coagulation of any lyophobic sol.

"The phenomenon of preventing the coagulation of a lyophobic sol due to the addition of some lyophilic colloid is called **sol protection or protection of colloids**."

The protecting power of different protective (lyophilic) colloids is different. The efficiency of any protective colloid is expressed in terms of gold number.

Gold number: Zsigmondy introduced a term called gold number to describe the protective power of different colloids. This is defined as, "weight of the dried protective agent in milligrams, which when added to 10 ml of a standard gold sol (0.0053 to 0.0058%) is just sufficient to prevent a colour change from red to blue on the addition of 1 ml of 10 % sodium chloride solution, is equal to the gold number of that protective colloid."

Thus, smaller is the gold number; higher is the protective action of the protective agent.

$$\text{Protective power} \propto \frac{1}{\text{Gold number}} \qquad \qquad \dots (5.21)$$

Table: 5.4: Gold numbers of some hydrophilic substances

Hydrophilic substance	Gold number	Hydrophilic substance	Gold number
Gelatin	0.005 - 0.01	Sodium oleate	0.4 - 1.0
Sodium caseinate	0.01	Gum tragacanth	2
Hamoglobin	0.03 - 0.07	Potato starch	25
Gum arabic	0.15 - 0.25		

Congo rubin number: Ostwald introduced congo rubin number to account for protective nature of colloids. It is defined as "the amount of protective colloid in milligrams which prevents colour change in 100 ml of 0.01 % congo rubin dye to which 0.16 g equivalent of KCl is added".

Mechanism of Solution Protection

The actual mechanism of sol protection is very complex. However, it may be due to the adsorption of the protective colloid on the lyophobic sol particles, followed by its solvation. Thus, it stabilises the sol via solvation effects. [Fig. 5.33]

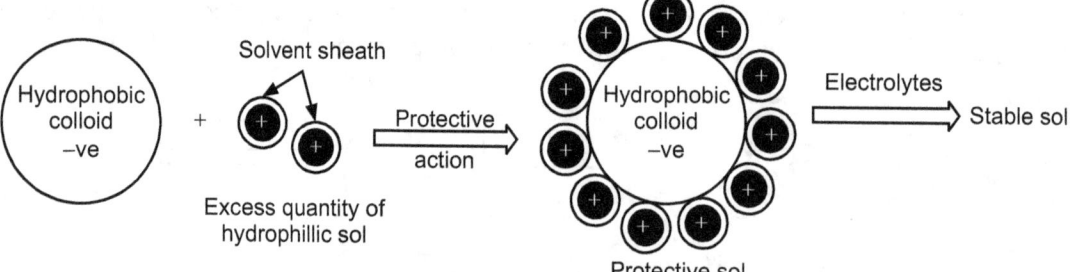

Fig. 5.33: Protection of colloids

5.14 PHARMACEUTICAL APPLICATIONS

1. **Therapy:** Colloidal systems are used as therapeutic agents in different areas.
   Example:
   (a) Silver colloid used as germicidal,
   (b) Copper colloid used in cancer treatment and
   (c) Mercury colloid used as antisyphilis.

2. **Stability:** As already stated, charges play an important role in determining the stability of a colloidal system. Colloids; especially lyophobic colloids having like charges on particle surface repel each other and prevent flocculation in suspensions. Example: Colloidal dispersion of gelatin is used in coating over tablets and granules which upon drying leaves a uniform dry film over them and protect them from adverse conditions of the atmosphere.

3. **Absorption:** As colloidal dimensions are small enough, they have a huge surface area. Hence, the drug constituted colloidal form is released into the vicinity in large amount.
   Example: sulphur colloid gives a large quantity of sulphur and this often leads to sulphur toxicity.

4. **Dissolution:** Due to huge surface area, the dissolution rate is very large.

5. **Targeted Drug Delivery:** Liposomes are of colloidal dimensions and are preferentially taken up by the liver and spleen. Hence, principle of colloids is also used in targeted drug delivery system.

QUESTIONS

1. **Short Answers Questions (3 Marks):**
   1. Briefly explain about protective colloid. **[SPPU - 2015, 2014 and 2010]**
   2. Write about Hopmeister lyotropic series. **[SPPU - 2015, 2014 and 2012]**
   3. State the Shultz-Hardy rule. **[SPPU - 2014 and 2012]**
   4. Write note on properties of lyophilic colloids. **[SPPU - 2014]**
   5. Differentiate between Zeta potential and Nernst potential.
      [SPPU - 2014, 2013 and 2011]
   6. Briefly Explain about sensitization of colloids and protective colloid. **[SPPU - 2013]**
   7. Write note on properties of lyophobic colloid. **[SPPU - 2013]**
   8. Differentiate between lyophilic, lyophobic and associated colloids. **[SPPU - 2013]**
   9. Define and differentiate between electrophoresis and electro-osmosis.
      [SPPU - 2013]
   10. Explain gold number with example. **[SPPU - 2011]**
   11. Enlist applications of colloids. **[SPPU - 2010]**
   12. Differentiate between true solution, colloidal and coarse dispersion.
   13. Why colloidal particles show Brownian motion.

2. **Medium Answer Questions (5 Marks):**
   1. Write short note on kinetic properties of colloids. **[SPPU - 2015]**
   2. Write note on DLVO theory. **[SPPU - 2014]**

3. Write note on electric double layer.   **[SPPU - 2014]**
4. Write note on Donnan membrane equilibrium.   **[SPPU - 2013]**
5. Write note on optical properties of colloids.   **[SPPU - 2011]**
6. Explain Faraday - Tyndal effect.   **[SPPU - 2010]**
7. Write properties of associated colloids.
8. Explain factor affecting the stability of colloids.
9. Write methods for preparation of colloidal dispersion.

3. **Long Answer Questions (10 Marks):**
   1. Elaborate on electric properties of colloids and its role in stability of colloids.
      [SPPU - 2015, 2014 and 2012]
   2. Explain the DLVO theory and its pharmaceutical application. Highlight the stability of a lyophobic sol.   **[SPPU - 2010]**
   3. Define colloids. Write an account of optical, kinetic and electric properties of colloids.   **[SPPU - 2013]**
   4. Explain in detail types of colloidal dispersion.

■■■

APPENDIX

Greek Alphabets

α	Alpha	ι	Iota
β	Beta	κ	Kappa
γ	Gamma	λ	Lambda
δ	Delta	μ	Mu
ε	Epsilon	ν	Nu
ζ	Zeta	ξ	Xi
η	Eta	o	Omicron
θ	Theta	ω	Omega
π	Pi	χ	Chi
ρ	Rho	Ψ	Psi
σ	Sigma	υ	Upsilon

■■■